Wanderlust

L. Costevelos

Printed in the United Kingdom

First Printing, 2019

Cover design by Alex Storer

thelightdream.net

Paperback ISBN: 978-1-9160189-0-7

eBook ISBN: 978-1-9160189-1-4

L. Costevelos Publishing
Bartley Green
Birmingham

To my little sister, Molly.
Many years ago, your eyes would light up when I read you my stories. Twenty years later, they still light up. Thank you for always listening to my stories.

PROLOGUE

I'm not sure if you can hear me, Mia, or if you can hear anything for that matter. I mean, what can a foetus hear really, except a few jumbled sounds through the stone walls of a uterus? The chance is unlikely, but I'm hoping this will work because I promised him I would tell you this story. All of it – even the bad bits, and as you and I have limited time together, I guess now is as good as any time to start, right at the end, as I lay next to my husband, bleeding out on the living room floor.

I watch him vigilantly. His thin lips gape, revealing fragments of sharp white teeth, and his cloudy eyes are still stretched in horror. Eyes that are too wide to lie, but Dan was always lying. Lying came as naturally to him as breathing did to a middle-aged yoga-teaching spinster.

'For better or for worse,' he said. 'In sickness and in health, till death do us part.' But what he really meant was: I will love you for the foreseeable future, until I see you for who you actually are, and I run for the hills.

No running now.

Trying not to inhale the dank stench of blood, I breathe in through my mouth. But already, it's everywhere, spiralling through the muggy house, and staining everything in its path; the drawn magnolia curtains, the Venetian cream rug soaked black beneath us, the coffee table Dan whacked his head on before he went down, and the swanky beige sofa I'd flung myself onto only minutes before.

Nothing would ever rid the house of that pungent scent of death, but I guess domesticated chores would no longer be the bane of my existence. No more scrubbing floors, pretending to be grateful for a husband I despised. No more false cheer at the kitchen sink. No more folding laundry while fantasising about thrusting the kitchen knife into his secretive little skull, over and over again. No more lies.

Well, maybe just one.

Swallowing the lump in my throat, I gaze up at the blood-splattered ceiling, going over the promise I made to keep you safe, Mia. Only now, it seems near impossible since I'm the reason he's dead.

I can't remember doing it, just flashes. I remember the knife in my hands, the sound the blade made when it connected with his spine, that great eruption of blood. What must he have thought when I issued the first blow? Why hadn't he told me the truth? If he'd told me the truth, all of this might have been avoided.

Might have.

Blinking away hot tears, I stare at him sprawled out with his arms above his head. Blood leaks out from his chest. Black, and glutinous, I feel it pooling up in a sticky puddle beneath us as I cling to the kitchen knife.

Contrary to what you believe, I did love him once, Mia. I guess I still do, but what good is love now? Love won't bring him back. Love won't undo his lies; love won't keep you safe.

Focusing on the blue lights grazing the ceiling, I blink furiously. Police sirens wail outside. They're coming for me, but I'm not afraid, not like I was before — the front door hammers. Someone calls my name, his name, mine.

"Raine Black!"

"Dan Black!"

"Raine Black!"

More banging. My jaw throbs. I feel my front tooth coming loose. I run my tongue alongside the bloody gash on my lower lip as the front door smashes open. Cold air whooshes in. Raised voices puncture the silence. I can't make out the words, only sounds. My eyes sting as I glare at Dan's blue lips, his pale face. He should've told me the truth. They both should've told me, and now they're both dead.

I wince as I am yanked up from the floor. Cold metal is pinned against my wrists. I take one last look at Dan, lying there. Frozen, comatose, not much different from how he appeared when he was alive. Then, as the uniforms patrol me out of the house where I'd unveiled the greatest of wonders, just meters above me in my loft, all I can think to say is that I'm sorry, Mia.

I told him I'd tell you this story — all of it, and this is how it ended, with a murder.

.

CHAPTER ONE

Buzzing wakes me. A violent sound that scrapes away at my eardrums with jagged fingernails. Assuming it's a message from Dan, or an email from a client I hadn't returned, I nudge my head in an attempt to sleep in a little longer. The buzzing continues. My fingers tremble over the thin sheet placed on top of me. Not my sheet. Not my bed.

My brow collapses as reality rushes back to me. Every rancid memory flickers through my brain like a rambunctious blue furnace flame. Dan's bloated body. The knife in my hands. The surge of rage that had come over me. And him, not being able to save him. Jolting upright in bed, I blink at the warden watching me from the doorway.

"Come on, sleeping beauty. You'll have plenty of time to rest later," she tells me.

Understanding the buzzing noise must've come from the security code she'd just punched into the wall, I fall back in my bunk with the sound of sobbing from down the corridor dragging me back to the ward where I have spent the last six days.

"Come on," the warden pushes.

I lie there a moment, wondering if she'd get bored and leave if I didn't answer. She hadn't when I refused breakfast a few days ago, and when I declined my meds the night before. Taking my time, I unglue myself from my pit, then clamber down the steps from my bunk.

Landing on the cold uncarpeted ground, I scrutinise the hole impersonating a window to the right of me; the handprint in the centre, the rusted iron bars safeguarding the world, the sky spread beyond it. It's funny how your perception of the world alters based on what's compressed inside of your heart, Mia.

Three months ago, I would've thought the bulging grey clouds cast above the earth were dazzling. Thick and bursting with the abandon that possessed the ability to bring back forgotten life. Now, all I see is a roof the colour of year-old Weetabix.

"Come on," the warden orders.

Tearing my focus from the window, I follow her out into the corridor with no time for a coffee or a chance to brush my teeth, because those things are luxuries – a virtue I'd denied myself of since my incarceration at Raven House; the maximum-security mental health facility accommodating a murky cocktail of the most lethal and docile of human life.

Heading north, we march through the maze of disinfected corridors masking the scent of piss and vomit, past the reception where a nurse glances up expectantly, and the canteen buzzing with morning slurs from patients heaping their plates with as much processed crap as possible.

"Index finger down, little finger up, both thumbs down," I mutter, reminding myself I have to stick to my story if I want to do this properly. "Index finger down, little finger up, both thumbs down." It takes less than a minute before we halt outside of a steel door at the end of the corridor. Through the crisscross window, I glimpse a woman at a desk with straw hair scraped back so tightly her entire scalp seems endangered.

Struggling to make out her face beyond the glass, I flinch as the warden lugs open the door and stomps back down the corridor, leaving me alone with the suited stranger who swings around, smiling.

"Raine." Her voice is a silk knife, and all too quickly I am aware of how hellish this ordeal will be devoid of caffeine.

I take her in from the doorway — a woman born wearing shoes two sizes too big, and finally, proudly, filled. Blonde hair fastened neatly, eyes the colour of a bruise set above a plastic smile that seems too heavy for such a sallow face. A face that would never be caught hovering over a toilet in a bar, or rubbed raw because of boys who played games with hearts.

"It's nice to meet you, Raine. My name is Doctor Margo Watson. I am one of the clinical psychologists carrying out your psychiatric evaluation." She bobs her head at the empty seat in front of her.

Halfway there, her perfume whacks me. I clear my throat as the musky scent of rose petals lifts from her blazer, and gropes at everything with fat sweaty palms. The mahogany desk she sits at, three blue plastic chairs surrounding it, the drizzle splattered window to her right where limp mustard curtains hang from a metal rail, and a clock, ticking away on the wall behind her.

I blink at the low ceiling, then at the woman smoothing out invisible creases in her suit, before taking my seat.

"How are you today?" she asks brightly.

My lips crack, and I wonder if she understands the inanity of her question. How am I? That grin again, she doesn't. She waits for the word 'good' or 'fine' to roll off my tongue before jotting something down in a pad of paper. *Patient is unresponsive*, I imagine, or, *after six days, patient is still uncooperative.*

"I'm sure you are aware of the arrangement following Judge Rosturan's ruling," she asks as I eyeball a mountain of manila folders sprawled across the desk. "While the investigation into the death of your husband is being carried out, Judge Rosturan has requested you undergo a full psychiatric evaluation to assess your mental state at the time of the incident," she pauses, combing over my face for a flicker of understanding, anything human –

I give her nothing.

"My colleague, Doctor Elliot Pierce, and I will meet with you throughout eighteen sessions. During which time, a comprehensive diagnosis of your mental state will be reached, then discussed at your hearing to determine whether or not you are mentally competent enough to stand trial. And, if you were in the right frame of mind on the night in question. Do you understand?"

I do understand. I understand every single word. Still, prim and proper Watson ogles me as if mentally unstable somehow translates as deaf.

"If you feel uncomfortable, or distressed at any point during our sessions, feel free to let Doctor Pierce, or I know, and you can have a few minutes to compose yourself." Her eyes dip to a box of tissues ornamenting the table before she starts leafing through pages littered with question marks, and highlighted scrawls, and words circled in bright red felt.

Halting at a blank page, she smooths it down, then peers up at me with fresh hope.

"Raine, I was wondering if we could start with something light. How about you tell me something about yourself?"

Pushing back in the blue cushioned seat, I find myself

unsure of how to respond to a question she assumes she knows the answer to. A question that everyone believes they know the answer to. Who is Raine Black? Not a model citizen or even a rebellious one. Someone who flew under the radar and barely left a mark until she did. I am a liar; I want to tell her — a dirty murdering liar.

Pressing my lips into a tight line, I picture the hordes of crumpled up spouses gossiping to one another over their morning cups of coffee.

"Wife butchers husband after four years of marriage," they would gasp, secretly elated to have something to distract themselves from their mundane existence, before rushing off to their real lives. Lives where husbands visited mistresses on lunch breaks. And wives had friends over to boast about his bonus, and the new house, and the sex, oh god the sex! Monitoring their intake of wine. Drinking not enough not to slip up, but too much to keep the fantasy of a cold barrel of a gun pushed up against their well-groomed skulls at bay.

"Raine?"

I flinch. I can't tell her about you, Mia, not yet.

"We can start with the basics. You're twenty-eight? Your birthday is?" Watson waits for an answer as I take in her glossy eyes and sheen blonde hair. She is attractive, but it's the frosty sort of attractive most men are secretly afraid of. Most men want vulnerable, placid, compliant, even if they don't admit it.

"What do you really want to know?" I ask.

Her jaw tenses, and her eyes glimmer with expectancy.

"I want to know about you, Raine. Your hobbies your life, where you grew up. We can start slow. How about—"

"You want to dissect me."

"Not at all." She forces a smile. All teeth. "Can you tell me anything about your occupation? I understand you're an artist, and you have been for..."

8

I ball my hands into fists as her silky voice drills huge craters in my skull.

"I've researched your paintings; they're very... unique. Any exhibitions recently? Do you remember your first? That must have been quite a significant moment. Do you remember anything about that?"

Dropping my gaze, I study the desk. Etched into the wood are fingernail marks. Long strips of flesh coloured warning signs.

"Why?" I ask, stroking the dips the way one might do to an injured animal.

"To get an understanding of the type of person you are, Raine. What you tell us can potentially determine your future."

Just like that, my hand freezes above the desk. My insides implode. My heart, my lungs, my kidneys, everything shatters into a bloodied pile of puréed organs because if there's one thing I'm sure of, Mia, it's that my future has already been determined.

I will stay here; locked in a ward of murky eyed zombies and nurses who speak in voices that are six pitches too high, safe from myself, safe from the world, and most importantly, safe from you.

Watson clears her throat.

An image of him flutters through my mind.

Index finger down, little finger up, both thumbs down.

My heart trembles and I have to punch my chest to get it to stop shaking. Watson won't believe me if I tell her the truth. No one will, but I'm afraid if I don't tell someone, I might forget, and I promised him I wouldn't forget.

Meeting her hungry eyes, I take a ragged breath, confident if I have to start anywhere, it's at the beginning, before you were conceived, and before I was even married, Mia.

"The night of my exhibition," I mutter.

Watson lifts her pen; the motion goes hand in hand with the curve of her lips.

"I should've been happy."

"And weren't you?"

I shake my head.

"Back then I didn't know how to be. Dan and I had been together just under two years, but even then, it felt…" I pause, choosing my words carefully. "Staged."

JULY 2011

We stood in front of the mirror in an awkward embrace. Dan's hands were draped around my waist, and my chin was pressed to his shoulder. The gesture should've made me feel safe, but felt more like a subtle form of strangulation. Inhaling the sharp tang of his cologne, I squeezed my eyes shut tight. It was the cologne he'd douse himself in, on special occasions; the rare fancy dinners we treated ourselves to, the few birthday parties we attended of friends Dan actually tolerated, the cheap last-minute getaways.

The smell made my stomach hurt.

I studied us in the mirror, hunting for a couple in love, but all I saw was a boy, dressed as a man, holding on to a woman who wanted to throw away an intricately sculpted future. I licked my lips, waiting for the anxiety to pass. Lately, all I ever seemed to do was waste my time waiting; for a text, a call, a stroke of inspiration, a train, a bus, a feeling, a way out. I wondered if I were to collect all those squandered hours waiting, what would they amount to? A month? A year? A lifetime?

Would I waste my life waiting for a feeling I just didn't get with Dan? He was a good man, kind, funny, and attractive in a sharpened pencil sort of way. Tall, a little gangly, painfully neat, with dark hair that was always cropped short, fingernails that were always trimmed, socks he'd practically iron out every morning.

I cared for him – I really did, but I always felt as if I was anticipating this tsunami of emotion to take me by surprise and batter my insides with certainty that this was it. The revelation that this was the man I was destined to spend the rest of my life with. Only that feeling never came, and without it, I couldn't help wonder what we were doing, if not just coexisting.

I scanned the jumble sale of our flat from over his shoulder. Cramped, much too cramped for one person, let alone two, but lo and behold we were everywhere. Wedged in the floral wallpaper that dripped with Dan's coconut face cream, and pressed against the fibres of the paint brushes and canvasses propped against the burgundy sofa I'd bought from a charity shop.

This was our life. Our cheap, lived in life, where the ground was left uncarpeted because Dan claimed the floorboards looked more rustic painted mahogany – but really, it was because carpet was more than twenty pounds a metre. An extravagance on a waitress's salary where tips were scarce and Dan was still 'taking it easy' before real life started.

Chewing my lip, I tried fixing my face to look happy, and why shouldn't I be happy? Tonight, was the night of my exhibition. The night I'd dreamt of for years, and at twenty-two, it was more than an accomplishment. Bringing my attention back to the mirror, I searched for a spark of something, anything, but when I met my own dark eyes, all I saw was an unquenchable thirst to escape.

I knew I had to end it, and I had to do it tonight: Fresh starts, clean endings, and all that malarkey. I'd sit Dan down after my exhibition and tell him that I loved him, just not in the way I should've, and that I'd tried to make it work, but I felt like the parts I needed were missing.

I peered up hesitantly. He looked proud; the wash of emotion impossible to conceal even with his eyes closed. How would I tell him tonight? I imagined his muddy eyes clouding over, his voice quivering.

'Why?' He'd ask in a tone too wet, and I would take it back like I always did, terrified I was sabotaging my only chance of happiness. Terrified I just didn't understand this notion of love that everyone gushed about.

"You look beautiful, Rai."

I flinched, hoping Dan couldn't hear my rowdy thoughts.

"Like someone who's about to become a huge success," he added.

Shame tore through me when he smiled.

Dan was kind I reminded myself, and supportive when he wanted to be. Was I really going to throw that all away? I forced a nod, distracting myself from the wreck of my relationship by thinking of what would commence at the exhibition showcasing budding artists. An opportunity I'd been offered a few months ago while working a late shift at Del Sau – the café where I was employed as barista/waitress/cleaner/customer punching bag.

"Who's the artist?" a small woman with a long doughy nose had wheezed, eyeballing the painting I'd given to my manager, Barry, on the wall behind me. Usually, whenever a customer asked who painted the piece, I told them I wasn't sure, which wasn't entirely smart after I heard them mutter the word 'different' or 'interesting' in a voice that made my gut feel like it was being scraped against a cheese grater.

But there was something different about this woman. She wasn't a regular, and she smelt of those disposable soaps you find at airport bathrooms in first class, and so

I took a gamble and admitted it was me. She didn't say much after, only nodded then sauntered off to the far side of the café, watching me pretend to polish mugs that were already clean, and wipe down the counter, reeking of disinfectant.

Only after she left, did I feel the breath return to my lungs, and after clearing her table, sandwiched between an untouched americano, and a generous ten-pound tip, I found a card that read: *Call me, Sue Garner.* At first, I thought it was a joke. Some pyramid scheme in sales, or a low-key cult recruiting women who had lost all faith in humanity, but after a quick Google search, I learned Sue Garner was the curator of a renowned art gallery in London. Her list of accomplishments dating way back to before I was even born.

"This could be your big break kid," my manager Barry had told me, but I didn't want a big break – or at least, I didn't think I did. Reminding myself I didn't need a snooty old woman passing judgement on pieces that had taken months to complete, I had tried to shrug it off. Though every night my mind strayed to dreams I had as a child. A gallery swollen with my work. My paintings, hanging in homes of people who understood. A purpose, I thought. It would finally give me a purpose.

And so, hounded with 'what if's' and 'maybe's' I called the number, and after three months of procrastinating, and fantasising, and working at Del Sau until my feet bled to afford rent and art supplies, I was standing in Miss Garner's office with a wobbling view of London beneath me.

I remember watching her veiny hands leaf through miles of my work. Watercolour, and charcoal, and acrylic prints, all sprawled across the floor, giving the impression of a Crayola mass suicide. Before she nodded glibly, lifted her meaty nose, then offered to showcase my work at a young artists' exhibition.

Now, here we were. Granted, I had no idea of how the night would pan out. Still, I was hopeful. And that hope stretched its arms around Dan and me because I thought if I waited a little longer, the feeling we lacked, might just turn up.

With an hour to spare Dan suggested a drink. After following him into our tattered sunlit kitchen, I watched as he filled two glasses with cheap whisky. He was talking about his friend whose wife had left him for the mailman with the lazy eye, but I couldn't focus. All I could do was listen to the slosh of whisky hitting the glass.

Dan was always telling stories. A writer, he'd said when we first met, with a glint in his eye that reeked of his sheltered childhood. He was just finishing up his journalism degree. I hadn't even gone to university. I was too busy mourning the loss of my mother and drinking too much gin.

Dan told me I was too pretty to be waiting tables. A recycled line, I know – but back then I wanted to be someone else. I needed to step away from my grief, and anger, and the dismal grey blanket of my life – and so, I became the girl without a past. A blank sheet void of all the ugly red mistakes; no history, no shame, and I had been her for nearly two years.

"Poor bastard thought he was gay," Dan went on.

I struggled to look like I was interested.

Nodding when appropriate, biding my time till I could grab the glass, but even after downing the half-empty tumbler of whiskey, I couldn't shake that niggling feeling of waiting.

After a twelve-pound taxi ride that I paid for, and half a bottle of whisky I was sure to pay for the following day, we were late. Following Dan down a corridor decorated in posters advertising local pubs, and restaurants, and mobile hair salons, we rushed towards a mahogany double door marked EXHIBITION.

Dan kept ahead of me. The click of his tan leather shoes filling the corridor with misplaced excitement. *Click, click, click.*

"It's going to be great–" He kept telling me. "If not for your work, then at least for the free booze."

The zip of my black knee-length dress skinned my shoulders as I marched on, confident tonight would either be the beginning or the end of everything. Perhaps no one apart from Pam, the gallery manager (who had to be there) would even turn up. And after a few mortifying hours, she'd glance around the empty room and throw me a: sorry, art isn't really a career, try something in law or business- smile. And that would be that.

Dreams obliterated.

Focussing on a table stocked with bubbling champagne flutes outside the door, I took a deep breath, promising myself that whatever was about to happen, wouldn't be that bad. Even if people did grimace at pieces that had taken months to complete, it didn't mean I had to stop painting. What it did mean however, was that I wasn't actually good at anything.

About to tell Dan I was ready to face the music, I took an uneven breath, only when I looked up, my spleen coiled. He'd gone in without me. I rolled my eyes. Of course, he hadn't waited. On the taxi ride over, all he'd talked about was how hungry he was. If he waited a few more seconds, he might've withered away from malnutrition.

Swallowing hard, I forced my legs to rally through the hefty double doors. Punched by the aroma of expensive colognes and the soundtrack of clinking glasses, I kept my eyes pressed to the ginger floor, my heart racing, my legs liquefying, and when I was much too far to turn back, I peeked up, stunned.

The first thing I saw were the lights. Blaring fixtures dangled from the rectangular ceiling. Spotlights burst through the painfully white walls. Speckled bulbs ruptured the oak panels, each one highlighting the various artists' canvases tacked to the wall.

Ahead of me were fifteen fragments of myself, with my initials R.C. looming beneath them. Skimming through guests, I broke into a noticeable sweat, courtesy of the lights, when I saw people – real people. Amongst them, I spotted Dan's friend hiding behind a man with a bright red Mohawk. To my right, scattered in messy clusters next to a buffet, I noticed customers my manager had convinced to attend, most of them eyeing waitresses and waiters whooshing past, carrying silver platters.

Littered between the few guests I recognised, were the friends and family members of the two other artists exhibiting their work; Lui Yang, a Chinese art student whose ink and wash paintings, were famous in her native town. And Devon Calmer, a twenty-three-year-old undergraduate, raised in Hackney, who spoke as if he was babbling with a silver spoon jammed down his throat.

Then there was me, Raine Close, the twenty-two-year-old waitress who was trying, and failing, to end things with her emotionally redundant boyfriend because deep down she was terrified of being loved.

"Quite the crowd."

I jumped, then spun around quick enough to catch Dan swipe an impaled block of cheese from a floating platter.

"It could still go tits up," I mumbled.

"Ever the optimist," Dan replied, twirling the stick between his fingers with a grin that stung.

Raising a brow, I was about to tell Dan I was just being pragmatic when a cold hand gripped my shoulder, and when I turned, for the first time that night, the knot in my chest loosened.

The hand belonged to Lucile; my childhood friend whose silky laugh could bring an army of men to their knees. She wore a silver gown that clung to her hips and spilt out into a metallic puddle on the floor. With a drink in her hand and her golden hair pulled high, she beamed at me through eyes that were ruthless in disarming the most skilled at combat.

"These are brilliant, babe," she said, taking me in in that Lucile way that made you feel like you had turned up late for an exam. "And you look stunning! Doesn't she look stunning, Katie? Is that the dress?"

Before I had time to muster up a nod, Lucile pulled me into a one-armed hug, clouting me with the smell of cheap perfume and champagne, while Katie, my co-worker from Del Sau, peered down at her pudgy feet slipping out from the straps of her khaki sandals.

"Well done," she said in a mousey voice the same colour as her hair.

Thanking them both, I wondered how long they'd been alone together. On the rare occasions they met – (birthdays, dinners, the once attended spin class) they were like an alcoholic who loathed liquid. Most, felt dazed throughout the day if they'd skipped breakfast, or a shower, or a steaming mug of coffee.

Lucile felt that way if she wasn't dodging a court case, or being stalked by an axe-wielding neighbour whose prize possession was a telescope. Both of which had happened in the last six months. Though for Katie, who I'd only known a year, any mention of crisis would send her into a fluster with her brown eyes swelling twice the size of her face.

"You alright, Raine?" Lucile asked.

I forced a smile.

"I'm just feeling a bit overwhelmed."

"Enjoy it," Dan said.

Guilt sliced through me when I saw him grinning at guests he'd never met, and I found myself questioning if I should take him somewhere quiet and end things there.

"Honestly, Rai," Lucile said, pointing a red fingernail at my painting of two birds hanging on the wall adjacent to us. "That right there. I'd have that hanging in my flat."

I inclined my head, squinting at the chalk and charcoal canvas, envisioning it scattered somewhere in Lucile's cluttered one bedroom flat. Probably collecting dust on a table stacked with glossy magazines, or crammed between empty wine bottles, and unopened mail.

I peered at her hesitantly. I could tell she was thinking the same. Her lip twitched, her chin trembled, her eyes grew wet and before we could stop ourselves, we were laughing.

Three hours passed, and as a parting gift, left only the ghosts of feral conversation, and the dry memory of laughter. Katie, who only drank at Christmas had joined Lucile at the bar, and after six shots of tequila she'd fumbled through the crowd slurring, 'it must have been something she ate.' Lucile left after meeting an international businessman who owned a yacht, and was apparently passing time at the small-town exhibition.

Though, after I mentioned his outrage when he realised the bar tab had ended, and that he probably didn't own a paddling boat, never mind a yacht, she cursed men, laughed, swiped a bottle of champagne from the bar then disappeared into the night.

Dan and I were the last to leave. Bathed in darkness and the stale smell of success, we stood beneath my painting of an oak tree with red faces engraved into the bark.

"What a night," Dan yawned.

"Yep," I agreed, ignoring the girlish strands of laughter trickling down the corridor from waitresses counting tips. "Why do you think this one didn't sell?"

"Seriously?" Dan joked.

I turned to him, hurt. But what I didn't know then, was that the painting would spend the next six years hiding in a home that failed to be a home – facetiously observing the spectacle we would become. If I did, I would've run. I glanced around in the shadows. All of the nights spent pretending, afraid, hiding, were plastered across the walls. Yellow stickers dotted against eleven of my sold pieces.

The night had gone better than I could've imagined. People had turned up and paid for my work; the percentage I would receive was enough to pay next months' rent, and with the money left over I could buy new art supplies. I should've been filled with a tingly sense of warmth that screamed of my accomplishment, but I couldn't help feeling something was missing.

"It's scary, Dan," I admitted. "Putting your life out there like that. It's like cutting yourself open and expecting the world to be gentle with your heart. To everyone else, these are just pretty pictures and techniques and brush strokes, but to me, it's my life."

With a heavy head, I turned to the painting I'd slaved over for months. I began the piece around the time I started dating Dan. Two trees submerged in the emerald woodland, their faces contorted and rigid.

I remember sitting cross-legged on my studio floor for hours, while my phone lit up with those earlier messages. *Last night was great. Can't wait to see you again. You're lovely.* Then that feeling; that feeling I just couldn't grasp. Why could I never grasp that rush of emotion that came so effortlessly to so many?

"Rainey –"

I flinched then studied Dan warily, my boyfriend. Even after two years, the title sounded forced.

"If it's something wonderful, then it should be shared."

I offered a hearty nod, despite thinking Dan was wrong.

Not all wonderful things should be shared. Some things are too precious, and the second they are released into the universe, the magic inside of them fades.

We stood in silence, Dan tapping at his phone, me with my eyes sealed, and my nails cutting my palms. I knew it was the right time to tell him then. The words singed my lips. *Dan, I can't do this. Dan, I'm sorry. Dan, I don't love you. Dan, I feel trapped.* I opened my mouth to tell him when the cleaner jingled his keys.

"Come on," Dan said. "Let's go home."

Home. The word stuck in my throat like a boulder. I wanted to go home; only Dan wasn't home. Had he ever been? Had I always felt like I was holding my breath whenever he watched me? I stood there grappling with what might happen in the following hours if I were to tell him then. I'd have to pack his things. He wouldn't do it. He would fight, telling me I was just scared while he drank himself into a stupor and kicked cupboard doors that were already coming off their hinges in the kitchen.

I'd pack till the morning, the flat growing fatter, then emptier while the brown boxes stacked up in the hallway. Inside of them, you'd find the children's books Dan collected when I told him I never owned any. His grey Ralph Lauren shirt I'd cried into on the night he told me he loved me, and I couldn't say it back. The guitar he smashed up when I told him I was leaving the first time.

I watched him with the words scalding my tongue

when he leant down and kissed my cheek.

"I'm so proud of you," Dan whispered.

Timing.

The timing was always off. With that, Dan took hold of my hand and led me out through the barren hall. I was silent all of the way home, and when he offered to make tea, and when he asked if I wanted a sandwich or a nightcap before bed, and to be frank– I'm not sure he even noticed, Mia.

We had sex after. The passionless, comfortable, race to the finish line then reward yourself with sleep, kind of sex. Only sleep wouldn't come, and I couldn't remember the last time it arrived without force. I was waiting for something, anything, and when I heard Dan snoring next to me, I crept out into the bathroom, curled up on the cold tiled floor, and I cried.

I didn't know why I was crying or how to stop; all I knew was that the emptiness was too much. I stayed there sniffling and falling apart until dawn cracked through the thin slit bathroom window, before gathering what I had left of my energy and doing what I always did when loneliness took hold of me, I painted.

***

"That sounds like a massive achievement," Watson exhales. "You must have been extremely proud. Was that your full-time occupation?" Was – past tense, coffin lowered.

I shake my head because I never made enough money to guarantee a steady income. I continued waitressing, bartending, scrubbing tables, scouring floors, wasting hours polishing wine glasses people were too drunk to even notice were glasses. Often encountering that nasty little question when someone turns to you at a dinner party and asks:

'So, what do you do?'

To which you reply.

'I'm *just* a waitress.'

Eventually, I secured work as an intern in a small art gallery. Though the job was unpaid, it offered a scheme for progression. But after the two-hour commutes to work each day, and after four months of coming home penniless and drained, Dan encouraged me to quit. And when I gained regular clients who bought pieces to hang in rooms they'd never enter, his suggestion became a demand.

I had argued, insisting I needed something else: inspiration, a purpose, human contact. Dan didn't understand. And I guess most people would've found it reassuring that their partner was willing to work, while they pursued their dream. But Dan didn't want that. He wanted a Martha Stewart reincarnation that came in the body of a fuck doll, and when he realised that wasn't me – when it was harder to leave – things changed.

"How did you feel when—"

"It's bullshit," I mutter gripping a scar on my neck with both hands.

Watson's face blanches. She looks at me as if I'm about to strangle myself, and for a second, I want to, just to stop her pen grating away at my memories.

I watch myself in the reflection of her reading glasses. Brown eyes like the ends of cigarettes; red-rimmed and sinking into the pit of my face. Dry skin, chapped lips, all framed by long brown hair that hangs limply at my shoulders. I didn't always look this way, Mia. A moment of grief can age you quicker than a lifetime of cigarettes and booze for breakfast.

"When did it stop mattering?"

I peer at the clock behind her. 11.45. The session is nearly over. Pierce still hasn't arrived.

"Raine, what happened?"

Glancing back, I decide to test the waters.

"People say seeds have to come undone before they can grow, have you heard that?"

"Raine—"

"It seems like destruction when actually it's growth."

Watson's forehead pinches.

"Raine—"

"Sometimes it takes destruction, to build something strong."

"And do you feel strong?"

"I did."

"When?"

"After."

"After what?"

"Her voice."

"You heard a voice?"

I bite my lip then peer at the crisscross window where the warden is waiting.

"It wasn't important," I mutter, but Watson won't drop it.

"The voice, was there one, or more?" She studies me undecidedly before the morning ends in the exact same way it started; with a loud buzzing as the door is lugged open.

"I'll see you tomorrow," Watson says as I head out into the corridor.

I don't answer. Keeping my head bent, I focus on my hospital slippers slapping the floor.

"Index finger down, little finger up, both thumbs down," I mutter.

"Index finger down, little finger up, both thumbs down."

CHAPTER TWO

Following the same warden, down the same twisted corridor, we halt outside of the same crisscross window. Peering through the glass, I see a man at Watson's side. Pierce. His dark uncombed hair is streaked with silver; and despite the trend of beards sweeping the British nation, the stubble on his face only serves to make him look homeless.

His navy jumper doesn't help. Rolled up at the cuffs, it sags around his neck and chest. All in all, he seems to be an uneven man, who I imagine got milk on his upper lip often, and wouldn't notice until days later.

"It's nice to meet you, Raine. My name is Elliot Pierce," he says as I take my seat. "Before we begin, I'd like to apologise for my absence yesterday." His voice is soft, warm, the kind that can coil itself around you and pull out all of the little truths you forgot you had buried.

He is dangerous, I realise.

I watch him cagily, and before I can gauge whether Watson has told him about our session, they begin their interrogation.

Both speak side by side, with too much contempt

running alongside them for me to be blindsided into thinking they hadn't met before. Pierce asks a question, then Watson. Then Pierce. Their eyes fixed either on me or the mountain of paper and all too quickly I have become a child of divorce.

Watson asks if I have experienced any side effects on my medication – detached thoughts, slurred speech, headaches.

I nod through the checklist.

Pierce changes the direction of the inquisition, asking if I kept in contact with my friends over the years. Katie – now married with a son, George. And Lucile, who had changed her job fifteen times since my exhibition back in 2011.

When I tell him I have, something in his loitering gaze informs me that he knows I'm lying, and before I can rectify the slip, he brings a pen with teeth marks denting the lid to his mouth.

"Yesterday, you mentioned hearing a voice?" he asks.

I glower at Watson. Somewhere in the past twenty-four hours while I was staring at the blank walls of my cell, and she was probably sipping Rioja in her plush cushioned king size bed, she'd found time to tell Pierce about the hysterical woman who was hearing things.

"I was wondering if we could talk more about this voice."

"In your initial statement, you say Dan became violent," Watson pipes in. "Did you hear the voice before, or after, the abuse?"

"Index finger down, little finger up, both thumbs down," I mutter, moving my fingers around on the desk.

"Raine."

I glance behind them at the clock. 10.05.

"When was the first time you heard the voice? We don't need a specific date, just a rough estimate."

"What did it say?"

Heat sticks to my skin, and the tissue box on the table is screaming. Lowering my head, I take a deep breath, battling the urge to run down the corridor and hide under my blanket that no amount of disinfectant used, will ever stop it smelling of bile; but a voice inside of me shrieks I need to tell the truth. Not for them, or even for myself, but for you, Mia. And that meant going back to the night I met her.

"Raine."

My eyes tremble as I stare at the scratches etched into the table. Running a finger over the groove, I lower my head. She came after Dan and I were married. After we bought the house with the white picket fence, splintered with arguments and reconciliations, because without a job I had nothing but Dan.

Sometimes I wonder if she'd been watching me all along, biding her time until I was weak – I was weak then, a thread wrenched at both ends, and that was just the beginning.

"Her name was Esme."

"Esme?" Watson asks skimming through pages.

"She told me I'd save the kingdom."

At that, both their faces pale.

"Raine—"

"I didn't know what she'd make me do."

"Raine—"

"I didn't know."

JUNE 24TH 2018

I sat with my head bent over the kitchen table, and my eyes squeezed so tightly, I could see patterns dancing in my mind.

"What the fuck, Raine?" Dan shouted.

I tensed up. I hadn't heard him come home. Hadn't even heard the front door. I strained my ears, listening. He was stomping through the living room. Something shattered. The vase on the mantle maybe, or the glass ashtray we kept on the coffee table. "Again?" His voice came from the kitchen doorway. "You're going to do this again?"

I focussed on the patterns in my head, an intricately projected kaleidoscope, swallowing me. I wanted to be swallowed; gulped into the ravenous belly of life, but it wouldn't take me.

TAKE ME, a voice in my head begged. TAKE ME.

"Again, Rai? You never try."

I sensed him wrenching at his hair, tugging at it until it ripped out in thin brown wisps in his hands.

"This is bollocks, complete and utter fucking bollocks!"

I continued watching the colours, struggling to remember why I hadn't turned up for the dinner he planned. I got dressed; I knew that much because the black dress I'd chosen for the occasion was burning holes in my spine. But I didn't have on shoes. What stopped me from putting on shoes?

"This place is a fucking mess."

Cabinet doors hammered. Cutlery clinked, plates clattered.

I imagined him searching for a glass. He'd pour a tall glass of whisky when he found one. Slam it against the counter after it was drained. Smooth satisfaction wetting his lips, mouth wiped with the back of his deceptive hand. I felt him watching me. Hard eyes disassembling the mess of his wife at the kitchen table, too exhausted to even raise her head.

I held my breath. I thought he was going to hit me, and the truth was, I would've been glad, Mia, because after so much nothing all I wanted was to feel something. I waited, ready, but instead of feeling his fist against my jaw, I heard him bolting upstairs through the kitchen stairway.

I ground my teeth.

In my mind I saw him undressing; his shirt and tie plummeting into a crumpled heap on the bedroom floor that he wouldn't pick up. His trousers flung somewhere next to the bed. But unlike every other night, when Dan sought consolation with his whisky and words, I heard him thundering back downstairs.

"I'm not staying here tonight," he said. "I can't, won't, put up with this shit again. I'm going to the hotel to write."

My stomach tightened. This was new. He was almost daring me to look up; to question him, to beg him to stay, but fighting for lost love I'd learned was a lot like fucking for virginity.

"I'll get to work from there tomorrow."

I chewed the inside of my cheek, harassed by an urge to say something; confront him maybe, or tell him not to bother coming back at all. Hounded by a silent list of demands, I heard his Italian leather loafers striding through the living room, and crunching over the smashed glass.

My pulse punched my teeth as his car keys jangled, the front door creaked open, then slammed shut, smashing my heart with the truth that my shitty little three-year marriage was over. And for the briefest moment, I was relieved.

I stayed at the table. Inhaling the cinnamon ironed into the creases of the wood, exhaling. Trying to keep it together, failing, and when I was sure Dan had left I lifted my head then groaned. 23.22. The digital timer on the stove prompted me to realise I'd been sitting there for hours, and as I fought to conjure the energy to drag myself up, I realised I couldn't even remember first sitting down.

I recalled waking up, showering; the water was cold, and so I ran the tap a while. I fed the cat, skimmed through emails, but what happened after? The afternoon was a blur, and recently there'd been too many of those. Cricking my neck, I hauled myself over to the light switch. Flicking it, my stomach turned.

Dan was right; the place was a mess. Mugs, and wine glasses, and plates were stacked high at the sink. Chocolate bar wrappers and ready-made meal boxes seeped out from the wheelie bin to the left of me. Above that, half a carton of milk dripped from the worktop, leaving a chalky puddle on the hardwood floor.

I shook my head, studying the place the way a nurse would regard a ward packed full of heaving bedpans. If ever there was a time to ditch my life, Mia, this was it. Toying with the idea I moved over to the sink, questioning who I'd be if I left. Someone who didn't take shit. Someone who wasn't afraid to speak up. Someone stronger.

I ran the tap. The water was hot, but I kept my hands perched beneath the faucet as clouds of steam puffed up around me, pounding their tiny fists at the window, leaving long wet streaks bleeding down the glass. Studying my foggy reflection, I wondered if I was making the right decision by staying. After everything Dan had done, staying felt a lot like surrendering, but then again, so did leaving.

Dousing the sponge in washing up liquid, I picked up a wine glass and went to work. Squaring up my shoulders, I scrubbed and scrubbed, but no matter how hard I scoured the glass, it wouldn't get clean. I bit my lip. When had I last drank wine? Dan didn't drink wine. *'Too vinegary'* he winced once at a dinner party. Dan preferred whisky.

Always whisky.

Wrinkling my brow at the mouldy stain at the bottom, I tried to work out whether I'd been drinking earlier, and if that was the reason I hadn't got dressed when I heard something behind me. I froze, listening to the drawn-out vibrations from the refrigerator; the branches scraping the window outside, the water exploding from the tap when I heard it again. Footsteps.

Glaring at the sink flooding with a watery pile of yesterday's leftovers, I swallowed hard. Had Dan come home? If he had, why wasn't he speaking? About to call out to him, I peered up at the sweaty window then noticed something behind me.

My brow puckered as I looked harder, and when I registered what I was seeing, my heart stopped. Someone stood behind me, and whoever it was, wasn't Dan. My cheeks flamed as I stared at the stranger inching towards me with their head bent.

Who was it? More to the point, what the hell was this person doing in my kitchen? Pushing my chin to my chest, I bit my lower lip as the sound of their raspy breath fused with the rushed melody of the water exploding from the tap.

I had to think logically – a weapon. I needed a weapon. Barely able to stand, I peered at the wineglass quaking in my hands. If I swerved around quick enough, I might be able to catch this person off guard and whack them over the head. That's what they did in the horror movies, didn't they? Stunned the intruder. But those ballsy people always died in the end. Their bodies skinned, their faces worn as a mask.

Perspiration dripped down the back of my neck as I clung tighter to the glass. Even if the stranger didn't go down right away, the blow to the head would startle them enough to give me time. All I needed was time. Glowering at my unsteady palms, I commanded my legs to jerk into action, to swerve around, to attack, but all I could do was stand there wide eyed, as the world collapsed around me.

What if the second I turned, the stranger grabbed me? What if this was all some twisted plan?

Come on Raine. Stop being a coward. Do it. Do it. Do it.

Swallowing the lump in my throat, I took a tattered breath then swung around and smashed the glass into the stranger's skull with as much force as I could humanly muster.

A violent clatter followed.

A desperate whimper escaped my lips, and when I glanced up, my skin prickled with humiliation. I was alone. I scanned the place desperately, searching for somewhere the stranger might've taken cover: the open cupboard doors, the messy worktop, the empty pantry, and when nothing jumped out at me but the smashed glass on the floor, my heart sunk with the realisation that Dan was right – I was losing my mind.

Scrabbling around on the ground in an effort to retrieve the smashed glass as quickly as possible, I blinked furiously. How could I have thought someone had broken in? We had an alarm, and the door was always double locked. Even if someone had broken in, why would whoever it was, have been standing behind me?

Resenting myself for my overzealous imagination, I rolled my eyes when a loud bang from upstairs made me jolt backwards.

Fuck.

I dropped the glass. A neat red incision scraped my palm from where I'd held the stem too tightly.

Fuck. Fuck. Fuck.

Wiping the blood on my dress, I gulped, waiting for the sound to come again. Silence leaked through the kitchen and before I could convince myself the sound was probably nothing, the lights went out.

I jumped. The banging sounded again, louder this time. What the hell was going on? Had the electric gone out? I palmed my cheek. The electric couldn't have gone out. I'd paid the bill last week. Even if it had, where was the banging coming from? Ambushed by darkness, I cleared my throat.

"Hello?"

At the sound of my voice, the lights flicked back on. I scanned the place wearily, my palm still bleeding, my face a sweaty puddle of fear. The place was motionless, silent, and just as I was about to stand and dispose of the glass, the light bulb flickered. My brow puckered as I gazed up, bewildered.

An elongated buzzing sound ripped through the stillness as I clung to my knees, shaking. Moments later, the light bulb began flashing amber, then black, then amber. What was happening? Hunting the wreck of my mind for an explanation, I ground my jaw when it hit me.

Jinx. The cat had probably woken up from one of his sixteen-hour naps and decided it was time for feeding.

"Jinx," I called as the kitchen continued to blink heedlessly. Each explosion of light striking the glass on the ground. "Jinx."

I stared at the trembling ceiling, my heart pulverising my chest. What if someone had broken in? I would have to call the police. What would I tell them? I heard banging coming from upstairs, and it may, or may not have been the cat? Oh, and by the way, there was a stranger in my kitchen who just happened to disappear.

I hung my head. I couldn't risk Dan coming home and seeing the officers shaking their heads at me dolefully. I couldn't give him more of a reason to justify his actions. No, I had to sort this out myself. Picking myself up from the mess on the floor, I clung to the kitchen counter when the sound came again.

BANG. BANG. BANG.

"It's just the cat," I whispered, forcing my legs to advance towards the mountain of steps. "Just the cat," I mumbled, climbing the first step.

BANG. BANG. BANG.

"Just the cat." Clinging to the melting bannister, I mounted the stairs clumsily, and after reaching the top, I frowned. The sound was coming from my loft. The dusty little space where I spent the majority of my life, working, and admittedly hiding.

How could the cat have gotten up there? Studying the panelled ceiling, I reached out and gave the golden stair cord a hefty tug. From the jolt came an eruption of steps. Each one unfurled with a drawn-out creak, punching me with the musty scent of chalk and used up paints.

Nodding at my feet, I started climbing the steps with a plan to retrieve the cat and put him outside. Self-assured, I dragged myself through the hole in the floor before stumbling through the darkness to the light switch, only after reaching it, something warm shuffled past my ankle.

"Jinx," I whispered.

A floorboard creaked behind me.

"Jinx?"

My legs turned to paste.

"Jinx?" Clinging to the wall, I blinked heatedly, and when his distant meow sounded downstairs, my chest caved in. I shook my head, convinced the moment I flicked the switch I'd find this was all in my head.

Just in my head. Just in my head.

My face dripped with sweat as my fingers scrabbled over the plastic.

Just in my head. Just in my head.

"Raine," someone whispered.

I gasped, flicked the switch.

Fighting to catch my breath, I scanned my studio for the stranger who'd just spoken. Paintbrushes, and pastels, and watercolours were crammed on a wooden shelf to my right. Mounted easels were stacked next to the thin slit window. My finished paintings were piled against the rust coloured wall behind me.

Despite the place appearing clear, I remained stagnant, waiting for some crazed butcher to jump out and attack me, and when no one did, my eyes stung with tears. I cupped my clammy face in my hands. Is this what failing to confront Dan was doing to me? Making me lose my mind?

Ready to put the antics of the night behind me, I turned sharply when the banging sounded again– only this time it wasn't so much banging, as knocking. I examined the place with my shoulders stapled to my ears, and when I gathered where the sound was coming from, my jaw collapsed—

the mirror.

Someone was knocking on the other side of the mirror. A dusty antique, tucked in the corner of the room, how? Crossing the room, I watched it tremble and quake, the gold edges quivering, the dust pouncing from the glass, and when I set eyes on my reflection, I released a dry laugh. It was wrong; it had to be wrong.

Pressing a hand to the wall, I fought to keep myself upright as I examined myself in the glass. Wide brown eyes wedged on a pale face decorated with terror. Behind me, were an army of trees. Veering round, I scrutinised Dan's boxes sagging with clutter; old books on marketing, a few broken kitchen appliances.

Taking a deep breath, I told myself that when I turned back, the trees would've disappeared.

KNOCK. KNOCK. KNOCK.

I would go downstairs and make a fresh pot of tea, and

hopefully get some sleep.

KNOCK. KNOCK. KNOCK.

I glared at the cardboard boxes, a vein in my head ready to break through my skin. Swinging around, I almost lost my balance. The trees were still there, swaying behind the glass, taunting me. Pushing my hand to the glass, I closed my eyes, debating whether it would've been wise to call Dan and end things now. Keeping quiet must've been taking a toll on my health.

Riddled with uncertainty, I clenched my eyes shut tighter when the strangest sensation came over me, Mia. I felt like I was falling. My chest tightened, my fingers tingled, my hair flustered about my face, and when I opened my eyes to check my studio for a draft, bile lurched up my throat.

It was gone. Everything was gone. No longer was I in my studio– or even my home. Staggering backwards, I widened my eyes at the jungle of trees surrounding me, the lanterns splayed at their feet. I was in the same place I'd just seen in the mirror.

Was I dreaming? Perhaps I'd passed out from shock. That was it! I was shocked by the events of the night, and I'd passed out because people don't move through mirrors. Only crazy people thought that, and I wasn't crazy. No, I was as sane as they come (give or take a few minor breakdowns.)

Thumping my thigh with a fist, I hoped the jolt might wake me. When it didn't, I threw back my head, studying the sky. A gargantuan red moon glared back challengingly while the wind whipped at my hot cheeks. How was this possible? It was like I'd just stepped into an episode of the twilight zone.

Shaking my head at the bark smattered ground, I was about to continue thinking up ways I might be able to wake up when something crunched behind me.

My lip twitched as I waited for the noise to cease, but

instead, it came again — louder this time, closer. A trampled leaf, a wounded twig, a snapped bone. My brow sagged and when I looked over my shoulder to check I was alone, the world as I knew it ended, Mia.

This is how it started, with her.

Dragging herself forwards with a wooden cane, was a silver-haired woman with two dark voids in the place her eyes should've been. My legs buckled as she skulked closer, her movements rough and disjointed, her black gown catching a carpet of gold leaves. Backing away, I stared at the scraps of flesh hanging from gaunt face, exposing red pouches of fat and fragments of bone.

"This isn't real," I whispered as the monster drew nearer. "This isn't real." My eyes throbbed, and when she lifted her head, I froze, gazing into the pit of her sunken eyes.

"Finally!" the dead woman gasped. "you're here."

"What… what are you?"

"You don't remember me?" the dead woman said, her hot breath whacking me with the scent of rotting corpses. "Well... you were only a child when I saw you last; such a lovely child!"

"How did I get here?" I whispered, struggling to keep my voice steady.

"You moved through the mirror."

"The mirror?"

"The glass in your studio," she replied.

"I know what a mirror is. I want to know how."

"How?"

"Yes, how? People can't– they can't–" The words tasted like cardboard in my throat.

Up close, I saw the mottled insides of her brain. Red and raw, with blood vessels that looked ready to burst. She grinned, a gesture so wide I thought her skin would split.

"This isn't real," I repeated.

"Oh! You claim it isn't real, and yet it is happening?" the woman growled. "How many times have you claimed something isn't real amid your darkest hours, Raine? Now you are in your brightest hour, and still, you claim it isn't real?"

Unsure of how she knew my name, I skimmed the forest, convinced at some point I'd wake up.

"Raine," the dead woman whispered.

I didn't want to look at her. My heart thrashed my ribs as I glared at the lanterns spewing orange light into the mist, the dimpled tree stumps decorated in moss.

"Raine," she giggled.

I chewed my lip.

"Look," she whispered, nodding behind me, but I was terrified the moment I did, she'd grab me.

"Look." Her bloody lips drew together, and when I managed to swivel around, my heart plummeted.

Somehow, the trees had parted, and in the clearing sat an array of furniture: rotting tables, broken chairs, dilapidated dolls' houses, run down dressers, all scattered around messily and glittering in the light of the lanterns.

Recognising each bit of mismatched clutter, I lumbered towards them. Slowly first, then faster. Mannequins, dressers, old journals. They were all mine. Shards of crockery sliced the balls of my feet as I hurried through the maze, panting, and gasping, and choking on sharp chunks of winter air before I stopped at a shabby peach sofa.

Collapsing next to it, I widened my eyes. I would sit there with my dad when I was a child; I was positive. Despite the scent of decay seeping out from the timeworn fibres, I smelt that cheap perfume my mom would spray on her neck each morning.

My throat constricted as I stroked the damp fabric, recalling the way my dad would bounce me on his knee and belt out old British rock songs that when I was older– I could never recall the names of. Then of the flash of anger in his eyes when I spilt juice over one of the sofa cushions. Anger that was enough to kill a man.

I was playing, laughing, my hand slipped, then there was screaming. Too much screaming.

Always screaming.

"You never sat there again, did you?" The dead woman's voice made me flinch.

Jumping up, I turned to her heatedly.

"Where am I?" I demanded.

Stroking a scrap of white skin dangling from her chin, she tilted her head.

"You are home, syrup, back where you belong."

"No, my home is with Dan."

"Is it?" she countered.

"Yes." Even then, I sounded uncertain, Mia.

"But you weren't happy there," the woman croaked. "Surely a place you are unhappy, isn't home?"

I tottered back as she grinned, exposing a mouth packed full of sharpened gravestones.

"You don't remember me? We would play such wonderful games when you were a child. We would dance and sing, and ohhhh!" before I had a chance to scarper, she grabbed my cheek with scabbed palms.

"My," she muttered. "You have grown into a fine woman, and those eyes, how marvellous."

Shrugging myself free, I stared at her indignantly.

"Who are you?" I muttered.

At that, the dead woman drew back her shoulders. The click of her spine sent a shiver ripping through my teeth.

"I, my syrup, am Esme," she said. "And I have come to save you from the hell you call a life, and in return, you will do something wondrous for us all."

I shook my head as she sashayed away through the amber light.

"Would you like supper?" she called. "Something to drink perhaps? Of course! You must be starving! So empty you are, no longer full of hope, never full of love. You must be ravenous! We'll fix that. Don't you worry, we'll soon fix that."

My face twisted as she started waving her hands in large sweeping motions. Her black gown lifted at her ankles, her grey hair thwacked her spine. Moments later, a stove plummeted from the sky, sending a crisp tornado of crisp autumn leaves dancing around her head.

"Why can't I wake up?" I shouted.

"Maybe because you're not asleep," Esme replied, lugging open the oven door.

"I must be."

"Oh, you must, must you? Must, must, must, because all the things that must happen are bound to happen aren't they?"

My face crumpled as she rummaged around in the rusty compartment.

"You were in my house," I said.

"Oh, yes!"

"Why?"

"To meet the creature who would save us, of course."

"Me?"

"Yes, Raine, you. Resident of 34 Bluemont Avenue, married to Daniel Black for three years, happy not a single one of them."

My gut roiled as thick blankets of smoke seeped out from the oven, drenching the forest in the charcoal odour of burning. "Our kingdom is in grave danger, and only you can save us. But the question is, will you forgive him, or will you run."

"Forgive who?"

She didn't answer. Instead, she pulled herself up, and when I set eyes on the small body in her palms, I flung my arms across my chest, certain I had to wake up. Skimming the forest for a way out, my eyes raked over a mildew infested mannequin and mismatched shoes dangling from tree branches, before settling on a chipped blue door leaning against a tree a few metres away.

Praying it might function as an exit, I hurried towards it.

"You shouldn't go, Raine," the woman called as I skirted around a rotten dresser. "Think of all the magic you could unearth in a place where you can start again."

Darting past a row of burning lanterns, I winced as my ankle knocked the metal casing.

"Don't leave us now."

I was nearly there, my hand inches away from the gold doorknob, my eyes set firmly on the rusty number seven in the centre, and had the dead woman not have said what she did next, my life may well have turned out differently, Mia.

"Happy birthday."

My lips parted as the sound of crunching glass behind me grew louder.

"Daniel didn't even wish you a happy birthday," she wheezed. "He waited for you in the restaurant, but he was glad you didn't show up."

I expelled a sigh of disbelief, and just as quickly as the tears took to fall, the memories flooded back. Dan had arranged a meal at his favourite Thai restaurant. I'd bought a dress – this dress – he kept texting all day claiming he was excited, and I kept staring at my phone wondering why he was pretending, why I was pretending.

"You have no one left in your world Raine," Esme said from behind me. "But in this place, you are set to accomplish great things. Believe me, and allow your heart to consume all of the wonders he stole from you."

Wiping my eyes with a fist, I turned to her like an old wounded dog. Half fear, half faith. She offered what she'd pulled from the oven. Her butchered face soft again the crimson moonlight, her palm extended. Then, against every instinct screaming for me not to, I took hold of it and winced.

Lissey. It was the doll I'd lost as a child. The doll I clung to, whispered to, promised everything would be okay to, every time the world went up in flames, only it looked as if someone had taken a mallet to her face.

"Let Esme take care of you," Esme whispered.

I was too busy studying Lissey to answer. Her jaw was smashed, and her doughy blue pupils were empty like the monster in front of me.

"Look at you, poor child. Look at the mess you have become. Is this truly the life you dreamt of as a girl?"

I peered up to argue I wasn't a mess. I was a woman with a career, and a home, and friends, and a husband who loved her. But the words were hindered, because there in the crackling woodland, as I clung to my childhood doll, the truth flickered in the glow of a thousand lanterns, reflecting right back in Esme's empty eyes – I was a fraud.

Bringing Lissey's face to my own, I stroked her cheek when something crawled out from her left eye; the movement similar to a beckoning finger. Releasing the doll, I gasped as she flailed to the ground and shattered into a million wistful pieces at my feet.

From the wreckage of porcelain came a hoard of chubby white maggots, each one wriggling above and below one another.

"Things that are broken shouldn't be held so tightly," Esme chuckled, stepping on Lissey's fractured arm.

"I need to go," I said.

"Go?" Esme breathed. "But you've only just arrived. Why leave, when you can be part of something magnificent? Something you were destined for. Are you really going to cheat your destiny, Raine?"

Convinced I could ward off this warped creature, I tried moving past her when she dove sideways, blocking the doorway with her cane.

"Let me go," I said.

Esme's shoulders snapped back. She studied me thoughtfully. Her face lit up, her empty eyes widened, and just as I began to fear she may massacre me after all, she lowered her shoulders.

"Go," she smirked. "But before you leave, I need your word you will not tell a living soul you have met with me."

I nodded, certain I wouldn't want to.

"Say it," she hissed. Spit escaped her lips as she dove forwards.

"You have my word," I muttered.

"That…?" Esme whispered, her hot breath turning my stomach.

"That I will not tell a living soul I have met with you."

"Marvellous!" she exclaimed. "Now open your mouth."

"I'm sorry?"

"Open your mouth, Rainey. You have agreed to give me your word. Have you not?"

My lips cracked as I glared at her with a million questions swimming through my frantic eyes, and before a single one of them could make it to my lips, she knocked me to the ground.

A flash of brightness blinded me. I fought to sit up, but there was something cold pressed against my throat: something dry, her hand. My insides twisted as her hot breath smacked my nostrils. What was she doing? Staring into the pit of her eyes, I flinched as she stooped lower, a scrap of her flesh swinging from her chin and grazing my nose.

I shook my head as she brought her hands up to my face, and just as I was about to demand she let me go, she ripped apart my lips. I winced. The sensation similar to someone pouring battery acid down my throat. Everything burnt, simmered, smouldered.

I screamed, clinging to the bark at my sides and gulping in air that refused to enter my lungs. Distant laughter crashed through the air as her fingers became snakes, slithering behind my tongue and crawling down my neck.

I retched, tasting year old decay as her fingernails buried themselves deep within the trench of my stomach, and a scrap of cold flesh lay dormant in my mouth. My head throbbed as the red moon behind her swayed. I was about to lose consciousness; I was sure of it. The world was hazy, distant. My teeth pulsed, my jaw ached.

I fought to keep my eyes open, but everything was going slow and it hurt to breathe, to think. I was going to be sick, but I couldn't, because if I was sick, I would choke and die anyway.

I coughed. My face drenched in cold sweat, my throat a pile of bloody pulp, and when the world was nothing more than a distant afterthought, her grip loosened. Gulping in moist air, I strove to sit up, but my chest rebelled against it. Seconds later, I fell back with my cheeks pushed against shredded letters, my letters.

'Mrs Black, we are writing to inform you, you are overdrawn.'

Glancing around at the woodland, I saw her striding off with a glistening blue orb dangling at her side. I wrinkled my brow as she looked over her shoulder, and flashed me an uneven smile.

"I have your word," Esme announced. And then, she disappeared.

***

"You started seeing things?" Pierce asks, failing to hide the scepticism in his tone. "What happened after?"

I shrug, staring at a single word written on his page, thinking back to the morning when I'd woken up and reached out for Dan. The empty space next to me reminding me I was barricaded in this stale marriage, either waiting for him to come home and pretend nothing had happened, or face the truth we kept running from.

I remember stumbling out of bed when I heard a car pull up outside, but even then I knew it couldn't have been Dan, Mia. A simple dispute wasn't enough to make him come home. Maybe he felt guilty, I thought as I threw on my dressing gown, only when I caught sight of my reflection in the bedroom mirror, Dan was the last thing on my mind.

"Had Dan acted that way before?" Watson presses.

I force a nod, because my solicitor, Peters, is basing my case on battered woman syndrome, and if I want the charges to be lessened, I must play up to the role of derailed housewife, but people don't have to use their fists to be violent, Mia.

Lowering my head, I think back to the morning when I'd traced the slashes against my neck — Purple, almost black.

"Did you ever see this sort of thing again?"

Again, I nod. This time it's the truth because when Dan came home and apologised, I saw her rocking on her heels behind him. I heard her whispering when he typed beside me at night. Humming, when I stirred my morning coffee. And on the evenings where we'd switch on the television to avoid the passionless silence, she'd call my name, begging me to go back.

Tucking a strand of hair behind my ear, I blink at Pierce's page before he catches me then flips it over, but it's pointless because I've already seen the word.

– Hallucinations.

CHAPTER THREE

Watson is late. Dashing inside, she drops her bag, then sighs. Inside her red leather satchel, I glimpse a cluster of lipsticks, half a pack of cigarettes, a compact mirror, a perfume bottle, and what appears to be a bright pink pencil case. I eye it hesitantly, certain if I hadn't seen the designer label tacked to the front, I would've suspected the bag belonged to a rebellious schoolgirl– never mind a doctor in her early thirties.

"Sorry," she pants, pushing her bag forward, so the contents sit out of my view.

"Traffic?" Pierce asks, grinning.

She rolls her eyes before they begin. They ask me: how long was I seeing things? If there was one voice or more? Did it seem angry? Did it force me to do things? Did I feel like it was my fault? Did I think it was right? To all of their questions, I respond with a shrug.

"So, you went to this place..." Pierce says, rubbing a strappy tan line on his wrist, most likely from a second-hand watch. "Did you ever go back?"

I consider shrugging again, mainly because Esme was right. She knew about the void in my life I was desperate to fill, and the other part is because they wouldn't believe me. I wouldn't have believed me five months ago.

"Okay, so assuming you did go back, why?"

"It was an escape." The word dances from my mind to their pages.

ESCAPE.

"An escape from what?"

"Dan?" Pierce chimes.

"Yes," I mutter, because Dan was everywhere, Mia.

Buried in every phone bill. Tucked inside of every photograph. Pressed against every unnecessary household appliance he ordered on my credit card. He was always there, lingering in a house made of windows. But going back there made it seem as though all of the darkness from my past– everything Dan brought back in heed of his own self-righteous entitlement– disappeared. Everything was new. I was new. I wasn't that broken girl anymore.

"It was the only place I felt alive."

JULY 8TH 2018

After days curdled to weeks, I managed to convince myself that lack of sleep was responsible for my overactive imagination. I researched vivid dreams, watched documentaries on sleep paralysis, I even considered telling Dan about the woman in my nightmare, but despite all of the rationalisations I explored, the marks on my neck were still there. A pulsing reminder that something– whatever it was, had happened.

I tried to relax. But the more I tried, the more agitated I became. A painful numbness swelled inside of me, and I was constantly torn between ripping my skin off to feel something, or screaming until my throat bled because I felt too much. After spotting the marks on my neck, Dan became anxious. Not the concerned kind of anxious, but the sweaty kind a shoplifter grinning at a store manager might experience, after skulking through a security door with a backpack full of stolen goods.

I remember him standing behind me while I applied lotion to the scratches on my neck. Assuring Dan I'd scraped my neck during the night, I'd held my breath as he nodded, smiled, then, after swallowing my lies as punishment for his own, he strolled out of the bathroom and retreated to his study.

Dan didn't have to tell me he wanted out of our pitiful marriage; it was clear in every moment we shared, or rather, failed to. I could've changed it, I guess. I could've dressed provocatively, listened more, confronted him. I should've confronted him. But the damage had already been done, and I couldn't forgive Dan for his indiscretions, or even bring them up unless he was willing to admit them.

All I could do was wait for him to confess. And in the process of waiting, one night, he suggested he slept in the guest room.

"Just to get you back on track Rai, it will be good for us both."

I stared at him leaning against the bedroom door with that shoplifter smile, and before I could argue, Dan was bundling pillows under his arm and setting up camp in the guest room. Dan had no idea he was killing me. But there, in his eyes, I was dying fast.

Days after Dan became comfortable in the spare room, I stood next to our wardrobe planning a new piece. For the first time in months, I was hopeful. Summer had arrived bearing suitcases stuffed with fresh beginnings, and a gentle gust of wind that whispered of its strength to carry off ugly scraps of the past.

Throwing on an old t-shirt, I marched into the hallway,

before tugging down the cord to my studio steps. Climbing the stairs, I ignored the smell of Dan's aftershave bruising my cheek from where he'd kissed me goodbye. *'I'll see you tonight.'* Liar. His words strummed around in my head while I tried to focus, and the more I did, the more ridiculous I felt for postponing work for something as trivial as a nightmare.

I had pieces to sell, emails from clients I hadn't returned. Dan would've called me stupid. I needed to be stronger. Reaching the top, I skimmed the place uneasily. Everything seemed less sinister in daylight. Sunlight slinked through the windows, kissing the red brick walls and the magnolia bedsheets strewn about my finished paintings.

Behind me, a stepladder was stocked with plastic plants, and books on nineteenth-century art, scattered between a few Bukowskis. Ambling through the musty scent of used up oil paints, I stopped at the mirror. Searching my reflection for a glimmer of something, anything, I sighed when nothing jumped out at me but a mousy little woman who looked like she hadn't slept in months.

Sealing my eyes shut tight, I visualised what I would paint. Something vivid, maybe. Reds and blues tousling through veiny leaves. A burgundy river set alight by the sun. I hadn't even realised I'd lifted my hand until I felt the cold glass hit my fingertips.

About to grab an easel from behind me, an enigmatic whoosh of calmness flooded my temples. I shuddered as the sounds of an oncoming train burrowed deep within my skull, clanging, and clicking against the tracks, stuffing my chest and ears with cool bursts of air, and when I opened my eyes, I was walloped by an urge to scream.

I flew back, stunned. No longer was I at home, or even in the forest from my nightmare. Instead, I was in some sort of field. My face blanched. Carpeting the ground was a sea of sunflowers that reached way up past my waist, painting the world beyond me in vibrant dashes of yellow and brown. No, no, no. I spun around, my eyes burning.

I had to have been asleep. Only seconds ago, I'd been in my studio, and now I was trapped in some sort of flamboyant Van Gogh painting. Searching the dusty pink sky for answers, I was pummelled by more unwarranted uncertainty. Hanging low in the centre, was a huge red sun.

My eyes glazed over as I stared at its edges glimmering a fuzzy orange, making it seem as though the sky had been stubbed by a cigarette and never fully recovered. What was this place? Behind me, two trees were fixed opposite one another, their mighty branches enveloped in a rich tapestry of purple and gold blossoms.

Moving through the heavy scent of wild, uncombed pastures, I paused next to one of the trees. Stroking its cracked bark, my heart raged with doubt and the sour taste of insanity when a woman's voice made me spring backwards.

"Will you get away from my husband you harlot!"

Shit.

Clawing my palms, I turned shakily, but after giving the place a once over, my brow sagged. I was alone. I waited for the voice to sound again, but the world was silent and bursting with humidity that made t-shirt stick to my spine. Figuring I'd probably imagined the voice, I set off into the field in the unlikely hope I might find someone who could explain what was going on when she spoke again.

"Going somewhere?"

My chest rattled as I glanced at my feet. A shadow rocked overhead of me. The silhouette swayed back and forth, back and forth, but there wasn't a whisper of wind around for miles. Forcing my legs to jerk around, my eyes raked over the sunflowers, the fuzzy sky. Settling on the tree closest to me, my heart shrivelled to dust.

Etched into its mighty stump, was a face. Lurching backwards, I glared at two slanted eyes, set above a mushroom-shaped nose.

"This… this… isn't right," I gasped, ogling the monstrosity with eyes bigger than my face.

"Don't start that nonsense with me." the tree barked, lunging so swiftly the sunflowers at my waist shivered. "I saw you stroking my husband."

My lips puckered, but I couldn't answer; I could barely work out what was going on. Not only was this tree talking, but I was pretty sure I was about to become its meal ticket.

"Well?" it roared. "Fairies like you, flying about. Go around and fondle everyone's husbands, do you?"

Fairies?

Sliding past the overgrown plant on legs that had become nothing more than two useless strings of spaghetti; I stared at the great entry to its mouth with my brain threatening to implode.

Wake up, Raine. WAKE UP.

"You should be ashamed of yourself!"

Sweaty and disoriented, I inched back further then bashed into the tree behind me and froze.

Hearty laughter followed. Pressing myself to look over my shoulder, my eyes pricked with hot tears when I saw it. Like the first tree, engraved into its wrinkled bark was a face. Only in place of a scowl was a heavy toothless grin. Crumbling under the realisation of what I was seeing, I threw my arms over my head.

"I quite enjoyed it, Marie," The male tree chuckled in a voice so deep the earth trembled. "Haven't been touched like that in a while."

"Edward!" the female tree cried lunging at him.

"Yes, syrup?"

"Don't yes syrup me, Edward. It had its hands all over you!"

Throttled by an urge to sink into the earth and never come up for air again, I shook my head. I was going mad. I had to have been, to imagine these trees were bickering with one another.

"It didn't know we're married," Edward reasoned. "It can't see our rings."

"Rings or no rings, this is the pixie fiasco all over again, Edward."

"It most certainly is not, Syrup. Besides, I expect the creature mistook me for a fern, you know ferns aren't really fans of commitment."

Enough.

"I'm sorry," I interrupted, glaring at the trees through watery eyes. "But how is it possible you're both talking?"

My cheeks stung as the trees gawked at me, baffled. In the silence that proceeded, I waited for them to tell me they were genetic mutations of some sort. Or figments of my imagination, but to my complete and utter dismay, both began laughing.

"What's funny?" I shouted. "Can you please tell me where I am?"

"You're right, Marie!" Edward tittered. "It must be sick."

"I'm not sick, can you please just tell me where I am?"

"How did you get here?"

"There was a mirror—"

"Ah, a mirror! Oh, heavens," Edward guffawed wiping his eyes with a branch.

"Please, will you help me?"

"You better get back to your hole, fairy," Marie said. "And don't go about touching anyone else's husbands."

I tried to tell the trees I didn't live in a hole, and that I wasn't a fairy, but after shouting until my lungs were as hollow as theirs, I realised it was pointless.

Defeated, I set off into the muggy field with the trees' laughter growing fainter, and the sound of my heart becoming riotous. Trudging on for what felt like hours, I stopped when I heard a piano being played. Heat pressed against my head like an iron as I scanned the hazy stretch of land.

The place was motionless, and just as I was about to continue moving, the earth beneath my pumps pulsed. Lowering my head, I caught sight of a hole the size of a fist.

"Hello?" I called.

Suspecting there must've been an underground bunker underneath, I crouched down, when I heard it again — a piano. With my palms pushed against dry soil, and the scent of moss and dirt bruising my lungs, I wrinkled my nose as the hole amplified, the ground shook harder, and before I had a chance to work out what was going on, I was pulled through the tiny space.

Terror ripped through me as I kicked my arms and legs about. Submerged in sandy darkness, I screamed, but even as the sound surged through my lungs, I couldn't hear it. I'm falling, I thought. I'm falling into a miniature hole, and I may never be able to get out. There was too much air. It jammed my ears and lungs, and throat, and just as I began to dread I'd entered an everlasting abyss, I was welcomed by the smash of cold concrete.

I winced. My shoulder hit first. A bone skated out of place. My head spun. Debating whether or not I'd just landed underground, I flinched at the sound of a gruff voice.

"Careful, syrup."

I stiffened, but couldn't find the strength to answer. My chest ached, and my neck throbbed so viscously, I feared it was broken.

"Where's your cushion?"

Cushion?

With my chin quivering above concrete, I peered up slowly. Two scuffed black hooves clipped beside my face. Widening my eyes and forgetting the dismal state of my body entirely, I leapt up, gawking at the creature in disbelief.

He had the face of a man; thick black brows set above eyes the same colour, with his hair fastened in a ponytail. His torso belonged to a man too. Beefy shoulders that practically leapt out of his ears, a sculpted chest smattered in wiry hairs.

If kept my eyes averted from his waist, he would be a man. Only when I forced my focus on his legs, my heart slipped out from under me. There were four of them. Each one covered in rich tan fur, giving the impression they'd been sawn off from a show-stopping racehorse.

Fighting to work out if my eyes were playing tricks on me, I stared at a sleek whip-like tail thwacking out behind him. As a child, I'd heard tales of centaurs, but they were just stories, narratives about mythological creatures that didn't exist. That couldn't exist.

"Not easy to get these like this," the centaur boasted, flexing his bicep, and mistaking my horror for a sign of admiration.

I nodded, scanning the cave for a way out. The walls were built of stone, the floor dusted in tiny pebbles. Peering up at the ceiling almost forty feet away, I could just about make out the hole I'd fallen through.

"Are you okay?" The centaur asked.

Despite wanting to scream NO, I felt myself nodding.

"You must recognise me," he said.

"Recognise you?"

"From Bat fire, our national sport, I was the champion years back, the crowd loved me."

"Bat fire?"

"Fall must have frazzled your thinking more than I thought," the centaur chuckled, prodding his skull with a stubby finger.

Nodding politely, I averted my gaze from his bemused face then glimpsed a wooden door behind him.

"You honestly don't know what Bat fire is?"

I shook my head, wondering if I could sidestep him and make a run for it.

"All contestants, sixteen of them, fastest and strongest centaurs in the kingdom, we run."

"So, it's a race?" I asked, trying to keep the conversation light.

"It's more than a race! We have a spear. The aim is to reach the finish line without getting hacked up.'"

"Sounds brutal."

"It is," the centaur smirked, twisting out his front leg so I could see a healed pink scar whittled against the fur on his knee. "Got that in my last game. Would've still been playing if it hadn't been for that." Gripped by a memory, he shook his head before his tone became professional.

"ID," he said, extending a hand with surprisingly neat fingernails.

"ID? Is there a way I can get out of here?"

"Jumpers inside," the centaur shrugged. "Not going to stick around for one?"

I faltered, wondering what this *one* was when he smiled a wry smile.

"Okay, Okay," he whispered, yanking open the door. "In you go, only this time mind, since you forgot your cushion."

Eager to set eyes on the jumper as soon as I made it inside, I shuffled past him, only when the thin sheet of wood clipped shut behind me, the jumper was the farthest thing from my mind.

Pushing back in the doorway, I scanned the place guardedly. It appeared I'd entered a bar; an underground lair with stone walls, and a dusty cobbled floor that leaked with the perfume of fresh terrain. A piano was being played, a sparky melody that sprinkled the spacious chamber with a flicker of joviality.

Astounded, I peered around, hunting the room for a ladder. Metres ahead of me was an ancient tree stump stretching right the way up to a muddy ceiling. Dangling from its many branches were an assortment of colourful lanterns casting a buttery glow upon dozens of wooden tables. I held my breath, studying the tree. Unlike the trees I'd encountered earlier, this one didn't have a face. Encrusted around its dented stump instead, were an assortment of twinkling white fairy lights.

What was this place? And if it was underground, how would I leave? To my right, was a long mahogany bar where two women with sleek red hair, waited for what I assumed was the attention of a shirtless bartender. Shifting my attention to a stage on the far side of the room, I bit my lip. A single spotlight burst from the dusty ceiling, illuminating a stout man in a snug black suit, playing a grand piano without keys.

I inclined my head as he threw down his palms, whacking the empty keyboard, and when he lifted his head, I gulped, realising I hadn't been staring at a man at all, instead, playing the keyless piano was a chubby creature with the head of a mole. My cheeks moistened as I took in his long pink snout, and eyes that were barely visible beneath his inky black fur.

Horror dusted my face as I skimmed the place desperately, and the longer my eyes raked over the bar's inhabitants, the harder I had to stop myself from screaming.

None were human.

At a wooden table closest to the stage, was a creature

with tall white ears and buck teeth. Behind him, was a tubby shirtless man who couldn't be taller than three foot at best, who had feet larger than his body. Shifting my focus to the bar, I stared at the red-haired women and when I caught sight of a bushy red tail thwacking out from one of their hinds, I rushed to the table closest with my head in my hands.

I'd lost the plot, clearly. I'd probably passed out in my studio. Dan would find me and send me to a psych ward. He'd have them lock me up and throw away the key. 'It's for your own good," he would tell me, and I would hate him. I punched my thighs, endeavouring to stay strong, but I didn't feel strong, I felt like an army were discharging their weapons in my brain.

Stiffening as the rabbit creature strode past me, I watched as he marched towards a door, metres away. Yanking it open, he slipped into a room that appeared similar to the place I'd just landed. Only wedged in the middle of the pebble-soaked floor was a yellow circular platform.

I narrowed my eyes as he convened on the circle with his hands on his hips and his pale cheeks puffed out. Raising a brow, I leaned across the table when the circle launched him into the air, leaving me with the grim realisation that the jumper, was literally a jumper.

The piano melody struck the walls of my heart as I fought to work out what I should do. Leaving was probably my best option, but if I exited by the jumper, how could I know for certain it wouldn't launch me into some other lair filled with warped oddities?

Wracked with doubt, my eyes swept over the tubby man a few tables away. Fiddling with a small plastic packet of glitter, he peered at the bartender from over his shoulder. The creases around his neck deepened, then disappeared as he turned back to the table, threw back his head, then tipped the contents of the packet down his tiny gullet.

"That's some good stuff!" the man laughed, slamming his fist into the table.

Stooping lower, I glared at his sweaty face when something law defying began taking place, Mia. Both his eyes were flooding with colour. Whirling tangerine then purple then lime, until all that was left were two nonsensical pools of paint the size of saucers.

"I've warned you, Henry!" the bartender shouted. "No magic inside!"

Magic?

My mind worked up a sweat trying to connect the dots.

"No magic inside," Henry mimicked, elevating from his seat and thundering through the air like a heedless cannonball.

"You've been warned before, you dim-witted elf," came a voice from behind me.

Elf?

This creature was an elf?

Not only that, a flying elf?

"This time we're going to the authorities!"

Swerving around, I saw the doorman trotting across the room with his tail whipping the air behind him. Seconds later, the bartender galloped over the counter, revealing legs that were identical to the doorman's.

My heart throttled my ribs as the mole played louder, and the vines from the ceiling smacked the air furiously.

"Catch me then," sang the elf. "Come on!"

"Get down now!"

"Grab him!"

It was the perfect picture of anarchy. Bar stools clattered as the centaurs lunged, stumbled, then missed. But it was only a matter of time before the elf was apprehended. Whatever he had taken was wearing off. Like an injured bird, his body fluttered feverishly but couldn't quite make it to the ceiling. His eyes began losing sparkle. His belly vibrated as he fought to hurl himself up higher.

He was sinking. Inches from the ground, the doorman seized him by a toe, then flung him head first across the room where he landed in a hysterical pile at my feet. I shivered as the elf's hot breath smacked my ankles, and the clipping of the doorman's hooves grew louder.

Hunching lower, I prayed I'd go unnoticed. The doorman grunted. His breath whacked the back of my neck. Peering up, I saw him trotting towards the door to the jumper with the elf dangling at his side.

"Foolish elves," the bartender muttered. "All magic fanatics."

Positive I had to leave, I held my breath as the doorman disappeared beyond the door. This place was too dangerous. I could still hear the elf's skull shattering; I saw his eyes fading from a vivid magenta to a sorry shade of blue. Though, I feared if I didn't ask the question bludgeoning my brain, I'd be faced with a different kind of danger, regret.

With that drunken logic in place, I stood then started inching towards the counter where the bartender polished a mug with a dirty rag.

My feet tacked to the gummy cobbles as I watched him, ready to ask where this place was and get some solid answers. Only, after making it halfway, I stopped. What did I expect would happen if I told the bartender I'd accidentally stumbled upon this world through a mirror? That he'd pat me on the back and offer me a drink?

On the precipice of hurrying back to my seat, I froze when he looked up and smiled.

"What will it be, syrup?" he asked.

My lips cracked as he eyed me warmly.

He had the kind of face that belonged to a man who strove for the simple things in life, and had I not seen the spectacle moments before, I wouldn't have believed he was capable of anything remotely violent.

"I was just wondering," I said, forcing my legs to go the rest of the way.

"Yes?" the bartender asked, raising a bushy brow.

"I erm," I glanced at the mole, then at the women towering above him on the stage to my left.

"What are you?" the bartender quizzed.

My heart stirred as I turned back. Up close, I smelt the year-old sweat sticking to his bulky chest, and I saw a rabid hunger in his eyes I hadn't noticed before.

Licking my lips, I questioned how I would respond, a woman? A human?

"Ah, you're a Mithel!" the bartender decided before I could answer. "A little on the scrawny side for a Mithel aren't you?"

"Yes," I heard myself lie.

Why did I lie?

My throat boiled as his eyes wandered shamelessly across my body.

"And your eyes, and hair, why are they so dark?"

I shook my head, fearful he could hear my insolent heart.

"What are you doing here?"

"Just passing."

"I thought you Mithels stayed in packs, only gallivanting to your formal affairs. Were you sent here?"

I shook my head again.

"So what are you doing on this side of the grass?"

"Just taking a walk."

His eyes met mine, dark and full and empty.

"So, what are you having?" the bartender shrugged, gesturing to the bottles above the bar. "It's on me, being a Mithel and all."

Releasing a painful breath, I skimmed the bottles lined up on deep copper shelves above the bar. Tiny flecks of dust pounded the glass inside. Yellow and bronze and turquoise, shades ranging from a fizzing pink to a glistening black.

"What are they?"

"Unicorn tears, I have gold if you prefer? Keep the special bottles downstairs. Some folks in here get a little handsy."

"Unicorns?"

"Finest and best breed."

"How?"

The bartender's eyes amplified.

"How? Farms on the fifth region. You bang your head or something?"

Resisting the urge to tell him I had, I changed the subject.

"That elf," I tiptoed. "What did he take?"

It was a question uttered like any other, but the words hit the bartender like a jackhammer. Exploding backwards, he stared at me with his fluffy brows buried somewhere in his hairline.

"You have been sent here," he hissed. "I knew it."

I tried to rearrange my face to seem disinterested, bored, unappeased, but my cheeks were reddening, and I couldn't stop my lips from trembling.

"I… I haven't. I was just curious."

"Why?"

"I… I don't know."

He stared at me for the longest time, before rolling his eyes.

"Saturated sprite powder," he grunted.

"Pardon me?"

"Fairy dust!" he snapped. "Not that you need to be told that, and he didn't get it from here if that's what you're wondering, so there's no need to spread stories about my respectable establishment."

I nodded, confident he'd mistaken me for someone

else. Someone he was afraid of. Someone he couldn't attack. Clearing my throat, I tried my best to play up to the character.

"I was just wondering," I said in my best authoritarian voice. "If you might tell me where we are."

"Goldman's tavern," the bartender replied, emulating my tone.

"And where might that be?"

"Wonder often, wander always," he said, tapping his nose.

"Pardon me?"

He opened his mouth, uttered a sound, then watched me as if I were mad, and when he replied, I wondered the same thing.

"The third region of Wanderlust."

***

"How did you leave?" Watson asks.

"After I spoke to the bartender, everything went dark, and I was back in my studio. Just like that."

"Just like that," she repeats, scratching her mouth with a bright red fingernail.

"Was Dan around at the time?"

"Was Dan ever around?" I mutter.

Pierce raises a brow.

"No," I tell them, and it's the truth because even when Dan was there, all I needed was the collision of our eyes to tell me he was gone. That crash of a glance, always searching for a way out, only Dan was too complacent to ever find one.

"That must have been difficult, not having your husband there when all of this was going on."

I shake my head because Dan's inattentiveness made it easy, Mia. Trouble only surfaced when he came back – when he asked questions – when he tried stopping me, but I wouldn't let him. In the end, he learnt that the hard way.

CHAPTER FOUR

Ten a.m. and we've already meandered through my mental state in the lead up to the '*accident*' they keep branding Dan's death; only it wasn't an accident. It was a cold-blooded act of revenge. They ask how many times I went back, why I went back, but the truth is I can't remember why, Mia, just that I had to.

Pierce flips his page, coughs.

"And it was the same things you saw... a bar, creatures..." he looks up at me shaking my head. "Well, what was different?"

"Raine, did anything significant happen around the time you were experiencing these things? Anything stressful?"

They're probing. Urging me to admit what they think they already know, but it's a lie. It's all a lie.

"Can we talk about Dan? Let's start at the beginning when—"

"He didn't believe me either."

Watson glances at Pierce for the first time this morning.

"When did you tell Dan?" she questions. "Was it after

your first GP visit?"

"Before I killed him."

Watson grimaces.

Pierce barely reacts. He watches me closely; his full-fat hazel eyes deconstructing me.

"What did you tell him?" he probes.

"Everything."

"You told him everything?" His brow lifts, and when the room floods with silence, he places his hands on the desk. "Okay, so pretend I'm Dan."

I'm not listening. I think of the tavern, Instead. I was fascinated by it. The colours, the creatures, their bizarre antics, and it was only the beginning, Mia.

"You need to trust us," Pierce instructs.

Looking up, I see his palm inching closer to mine from across the table. I incline my head, then, unexpectedly even for me, I release what sounds like a laugh. A flat, dry, ugly sound that knocks both Pierce and Watson back in their seats.

And once I start, I can't stop, because it's in that tactile demand I recall what a precious gift trust is. A prize we cling to fiercely, scared it may fall into the wrong pair of hands, but in times of desperation, trust is tossed from our fingers as if it were burning coal. But I'm not desperate anymore.

"What's funny?" Pierce asks, hiding his hands under the desk.

"Nothing," I tell him. And for the most part, it's the truth.

JULY 12TH 2018

For the next four days, I was hooked.

Wanderlust became a drug. The mirror, my dealer, and I, its quivering junkie. Anticipating the rush of colour that would thunder through my periphery every time I was pulled through the mirror, I'd stand there with one hand pressed against my reflection, waiting. Sometimes it would take seconds, other times hours, but it would always arrive, the glorious abandon wading through my chest when I opened my eyes and found myself back in the tavern.

Hoping I'd go unnoticed, I would dart over to the table nearest, studying the place with an insatiable thirst. In those earlier days I saw all sorts of creatures, Mia. stout men with gold marble eyes, gangly women who resembled foxes, creatures with sleek blue skin and long silver manes.

All entered through the door where I'd encountered the centaur, and after chatting amongst themselves, or squabbling, or waltzing to music the mole played on stage, all left through the door to the jumper. It was bizarre, and magnificent, and terrifying all at the same time, and as the days unfolded, I managed to trick myself into believing the world I came from was just a dream, and this chaotic mixed up world was mine.

I'd feel myself drifting after a few hours. It began with a timid fizzling in my skull, followed by a soft pulsing of my fingertips. Each one jittered and quaked with the viscous reminder I was going back to the vacuum I called my life. Seconds later, I'd find myself back in my studio, eyeballing the mirror, and biding my time till I could return.

My descent wasn't entirely a problem. If anything, it was convenient, in that it allowed me to keep up the charade with Dan, and still feed me with the freedom he stole. But like most good things, my venture would be cut short, and this mystical escapade came to an end on the fourth day.

Stumbling through the mirror, I skimmed the bar for

the usual commotion. The place was more or less empty. Upon the stage, the mole played a sombre tune, dry and melancholy and painting the room in a dull shade of loss. Across from him, partially hidden behind the mighty tree stump, the doorman was midway through speaking to a woman who had limbs like his. I raised a brow as she tipped back a glossy head of auburn hair that fell past her sculpted torso and settled at a matching tail.

Apart from them, there was only one other creature in the tavern. Dressed in a finely tailored black suit, he stood at the bar with his back to me. Slumping down at the table closest, my eyes danced across the emerald creases enveloping his bald scalp and the thick jade tail falling from his hind.

"Dangerous?" the bartender asked the creature. "How so?"

"...All sorts of dark magic—" the tailed creature replied in a raspy voice.

Hoping neither would catch me eavesdropping, I focussed on the mole playing the piano. Though, a few verses later, the melody came to a standstill, and after rising from the bench, the mole shuffled down the steps and left through the door to the jumper.

I lowered my head. Without the music the voices behind me were easier to pick up, but with the growing absence of creatures, it was becoming increasingly obvious I was an intruder.

"I have been informed by the king himself, it slaughtered an entire village with its bare hands," the conversation continued.

"And his majesty is offering a substantial reward."

"How much?"

"A lot."

"What class?"

"Well, that's the thing," said the tailed creature. "You

see, the creature does not possess any identification."

Releasing a high-pitched whistle, the bartender pushed his palms against the counter. Seemingly not a fan of theatrics, the stranger turned enough for me to catch a fraction of his sunken face. It was the colour of a shattered beer bottle, and his features appeared similar to that of a reptile.

"What region?" the bartender asked.

The creature lifted his empty glass.

Pulling a face, the bartender filled the glass with a thick gold liquid, then waited while the creature drained the contents.

"It's irrelevant," the creature said, slamming the glass against the counter.

If the bartender was offended by his lack of admission, it didn't show. Instead, his eyes swept over the bar like he was coming out of a bad dream.

"Imagine that," he breathed. "A creature without identification. Do you think it was the same creature that the Siren—"

Leaving no room for him to finish, the stranger flung himself against the counter, and though he barely reached the bartender's chest, it was obvious the bartender was terrified. Everything belonging to him shook. His brows, his jaw, even his burly shoulders juddered as if he'd just ingested an alarm clock.

"No!" the creature hissed. "And if you so much as think about that incident again, I will slit your throat personally, do you hear me?"

"Yes…Yes sir," the bartender replied.

A lengthy silence followed, in which I envisioned the creature's luminous eyes brightening at the bartender's distress, but when he spoke again, his voice sounded less brutish then I'd anticipated.

"So, Rodrigo, I have your word, every creature must be inspected before entering and leaving your…

establishment?"

Inspected? My forehead drooped as I swung back around to the table.

"Yes…Yes, sir. You can tell his majesty it is an honour to serve him. And if…"

I heard the click of the creature's heels whacking the floor. He was leaving. My chest stirred as I glared at the table, concerned that without identification, they may have mistaken me for the creature responsible for the crimes they'd spoken of.

Plagued with anxiety, I lowered my head as the creature continued towards the jumper. The place I sat adjacent to. The place he was sure to see me from. I held my breath as his footsteps grew louder, stopped. My cheeks flushed as I peered at a shadow draped against the stone wall.

He was standing behind me, I was sure of it. I felt his eyes ripping holes in the back of my skull. My cheeks stung as I fought to convince myself that when I turned, I'd be able to explain I was just passing like I had a few days ago.

Sweat beaded on my palms as I peeked over my shoulder, and when I set eyes on the beast, the walls of my mind collapsed so hard and so fast I lost my balance in my seat.

He watched me through the eyes of a snake. An incandescent yellow wedged into skin that was a dead shade of green.

"What are you?" the creature hissed.

My chest rattled as I glanced at the silver claws protruding from his skeletal fingers. He was comparable to one of those monsters mothers warned their offspring about when they've been bad. Creatures that lurked in forests and preyed on the souls of misbehaving children, and despite his slender stature, he carried the air of someone who'd snap bones for pleasure.

"She's a Mithel," the bartender called. "You should know that, Candimore."

My cheeks burnt as the creature shook his head slowly.

A thin black slit in his yellow eyes expanded as inhaled through two cavities in the flat surface of his nose.

"That is not a Mithel," he spat. Darting forwards he hauled me up by my arm. I flinched, staring at the blue veins etched into his skull.

"Where is it?" he said. "Where is it?"

I winced as the flesh tore on my arm. My eyes watered as I squirmed, fighting to ward him off, but his grip only tightened until I shouted,

"Where is what?"

With that, the creature slinked backwards.

My legs crumbled as I peered at my wrist. Five wet punctures dented my skin, and a trickle of blood ran down my index finger.

"Your ID," the bartender called.

"Where is it?" the creature goaded, thrusting his arm in my face, jabbing me with the whiff of bubbling swamps.

Jerking backwards, I glimpsed an inscription blistered into his wrist.

CANDIMORE, REPSIL, 2.

"Where is it?"

I shook my head, understanding their ID's were something that couldn't be counterfeited. They were carved into their skin for the world to see, and without it, it was clear I was an intruder.

"I didn't—"

The ground shook as I backed away,

The bartender whispered something. The centaur crept closer. My eyes hammered mercilessly as I struggled to find the words to tell them this was a mistake. My legs liquified. The words dried up in my mouth, and before any of the monsters had a chance to attack me again, I ran.

All havoc unleashed behind me, but I didn't turn. I had to get to the jumper. It was my only chance of survival. Swerving past the tree, I pushed my legs to move faster.

"Catch it," the woman squealed.

"Kill it," someone else shouted.

My brow pricked with sweat as the sounds of galloping hooves and shrill laughter tore through the air, forcing me to run faster before I burst into the room with the thick rubber platform.

Breathless, I mounted the circle. Springing up and down, I willed it to launch me into the sky as it had with the other creatures, but I had no such luck. The other creatures I'd seen use the jumper had stood still, but I couldn't risk waiting, not when they were so close. My chin quivered as I groped the stone walls in search of a secret switch or lever to hurl me through the air.

Nothing.

My eyes smouldered, and the Repsil was nearly there. From the door, I saw him schlepping through the room, not even bothering to run now that he was so close. The creatures behind him watched as I bounced on the circle.

Work, I begged. *Please work.*

The Repsil reached the door, his shoulder knocked the latch, his eyes brightened, his thin, bloodless lips curled into a tight smirk, and just as he was about to reach me, the platform plunged deep into the pebble soaked-floor, and launched me into the air.

I screamed, tasting wet earth. My eyes bulged, my insides tingled as my head burst through something compact. I gazed up, dizzy. It looked like the same place I'd come from a few days ago, the flushed cerise meadow, the everlasting stream of sunflowers, the thick cloudless sky.

Springing to my feet, I tottered forwards, blinded by violent flashes of pink and blue and yellow as I spat out hot soil, with the remnants dribbling down my chin. I had to escape; I had to get away from the hole before they shot up after me. Rushing through the sticky field, I battled through a crowd of sunflowers on legs that kept clicking out of place, and when my eyes finally adjusted to the sunny strip of land, I stopped with an itch to scream.

The field was flat.

There were no trees to hide behind, and no shade to obscure me from their view, so when they did eventually burst through the hole, they'd see me. Pressing a palm to my brow, I went over my options. I could carry on running in search of shelter, crouch down beneath the sea of sunflowers hoping they wouldn't find me, or, I could call for help.

Scrutinising the sparse patch of land I believed I'd come from, I rolled my eyes, then shouted,

"Help!" My voice bounced into the stillness then bounced right back to where I swivelled on the spot.

"Well done, Raine," I muttered. "You've really done it this time."

I thumped my thighs, and just as I was about to continue running, I heard a voice.

"Here," it said.

Scanning the field, I was bombarded with thoughts of travellers so deprived of sustenance their charred brains conjured up mirages of things they craved most.

"Hello?"

"Here," it said.

Lowering my stare, I caught sight of a twig swivelling in the ground ahead of me. It turned left, then right, then dipped back into the sugary earth. Creeping over to where it had disappeared, I flew back when the long-crooked branch popped up from the ground.

"Can you help me?" I asked, deliberating whether I'd just been speaking to the branch.

"Shh," came the voice.

"I need to get home. Please, will you help me?"

"Come closer," it said.

Reluctantly, I crouched amidst the sunflower stalks.

"Closer," it said.

Swallowing the fear compressing my throat, I tipped my head even lower, detecting a hole about two inches wide. Pushing my nose against the cavity, I tried to work out whether it was similar to the tavern's entry when the answer walloped me.

Tumbling through the inky darkness, I gasped. My hair whipped around my face. My t-shirt filled with huge bouts of dusty air, and just as I began to fear the collision of cold concrete, my body plunged into something spongy.

Grateful for the rush of air, I looked up, my heart still pounding. I'd fallen into a muddy little burrow. Like the ceiling, the floor was carpeted in soil. My lip twitched as I inspected the pool of pink satin pillows that had broken my fall. Fifteen, maybe twenty of them, pushed against the grimy wall behind me.

What was this place? It looked like a jeweller's *'in case of Armageddon'* hideout. To my left, was a large glass cabinet, fixed from the floor to the ceiling. Displayed upon its many shelves were an assortment of glittering jewels: white diamond necklaces, ocean blue rings, deep emerald earrings.

Rubbing the back of my neck, I took a tattered breath, detecting the subtle hint of peppermint tea. In front of me, a single candle flickered on a coffee table. Focussing on the riotous flame, I relaxed, understanding it was probably safer to stay hidden in this underground bunker than to traipse about in the sunny field being hunted, and before I could make myself comfortable, I heard someone clear their throat.

My brows shot up as I skimmed the place uneasily. The soil smattered floor, the walls decorated in ruby pictureless picture frames, the earthy ceiling that looked close to tumbling down, then a door, metres ahead of me. A figure lurked beyond the entry. Its features obscured by the shadows.

"Hello?"

At the sound of my voice, the stranger waddled forwards, his meaty head bowed, his hands clasped at his bulging waist, and when he materialised in light of the candle, my face dropped. It was the mole from the bar. Since exiting the tavern, he'd changed into a much too tight crimson robe. Had I not been trapped underground with him, I might've laughed.

"Pleasure to make your acquaintance, syrup," the mole said, extending a paw the size of a baseball glove. "Bildred, Baderello four."

"Raine," I said, keeping my hands at my sides.

"Ah," Bildred exclaimed, pointing a claw to his snout. "You must keep your mouth shut on the jumper."

I nodded uneasily, staring at the mole with my skin crawling. If Danny DeVito were an animal, I'd be looking right at him. Robust and half my size, the mole studied me through black beady eyes submerged beneath fur the same colour.

In an effort to stop my hands shaking, I clasped them in my lap when a wet grunting behind me caused me to jerk forwards. Startled, I peered at the mole. He grinned at something behind me, following his stare to a dusty keyless piano, my heart skidded out of place.

Drinking me in through thin brown tentacles, beneath the instrument, was what could only be described as a slug, the size of a handful of small children.

"Ah," the mole exclaimed. "That's Beatrice."

"Beatrice?" I whimpered.

"My pride and joy. Would you like to meet her?"

"No!" I gasped. Hoping I hadn't offended the mole, I offered a shaky smile.

"Do you live here?" I asked, struggling to wash the terror from my voice.

"Live?" Bildred said, twirling his whiskers between thick yellow claws. "Live, no. Sleep, potter. Living I do in the tavern when I play."

I bobbed my head, searching the cluttered lair for a way out when a clump of soil tickled my throat. I gulped, attempting to swallow the speck of earth, but the soil refused to go down, and moments later I began choking.

"Let's get you some dragon urine for that cough," the mole giggled, swerving round to the doorway while I fought to catch my breath.

"No, no, I'm fine," I wheezed, but the mole had already vanished, leaving me alone with the slug who looked close to erupting. Wiping my eyes with a fist, I sat forward as its tentacles expanded.

Don't come closer. Don't devour me. My skin would taste of paint and desperation.

"I think you may be in a spot of bother," the mole announced, popping out from the doorway.

"Would you like a biscuit? I don't often get company. It truly is a pleasure."

With that, he disappeared again.

This time the room was filled with a clatter, a gentle clang, a brief whoosh and slam.

"No, thank you," I called, my throat still stinging. "I need to get home. The people from that place... the tavern, they're looking for me. They don't think I belong here."

I heard running water, the plunk of a bottle, before the room went silent. Too silent. Glaring at my bloody wrists, I hoped I hadn't said too much when Bildred burst out from the doorway.

"But you don't belong here," he chuckled, wobbling over to me with a silver platter clasped in his paws. "You don't need anyone to tell you that. Surely, you know already?"

I held my breath as he set the tray on the table, then sunk into the seat next to mine. Ignoring the scent of his damp fur, I eyed the platter hesitantly. Upon it was a handful of blue biscuits shaped like stars. Taking a biscuit, Bildred began nibbling one of the points.

"Never mind them, syrup," he said. "They're harmless, a bunch of bored ignoramuses if you ask me, they can't do a thing to you here!"

I mustered an unsteady laugh as he continued to chomp loudly, crumbs of biscuit bursting from his needle teeth. And just as I began to feel a little safer, he asked a question that brought back all of the dread I'd felt in the tavern.

"If you don't mind me asking," he whispered. "What are you?"

"What am I?"

The mole nodded. Cradling his face in his coarse palms, he leant closer.

I looked away. I was pretty sure I couldn't tell him I was a human, not after what had happened in the tavern.

"Go on," Bildred pushed. "I'm not one to judge. We all have our demons."

I gnawed my lip, thinking maybe if I told him the truth, he might be able to explain all this. After all, he had offered me refuge. Looking him in the place I believed were his eyes, I took a gamble.

"I'm a human," I admitted in a small voice. "A person."

Bildred's jaw dropped, showcasing the gooey remains of a half-eaten biscuit. My heart thudded as visions of his teeth tearing away at my flesh stampeded through my mind.

"Fascinating," Bildred breathed. "Just as I suspected. I knew it the moment I set eyes on you. Biscuit?" he offered, jutting his flaky scalp at the table.

Relieved he hadn't attacked me, I felt the breath return to my lungs.

"Is there a way I can get out of here?" I asked.

"Of course!" the mole said. "But the way out is not always the same as the way in."

"Then how will I leave?"

"Patience! You must have patience, human. How about you tell me the tale of how you found yourself in this world? Biscuit? I really do insist. The jumper takes a great deal of energy from those who use it." Bildred pushed the tray closer, and in a bid not to appear rude, I plucked up the sugary treat.

"Go on," he insisted. "They're really good."

Sensing the mole wasn't about to let up, I took a bite then softened as a warm explosion of butter, and lemon, and hazelnut burst on my tongue. I took another bite, then another, chewing, and swallowing with my growling stomach voicing its thanks. All the while Bildred watched me eagerly, waiting to hear the story I hadn't told anyone.

"It started with a mirror," I said, wiping my mouth with the back of my hand. "There was this knocking sound coming from the other side, and when I went to check it out, somehow I ended up in the woods with stuff from my childhood everywhere."

"A museum of the past!" Bildred clapped. "How marvellous!"

"Not exactly," I mumbled, recalling the dead woman who'd assaulted me. "I thought it was a dream, I mean, things like this don't usually happen, not where I come from anyway."

The mole bent lower, his hot breath smacking the spaces between us.

"And then you came here?"

I shook my head.

"A few weeks later I went to check the mirror. By then I was convinced that what happened was all in my head, but then it happened again." My brow creased as I scrutinised the glittering biscuits on the table. "I moved through the mirror, and there were these trees that could talk."

"Ah, Forkels," the mole sniffed. "Guides of the fourth region. Not very helpful, were they?"

On the verge of shaking my head again, I flinched when the slug grunted.

"Forkels claim to give direction," Bildred said, hushing the gurgling creature with a paw as if it were an infant. "Though I myself can't see how a weed that has stood still for over a century, can possess any knowledge on direction."

"This place," I muttered, gazing up at the white strings of dirt hanging from the ceiling. "I'm pretty sure it's all a dream."

"Oh! This is all very real, syrup." Bildred exclaimed, gesturing to my wrist. "May I?"

I opened my mouth, with every reason I shouldn't offer my arm, hammering away at my brain. *He might yank it off; he might feed it to the slug behind me; he might club me to death with it.* Unable to come up with an excuse quick enough, I stiffened as he tugged up my crusty sleeve.

"You aren't identified!" Bildred gasped.

Dropping my bloody palm, he yanked up the sleeve of his dressing gown, revealing the same inky lettering on his forearm as the Repsil, only his read,

BILDRED, BADERELLO 4.

"What does that mean?"

"Baderello is my form. Four is my class. It really is enlightening to meet one of your kind. A moment in history I would go as far as to say." Bildred smirked, and when his eyes flicked from my wedding ring to the glass cabinet, my brow blistered with sweat. In that brief slip, I imagined my finger on one of the shelves, and Bildred gloating to his future guests about the human he'd maimed.

"Your class?" I muttered, fighting to keep my voice steady.

"It's a ranking system. The lower our numeral, the higher our status. Goblins, Repsils, Mithels stand at two. Sirens and other deathly creatures stand at seven."

"I'm sorry, Sirens? Repsils?"

The mole laughed, the stomach full of air making his robe come undone.

"Heavens, you really aren't from here are you?"

"The centaur thought I was a Mithel."

"Ah, Mithels are his majesty's form of defence. Beautiful creatures, not quite like yourself."

My cheeks flamed as he leant closer, his voice dropping to an oily whisper.

"Tell me human, do you devour the organs of livestock? We hear tales you see, stories read to us as infants. We never imagined we would meet one of your kind. Are they true?"

"I don't…" I paused, unsure of what he was asking, and hoping at some point, he'd tie up his robe. "The things outside, will they get me?"

"Don't worry, human," Bildred hooted, waving a paw. "No one ever suspects pleasant old Bildred."

"They wanted to hurt me."

"Oh, but they can't."

"Why not?"

"He won't let them."

"Who?" My lips jerked as I stared into his minuscule

eyes, certain that something awful was about to transpire. And just as I was about to jump up and hide, the mole laughed so hard his belly vibrated. I watched him anxiously. He had the kind of laugh that belonged to someone who never grew lonely due to the ceaseless nature of their imaginary friends.

"Never mind that, human," Bildred said. "Tell me about your world. Were you strapped to a bed?"

I raised a brow, positive this creature was insane, but before I could inform him I was leaving, a euphoric sensation flooded my temples. My shoulders sagged as I fell back against the cushions. Pretty sure I was about to drift off, I decided it was probably safer to distract Bildred until I disintegrated.

"You play the piano?" I asked.

"Ah yes," the Bildred breathed. "I was trained in the palace."

"The palace?"

Bildred nodded.

"I don't mean for this to sound rude," I yawned. "But where are the keys?"

"Keys!" Bildred gasped. "Keys? Syrup, keys are unnecessary when music is born from our soul. A great melody is the passage of one's being, not flesh pounding away at an instrument. Heavens, if that was the case, any creature could play."

"I'm sorry, I wasn't..."

Bildred raised a paw. With the other, he pushed the plate closer, but I couldn't take another biscuit, even if I wanted to.

My bones were congealing to cement, and my head kept lolling to my shoulder.

"I played for royalty. The grandness of it all! I played for hours while they listened, creatures from all over the kingdom, they drank, and they danced. Oh, how they danced!"

"What happened?"

"Things changed. Everything changed. I was sent away, as were the others."

"The others?"

"Many of us. It's hard to remember now. Only a few travel through the palace, apart from the rituals of course." His voice thinned, and it hurt to pick up the sound.

I strained my eyes as his face doubled over. There were two of him, then three, then four. Exhausted, I battled to keep my eyes open.

"I myself, expect to be invited there soon."

"What do you mean?" The words refused to leave my mouth. Sweat pricked my brows as I struggled to unglue my eyes. I couldn't, and when Bildred's hot lips brushed against my ear, my gut churned.

"No more biscuits for you," he chuckled.

Bile coated my throat as I tried to work out what was happening.

"I had to do it," the mole whispered.

Do what?

My lip trembled as I strained my ears to pick up the sound of his voice.

"The king will be delighted when I hand him a real human."

The king?

Bildred's claws grazed my shoulders, the slug groaned, its cold breath whipped my cheeks, and then, there was nothing.

***

"How was your relationship with Daniel?" Watson asks.

I stare past her as my mind strays to Bildred, the putrid little creature who'd sold me out. I loathed him, but more than anything I loathed myself for ever trusting him. Still, if I hadn't stumbled upon his grotty little lair that day, Mia, I guess I wouldn't be telling you this story.

I can't lie and say that what happened wasn't a mistake. And that when I woke up, I wasn't terrified, but sometimes it's the mistakes in life that steer us to the places, and people, and adventures, that have been in our hearts all along.

"He should have told me the truth."

"Who should—"

"Index finger down, little finger up, both thumbs down," I whisper as they exchange nervous glances. 'Index finger down, little finger up, both thumbs down.'

.

CHAPTER FIVE

"Did you ever feel as if you had a gift?" Watson asks. "A different way of thinking, or something supernatural, or otherworldly?"

"Was it only in your studio you believed you could leave?" Pierce tries.

I ignore their questions because both have already gotten it into their heads that the mechanics of the human brain are so easy to determine. Instead, I think of Amanda; the woman I have shared my cell with, since my incarceration. The woman, torn between suicide or optimism, which in itself was suicide, because Amanda was afraid of everything.

It took a few days of sharing a room with her before she gave up trying to attain a response to her hesitant: 'How are you's' and 'when do you think you'll be outs?' But after my session yesterday, it seemed Amanda had forgotten I was the psychotic monster muttering my apologies to you in bed every night, Mia.

"…Danny said he's so advanced for his age. He'll be talking soon. I think we'll send him to private school. I didn't go to private school, but I didn't have much to work with if you know what I mean. I bet he'll be a doctor or a surgeon or maybe something to do with maths, what do you think?"

Eyes sealed, I hovered beside my bunk, while she rambled on about how she'd be discharged soon. Three weeks, and four days. Regardless of her neuroticism and failed suicide attempts, Amanda had a home. A place restlessness is obliterated between timeworn bed sheets, and dusty mugs collected on drunken holidays, that tasted of a future. I don't have a future, only a past these butchers are attempting to dismember and attach explanations to for their own gain.

Watching Watson's lacquered mouth open and close, I realise I know nothing about them. I have no idea if Pierce lives in a rundown, shabby house, cluttered in cigarette butts and letters to old girlfriends he'd never send. Or, if he spent his days in a modern apartment with a never-ending stream of guests waltzing in and out of his empty Gatsby life.

I was clueless if Watson ever allowed a stranger to ravage her glossy hair, or smudge her ruby lipstick. Or, if that same stranger left her with her bright eyes rubbed raw, her face an inky portrait of mascara blemished regret.

"Are you married?" I interrupt.

Watson's eyes stretch, and her chest heaves through her beige silk shirt.

"I'm not at liberty to discuss my personal life in these sessions, Raine."

"But you ask me questions."

"Because it's my job. Without asking questions, we can't help you."

That word again.

Help.

As if any of this is actually helping. She pushes her shoulders forward then taps her pen while I wait for

Pierce to swoop in, offering a reason why I should end my interrogation, but the only sound comes from her buoyant pen.

Tap. Tap. Tap.

"No," she answers. "I'm not married. Now when you say—"

"Do you have children?" Watson's eyes flick to mine. Something real, an unspoken plea to make me stop.

Pierce turns to her with his brow raised, intimating for her to go on, and before I can mask my surprise, she emits a sound like a punctured balloon.

"I have a son." A son, someone as orderly, and refined as Watson has a son.

"What's his name?"

"Liam."

"How old?"

Watson glances at Pierce, then at the table.

"Twelve."

Pushing back in my seat, I imagine her slipping off this painful second skin. Her platform heels, and trim jacket thrown in a pile on the sofa as she stirs a pot next to a fridge tacked with letters for sports days, and Parents' Evenings, and school trips. Beneath them, colourful scrawls from Liam as a child.

"And you?" I ask Pierce. "Are you married?"

He half coughs then laughs – a muffled sound held together by a timid smile.

"No, no, I was a long time ago."

"What happened?"

At that his jaw tenses, and I can tell he's debating whether to answer or dismiss me.

"Things didn't work out. Life got in the way, I guess."

"How?"

"I don't know, Raine. I guess, sometimes things just happen. Now, when you said you couldn't come back, how did—"

"What things?"

His smile dissolves. In its departure, I wonder if this is the question that jolts him awake at night. Everyone has a question. Incessant words we hope to silence in bottomless bottles of whisky or the taste of a nameless stranger.

Pierce places his palms face down on the table and offers a carnivorous smile.

"These are your sessions Raine, not mine."

"Do you have children?"

"Raine." His eyes harden. "Need I remind you that in fewer than two weeks, you have a hearing where myself and Doctor Watson must give our professional opinion as to whether or not you were acting rationally on the night your husband was murdered." He searches my face for a flicker of fear, but my eyes are just as bold as his.

"If you don't cooperate, it's likely the charges won't be lessened to manslaughter." Sweat punctures his upper lip as he clears his throat. And before he can offer any more sugar-coated threats, in a voice much calmer than his, I tell him:

"He didn't scare me either."

JULY 24TH 2018

It was cold, and the world was buried under the lazy kind of peace you find on a Sunday morning, where you don't really care if things make sense. I nudged my head, dreading Dan's questions. *Have you fixed breakfast? Why didn't you answer your phone? Why aren't you trying?* Resentment whirled around in my gut, and I yearned for it to have been dawn so I could stay in bed a little longer.

Attempting a yawn, I flinched when my lips refused to part. There was something hot pressed against my mouth. I tried again, nothing. My throat tingled as a crushing sensation unfolded in my temples. A vice, squeezing, the handle straining. Certain my brain was about to explode, I pried open my eyes, remembering Bildred.

Struggling to focus, I swallowed. The room was spinning, and everything glittered. The walls, the ground, even the ceiling that stretched too high for me to see, spat mouthfuls of frost down at me. I shuddered. I was still in Wanderlust. But how long had I been here? And where was here? A shiver tore through my spine as I forced my attention on the walls, built of glass, or ice, which one, I couldn't be sure.

The panels stood hundreds of feet tall, with roses that looked like fists carved alongside the edges. I could just about make out my reflection in the wall closest. I lay on my side, with my cheek pressed against the frosty ground, and my arms and legs bound behind my back. Someone had done this to me, but who? The mole seemed too puny to carry out something so tactical alone, but if it wasn't him then who was it?

I tried hoisting myself up. My chin barely made it off the ground. Seconds later I'd smacked back into the sheet of ice with a throbbing pain conquering my spine. I huffed, willing myself not to acknowledge the pain, not when I had to find a way out of this mess, but even if I did manage to find an escape route, I'd have to untie the ropes first, and that felt near impossible.

My eyes skated across the polished ground, the arctic walls, the mountainous ceiling, before settling on a great mahogany door that seemed tiny in the distance.

A way out.

I fought harder, glowering at the door while steam poured from my nostrils, slapping my upper lip in long wet streaks. My teeth chattered, my jaw ached, and before I could release the scream tearing a hole in my lungs, a voice brought my trembling body to a standstill.

"Ah, our guest awakes."

Peering up, I caught sight of something I'd missed. Fifteen metres or so away, glass steps led to a block of ice, posing as a stage. Behind it, a mountainous black hearth reached way up to the ceiling, and spat tangerine embers across the hall like burning bullets.

I strained my eyes, attempting to make out the figures seated at a long glass table upon the stage. The voice had come from the Repsil. He sat in the middle with his flat tongue dipping in and out of his mouth as if he'd just detected meal time.

My insides swam with anger. The mole had tricked me. He'd probably offered me up in exchange for some puny reward, but for what reason?

Lowering my head, I kicked my feet, fighting to loosen the ropes, thinking maybe if I managed to fray the rope enough, I might be able to make a run for it.

Unknot the rope and get to the door. Unknot the rope.

I jerked my ankles, thrashing harder and faster until I heard laughter. My heart stirred. It came from a bald man seated next to the Repsil. A beastly thing, with small piggy eyes and great flapping ears planked on a head that looked like a rotting potato. Toasting me with a glass beaker, he chuckled louder as I turned to the remaining creatures on the right of the Repsil.

A male and female with thick blonde hair and deep blue eyes who looked to be somewhere in their early twenties. I widened my eyes at the couple, hoping one might take pity on me. The woman smirked, before running a tongue along her upper lip.

"You have been brought here with the privilege of kneeling before us for trial," She hissed in sickly sweet a voice. "Do you understand?"

I clamped down hard on my tongue, when something wet dripped behind me, blood! It skated down my wrists and moistened the ropes. A flicker of optimism surged through me because I thought if I managed to wet the ropes enough, I might be able to slip my hands through and escape.

"Or do you need us to speak slower... human?" hissed the Repsil.

"State your class and form before the court," called the blond man.

But I couldn't state anything. All that came was a muffled humming as my teeth vibrated behind my lips.

"The charges are as followed: The practice of magic, intrusion, and murder."

Murder?

"Evidence has been put forward prior to your trial, and judgement will commence now."

I blinked, questioning how I would tell them they were making a mistake if I wasn't even able to open my mouth. Forcing my focus on the hearth, I caught sight of a throne behind the creatures. Facing flames, all of it was concealed, but the golden headrest that shone so violently it seemed the blaze was roaring inside of it.

"How do you plead?" hissed the Repsil.

"Perhaps its silence is a confession," said the woman. "I've seen the crimes it has committed. Terrible, terrible crimes."

What crimes were they talking about? I squeezed my eyes shut tight, visualising my studio, thinking maybe if I focussed hard enough, I might be able to force my way back. I pictured the blank canvas I'd stared at like a stranger yesterday. I had the paints ready, but I couldn't pick up the brush. Every time I tried, the word coward fluttered through my skull like a moth set alight.

"Proceed to the punishment!" the small man yelled.

My heart rattled as I pressed myself to keep calm, only when I lifted my head, I saw something that made the universe come to a crashing halt, and after, I felt there was nothing left but to panic.

Placed a few inches from my face, was a pine bench. Upon it, an axe. My brain ballooned with terror as the world beyond it dissolved.

"It confessed!" someone screeched.

"Boris," the woman whined. "May I be the first to drink?"

My stomach dipped.

"No," the man whispered. "This one is mine."

Leaning over the table, the man tilted his head, watching me with this cold blank expression. Twisting my hands against the rope, I blinked as the hall began fading.

Was I venturing back?

Hopeful, I squinted at the man's face. His lips were thinning, turning crisp, and taut until there was nothing left of his mouth but a thin black slit. His eyes were altering too. Sapphire sifting to tar. Black cloaking the entirety of his retina until what looked back at me was a creature with chalky skin and murky pupils.

I trembled as the room slipped from my sight: the arctic walls, the stage, the creatures. In its place I saw hordes of deformed bodies. I heard screaming. Bones snapped, ligaments torn. Arms and legs splayed, bodies mounted above one another, blood dripping onto the ones lower.

Fighting to snap out of the blanket of images swarming my mind, I thrashed my head, but the sounds were still there, drenched in the smell of burning, so much burning. I gagged, assuring myself if this was going to be the end, I would not die afraid. I'd spent too much of my life being that fearful little woman. I wasn't about to allow my life to end in the same manner.

Regaining sight of the monsters ahead of me, I steadied my focus. Icy beads of sweat trickled down my skull as I strained my ears. I heard the Repsil reading.

His words were distant, but each one was growing steadier, sharper.

"Under strict commandment of the king, due to your guilty plea to all of the offences stated…" my heart hammered as I urged myself not to be beaten by the sea of images. "You shall carry out the maximum sentence imposed on perpetrators of such nature." When the smog began to clear, I saw my reflection in the blade.

Red eyes raging, my body fastened like a piece of meat hanging in a butcher's kitchen.

"Beheading." I stiffened at the sound of footsteps. Heavy, and so close, the ground beneath my chin quavered.

"Any last words?" the Repsil hissed. Glancing sideways, I caught sight of a pale foot with four hairy toes, each one the size of a fist. Bile glazed my throat as the cold edge of the axe was pinned against my neck.

"Anything at all?" teased the blonde woman. Like his, her cheeks were sunken, her eyes hollow.

"Boris, we shouldn't taunt the creature," she giggled.

"Yes, proceed. Get to it," said the creature on the end.

"Very well then," smirked the Repsil. "By order of the king."

I heard the blade lift. I imagined the swipe as it sliced, my blood splattered across the creatures faces, the thud of my defeated body. What would they do with my head? It was an odd thought to have in my final moments, but I did wonder. Would they keep it mounted somewhere as hunters did with deer, or would it be tossed in a pile of rubbish where it would decay and putrefy to nothing?

What would happen when I didn't venture back? Dan would've assumed I'd run away. Is that what happened to all of the people who went missing? Had they discovered this place and been beheaded? Would Dan have cared? Probably not. I imagined him leafing through my unsold paintings, before sipping tepid cups of tea, and forgetting.

Had he not forgotten before all of this?

I wondered if death would hurt. So close to the end, it was only then, I understood I hadn't lived my life to the fullest, Mia. In fact, I'd barely lived at all. A lump formed in my throat as I thought of all the things I wished I could take back. The time I'd shouted at my mother and seen this haunting look of sadness sully her features.

The stranger I'd kissed in an alley. The shame I'd experienced when he slipped his hand up my skirt. I thought of the night I'd agreed to marry Dan, hazy from cheap wine and clumsy sex when he placed a ring on my finger with hands that were too steady. I remembered the word NO pressed against my tongue when he kissed me. Would things have been different if I had said no? Would I have been happy?

As I cowered on the floor in what I believed were my last moments, I realised all I had threading me together was regret. And suddenly I was furious at myself for all of the times I was too afraid to say something, to do something, and now my life was about to end and there would be no going back. I blinked furiously, promising myself if I made it out of this alive, I wouldn't be that person — no more cowering from what I wanted. No more being afraid.

It was for that reason I forced myself to glare up at the blond creature. As his tarry eyes twitched, I caught sight of something sweep through the fire. The movement was so swift, it could've easily been mistaken for the throne casting shadows, or the flames rebelling against their making. Looking closer, I saw the outline of a woman.

My eyes watered as strands of her hair spiralled through the blaze like dancers set alight. In the centre, two dark spaces where her eyes should have been. Esme. My gut rattled as I stared into the snarling fire, trying to work out whether my desperation was getting the better of me, and just as I was about to dismiss the figure – her voice dripped through my ears.

"Do not fear him," she whispered.

Gazing into the inferno, I saw her outline dwindling. Her shoulders spiralled back into the combustion, her hair, her lips, her eyes, every feature simmering back into the amber blaze, and when she disappeared completely, my hands fell limp behind me.

I gasped as shooting pains carved at my core. Esme had freed me, but why? Would that mean I'd be back in my studio soon? Taking a rickety breath, I expected to find myself back in the nothingness I'd spent so long calling my life, but when I opened my eyes, I saw I was still in the hall.

"On the date of…" Before the Repsil had a chance to finish, I released an agonising shriek that was more animal than human. The sound bled through the walls, the ground, even the glittering chandelier above me shivered. The moment that followed may well have lasted a second, Mia, but with my blood boiling, and the adrenaline coursing through my veins, it seemed to go on forever.

Ungluing myself from the floor, I stumbled forwards.

"D….d…da…dark magic!" the bald creature at the Repsil's side squealed.

"Quiet goblin," the Repsil spat. His gaze hadn't left mine, though his lips had curled downwards, and both continued to sink lower as I skulked towards them, forcing one numb leg in front of the other. "How have you, how…." I continued staggering forwards, my joints aching, my head a minced heap of exhaustion, but I wasn't afraid of them. If anything, the creatures seemed more frightened of me, and just as I reached the bottom of the steps, I learnt it wasn't me they were afraid of, it was him.

"Leave," a voice uttered with such poise it seemed hazardous. I glanced through the fretful faces, searching for the creature who had spoken. Candimore was studying the table, the blonde couple were pushing back in their seats, getting ready to leave. I tugged my earlobe. The voice must've come from the throne. Someone had been sitting there, and whoever it was, had been too gutless to witness the absurdity that would've taken place.

Staring at the light pouring from the edges of the headrest, I held my breath as the creatures shuffled down the steps. The blonde creatures led first; their features inflated as they passed. Deathly eyes expanded to full blue sapphires, greying strings of hair flourished to honeyed trickles at their shoulders, and when the Repsil reached the last step, ignoring the goblin shivering at his waist, he looked over his shoulder at the throne.

"Master we can still—"

"Now, Candimore," growled the voice. With that, the Repsil continued towards the entry with the goblin sprinting behind him. When both had disappeared, I wondered if I should leave too.

"And you," the creature said.

Knotting my forehead, I was about to ask where he expected me to go when the sound of footsteps thumped me with the reminder I was not alone. Glancing over my shoulder, my stomach dropped. Marching towards me was a creature the size of a house with a brown linen cloth at his waist wavering like a flag.

Flinging my arms over my face, I waited for the monster who would've beheaded me to seize me by my shoulders as he lumbered past me to the door. Crouching lower to fit through the gap, I lowered my arms as he balled his body into a huge marble then scooped low enough for me to catch sight of a single eye in the centre of his forehead.

A cyclops? The eye blinked once, twice, before the monster crawled out into the shadows, leaving nothing but the sounds of his fading footsteps to spill through the stillness. I shook my head as the embers crackled and popped, speckling the frosty walls and making them weep burgundy tears.

"Who are you?" the stranger asked.

This time, all I heard in his voice was terror.

Turning to the stage, I was whacked by an unexpected bout of rage, because this creature was about to execute me and he couldn't even be bothered to learn my name? Something shattered inside of me then, Mia. Perhaps it was the death of the girl I was pretending to be, or maybe, the birth of someone stronger. To this day, I'm still not sure, but what I know for certain, is in that moment the timorous little Raine Black was gone.

"Who are you?" I shouted back. My words hurtled towards the stage with all of the indignation and uncertainty of suicidal soldiers, but if I thought they would elicit a response, I was wrong. "You brought me here. Shouldn't you be answering to me?" Dry blood willowed to the ground as I threw down my fists, waiting for him to answer, and when he didn't, I began making my way to the stage.

I climbed the steps furiously, my breath heavy, and my eyes fixed on the throne. Reaching the top, I looked over my shoulder to make sure I was alone. I was – and the room was bigger than I first thought. Bare, windowless, and starved of affection, it was the size of a small football stadium, with a crystal chandelier dribbling from the ceiling.

Beneath it, lay the axe. Next to that, a glistening silver string, I imagined had held me in place. Studying my bloody wrists, I skirted around the table with the breath of the fire making strands of my hair wisp out and stick to my face. Brushing them away, I scrutinised the bursts of emerald and ruby breaking from the skin of the throne when he whispered,

"You shouldn't be here."

About to ask why, my chest heaved as the throne grazed the ground, and the creature hiding, stood. He moved like a frightened child, biding his time before straightening up and gazing at me from over his shoulder. I held on to the table, staring.

Just staring.

Of all the monsters and men, I had seen in my life, Mia, he was something else. His face was ageless; not young, or old, but in his wide golden eyes I witnessed something painful, like a bird with a ruptured wing disappearing behind a thick blanket of clouds. He bent lower. His head tilted so that one side of his face was hidden, but even in that crooked stance, I reached just below his shoulder.

My eyes slipped to his shirt — the dull white material wore thin from years of neglect. The cuffs frayed, the stitching around the hem of his collars coming undone. I shook my head with a hunger to ask who he was, or why he'd captured me, but my voice was lost, and when he turned, and I saw the remainder of his face, I stepped back, perplexed.

Beneath his right eye, were the faintest tufts of fur matching the chestnut stubble on his jaw, and set between perfectly straight teeth were two sharp fangs.

"Who sent you?" he asked again.

I shook my head, staring at his trembling palms. The edges were rough like the glove of a carpenter – the tips pierced with thin black claws. Upon his little finger was a silvery black ring, blinding and beguiling like a million stars colliding against one another in the silent night sky.

Lifting my chin, I watched him bear his teeth in what I imagined was his best attempt to frighten me, but I wasn't afraid of him, not like I had been of the Repsil, or the hollow creatures, or the goblin. If anything, I was curious of how in spite of everything, he watched me as though I was the beginning and the end.

"Who sent you?" he asked louder.

"You brought me here." I reminded him.

"Before that," he grunted. "Humans are banned from Wanderlust, and they have been for sixteen years."

"Humans? You mean others like me have been here?"

He pulled back his head with a look about him as if he was about to burst out of his skin.

"Why are you asking questions when I've demanded you leave?"

"Because," I said, fighting to keep my voice from breaking. "Coming here led me to believe I was going mad, but if other people have been here too, well then maybe—"

"Maybe what? Maybe you're not insane?"

"Maybe I can make sense of what's going on instead of feeling so damn alone!" My chest gave way as I gazed into the fire, trying my hardest not to cry. I could hear him breathing heavily; I felt rage emanating from his skin. Beneath that, there was a sadness that was all consuming.

"Most humans only stay for a brief amount of time," he said.

I glanced at him, stunned. He was studying his claws with his chin tucked to his chest, and his voice reminiscent of sizzling timber.

"When they return to your land, they tell tales of Wanderlust, stories of creatures they have seen, the wonders they have digested, the Wolpels hear them begging to be taken back."

"Wolpels?"

"Creatures in Wanderlust," he said. "But you, you stay here longer."

"How do you know that?"

He shook his head at his scuffed black boots.

"You've been watching me."

He shook his head again, but everything about the way he carried himself told me he was lying.

Gripping hold of the frosty table, I stooped lower to meet his eyes.

"Are you in charge here?"

"I am the king."

"The king?"

I pulled a face when he nodded.

"Does that shock you?"

I shook my head, but in all honesty, I was more than shocked, Mia. This creature barely seemed in control of his own emotions never mind an entire nation.

"Why did you bring me here?" I asked.

"Does it matter?"

"Well, as a matter of fact, it does actually!"

Jolting backwards, he opened his mouth to speak, but my rage had taken over because this creature, king, whoever he was, had brought me here to behead me and he was going to act as if it was nothing but some extracurricular activity he couldn't be bothered to tend to?

"It matters because you were going to kill me, and you think that's okay?" My voice cracked as the fire roared louder. "Just because you claim you're the king, it doesn't give you the right to behave the way you did."

"I'm not claiming anything," he said tightly. "I am the king."

"Well then act like one."

His eyes swooped up to mine. For a second I was afraid he'd call back the Cyclops or the creatures with the sunken faces, but instead, he watched me with his sad eyes chipping away at mine, filling me with this feeling that we'd met someplace before.

"I'm sorry," he said.

I shrunk back, watching him watch his boots. Big hefty biker boots that didn't go at all with his title or suit. It was the word I'd been waiting for, just not from him and as it poured over me, a burden that had wrapped itself around my heart, snapped, and for the first time in months, I could breathe.

"What I did was wrong, and truly, I am sorry," he continued.

"Then why did you do it?"

He gave me a look that told me not to push my luck, but I wasn't going to drop it because it was only moments ago, he would've ended my life, and I deserved an explanation as to why.

"You need to leave," he said.

"Why?"

"Because it's the law. Humans are banned from Wanderlust, they are a danger to—"

"But I'm not dangerous."

His forehead puckered as pulled back his shoulders. I think he expected me to flinch, or recoil, but I couldn't, because in that wide gold stare all I saw was his own unadulterated fear, and before he had an opportunity to growl some petty order, I whispered,

"Please."

His face loosened. He looked at me then, Mia. Really looked. It was the first time I felt anyone had actually seen me in longer than I could remember. His eyes glimmered with my broken reflection, his jaw slackened, and before I could ask why he hadn't harmed me, he turned back to the fire, leaving me to stare at the valley of his shoulders.

"Never come back," he ordered.

***

"So, this creature tried to frighten you?" Watson asks. I feel as though someone is kicking me in my stomach and laughing. The room is too still, and somehow the world does not seem grief-stricken enough.

"His name was Nicholas," I mutter.

"Who is Nicholas?" Pierce questions.

"Nicholas…" His name bruises my lips. "Nicholas was my friend."

CHAPTER SIX

The insects are in my mind again, Mia. Each one flutters its putrid little wings and burrows so deep into my brain I feel that if I were to cough, I would spit out a million fizzling beasts. I jolt my head. The medication works against my memory like a steel wall, making it difficult to remember my name. I say it in the back of my mind – *Raine. Raine. Raine* – it sounds wrong, flapping against the walls like the bugs, and somehow, the only name scraping my tongue is his.

Pierce and Watson are still speaking, but I can't hear them above the insects. I saw her yesterday. It happened in the recreational room; the place we are encouraged to '*let our creativity flow*' despite having three paintbrushes between twenty-six women. I was backed against the wall when she came to me like a bad dream. Swift, inescapable and showering everything in the stale taste of death.

"Papers said she was jealous," a woman with fire engine red hair said. Bent over a table in the middle, she rammed her paintbrush into an A4 sheet of paper, sending bright splatters of blue paint bouncing across the pages of the girls around her.

"No, no, no. My Val said it was self-defence. Couldn't take it no more," A plump Latino woman argued. "Came in with a bust lip and her hands all fucked up, daft cow, should've done it sooner." All of them were staring. Grey faces, and milky eyes, dismembering the mess of me.

In all honesty, their discussion hadn't come as much of a surprise, Mia. Since my incarceration I'd received truckloads of letters from people who didn't know me, who didn't want to know me, who simply loved the glitz of a scandal, behaving as if taking time to put pen to paper would somehow absolve them of their sins.

Women should unite and stick together in times of crises – some scrawled in big curved letters. *Break free from the confines of patriarchal oppression* – others wrote. One even sent me a token of her gratitude in the form of sixteen eyelashes, addressed from Rita, from the small town of Presteigne, Powys, population two thousand, plus her cat, Tibbles.

Then, there were others, half – if not more – who condemned me to an eternity spent burning in hell. But what struck me as odd, was that throughout all of the letters, and all of the bolshy girls on the ward, not one person questioned whether I'd actually killed Dan.

"Why did your wife leave you?" I ask Pierce.

My voice comes out small, my throat still sore from the night before.

Wrestling to block out the girls' voices, I'd closed my eyes when I heard a whisper. Someone was calling my name; the voice was gentle, sweet. Pushing against the wall, I'd willed myself to keep my eyes closed, but old hope was pressed against my neck like a blade, and when I opened them, the blade sliced so swiftly, I screamed from a place that poured out from someplace deeper than my lungs.

The girls' laughed. A little blonde one in the centre swayed, her arms strung out and a slipper dangling from her foot. But I couldn't see the girls – all I could see was Esme, glaring at me with her flayed face cupped in her palms.

She'd found me.

"You killed him," she whispered.

I stared, stunned, and before I knew it, I was racing through the rec room. Rushing through the girls' laughter, I flew out into the hallway. My gown chased after me, my footsteps battered the sterile floor, and when my lungs were on fire, and my legs had crumbled entirely, I screamed.

Once I started, I couldn't seem to stop, Mia. I screamed louder, enveloped by a sound that was raw and wonderful. The emptiness, brilliantly terrifying, and it was no longer inside of me. It was everywhere, littered in the girls' mating calls and the light bulbs flickering above me in a neat line. Last night I was so empty, that for a crucifying moment I was full.

"No," I mumble.

Pierce looks up, startled. But it is Watson who speaks.

"Raine, these are—"

"I'm not going to tell you anything unless he tells me what happened."

Stunned disbelief dances across both their faces as I turn to the window, retreating to a place that came long before the end.

"Index finger down, little finger up, both thumbs down," I mutter, drumming my fingers against the desk.

JULY 19TH 2018

Mornings stretched and nights crumbled like stale biscuits left at the bottom of the packet. Dan came and left. I fed the cat, paid the bills, washed dishes and wasted hours staring at a blank canvas. I couldn't paint, couldn't think, couldn't do much of anything. Showering, washing, brushing my teeth – everything that had once been a routine task turned into a two-hundred-mile marathon, and I was the puffed out overweight failure, panting at the starting line.

I was haunted; plagued by images of a place I wasn't even sure existed. Wanderlust; the word skinned my tongue, every minute, of every day, and every time there was too much silence, and the 'too beige' beige walls began closing in on me, my mind would stray to his eyes.

Huge sad, lonely eyes, spinning golden myths in the light of the fire. Never had I seen eyes sadder than his, and it was that, more than anything, that hauled me up to my studio that day. Moving past an audience of blank canvases, I gazed out of the window where a cloudy afternoon glow permeated its way through the glass, painting everything in a strange shade of old.

The creature in the hall had insisted I had no place in Wanderlust, but I didn't believe it – not when it was the only place I felt I was seen. Turning to my reflection, I kept my hand pressed against the glass long enough to be conquered by that same sensation of falling through light, and space, and time, and when I opened my eyes I saw I was back in the hall.

Was it magic or insanity? The two were beginning to merge into the same disorganised blur that I found myself caring about less and less. My shoulders relaxed as I scanned the place. I was alone. There were no creatures cradling axes, or wielding pitchforks. Instead, the hall was as it had been on the night I was captured, only colder without the fire.

With my breath whipping out in front of me, I climbed the glacial steps to the throne. The creature who'd sat there wouldn't have filled it, not by a long haul. I pictured him residing there, passing judgement. His gold eyes sealed, his fangs ready. When had he sat there last?

I paused next to it. The frame seemed dull without the fire, the emerald and burgundy jewels lifeless, and before my greedy fingers could brush against the cold metallic edges, I heard something grunt behind me. I jumped as it grew louder; booming across the frosty walls and stuffing the hall with a boisterous roaring until I had no choice but to look over my shoulder, and when I did, my legs gave way.

Sleeping at the back of the room, was the Cyclops. I widened my eyes, wondering why he was napping in a room that was practically a freezer. Struggling to catch my breath, my eyes flicked to the door, then to the creature, then back to the door in a hesitant game of ping pong, before I started creeping down the steps.

A gentle clipping sound filled the hall as I watched his giant mouth blubber open and closed. My feet were entranced, dragged forward by the thunderous grunting escaping his lips, and when I was close enough to see what he had clasped in his palms, my chest buckled– the axe.

The cyclops clung to it as if it were some sort of treasured comfort blanket. My pulse raced as I studied the wooden handle pulled to his chest, his saliva trickling down from his lips, spilling across the silver blade. Backing away as quietly as my feet would permit, I held my breath, but the second my heel clouted the floor, his fingers jerked around the handle.

My brows cannonballed to the sky. He was waking up. My lips trembled as his shoulder shook. His thick brow juddered, and all too quickly his dirty sea green pupil fluttered open. He watched me blankly as I sprung back, my hands above my head.

Stupid. Stupid. Stupid.

Lowering my hands, I patted the air in front of me, in

a bid to show a creature, nine times bigger than me, with a weapon that could annihilate me, that I meant no harm. Only the monster didn't leap up as I'd expected. Instead, he nuzzled his cheek against the ground, closed his single eye, then continued sleeping.

My jaw hung as I backed away, waiting for him to grab me by my throat or massacre me with the axe. He didn't. Was he aware I was the same person he would've beheaded days ago? Keeping my eyes pinned to the blade I scuttled back further, praying his brain didn't spark with recognition.

Halfway across the hall, I darted towards the door, clueless of where it led, only that I had to leave. On reaching it, I wiped my palms on my sides then tugged the brass handle; only the door wouldn't budge. The muscles in my chest tightened. I tried it again. Nothing. Straining my shoulders, I tugged the lever as hard as I could manage, glancing back every so often to check the creature was still asleep, and when my face was drenched in hot watery angst, the door unclicked.

A patchy breath escaped my lips as I slinked into the sort of darkness where beasts emerged all over the place. I moved on with my palms outstretched, and my head roaring with doubt while I skimmed the tunnel for a trickle of light. And just as I began to fear I'd walked into an everlasting stretch of black, I glimpsed a door.

I squinted at the light blaring out from the fracture, highlighting two further doors sandwiched alongside it. Drawing nearer, I could've cried out in glee. I didn't, and it was a good thing too, because the second I made it to the end of the corridor, I heard a voice.

"Marianne, will you fetch the saucers?"

The strings around my heart constricted as I pushed against the wall.

"Are you going to help me or are you going to continue to prance about?"

Unpeeling myself from the wall, I inched towards the open door. Peeking inside, my forehead puckered. It was a kitchen. A sunny little haven that looked a lot like a scene from a 1970s sitcom, and nothing like the arctic room I'd fled.

Bright floral wallpaper plastered the walls, upon them were beech coloured shelves stacked with saucers, and dishes, and glasses. I spotted the Repsil at a counter adjacent to me, thwacking away at what appeared to be a turquoise pepper the size of a football with a butchers' knife.

I watched my eyes in the reflection of the blade each time it sliced. Frantic, wild, untamed, and I continued to stare, right up until a woman in an off-white gown floated past the door. Shifting closer, I looked on as she pirouetted and jived. In her palms, a pan of gurgling water sent huge blankets of smoke whooshing around her face, and when the steam began to clear, and I saw her for what she was, I slapped my hands across my mouth.

I kept gawking at her, hoping the longer I looked, the more likely I would be to find some logical explanation as to what I was seeing, but the truth blared back at me whether I cared to acknowledge it or not. The woman – if she was a woman – had no head. Draped across her shoulders instead, was a deep cut soaked a gushy wine red.

My stomach churned as she continued dancing with the Repsil barking orders I couldn't hear above the racket in my mind. *SHE HAS NO HEAD;* I wanted to shout. *SHE HAS NO HEAD.* And somehow, even without eyes, I felt she'd seen me. Turning to the door on my left, I pressed my palm against the timber with sour hope grazing my throat. *Please*, I thought. The golden knocker made a soft jingling sound as I pushed harder, *please don't catch me.*

"That's too much salt, Marianne!"

Perspiration blistered my spine as I shoved the door, then inched inside of a shorter corridor lit by a stream of pillar candles. Ogling the burgundy satin wallpaper laced with golden swirls, I crept towards a single door at the end. Pushing through it, I found myself in another corridor. This one, shorter. Cemented at the end was a grand blue door with gargoyles and chubby faced angels sitting overhead.

Edging closer to the exit, I examined the stone fixture's button eyes, and gaunt faces, before pressing my hands against the chipped surface of the door, praying I wasn't about to walk into a slaughterhouse. Riled up by thoughts of chainsaws and bloody axes, I gave the door a gentle nudge. The lock gave way with ease.

Lumbering inside, I flew back, speechless. It appeared to be a grand hall, only it was far grander than any hall I'd ever read about or seen. Surrounding me were pearl walls stretching hundreds of feet tall, supporting a huge glass ceiling, where daylight splattered through and littered the blood orange ground in a tidal wave of colour.

Green and blue and red all simmered across the floor, caking the room in so much beauty it was intoxicating. Softening from the sudden shift in temperature, I turned to my left where a mammoth stained-glass mural of creatures with heads of lions, and tigers, and bears, watched me hovering in the mighty doorway.

Up ahead, thick plum curtains concealed huge bay windows. Between them, was a great mahogany door. My shoulders snapped back as I strode towards the door, grateful there was a way out of this bizarre fortress, though after reaching it, I felt there was something I'd missed.

Turning to check, my heart lurched with wonder.

Curling up for miles was a spiral staircase built entirely of glass. My lips parted as I scanned the balcony overhead where white marble pillars upheld a blood-red ceiling. I blew out my cheeks, gazing up at the glittering steps.

Each one stole fistfuls of light from the fracture in the door, flickering and coaxing out the child in me, but pulling me away was the adult I'd grown to despise. *Be sensible, Raine,* she hissed, and of course, she won.

Forcing my focus back on the door, I rammed it open, and after skulking behind the gap, I slapped a hand over my mouth. The place was magnificent. A winter wonderland set alight by a titanic red sun hanging low above a lake, about half a mile off. Softening from the humidity, I peered down at the mountain of stone steps spilling out from the palace door and unrolling into a plush carpet of blinding white grass.

Stepping down from the stairway, I rubbed my chin when I caught sight of a biscuit coloured cliff, east of the horizon where a white curtain of steam poured over the glacial rocks at its feet. Entranced by the way the light struck the lake, I took another step down, then another, and before logic could intervene, I began racing downhill with the thick summer breeze beating through my hair, and the golden glow of the world setting fire to a soul consumed by the desire to explore.

As you may have figured out by now, I'd never considered myself reckless, Mia. Anyone who knew me would have pointed out I was the opposite. 'Raine, the girl who never turned up late.' 'Raine the do-gooder who wouldn't put a foot out of line.' But as I raced downhill, I felt the weight of my past slip from my bones. I was a snake, shedding its skin and slithering into the off beaten path of the jungle, but what I failed to acknowledge then, is that despite shedding its skin, a snake is still a snake.

Collapsing beside the lake, I looked over my shoulder at the Palace. The whole thing looked like a weapon; an intricately sculpted fortress with arctic walls that towered high and pricked the unsuspecting sky with its copious rooftops and turrets.

I wrinkled my nose, wondering if it really was a palace. There were no guards, or gates, or hedges to block out the world and nothing regal about it except its stature. Turning back the pastel water, I watched it sparkle and gurgle. The colours exploding from its ripples, giving the impression of a million flashbulbs going off beneath the currents, and just as I lifted a hand, a voice jumped out at me.

"Don't do that!"

I jerked back, commanding myself not to move, or breathe, or blink as the sound of breathing behind me grew louder. My lips jerked as I waited for the stranger to say something. Introduce herself maybe, or ask why I'd fled the palace, but after a thunderstorm of silence, I knew I had to turn.

Someone was behind me, and I began to question what might happen if that someone was to push me into the lake. I gave it another minute, then gradually peered over my shoulder, only when I set eyes on her, I had half a mind to jump into the lake myself.

"Careful," she said, but I couldn't answer, all I could do was stare at a wolf dressed in a long black gown.

I widened my eyes as she ambled closer on all fours, studying me through luminous almond-shaped eyes. I cleared my throat. Still, no words arrived. I tried my luck at smiling, but when the grey-faced creature squatted down next to me, the gesture seemed as futile as my fight to speak.

"I apologise," she said. "I didn't mean to frighten you."

"It's okay," I managed, even though every instinct I had was telling me to run. "Why… why shouldn't I touch the water?"

"They'll grab you," the mutant wolf creature replied.

"They? Who are they?"

"The spirits that dwell beneath the waves."

"Spirits?" She nodded, eying me with a morbid fascination that made my skin itch. She was crazy; she had to be to believe spirits lived under the water. One of those odd spiritual beings who believed the wind guided you through life and the trees could talk. Only the trees here *did* talk, and I was having a conversation with a wolf.

"You shouldn't disturb them," she went on. "The spirits don't like being woken."

"I'm sorry, what spirits?"

"Those that live beneath the waves," she repeated, slower this time as if I was hard of hearing.

About to tell her my ears worked just fine, I buttoned my lips when she threw back her head.

"So, finally you have come," she sighed, addressing the sky. "I knew it would happen, but so soon. It doesn't seem right."

On the verge of telling her she'd mistaken me for someone else, I froze when her jaw plummeted, exposing an army of knives for teeth.

"Forgive me,' she exclaimed. "Where are my manners? I have not introduced myself. Morgana, Wolpel 3."

Morgana watched me expectantly but she didn't extend a paw. Gazing into her calculating amber eyes, I wondered what might happen when she realised I wasn't who she was expecting.

"Raine," I mumbled pulling back a little.

With my heart in my throat, I waited for the shock to resonate on her face, but Morgana didn't attack me as I'd envisaged. Instead, she smacked together her gums, tasting my name and spinning syllables on her furry tongue until she was satisfied.

"Raine."

I offered a nod, still not sure I was safe.

"Did you come from the palace?"

"Sort of."

"I take it you were escaping."

"From the palace?"

"No," she smiled. "You were trying to escape something else."

"Such as?"

"Your life."

My heart stopped as she watched me knowingly.

"Pardon me?" I asked, wondering if she had been waiting for me.

"You were trying to escape your life, Raine," she said, wrapping her arms around her knees.

"I'm sorry, but do I know you?"

"No," she shrugged. "But I know you."

"How?"

"I know most things. All Wolpels do, it serves as both a gift and a curse."

"Wolpels?"

"My kind. There are only a handful of us left now. We're a dying breed."

I pressed a hand to my scalp. The creature in the palace – king – whoever he was, had mentioned Wolpels, I was sure of it, something about them being able to hear humans. If that was the case, I wondered if she'd heard me.

"What is it you think you know about me?" I asked, failing to hide the scepticism in my tone.

"I know where you come from," she replied. "I see the darkness you have fled. I taste the tears from nights you have sobbed for things you cannot change. I feel the wounds you wear on your skin like armour, I smell the hope in your veins when you sit alone, painting and dreaming of a life greater than the one you are bound to, and I know…" she paused as I watched the sun glint from her fangs. The bottom set slightly darker than the rest.

"Know what?"

"I know that here in Wanderlust, you will find what you have always been searching for.'

"Which is?"

"Happiness," she replied.

Eyes stinging, I blinked at the skirt of my plum summer dress. Happiness, it was the emotion I'd been chasing after desperately, but never truly caught. Perhaps it was harder to catch when my hands were full with pretending I was happy. I studied her thoughtfully. Her eyes were locked on the ground, and her thick brows were clumped together so that the fur on her forehead stuck out in oily clusters.

"You know me," I asked, but the words rearranged themselves into a statement.

"I think you'll find the question is do you know yourself."

"I do."

"But you've spent so long pretending to be someone else, how can you be sure?"

"I don't—"

"You're running," Morgana said. "But it will never work."

"What won't?"

"Running from yourself." Just then, she lunged so swiftly I didn't have time to pull back when she started sniffing me. "Can you smell that?" she asked.

"Smell what?" I gasped staring at her wet nose.

"You've lost your sense of wonder. But coming here seems to be restoring it." With that, she shook her head at the sky.

"When do you last remember having it?" she asked.

"Having what?" I mumbled, sitting up.

"Your wonder," Morgana said. "That childlike sensation of waking up with your heart stuffed full of an adventure waiting to happen?"

Unsure of how to respond, I shook my head at the lake. When had I last felt that way? Apart from the tavern, I couldn't recall a day I felt slightly excited about life, not even as a child, definitely not with Dan. Trying to appear ambivalent, I knotted my forehead but when I caught sight of my wedding ring on my finger, hot tears impaled my eyes and the words seemed too profound to swallow.

"I can't… I can't remember," I admitted. "I'm not really sure of anything anymore, the only thing I'm sure of, is that I haven't felt like myself in a very long time." My gaze flicked to the limitless lake, the thick gold sky, the arctic field, anywhere but her eyes, and without warning, I heard my words spiralling into sentences, without breaks, or pauses, or second guesses.

In the minutes that came after, I told her everything; who I was, what I did, where I came from. Morgana didn't seem fazed by my admissions, if anything it seemed I was regurgitating things she already knew. After spewing up everything I'd buried inside of me for years, she began telling me about Wanderlust.

She spoke of the ranking system segregating creatures to their own regions based upon their IDs at birth. Those with lower numerals were higher up in the hierarchy and lived in lower regions, and those lower lived in higher regions. Seven regions, seven classes, and an infinite number of creatures residing in each sector, their names bouncing from her leathery lips and pummelling me with so much disbelief I found myself gasping at every second interval.

Trolls, goblins, fairies, centaurs, all of the mythical creatures I'd read about as a child residing in this magical place I'd discovered. Then there were creatures

I hadn't even heard of, Flemgrils, Rosterils, Milotes, Fawndrakes. I listened intently, though at times I had to silence the troublesome feeling I had that the casting system was somewhat unfair.

At the top of the hierarchy, Morgana mentioned Sirens; creatures imprisoned in a region known as the Blacklands, only I couldn't fully grasp how something could be pigeonholed as good, or evil, from birth, or how an entire future could be set in ink, regardless of experience, or pain, or growth. Rather than voicing my concerns, I kept quiet, nodding when appropriate and trying my best not to be mauled by the odd wolf creature.

Hours passed. In their departure, a mellow stillness perched between us. Hungry and full I sat there, wanting to ask more about the humans who'd stumbled upon Wanderlust, then of the creatures who resided in each of the regions. I wanted to ask how they survived, and if their homes were underground like Bildred's, or somewhere up in the clouds, but mainly, what I really wanted to know about, was the creature I'd spoken to in the palace.

"The man and woman in the palace," I said, easing my way into the conversation. "Why did I see those things in their eyes?"

"Were you afraid of them?" Morgana asked.

"I tried not to be."

"Good," she nodded. "They're not people Raine, they're Mithels."

Mithels?

They were the creatures the bartender had mistaken me for. Bildred was right; we did look different. If anything, I was a Mithel in reverse. "They claim to help enforce the law here in Wanderlust. However, I believe their judgements are rather biased."

"What do you mean?"

"I mean," she exhaled. "They are called upon as they have the power to wheedle their way into the accused's memories, determining whether or not the creature is guilty. Though every hearing a Mithel attends will always result in a guilty verdict."

"Why?"

"Each Mithel creates violent recollections to store in the perpetrator's mind, claiming it belongs to them," she replied.

My mind jolted with the memory I'd glimpsed in the palace. Stacks of butchered bodies infused with the glutinous stench of burning. Had they tried to blame that on me?

"Their beauty hails from fear. They feed off it, sucking every ounce of happiness you have left inside of you. Without fear, each one would disintegrate into nothing more than the soulless creatures they truly are."

"So, instead of reverting to their true form they'd rather…"

"Subject innocent creatures to a lifetime of suffering."

"But that's awful."

"It is," Morgana agreed. "At times, I wonder why he allows them to reside on the welfare committee."

"The welfare committee?"

"The panel of creatures elected to keep Wanderlust in order."

"Who?"

"The king."

I lifted my chin, understanding this was my chance. Allowing a moment to pass, I asked:

"Who is the king?"

The second the question left my lips, Morgana glared at me as if I'd whacked her. Her eyes glazed over as she flared her nostrils.

"Why would you want to know about him?" she

demanded.

I opened my mouth but found myself unsure of how to answer. Why did I want to know about him? I assumed he was an overgrown child with servants obeying his every need. Someone who wanted the world to fall at his feet without an idea of what the world was; but if that was the case, why was his apology knotted around my heart like a noose?

"Because," I said in a small voice.

"Because?"

My cheeks reddened as she glared at me with her fangs bared.

"Because he was the reason I was captured and I'd like to know why."

Morgana's face loosened.

"And this is the only reason?"

I nodded forcefully.

"The king," she paused, toying with a shard of grass between her claws. "The king is a creature who will be perpetually plagued by his demons."

"Is he dangerous?"

"He has the capacity, though anyone in power holds that trait."

"Then why didn't he hurt me?" I didn't mean for it to come out the way it did. A mess of pain and confusion, but I couldn't help it when it was the question that had haunted me ever since he first turned away from me. If he had wanted to hurt me, why hadn't he?

I waited, and when Morgana shook her head at the ground, I let out an exaggerated breath, understanding the conversation was closed. Pushing my palms to my eyes, I rubbed my forehead with everything she'd told me whirling around my brain like a Ferris wheel set in fast motion.

"Nothing seems real anymore," I admitted. "These things, this place–"

"And what would you class as real?" Morgana interrupted.

"Just things that make sense." I was about to continue when she laughed. Looking up, I saw her regarding me the way a traveller would observe a small child.

"You know," Morgana said gently. "Just because something doesn't make sense, it doesn't make it any less real, Raine. The problem you have is that you focus too much on how you believe things are meant to look, and you forget how you feel."

While I mulled over her words, she gasped.

"I have an idea!" she said. "Lie back and close your eyes."

Recognising that lying back and closing my eyes, would give her the perfect opportunity to slash my throat, I looked away. After what happened with Bildred I really didn't want to take my chances.

"Go on," Morgana said. "If I were going to hurt you, I would've done it by now, trust me."

I blushed.

"Raine," she pushed.

Taking a painful breath, I lay against the pastel sheet.

"Close your eyes," Morgana instructed.

Hoping I hadn't mistaken this act of kindness as a ploy to kill me, I closed my eyes.

"Now, tell me what you feel."

Refraining from telling Morgana I felt absolutely nothing, I shook my head.

"Let go," Morgana whispered, and as I did, little by little, I felt the sun weighing down on my cheeks while the sounds of the waterfall thrashed softly at my ears, and I began to grasp what she meant. Even if I didn't understand Wanderlust, I felt it.

"If all of this is real," I said. "Then I must've gone mad."

"Probably," Morgana agreed. "But madness is a gift.

Only the finest creatures live their lives bursting with abandon the rest of the world is too caged to appreciate, but to taint it with doubt, that would just be foolish."

I squeezed my eyes shut tighter, wondering if I had gone mad. Here I was, speaking to a woman with the head of a wolf, asking after a king who'd called for my beheading. Still, my former life felt more surreal.

I yawned as my bones soaked into the earth. A tingling sensation spread through my fingers. I was venturing back. I'd taken the journey too many times not to have recognised it, but before I drifted off entirely, Morgana shuffled closer then pressed a wet nose to my ear, and whispered,

"He wasn't born a monster."

***

The insects have settled. Some, are resting up for sleep. Others are clattering across my temples, only delicately now. Pierce and Watson are packing up their things, telling me tomorrow they hope I feel like talking. I roll my eyes, a childish gesture. But that's what I feel like, a child being told what to do. Watching them dust off their expensive suits, I promise myself I won't utter a single word unless they begin unravelling like me, Mia.

.

CHAPTER SEVEN

"Raine, if you're going to sit in silence, it's going to be difficult for us to help you," Pierce says, but they don't want to help me. They want to diagnose me and collect their pay cheques, maybe sell a story to a newspaper, or be featured in one of the crime shows Dan, and I watched another lifetime ago. '*It's crazy what some people are capable of Rai,*' he'd mutter. Now I was one of those people.

"Raine, do you think it may be possible that the places you went to, and the people…things, you saw may have been symptoms of a psychotic disorder?"

I bite my lip. 10:34. This to and fro has gone on through the duration of our session.

Pierce speaking.

Watson speaking.

Then me, babbling the same monotone question.

"What. Happened. To. Your. Wife?"

Watson chews her lip. Wrinkles crack through layers of her makeup.

"Did she leave you?"

"Raine," Pierce snaps. "Do you think it's conceivable

that the stress you suffered beforehand triggered your delusional frame of thinking?" The gruffly warmth in his tone has dissolved like cotton candy on a child's tongue, and I want to scream. "We are aware of what Dan was engaging in during the time you were having these… episodes. It's highly likely these are symptoms of schizophrenia. A mental disorder caused by both environmental and biological factors. Given the circumstances and your family—"

"Tell me about your wife."

JULY 26TH 2018

Travelling between realms became something of second nature to me, Mia. I began swapping my worn-out baggy shirts, for floral dresses smelling of hope, in a futile attempt to match the world I believed I was becoming a part of. Dan hadn't noticed the missing clothes from our wardrobe. If on the rare chance he searched for them, he would've discovered them in a box, labelled paints, tucked between frazzled pastels and diluted watercolours in my studio.

Dan was too busy for that. Dan was too busy for anything, never mind scouring the house for dresses. He had no idea that every night, at around nine p.m. after he stumbled home from all of his *extra hours* in the office, I'd throw on my torn painting clothes and rush downstairs to start dinner, having already ventured into Wanderlust.

Even before pushing through the mirror I'd hear the waterfall flooding the world, I'd feel the sun cradling the universe and igniting the lake. In those brief but pivotal moments I was free; the very sensation I was robbed of each time Dan came home from work. Whenever I heard his key in the door, there'd be this knot in my stomach. A tangled ball that was too overpowering to ignore, and it grew bigger, and uglier as he strode up to the counter where I sliced red tomatoes and green peppers.

"How was your day?" I'd ask.

He wouldn't answer right away.

He'd push up against me first. His chest to my back, his lip to my ear, his cologne fusing with the scents from the sizzling pan, filling the kitchen with the aroma of a Mexican restaurant stuffed full of businessmen ogling wide-eyed busty waitresses.

I'd cling to the knife, trembling. The knot about to tear through my stomach lining. Then, when he was just about satisfied by the wreck I'd been reduced to, he'd whisper his day had been fine.

I'd smile, nod, serve food, pretend to be grateful for my husband who chewed with his mouth open, and overused words like nidificate, and cynosure, to emphasise he was a writer on the up, and I was just a housewife.

'Remunerative whatever does that mean?' He'd love to hear me ask that, but instead, I beamed idiotically then asked more about his day. In those small words of kindness, the cordial war commenced.

I always wondered if Dan could smell Wanderlust on my skin. Part of me wanted him to find out. Part of me wanted to feel his knuckles against my jaw making me spit out teeth like a coin machine. I needed something, anything was better than the affable war we were battling pointlessly.

After three visits to the palace grounds, I hadn't seen Morgana again. I waited; eager she might return. After a whirlwind of curiosity on the second day I decided to explore. I'd marched alongside the lake – my excitement thinning to despair, then irritation when I'd encountered nothing but the barren land. And after trudging, and marching, and wobbling back to the same place I

WANDERLUST

started, I learnt the lake was no lake at all; it was a moat.

So far, my journey had been undisturbed, but on the fourth day, everything changed, stamped back then, by an unforeseeable end. That morning Dan had jumped into his suit, collected his briefcase, and left. Something that was becoming a breezy routine to him, and the relief that came after was mine.

Heading downhill, I inhaled the untamed scents of the meadow, praising myself on how easy it had been to leave. Dan probably hadn't even reached work, and there I was in my own private retreat, framed by the blood red sun hanging low above the lake. Plodding away, I was oblivious of everything but the sounds of the waterfall and my eager heart when I noticed a figure at the lake.

I paused, narrowing my eyes at the outline. It was the creature from the palace, the king. My heart rattled as I crept closer, studying him the way an unarmed hunter might stalk deer through trees. Cloaked in rusty sunlight, he watched the water with his hands flat out behind him and his legs pushed out in front.

For a moment I was gripped by the sensation of an eclipse, feeling as though he didn't belong there just as much as the sun brushing up against the moon. My lips parted as the sound of the waterfall flooded my chest, and before I could pretend I hadn't been gawking at him, he curved his head and caught me.

Crap. I flung my hands around my sides, grateful for the distance between us so that he wasn't able to see me blush, but I didn't look away. He wore that same exhausted stare. A look of disdain, and petulance, and uncertainty mixed up in a cocktail that tasted a lot like sealed beginnings.

While he continued to stare right back at me, I debated leaving, then staying, then apologising for being there in the first place. Torn between all options, I ended up hovering with one foot in the air, while the orange air burnt so hot with curiosity it set the whole world alight.

About to call out to him, I cleared my throat when he turned back to the lake. I frowned, waiting for him to swerve back around with a face built of steel because I'd assumed if a situation like this were to arise he'd be livid, surely. He'd told me not to return. Forbidden the very thing, and yet there I was, yards away from him practically sticking him the middle finger and he didn't seem the slightest bit fazed.

Skimming the hazy stretch of land, I tried to work out what I should do. I could leave, but where would I go? The lake wrapped its arms right the way around the palace and I knew my efforts would only prolong running into him again. Taking a frayed breath, I decided to walk right past him, to not acknowledge him or say a single word. I'd make a swift exit and sit someplace on my own.

Drawing back my shoulders, I continued downhill with my hands thickening to bricks, and the back of my neck pricked by giant needles. And when I was close enough to smell the sun bruising the places his shirt didn't quite cover – his neck, his calloused palms, the skin poking out from the top button on his chest – I felt a small earthquake ricocheting under my flimsy blue pumps.

It wasn't until I looked down, I realised it was me who was shaking. Punching my thighs with a clammy palm, I waited for him to say something, anything. For his mud-caked fingers to twitch or his face to flicker with even the slightest hint of recognition, but he remained painfully still with the wind lifting tufts of his messy brown hair.

Casting sense aside, I sat down next to him. I didn't know why I did it, Mia, curiosity, perhaps. Curiosity had been accountable for most of my actions leading up to that day, but I didn't think much of why – I was too busy wondering what he was thinking.

I examined his hands. Both were buried so deep in the dirt that at first glance they would've belonged to a man. A carpenter, or welder, someone who'd spent his life building things for others. No time for creams or potions. No point. Examining the frayed hem on my navy dress, I wrapped a thread around my finger then tugged it with my pulse hammering away at my throat.

I tugged harder, wondering how long he'd been sitting there, and why? Why wasn't he speaking? Did he suddenly decide to become a mute? I pulled harder, my fingers squeezed dry of blood and my mind clanging about with so many questions I thought my head was about to combust, right up until his smoky voice brought my hands to a standstill.

"Why do you keep coming back?"

My lips puckered as I turned to him.

He was still looking ahead. His gold eyes fixed on the lake, his full lips trembling.

Taking in his unyielding expression, yet again I found myself questioning who he was. To claim he was a king was completely out of the question, not only because he didn't dress the way I imagined a king would dress: (hefty biker boots, and a washed-out creased shirt) or even because he seemed too young, or too reckless to be in charge of anything. It was because of the uncertainty in his tone. Every word spoken sounded like he was reading from a script in a foreign language.

My eyes danced across the rampant waterfall while I mulled over the limp excuse of why I came back, of why I kept coming back. The truth that my life was a complete and utter shambles. I couldn't tell him that. He wouldn't understand. Even if he did, he wouldn't care.

"Because," I said without thinking.

"Because?" he repeated.

I took a deep breath then shook my head.

"Because I feel like I don't have a home." I cringed immediately realising how self-pitying it sounded.

"A home is a luxury," he said before I had a chance to disclose I wasn't literally homeless. "That's like a creature complaining they don't have gold. Gold isn't just handed to you, you work for it."

I wrinkled my brow. That was rich coming from him. I bet he'd never worked a day in his life. I'd scrubbed tables, mopped floors, worked till my feet bled, and I would have put my life on him never coming across a mop in his entire existence. About to question his diligent little stance, he cut me off with a:

"I suggest you work on what you have, rather than setting up roots in places you don't belong."

"And if I don't have anything to work with?"

"Everyone has something," he sniffed.

I pulled back my head, about to tell him it was fine and dandy for someone who lived in a glass fortress with creatures obeying their every command when he cleared his throat, then, in a tone a fraction louder than a whisper asked,

"Who sent you?"

I chewed my lip, deliberating if I should mention Esme. Even if I hadn't seen her in a while, she was part of the reason I'd stumbled upon Wanderlust, and she'd told me I'd do something great, and I questioned if this creature might be able to shed some light on to what that greatness might be if I were to mention her.

Pinching the skin on the back of my hand, I was about to tell him when the strangest sensation overcame me, Mia. From out of nowhere I felt cold hands grappling my windpipe. I flinched then tried to say her name again, but nothing filtered through my senses but a gentle tingling, avalanching into a steady burning, and all too quickly I was spluttering mucus all over the place.

"I can't… I can't—" Hot tears traipsed down my face as I dug my fingers into the earth, taken by the same feeling I had on the night I'd given Esme my word. Frozen hands crushing my throat. Fingers slipping down my neck. That searing pain in my lungs. Mortified, I clung to my chest, realising I couldn't say her name, because I had literally given her my word.

I peered up ruefully. He was still facing the lake, only now he looked concerned.

"How many times, Raine?"

"Pardon—" I choked, wondering how he knew my name.

"How many times have you been to the lake since I've asked you not to return?"

"Two."

"You're sure of that?"

I nodded hesitantly, and just when I was about to tell him it had actually been four – he met my eye for the first time that afternoon.

"You've been here four times," he growled.

Looking at him then, I swear I felt the earth lose footing. It stumbled, fell, shattered, then smashed into a heap of all things lost, and just as quickly as it had happened, all of the lights flicked back on and the world was how it was, raw and unscripted.

"You lied," he said.

Gnawing my lip, I began ripping powdered chunks of grass from the earth.

"If you knew I was lying, why did you even bother asking?" I mumbled.

"Maybe, I wanted to see if you were capable of telling the truth."

"Well, maybe, you shouldn't test people," I retorted, pulling the grass viscously. "How do you know how many times I've been back anyway? I haven't seen anyone here, and how do you know my name?" Lifting my head, I expected him to look away, but he kept his steely gaze locked on mine. I rolled my eyes. If he was trying to frighten me, it wasn't working.

"Listen," I said. "I'm not a risk to you, or this place, I promise."

"And what good is a promise between strangers?" he contended. "Especially when one of them is incapable of telling the truth."

"I didn't…" I paused, focussing on the snowy skyscraper I'd built of grass. "I didn't mean for it to be a lie. I don't even know why I said it. I just wanted to stay here a little longer."

"Why?"

"I just like it here."

"You like it here?"

"Yes, and I'm not a threat like the creatures at the tavern thought I was. I'm just an ordinary woman who has found something that allows me to be a little more than who I was before."

"And who were you before?" It was a question spoken like any other, but it knocked me for six. Suddenly I didn't know what to do with my hands. I placed them in my lap, then on the ground, then started running them through my hair, wondering how I could explain who I was to a stranger when I was a stranger to myself.

"Well?"

"I paint," I heard myself reply.

"What do you paint?"

"All sorts." From the corner of my eye, I saw him watching me with the reflection of the lake glittering in his eyes. He's being polite, I told myself. Or perhaps just weighing up the likelihood of me being a threat to his precious kingdom. Regardless of the reason for his sudden interest, I heard myself blurting out words my brain hadn't even given the green light.

"I try to capture a moment."

"A moment?"

"You know that moment when you're deep in thought?"

By the look of it, he didn't.

"That moment when everything in your head is deafening, and outside there's nothing but silence? I watch people," I continued. "And I try to translate that moment into colours."

"Why?"

"Why?"

He nodded while my mind strayed to all of the strangers I'd caught glimpses of in the past. An old man in a coffee shop studying his leafy hands. A child kicking a rock at a bus stop so immersed in whatever he was thinking he hadn't even noticed the bus drive by. A woman with smudged lipstick in a public bathroom, studying herself in a spit stained mirror through the eyes of a frightened child.

I didn't know why I painted them, just that whenever I watched them, I felt as though they'd pulled back their skin and I could see the darkened corners of their souls. All of the pain, and hurt, and disappointment, everything that makes us human, and it was beautiful and tragic, and soul-shatteringly honest.

"I just think it's in those moments we forget how much power we have to relinquish all ties to the past, and just watching them, reminds me that regardless of however lost or hopeless we feel, we always have the power to change."

"You think it's possible to change?"

I peered up. His knees were pulled to his chest, and his chin tipped forward.

"I think everyone can change," I told him. "It just depends on how much you want to."

He nodded, his eyes raking over the currents ahead of us.

"Have you always painted?"

I bobbed my head, uncertain if he was interested or simply looking for the right moment to ask me to leave.

"I started when I was a teenager," I answered. "Whenever the world got too much, or I felt like I was just a kid who didn't need to be seen, I'd get this feeling that if I created something no one could take that away from me. I mean, they can try, but you hold it inside of you like some sort of internal medal, praising yourself on a piece of magic you created from nothing." Clearing my throat, I realised I'd balled my hands into fists so tight my nails were slicing my palms. "Then I got older, sold a few pieces, and that's that," I finished breezily.

"You don't paint anymore?"

I shook my head.

"Why?"

I stared at him as if he'd uttered a curse word.

"Why?"

He nodded as I shifted my focus to the palace behind us. A misty shade of orange had settled above the highest point, and the sky had broken in places where night hadn't quite caught up.

"Well?"

Turning back, I reminded myself he didn't care, but something in the way he watched me made me feel like he did.

"It's just the moment I get to the canvas, it's like everything in my head is stunted. I'm constantly worried what I paint might be rubbish or a complete waste of time." Tucking my chin to my chest, I exhaled. "It's stupid really, basing your life on something you're not sure is any good."

"Brave," he said.

My eyes darted back to him, but he wasn't looking at me, he was studying the lake.

"I'm sorry?"

"It's brave," he repeated. "I'll never understand why humans seek validation from others. If you enjoy it, nothing else should matter. Forget the world."

I shook my head as his words poured over me. Brave, that was a first. Weird maybe, a loner, but not brave, never brave. Dan had called me a recluse once, and it had stung because he was right. Whenever I locked myself in my studio it wasn't the canvas or the paints I found comfort in; it was the aloneness that wrapped its arms around me. When I heard my chest pumping, each palpitation reminding me I was more than my casing, more than my parts, more.

I nodded awkwardly, wondering if I'd gotten this creature wrong, not only because of the compliment that was sitting between us like a bad smell but because of the way he saw the world. It was as if he saw the heart and bones of the earth, and not just the pretty decoration hung out in front.

Watching the heavy waves crash against the mountain foot, I caught sight of something fluttering towards us in the distance. I knotted my forehead as it swooped closer. A butterfly? I squinted at the insect, and when it drew nearer, I glimpsed a woman's head attached to its black leafy wings.

My eyes bulged as I studied the spindly creature, understanding this was the perfect opportunity to showcase how easily I could fit into this inexplicable land. Sitting on my knees, I held out my hand. My palm itched as the creature landed. Taking in her bright blue hair, and huge doughy eyes, I bit my lip as she bent lower, smiled a wicked smile, then bit me.

"Ouch!" I gasped, flinging my finger in my mouth. "That butterfly just bit me!"

His forehead wrinkled as the creature flew off giggling with my blood smeared across her lips. For a second I thought he might laugh, but instead, he looked at me as if I were a piece of lettuce he couldn't get out of his teeth.

"That butterfly is a pixie," he muttered. "They tend to the gardens..."

"And bite people?"

"Most creatures don't disturb them. What did you think would happen? Because it's pretty, you thought it wouldn't harm you?"

"No, I just…"

"You just what? Beautiful things often hurt most. It's the deception rather than the blow."

I nodded, feeling stupid. No longer was I the woman he'd regarded as brave. I was the stupid girl dipping her toe in places that didn't concern her. Stupid, sitting next to someone who wanted her to leave. I was a homeless door salesman someone accidentally let into their house, sipping a cup of tea and making it last.

Inhaling the muggy air, I tried my best just to sit comfortably and enjoy the silence, but the sky was spreading over us like a fuzzy violet blanket serving as a warning I'd disappear soon, and I knew the moment I did, I'd regret all of the things I didn't ask. Silly questions popped into my head.

So are you actually the king? How many creatures live here? Why am I the only one who can stay in Wanderlust? Why don't you wear a crown? Is there a reason you're still sitting here in silence?

When I finally decided on the right question, it arrived so suddenly he jumped.

"What's your name?"

"My name?" he asked, turning awkwardly.

I nodded, wondering if he even had a name.

"Nicholas," he answered.

"Nicholas," I repeated.

He raised a brow as if I were about to ask a question, and why wouldn't he when I'd just said his name? My

132

cheeks prickled as I tried to think, but nothing I wanted to ask before sprang to mind.

"So…" I began too boldly. "This is the spirit lake?"

"Who told you that?"

"Morgana." I watched his face, searching it for a sign he may have been acquainted with the odd wolf creature but it was just as straight as before.

"What else did she tell you?"

"General things about the kingdom, and how creatures are confined to their own regions."

He didn't answer.

"I don't think it's fair," I added.

"Oh," Nicholas replied.

"Yes, oh," I fired back.

His lip twitched as he turned to me with a raised brow.

"I just don't understand how you can determine whether people– creatures, are good or bad before they've even had a chance to prove themselves."

"So what would you suggest, have them all roam about with each other instead?"

"Well, yeah."

Taking a deep breath, Nicholas scratched his jaw.

"With all due respect Raine, you know nothing about Wanderlust."

"Well, then teach me." There was too much hope in my request, and judging by his face he heard it too. "Start with the lake," I said, less enthusiastically. "Creatures come here when they pass?" I held my breath as his chestnut eyes flicked across the lake, then to the sky, and when they settled on his knees he squeezed them together so tightly lines appeared around his temples.

"They don't come here," he said quietly. "It's an illusion. When a creature passes their soul leaves their body and their energy lingers inside of the lake."

"So where are these spirits?" I asked.

"They are only seen by those who loved them."

"Do you see anyone in there?" As soon as the question left my mouth, I knew I was asking too much. This stranger had asked me to leave, and here I was asking after the scars that kept him awake at night. I held my breath, expecting him to tell me to mind my own business, but instead he replied:

"My parents."

Something sharp twisted inside of me. Regardless of our status, or pasts, we had something in common. We'd both lost our parents. I watched him undecidedly; wondering how old he was when it had happened. If he'd lost them at an older age, perhaps he may have had the tools to grapple with his grief accordingly, or maybe, like me, he'd lost them too young and internalised the world as if it were one of those whiteboards where everything gets wiped away when the day is done.

"Nicholas," I said quietly.

His shoulders fell forward as he turned to me.

"Tell me something about yourself."

"You already know about me," he said. "Everyone does, I'm the King."

"That doesn't tell me anything about you," I pointed out. "Are you a man?"

"Do I look like a man?"

"No, but you don't look like a creature either."

A bolt in his face came unhinged.

"Does that frighten you?"

"Not really."

"Why?"

I rolled my shoulders, focussing on his hands buried under the silver grass. His fingers kept twitching, making his black ring shimmer.

"Why aren't you afraid of me?"

"Why do you need me to be?"

"I don't."

"Clearly," I sniffed.

Taking a deep breath, he ground his jaw.

"Tell me why you're not afraid of me."

"Well," I thought aloud. "Like you said, we're strangers, so how can you expect me to be afraid of someone I don't even know?"

He mulled over my words then blinked as if it would wash the soreness from his eyes.

"You just…"

"I just what?"

"You need to leave," he barked.

My heart slipped down to my gut. Perhaps it wouldn't have fallen so hard, or so fast if he hadn't asked about my art or called me brave.

"Fine!" I snapped. Springing up, I nodded at my feet. I wasn't about to stay where I wasn't wanted, and I most definitely wasn't going to fool myself into thinking Nicholas cared for this drab conversation. On the verge of heading to the palace steps, my brow collapsed when he spoke so quietly, I thought I'd misheard him.

"I'm sorry did you just say…"

"I don't want you to go," he repeated.

From over my shoulder, I saw him watching me with the muscles in his jaw twitching.

"You don't?"

Nicholas shook his head.

"Then why would you   "

"Because it's the law."

"But you're the king. Surely, you have some impact on the law."

"It's not that simple. …" He licked his lips then skimmed the red hue spreading over the sky with a secret battering his eyes. "This place isn't what you think it is, Raine. It's not all beauty and wonder. It's ugly and cruel, and there's darkness here that shouldn't concern you."

"I don't care," I told him. And it was the truth because darkness existed everywhere if you looked hard enough, all I wanted was somewhere I might rest from the chaos.

"Fine," Nicholas said.

"Fine?"

"Stay," Nicholas shrugged.

"Seriously?"

He gave a faint nod.

"You're only going to come back anyway, what more can I do?"

Caught off guard, I crouched down next to him with my knee grazing his.

"Are you sure?"

He bobbed his head.

"Positive?"

"Why do you keep asking?"

"Because I'm afraid you might change your mind."

"Keep asking and I might." Quietening the urge I had to tell him I could still come back if he told me to stay away, I realised if ever there was a chance to explore Wanderlust, this was it.

"So, is there a way I can get past the lake?" I asked.

"Away from the palace you mean?"

I nodded, detecting a blade of unease in his tone.

"I've seen parts of the kingdom before. The tavern, the trees– Forkels, and I'd like to see the rest."

Nicholas looked as if he was thinking, or maybe he was just searching for a way to tell me to stop taking liberties.

"You want to travel alone?"

I pulled a face.

"You think because I'm a woman, I'm somehow incapable of travelling alone?"

"No," Nicholas answered. "I think because you're a human, you may struggle."

I looked away then cursed my cheeks for glowing.

"I'll manage."

"You want to leave the first region?" Nicholas asked, his lip curling.

I nodded.

"You're sure?"

I bobbed my head again.

"Positive?"

"Why do you keep asking?"

"Because I'm afraid you might change your mind."

My lips parted as he watched me playfully. Caught off guard by the sudden burst of warmth chiselling his eyes, I raised a brow, and before we could fall into a gentle two and fro, he hoisted himself up.

"I'll tell you how to leave," he said, patting the snippets of grass sticking to his trousers. "But first, you have to do something for me."

"And what might that be?"

Nicholas didn't answer. Instead, he started marching back uphill. Staring after him, I questioned if I'd just been the butt of some cruel joke. Had he been humouring me while his army assembled? I scanned the land nervously before he stopped in the centre of the field, then turned and stared up at the sky.

"Well?" I shouted.

Nicholas flinched, then looked back at me as though he'd forgotten I was there.

"Next time you return, I'd like you to come to the palace and paint my portrait," he called.

I repressed a laugh, staring at this creature who was obviously in love with himself. A narcissist, of course he was, what else could I have expected from a king?

"And if I refuse?"

"That's your choice, Raine," he said. "Just know that I see you." I frowned, and before I could ask where to meet him, or when, or even why, Nicholas continued uphill with the leftover scraps of sunlight pouring across the contours of his shirt.

It was when he reached the peak of the hill I was whacked by the familiar sensation of falling. My lungs lightened, my head spun, my fingers tingled, then it was gone. All of it, Wanderlust, the palace, Nicholas, and that nostalgic feeling of hope I'd tried so hard to hold on to.

It took a second for me to adjust to the beamed ceiling, the smell of candle wax, the stepladder wedged in the corner of the room, then Dan. He was standing over me. His face was wild; I blinked at his open palm. There was blood on his hands — my blood.

"Raine!" he gasped.

"Leave me alone," I whispered, scuttling backwards. "Please."

***

Pierce and Watson are silent. Watson twirls her pen around her fingers as I replay that day in my mind, Mia. The comfort of being heard, the gift of being seen. Then the moments after. Dan said it was my fault. It was, I know that now. Focusing on the pasty yellow wall, I feel the distant ache of my heart as Nicholas's voice fills my mind.

'*Forget the world,*' he'd told me. That's exactly what I did.

.

CHAPTER EIGHT

Pierce studies me with all of the desperation of a man who's about ready to sell his soul.

"Raine, it's been two sessions and you still haven't spoken. If you stop now, we'll have nothing to offer at your hearing."

"Why did your wife leave you?" I mutter for the fourth time.

He blinks, his face swollen with irritation since Watson left to fetch a pot of tea. Scratching a fresh cut beneath his stubble, he blinks at his hands.

"Why does that even concern you? It doesn't change anything you tell us, so why would my personal life be of any relevance to you?" *Why would his life be of any relevance to me?* Maybe because he's taking everything, and giving nothing back but fancy words, and a higher than mighty attitude.

I grit my teeth in an attempt to suppress the rage bubbling inside of me, but the sensation is ploughing away at my heart like a lawnmower. Before I can grapple with what I'm doing, I've leapt up from my seat.

"Because," I spit, glaring at the poor excuse for a man

in his tattered jumper and 90's boy band haircut. "You're not asking me for timelines or dates. You're asking for memories. Memories that are mine."

Pierce pushes back in his chair. His eyes dart around the room. This is what he wants, isn't it? Deranged ramblings, violent hysteria, something he can pass off as a symptom, and although I'm aware I am playing right into his hands, nothing calms the anger surging through me.

"Would it matter if I told you my father beat my mother every night until I was eleven. Or if I told you my husband, the man I trusted, the man I wanted to love, destroyed me in pursuit of his misogynistic caveman gain."

His eyes scour mine, hunting my retinas for a flicker of defeat. There is none.

"Or if I told you it was me who destroyed him. Me who couldn't deal with the emptiness anymore." I bash my palms into my chest; my eyes sting with tears. "Whatever I tell you, the outcome will always be butchered down to the same thing. Any label you stick to me will always mean insane."

"Raine, that's not—"

"It is! You don't see me as an equal, or even a person. You see me as a job. Someone lesser than you that you can pull apart and attach a diagnosis to. Do you understand how it feels to bury a piece of you? Something magical. Just dismissing it like it never happened, only to have it resurrected by strangers who tell you, you're not their version of normal?"

Pierce opens his mouth, but I won't let him speak.

"No, no you don't. Because you don't care. None of you care. Margo will go home to her son. You will go home to your shiny twenty-something-year-old fuck toy girlfriend, and everything will continue to spin in your egocentric worlds because you have enough of my blood on your pages."

"Raine!"

"You're killing me!"

Peirce's face blanches and when he's certain I won't back down, he holds up his hands.

"Fine," he says quietly. "But not now."

"When?" My voice breaks as the clatter of heels smacks down the corridor. I know Pierce won't divulge anything in Watson's presence. Not because it defies ethics, or professionalism, but because there is a secret wafting between them. Something ugly that prohibits pleasant conversations most colleagues are socialised to act upon.

Staring into his muddy eyes, I make it my mission to find out when she enters with three cups grasped under the arm of her sheen black suit.

"Everything okay?" she asks brightly.

"Fine," Pierce replies in a tone much too high for it to have actually been fine.

"Tea?" She places three polystyrene cups on the table. "It's green tea. Very cleansing. Not my usual brand but I'm sure it will be fine." Pouring the tea from a porcelain teapot, Watson leaves the dusty smell of caffeine to spill between us. "Are you sure everything's okay?" she glances between us as Pierce stares down at his empty jotter.

Forcing a nod, I chew my lip as Watson hands me a cup. Placing the other at her side, she leaves the third empty.

"So, around the time you were travelling to this place..." Pierce begins. "How were your relationships with the people around you?"

"I hadn't seen anyone in a while."

"Can you recall the last time you saw any of your friends, colleagues, maybe a neighbour?"

"No."

Watson eyes me thoughtfully, stirring her tea.

"Do you remember when you engaged in anything sociable? An event maybe, or a get-together?"

I stiffen. He wants to know about Dan's book launch. By then the world had already collapsed. Skyscrapers lay dormant at my feet, palaces and squats all jumbled together in a non-existent heap of rubble. Witnesses came forward, Dan's work colleagues who claimed they'd seen me scrambling through the rain that night; which wasn't entirely a lie, but that happened after.

Pierce is nodding, but for him to understand that night, I have to go back to the beginning, one week before I learnt about Wanderlust. I didn't know the truth then. How could I have? It was the morning of the evening I found out.

"It was one week before I first saw Esme," I mutter.

JUNE 17th 2018

"You need to get out, Raine," Dan was saying. He was hunched over the floor, scrubbing the mustard accident the cat left on the floor with a bleach-soaked washcloth.

Chewing what was left of my nails, I watched him work up a sweat. I didn't want to venture out today. Not like this, I wasn't ready, and that posed the question of: *ready for what?* Sunlight slinked through the windows, licking the beige floor length curtains, and prudent beige walls, and suddenly everything was too beige.

The colour was Dan's idea. Minimalistic he'd said, but I thought the place looked more like a glorified bachelor pad. The forty-inch plasma TV screen, the bare magnolia walls, the cream granite mantle, the black marble coffee table, the purely ornamental hearth that was never lit, because it couldn't be lit. All of it screamed single man shag pad, and I realised if we were to leave one day, there would be nothing left to tie me to this place.

"If not with your friends, then at least go into town or something."

"Can't I stay in and paint? We could get a takeaway or—"

"No, Raine," Dan shook his head at the stain on the floor. "This is becoming seriously unhealthy. You're turning into a hermit, spending all of this time on your own. It's not good for any of us."

My stomach twisted as he headed into the kitchen.

"I'm getting worried about this business. Lately you seem so distracted." Struggling to ignore the blame in his tone, I focussed on Jinx curled up on the sofa.

The cat had completely transformed from the ginger stray Dan and I discovered in our shed nearly a year ago. I remembered it clearly. We were in the kitchen; Dan was re-reading his tattered copy of Jack Kerouac's On The Road. I was midway through sorting the pantry. Holding up a tin of tuna, I'd squinted at the soggy label when I heard moaning coming from outside.

Creeping over to the window, I pulled it open then listened as the sound bled into the kitchen. Dan refused to help me look. He assured me it was probably the TV next door, or the rain in the gutters, or the water heater on the blink again, but after asking for the fourth time, he groaned then skulked out after me with a torch.

"I'm telling you, it's nothing," he said as we clambered through wild strings of grass leading up to the shed. Pulling open the rusty door, Dan waved about the torch, illuminating scattered supplies: corroded tools, a lawnmower, an old bike I'm sure still worked. Then, curled beside the bike, was a ginger stray who looked as though he'd been dead weeks.

Leaning down to untangle the stray from the six-pack of beer wrappers stuck around his neck, the cat had hissed and puffed out what was left of his chest with so much pluckiness you could only admire him. Eventually, we managed to release the cat before we set off back to the house. Dan continued reading; I continued scouring the pantry. Silence. Normal.

Weeks passed, and every day when Dan was at work, I'd leave out chicken and salmon, watching as the cat performed miracles from the kitchen window, making food vanish in seconds. It took a month for Jinx to strike up the courage to amble through the back door.

I was sitting at the kitchen table, leafing through mail from old clients and sipping a tepid cup of coffee with a sour question scraping my tongue: *Is this really my life?* When I noticed the ginger ball of fur at my feet. After that, Jinx never left.

"...And it could help you unleash some of that inspiration," Dan said from the kitchen. *Fuck*. I'd drifted off again. An occurrence that wasn't entirely uncommon. Dan was right; I had been distracted. Sometimes it was as if all of the thoughts in my brain vanished, leaving behind a vast galaxy of twinkling stars imploding between my temples. Other times, there was nothing but black.

Whenever Dan caught me spacing out, he'd take hold of me by my shoulders. 'Rainey, what the fuck,' he'd shout. To which I would muster up a breezy, 'I'm fine.' But when I padded over to the mirror, my reflection screamed bullshit.

I blinked at the stranger. I didn't look human, never mind twenty-seven. My skin was translucent and the rings circling my eyes ran so deep it looked like I'd whacked two coffee mugs on my face and forgotten to take them off.

"Fine," I called, pinching the skin under my eyes.

"Good!" Dan said, popping out from the doorway.

I held my breath, watching him slip over to me from the mirror. The years had been kind to Dan's face; kissing the skin around his eyes and chiselling his jawline. No longer was he the awkward boy I'd met in a coffee shop. Dan was a man. And all at once I felt a pang of annoyance for men who grew more charismatic with age, when all experience did for women was play games with gravity, and pull everything to the ground.

Wrapping his arms around my shoulders, Dan blanketed me in the sharp whiff of an aftershave that reminded me of fireball jawbreakers. I knew I should've been grateful. Grateful I had someone who believed in me, who despite everything was still there wrapping his arms around me.

I should've been grateful; only something wouldn't let me. Lately, it became almost predictable for our conversations to end in one of Dan's loud frowns, or that look of frustration that screamed I didn't understand him. I'd attributed it to his second novel being published, or at least, tried to.

And after the tumultuous failure of his first novel, of course, he would be anxious, of course, it wasn't me, how could it be when I was doing all that I should as a wife? I'd supported him when he spoke for hours about characters that lacked depth, the storylines that dragged, the inability to have yet another unsuccessful novel.

But deep down I knew there was something else, and the longer I stood there with his stubble grazing my neck, the more I understood it was me.

"Thanks," I whispered.

"What for?" Dan asked.

"For always being the man I married."

There was a long pause before Dan chuckled. A deep gravelly sound that hung in the air like a pine air freshener in a cigarette fumed car.

"Well then," he said, heading back to the kitchen.

"Thank you for always being the woman I married."

I flinched. It was a backhanded compliment that whipped at my cheeks, because I hadn't been the woman Dan married, not for a long time. That bright sparky sensible girl was gone. Maybe she'd never really been there to begin with, just a version of myself I wanted to be, but as the years dragged, the guise was slipping.

It fell on simple days. Mornings I wanted to be alone; nights Dan expected fireworks when I could barely stand to be looked at by another person. Afternoons he'd rattle on about how many holidays he'd taken with his parents, when the closest I ever recalled to a holiday as a child was when social services carted me away after a complaint from a neighbour.

Studying myself in the mirror, I forced myself to stare at my lifeless skin and chapped lips long enough to feel sickened, and as the minutes stormed by, I vowed to be better, for both of us.

"You better leave before it gets dark," Dan called. "You never know who's lurking around these days." He was referring to the attack on Mr Thompson from next door, who'd finally been released from the hospital after a burglar had broken into his home and fractured three of his ribs with a baseball bat.

Dan was right; maybe some air would do me good, perhaps it would stop the thoughts of jumping out of my studio window from impregnating my skull each night.

How high is high enough?

"No," I said, heading into the kitchen and passing him at the sink. "I'm meeting my friends for lunch."

Clambering up the stairs, I slipped through the hallway and into our bedroom identical to the living room in its pristine shag pad features. Sifting through the clothes from our wardrobe, I rummaged around in search of

146

something that told the world I wasn't a complete and utter waste of space. Blouses, shirts, skirts I'd worn to the gallery, an old Christmas jumper Dan's mother had knitted with one sleeve longer than the other.

"Besides," I shouted, halting at a navy summer dress and throwing it over my head. "They've gone out of their way, and you know what they're like when they're together." I started buttoning up, noticing midway it smelt different. Musty, and doused in a perfume I didn't recognise. "Plus, I'd like to see our godson. Katie said she'd bring him."

Smoothing out the creases in the dress, I moved over to the dressing table, attempting to salvage something of my face. Knotting my hair, I looked over a post-it note Dan had tacked to the mirror. 'Milk' it said. Making a mental note to stop off at the shop, I picked up a tube of mascara, going for a look that said: broken? No, I'm perfectly fine. I haven't spent the last four nights hiding in my bathroom and crying for no reason at all.

I dabbed my lips, a bit of pink, a stroke of blush, a flick of... I jerked back when the car door slammed outside. My heart sank. Dan was probably getting something from the car; I was safe. Closing my eyes, I took a deep breath, preparing myself to face the friends I hadn't seen in months.

It took forty minutes. After cursing the traffic and parking the car, my sandals slapped down dusty pavements in search of the restaurant Lucile had suggested. Since venturing into town over a year ago, everything had changed. New attractions were scattered across the city like ant hills, others had collapsed like washed out old business men dabbling into too many drugs.

The pub Dan and I would amble into after work had become a gym. The bookshop I used to visit on Sunday mornings, a brightly painted launderette. I continued through the silky battlefield of teenagers with fake tans, and oversized bags, understanding all too unexpectedly the temporary nature of life. All those memories bulldozed, forgotten.

No one would ever know that one blustery Thursday night, after work, I'd stumbled into the pub and found Dan singing '*I will survive*' at the top of his lungs when he failed to get a promotion at work. No one would know about Mr Harrison, the silver-haired man who'd sit at the front of the bookshop with two cups of tea, reading Sylvia Plath to a picture of his late wife, Edna.

It was a sad realisation, and suddenly I felt very small, and very still. Dodging shoppers dressed in shorts and tank tops, I trudged on with an overwhelming urge to jump back in my car and abandon ship. I turned a corner with the thought flickering through my mind like an electrocuted butterfly.

Just go.

I would drive past the motorway and stop when I reached the coast. From there, I'd race down to the seashore before throwing in everything I owned: my phone, my keys, my wedding ring. Dismissing the thought, I marched on, and after six minutes of searching, I found Smooch crammed between an Indian deli and a discount shoe shop.

Warm gusts of spices bustled out from the deli and laced the soles of the shoes outside. It didn't seem like the usual place Lucile would recommend. It wasn't loud, or overcrowded, and from the Italian menu tacked to the window it didn't seem overpriced.

I spotted them sitting near the back. Glimpsing me in the window, George bounded across the room like a baby deer first discovering his legs. Pushing through the door, I inhaled the bunged-up smell of microwaved Italian cuisine, assuring myself everything would be okay. These were my friends. I could tell them the truth.

"Nee's here! Nee's here!" George cried lunging at me before the door had a chance to jingle shut.

"Hey, George," I said, conscious of Katie watching us from the edge of the restaurant.

"I's no' George any mo'e!" George panted as I bent down to kiss his sticky cheeks. "I's Mr Parker!" George looked like his father. Amber hair and plump cheeks that were always flushed burgundy. I could only hope one day, he wouldn't wake up in a business suit, quoting Bill Gates.

"I do apologise, Mr Parker," I replied.

Satisfied, George took hold of my hand and led me through the land of the dining dead to where Lucile sat tapping at her phone, and a recently thinned Katie smiled at me in her oversized t-shirt. Since having George, Katie had traded her junk food diet for an alternative vegan lifestyle, encouraged entirely by her husband, Rob the banker, who was just as round, if not rounder than when we first met him.

"No, we haven't changed his name since you last saw us," Katie cooed.

I smiled, ignoring the lacquered knife in her words before glancing at Lucile who still hadn't looked up from her phone. Her hair was pulled into a tight bun, and she had a red lip jammed between her teeth.

"He's watched Spiderman recently, and he seems to have gotten into his head that Peter Parker is the superhero."

I peered at George, attempting to mount his high chair, growing redder in his endeavour before Lucile smashed her phone into the table and sighed.

"And done!" she exclaimed. "Took me fifteen minutes to do that."

"To do what?" I asked.

"Lucile was writing a complaint to West Midlands

Travel," Katie explained, narrowing her eyes at George who had given up trying to climb the high chair and had switched to mimicking Lucile by thumping his fist into the seat next to me.

"The train was twenty minutes late yesterday, and so I didn't have time to get back to my car, and it was clamped," Lucile said.

"Tell the truth, Luce," Katie laughed, the maternal streak in her voice doing cartwheels.

"Fine," Lucile groaned. "I ran down the street in my wedges – brand new may I add." She nodded twice to emphasise BRAND NEW. "And I twisted my bloody ankle. It was only a few minutes late. But if it were on time, I wouldn't have had to run, and I wouldn't have twisted my ankle and got a fine."

"Or... you could have worn sensible shoes, and you might've made it back to your car on time," Katie pointed out.

Lucile looked like she was about to argue when I stated the obvious.

"There's no cast."

"That's not the point," Lucile howled. "It hurts and I have to wear these stupid things." She frowned at her black pumps with her eyes welling up as if at any moment there would be an unforgiving waterfall.

I peered at Katie for help, and in the amount of time it took to glance back at Lucile, her eyes were dry once more. That was the thing about Lucile; she could convince you the world was about to end, then in the blink of an eye we were immortal again.

"You're late by the way," Lucile said, leaning in and kissing my cheek.

"I hope I don't get an angry email," I teased.

Her lip jerked, but she didn't laugh. Plucking up a napkin, she dabbed the lipstick mark she'd left on my cheek, before tossing it in the middle of the table. They were talking, but I wasn't listening. I kept staring at the napkin uncoiling like a fist clenching a bloody heart. Why did I feel like that was the perfect depiction of my heart?

"Rai!" Lucile shouted.

I gasped. Italian music was playing, had it always been playing?

"Shit. Sorry, I was miles away."

"Rai!" Katie scalded, nodding at George.

Fanning my face, I mouthed my apologies.

"Great, another dinner where we have to be censored," Lucile mumbled. Katie didn't hear the remark. If she had, she was too busy licking her thumb and dabbing at George's face to respond.

"Have you guys ordered?" I asked, attempting to make eye contact with the boyish waiter who seemed more interested in the voluptuous bartender leaning over the counter.

"No," Lucile said. "We were waiting for you. I'm only going to have something light though. Have to be off in a bit. If I knew you were coming, I wouldn't have made plans."

"Plans?" Katie's eyes brightened, the way they always did when Lucile had a story, and Lucile always had a story. Whether it was the cross-dressing boyfriend or the white-collar criminal whose tyres she slashed when the city slept soundly, there was always a story.

"Nowhere important, just a bit of grocery shopping."

"Grocery shopping!" Katie gasped. "But you never do grocery shopping, Luce."

"That's true, when do you ever cook?" I piped in.

Lucile rolled her eyes, then picked up a menu.

"If I remember correctly," Katie started. "Wasn't it you who once said, 'people who cook are talentless robots with too much free time'?"

Lucile's eyes traipsed across the light bites section, and

while Katie continued to grill her, it clicked.

Connor was back in town. Lucile's ex whose drive in life was to create chaos, stapled by his go-to phrase, *Let's fuck shit up* – which is exactly what he did. Three years ago, Lucile had protested they were soul mates, and that he was the best fuck of her life, but when the police carted him away for the fifth time that year, she admitted love doesn't leave you with smashed windows and a sagging wallet.

Eventually, Connor opened a string of partially successful night clubs from his inheritance after his father's passing. Shortly after, he proposed to Lucile. Though, after three agonising weeks of cocaine-induced fights and boozy makeups, Lucile discovered him in her queen-sized lavender bed with two other women.

She hadn't told Katie this. She hadn't even told me. I gathered it in dribs and drabs, the night I found her with her cheek pressed against the cold bathroom floor. A bottle of vodka in one hand, a bright red gash spluttering down the other. So last week, when Lucile called to tell me Connor was opening a new club, I wasn't at all thrilled.

"I just hope you're careful this time," I said, but it seemed Lucile did not favour my cautious approach.

"And what's that supposed to mean?" she snapped, dropping her menu and narrowing her eyes at me.

"Nothing I just…"

"Listen, Rai, I'm a grown woman. I can make my own decisions. I don't need you giving me the third degree about everything."

I opened my mouth to tell her I was only looking out for her when she cut me off with a hand.

"I just thought it was time I tried something different. I'm twenty-eight years old. I don't think it's odd I want to brush up on my culinary skills, do you?"

"I didn't mean…" I peered at Katie for help, but she

was pointing at her menu and smiling.

"George look, they have a children's option," she whispered.

I rolled my eyes, wondering if she had a child solely for situations like these.

"People change Rai," Lucile sniffed. Lifting her Mulberry bag, she sifted through clanking items before pulling out a bottle of perfume and dousing her neck furiously. I stiffened as she waved over the waiter, ordered, then left me to stew in my shame.

The rest of the afternoon was spent chatting through plastic screens. We discussed work; George's nursery trip to London, a TV show about the secret life of prostitutes, a holiday to New York we planned on taking but were all secretly certain life would impede on, followed by more work. Katie told us Rob had relocated to Cheshire, and that she was excited about the prospects his job would offer their family.

Healthcare plans, George's college tuition, private schools, retirement provisions, but the truth was obvious to everyone but her happy go lucky son, Katie was miserable. And despite living the life girls who treasured pearls dreamt of; a five-bedroom townhouse with a pool the size of my house, a live-in nanny, and gym instructor, I was almost certain if Katie could go back to the night she'd met Rob at a family function, instead of agreeing to the bottle of Dom Perignon he ordered on his business card, she would've said no.

Katie left after a niçoise salad and half a bottle of Rioja. Kissing us goodbye, she promised to call later, but I didn't count on it. She'd probably scour her mahogany bar for a vintage bottle of red then spend the rest of the week working off the burger she'd wolf down in her drunken state. I kept staring at her with the words, *'you aren't happy, just tell us,'* clanging about in my brain, and when she kissed me goodbye I wondered if she was thinking the same about me.

Without George, the sound was deafening. I chewed my lip, listening to the ice cubes clinking in Lucile's glass as she stirred her vodka soda.

"So, how's painting actually going?" she asked.

"Fine," I lied, but plastic screens never worked with Lucile, she always had a way of smashing right through them.

"Bullshit," she smirked.

"I'm okay, honestly."

"Rai, no offence but you would tell a fireman you were fine if you were on fire." Leaning close enough for me to smell the musky perfume pressed against her collarbone, she dropped her voice to a whisper. "You know, there's no harm in asking for help, especially when there are people who are willing to give it. Burden me," she said, holding out her hands.

"What are you doing?" I asked, wrinkling my nose at her open palms.

"Lay it on me," she said. "Give me the burden."

I laughed, and when her eyes filled with concern, my throat closed up. I could never lie to Lucile. She was the closest thing I had to family. I told her everything, we both did. Jobs that ended abruptly because of her lack of boundary control. Drunken nights that ended with us hovering over a grimy club toilet, cursing someone, or something, or everything.

'Fuck it,' we would say, but this was different, we were older, we were supposed to have our shit together now. Her eyes softened, and I had to look away because that same lump was choking me.

"Rai?"

"It's just not working," I said.

"What's not? Painting?"

Yes, I wanted to scream, that, and everything else:

Dan, me, my life. Focusing on the smudged grey table, I tried my best to tell her the truth. I told her I felt I was unravelling, that at times I didn't feel I was there, and when I was, I didn't want to be. I told her it felt like wearing someone else's clothes. Everything felt wrong, and staged, and different, and I couldn't remember what it felt different from.

I left out the bits about Dan, about how a month or so after telling him, he suggested we tried for a baby.

'*Just to give you something to focus on,*' he'd said.

Each word had hit me like a gunshot.

I told him I'd think about it, pretended to be thrilled. But I couldn't subject a child to our grey sham of a life. It seemed unfair.

"It's as if..."

"What?"

"It's as if I'm disappearing."

"Has Dan been supportive?"

I nodded unsteadily.

"Good," Lucile said. "That's all you need. A bit of support, I'm sure it's just a phase." She covered her mouth with a hand as if to end the conversation, which wasn't entirely surprising considering our discussions regarding Dan always went like this.

To put it mildly, Lucile disliked Dan maybe even more than I disliked Connor. Years ago, she'd called him a leech. That word led to the biggest argument Lucile and I had ever had. Dan was selfish, maybe; egotistical now that I knew him, but a leech? I was penniless, and working back to back shifts as a waitress to afford rent. He was the one with the trust fund and a mother who jetted off across the globe every few weeks because she could. What did I have that Dan wanted?

I called her jealous. Even then the word stung, because despite Lucile's anarchic ways, I knew all she wanted for me was the best. Four months later, Dan and I were married. Lucile had been my bridesmaid, her father had given me away, and when the photographer swarmed around guests in huge floppy hats, Lucile had clung to my arm with a fierceness that was disarming. 'Remember,' she'd told me. 'I love you.'

It was when she pulled me in for a tight embrace; I sensed all of the unspoken words between us grow taller. I knew Lucile believed I was making a mistake by marrying Dan because I didn't love him in the romantic way I should've, but I couldn't love anyone like that. He made me feel safe. I needed safe, fuck fireworks.

The dislike between them wasn't entirely one-sided. Dan never said aloud he didn't like Lucile. He was much more covert; making sly remarks about her carefree attitude and ominous sex stories. He preferred Katie with all of her orderliness. Suggesting I invited Katie and Rob over for dinner, gushing almost daily over how Katie made a wonderful mother.

"Raine!"

I jumped then turned to Lucile groggily.

"I asked if you went to dinner with your friends from the gallery."

"Sorry. No, I was ill."

She peered at me with her thin brows furrowed.

"You seem really weird. Are you sure you're okay?"

"Yeah, I'm fine," I mumbled, secretly unnerved I hadn't noticed the waiter clear our table.

Lucile sighed before stroking my arm the way her mother did when we were hiding something.

"You know, Rai, if there's anything you ever need to talk about, I'm always here. Whatever it is, whatever time. I'm always here."

I nodded then rubbed my eyes, smudging the mascara I'd forgotten I was wearing.

"I know, Luce. I've just been tired."

"You're sure?"

"Yeah," I lied. "You need to go shopping, the market closes at six."

She glared at my inky knuckles as I untangled myself from the table.

"I'll see you soon," I promised.

Lucile looked at me as though she wanted to say something. I always wonder if things would've been different if she'd said something then. Would Dan have still been alive? All I needed was a friend, someone to listen.

"Well, bye then," Lucile shrugged.

I faked a smile, and with that goodbye set in place, I headed back into the battlefield, unaware my life would go up in flames in a matter of hours.

***

Pierce and Watson flick through their jotters, unaware I've stopped my recollection midway. They don't know what happened when I went home, what I found out. They're just glad I've spoken.

"And then you left?"

Five minutes until the end of the session, five minutes until I have to return to my room where Amanda will most likely hum chart songs in the bunk beneath me for hours. Staring at the clock, I think of George, then of you, Mia. I wonder if you will be taken into a family with siblings. Lucile and I were both only children. When we were younger, we'd pretend we were sisters.

Thinking about it now, I guess the games we play as children never end. To friends, we pretend we're happy. To spouses, we pretend we're whole. To the world, we pretend there's nothing missing inside of us, because pretending means we don't have to tell the truth, and no one really wants the truth.

We say we do, but when someone asks: 'how are you?'

the answer they're looking for is, 'fine.' I wonder what would happen if you told the waiter filling your glass at a top-notch restaurant, you were considering jamming the fork he set down, in your eye.

"What happened when you went home?" Pierce asks.

I glance up. Lying never used to come easy to me, Mia, but now it's oxygen.

"That was the first time he hit me."

CHAPTER NINE

Watson has brought back the teapot; perhaps she sees it as a good luck charm since yesterday was the first time I spoke so candidly about the past. Pierce cradles his cup, skimming my face, I imagine him trying to decipher whether today will be a session he can dissect for merit. Luckily for him, I am counting on his integrity.

"How was your relationship with Daniel when all of this began?" he asks.

Placing my palms on the table, I stare at the scars whittled into the creases. Scars that broke the mounds of my skin the night Dan died. Each jagged rip serves as a mind map. He didn't scream when he went down, didn't cry out in pain when the knife punctured his chest. He simply dropped to his knees, clung to his chest, then drifted off with his eyelids fluttering closed.

The investigators came to me last night, Mia. Two stone-faced officers dragged me into this very room. A colleague of Dan's had come forward and shed new light onto the investigation. New light that had completely discredited a witness who gave evidence that could no longer be used against me.

They questioned me for hours, asking if I knew what Dan was engaging in. If I had an inkling why the witness would withhold vital information. Of course, I knew, but I couldn't tell them that, I couldn't tell them anything.

I'd stared at the wall, tight-lipped and bug-eyed, even after my middle-aged solicitor, Shelly Peters had burst into the room, highlighting her incompetency with the oily piece of hair sticking up from her ungroomed scalp. After the officers left, she asked me why I hadn't told her anything.

'This can change everything,' she'd whispered. But I didn't want anything to change, Mia. I needed everything to stay the same.

"Raine!"

I force my focus on Pierce. His eyes are more lined than usual, and his face exudes a silvery sheen that arrives after a week of sleepless nights.

"When you were having these visits and going to these places, what were your feelings toward Daniel?" They keep saying his name. Daniel. Daniel. Daniel. Then, to stop the feeling of their pens grating away at my skull, I jam my nails into the dents in my hands.

"Was he abusive at that point?"

I glance at Watson, scribbling.

"You said Dan was supportive. When did the abuse begin exactly?"

Shifting my focus to the window, I think of Daniel. Dear sweet, never harm a fly, Daniel. Then of the feeling I'd get as I watched him prepare for work each morning. The genuine feeling of emotion that turned up one day, planted roots in my chest and sprouted out wildly from the dented stone of my heart. Only it wasn't love. It wasn't even the opposite, because the opposite of love is indifference and that came somewhere near the end.

No, the feeling I had was rage. Pure rage for the smiling boy who skinned my insides for fun. I remember him standing in our bedroom mirror, fastening his pinstripe tie, and buttoning his crisp Italian shirt that would've cost more than two months' rent in the crappy little flat we shared when we first met.

He would give me this smug little grin pasted beneath eyes that seemed too clear to lie. But those eyes were always lying, and in that smile, I felt so much rage it was riveting. I remember the hunger I had to turn to our bedside table and pick up the hand-crafted lamp we bought on holiday in Prague. Then, to walk over to him calmly.

I imagined he'd appear amused before I swung. Stunned, as I bashed the lamp into his secretive little skull, over and over again. Hitting harder, and harder, until his boyish face became a sickly shade of grey, while all of his secrets spilt out on to our pristine bedroom carpet.

"Was that around the time Dan became abusive?"
I look up smiling, that same half smile Dan gave me.
"Yes," I lie. "That's when the abuse started."
Pierce watches me undecidedly as Watson jots something onto her pad of paper, and before they can press me further, I drift back to the story I promised I'd tell you, Mia.

JULY 30th 2018

I wore a stone coloured dress. A flimsy thing I'd bought from a charity shop, years ago. Listening to the symphony of the lake splintering through the glass, I exhaled. The waves crashed and whooshed. Bashing into one another then retreating like high school lovers. I could almost taste the sea salt on my tongue, the sun stroking my face, the wind lifting my hair.

"What are you afraid of?" Esme whispered.

My shoulders shot up as I scanned my studio. I was alone, but seeing Esme again wouldn't have surprised me, Mia. Since returning from Wanderlust, I felt her everywhere. There were times I was washing the dishes when the smell of rot would fog up the air – or reading a book in bed when her silhouette would glitter from the corner of my eye. But every time I forced myself to look directly at her, she'd scatter to nothing more than a shadow on the wall.

Hearing her was different. It started two days ago when I was unloading the tumble dryer. I'd heard a whisper, a gentle murmur, like wind sprinkling leaves on an autumn day. *'Go back,'* she hissed. I tried to ignore her, but the more I tried, the angrier her words became. Each one bruising my eardrums until I was left with no choice but to run upstairs and lock myself in the bathroom with the water running to block out the sounds. *'GO BACK.'*

The only place I believed there to be silence, was Wanderlust. And despite my excitement to return, the truth was I was afraid. Nicholas had asked me to paint him, and I had no idea why, of all the creatures in his kingdom, he had chosen me. Maybe it was a ploy to ensure I'd be gone for good, or maybe, just maybe, he really did see something in me.

I'd gone over it countless times, pacing up to my studio, then marching back down to the kitchen table where I slumped down with my head in my hands. Plagued by uncertainty, I was afraid of so many things, but mostly, I was afraid of seeing him again. The afternoon I'd spent with him was anything but telling.

He'd asked me to leave, complimented me, insulted me, then told me he wanted me to stay. If ever I'd met someone who was more at war with themselves, it was him.

I skimmed my studio. Fresh darkness slinked through the windows, scraping everything in its path: the black lace curtains, my clay pot holders, the burnt-out candles stocked on the various cabinets, and my most recent painting backed up against the redbrick wall, of a lake the colour of a firestorm with two silhouettes watching the night unfold.

"Go," Esme whispered.

Refusing to give her the satisfaction of being acknowledged, I kept my eyes pinned to the mirror as I reached out, forcing my hand to stay there long enough to feel that glorious abandon flowing through my lungs, and when I opened my eyes, I saw I was back at the lake.

I spun around, inspecting the palace. The lazy sun hung low above it, making the crystal panels shimmer so brightly I had to squint just to take it in. Would it have been rude to have turned up? Nicholas had invited me, but where would I find him? I bit my lip as the heat weighed down on shoulders. It had been four days since I'd returned. Four days was long enough for him to have changed his mind, forgotten even.

Puffing out my cheeks, I shifted my focus to the palace steps where I noticed a figure. Nicholas. I dropped my head as he waved me over, but how did he know I'd come back today? And how long had he been waiting? My chest stirred as I took a deep breath, reminding myself I could do this. The painting would take a few hours at most, then it would be over. No more Nicholas, no more odd little moments where I felt him tunnelling into my mind with his steely-eyed gaze.

Lowering my head, I began trekking uphill with the

sun bumping against my shoulders and the sweet scent of wildflowers grazing my lungs. Halfway there, I peered up, then froze. It hadn't been Nicholas waving me over at all, but the headless woman, and the longer I watched her dancing around on the steps, the more I felt ridiculous for mistaking the two.

I hugged my chest. Was it too late to run off and convene on the other side of the palace? I peered back shakily. She was ushering me closer, propelling her arm higher and higher. Assuring myself she was probably there to take me to see Nicholas, I started moving. Why else would she have been waving me over?

To take my head, a voice in my head wailed.

Pressing myself to stay positive, I trudged on, only when I reached the middle of the stairway no amount of positive thinking could stop my heart from plummeting when I saw the wound cast across her neck. I winced, ogling the deep black gash cementing her shoulders. Brown blood caked the frilled ruffles of her dress, and a dull piece of marrow jutted out from the centre.

"Erm- my name is—" I stiffened when she thrust a hand in my face. "I don't know if it's wise. Nicholas… the king I mean."

Grabbing my arm, the headless woman hauled me inside.

"Nicholas asked me to paint him," I told her as the door slammed shut behind us.

She didn't answer, how could she without a head?

Peering up at the spiral staircase, I searched the balcony for a face, a creature, him. There was no one there. Skulking behind the headless creature in silence, I purse my lips, and when she moved a little ahead of me, I glimpsed two bloodstains the size of fists against her shoulders. Wrinkling a brow, I wondered if I had mistaken her odd little dance for lack of balance.

Continuing behind her through the candlelit corridor, I

focussed on my breathing, trying not to panic.

"Where are we going?" I whispered.

Her dress smacked the back of my legs as we moved faster.

"Can you hear me?"

No answer.

We were heading the same way I had escaped from, I was sure of it. Passing the kitchen, her grip on my forearm tightened as she led me into complete darkness.

"Can you hear me?"

This time she squeezed my hand, but before I could thank her for her impromptu response, light from the glossy walls illuminated the place where we'd stopped. My mouth went dry. We were outside of the ruby door where the Cyclops had slept with the axe. Swallowing huge chunks of air, I backed away as her pale fists pounded the door.

KNOCK, KNOCK, KNOCK.

My eyes expanded, and my brain swelled with all of the horrors that might've been waiting inside.

KNOCK, KNOCK. KNOCK.

What if there were Mithels inside? Or Candimore? What if Nicholas had changed his mind and he'd decided to behead me?

KNOCK, KNOCK. KNOCK.

My throat tightened as the headless woman pushed open the door.

The creak sent a violent tingle surging down my spine as she released my arm and sashayed back off into the shadows. Waiting a few seconds, I craned my neck to see inside. I could almost make out the chandelier dangling from the ceiling. An easel was set up in the middle. My lips cracked. Beneath it was a thin blue sheet.

The door screeched as I pushed my head in further, and when it was just as far it could be, I heard his voice.

"Raine."

I jumped and hit my neck on the doorframe.

"Ouch," I mumbled, massaging my collarbone. Nicholas was inside; it could've been worse, much worse. He'd upheld his end of the bargain, which meant now, I would have to uphold mine.

Keeping my eyes on the ground, I inched through the hall. Slinking past where he sat in his throne at the bottom of the steps; I reminded myself I had to face him if I wanted to cross the lake. Even though painting him seemed as though it were a terribly intimate request, I tried to think of it as it was, just a job.

Stopping at the blue sheet, I urged myself to stay in control, or to at least look like I was in control. Anxiety crawled up my throat like a caterpillar, balling up its thick body and stretching out lavishly. Portraits weren't my strong point; never had been. I'd always found it unnerving working in front of an audience, understanding what I envisioned may not live up to another's expectations.

Then there was the question of paint. I preferred acrylic. Acrylic dried faster, and I believed there was something honest about having an image set so interminably without the prospect of alteration, but the beauty of such a thing could be disastrous if the person painted found it to be tasteless. I wondered what sort of paints they used here, then if they even used paints when Nicholas cleared his throat.

I peered up at him from the side of the canvas. He sat with his palms on the golden armrests and the muscles in his forearms twitching. I could almost imagine an unlit cigarette dripping from the corners of his lips; a creature who flirted with danger but was too afraid to light the match.

"Thank you, for coming," he said.

"Well, I wasn't left with much choice."

His face twisted as I took in his attire. His shirt seemed brighter, and his boots had an indisputable shine making me question if he'd made an effort. He watched me in the same outlandish way that built forest fires in my chest. In a bid to dampen them, I thought of other things, vital things, like how I would do this.

For starters, I would take charge. King or no king, this was my domain, and if he didn't like it well, that would be his problem. About to tell him to move closer, I cleared my throat when he asked,

"Where would you like me?"

My lips parted as he arched a brow.

"Right there is fine." I jutted my head at the space in front of me.

In seconds Nicholas slung the throne over his shoulder. He strode forward like water; fast, smooth, and changing everything in its path, before setting down the seat and collapsing into the deep red cushion.

"So, how is this going to work?" I asked, hating myself immediately.

"Well, that depends on you," Nicholas replied. "You're the artist."

I uttered a sound that was a cross between a sigh and a snort, before skirting around the easel, grateful I had something to mask myself from his view.

The canvas stretched over a metre wide and was almost double that in height. What Nicholas was expecting would've taken hours, days even, and I didn't know if I had that sort of time. Stroking the stapled edges, I scanned the pallet wedged into the groove then widened my eyes.

Fixed in the easel were rows and columns of colours I'd never seen. Colours that didn't even exist. Tangerine trickled with black, cherry gleaming with daffodil, plum tangled with taupe, peach fused with sapphire, all of them glittered and made my fingers jitter with wonder.

"These are remarkable," I whispered. Tracing the pallet, I was taken by the same sensation I had as a child. The belief that the colours were an elixir, within them lay the power to transport you through time, and space, and cultures, to the mind of a stranger.

As I grew older, that feeling had been bleached out somewhat. The right shade of emerald reminded me of the winter coat my mother had sold to put food on the table. The right shade of ivory, the wedding gown I'd dreamt of as a child but itched like thorns against my skin when I walked down the aisle.

I stole a look at Nicholas. He hadn't seen anything I'd painted, and I had no idea if my work would even suit his taste.

"Listen, before we start, I need to tell you I'm not sure if this will be any good. I'm not sure how things work here, and I'm a little out of practice."

"All I expect is for you to try."

"And then you'll tell me how to pass the lake?" I held my stare, embarrassed I wanted to see an ounce of regret line his face, but he didn't so much as flinch.

"Yes."

My cheeks flared as I forced a hefty nod.

"Thanks, but portraits—"

"I'm sure it will be exceptional."

"No pressure then," I joked.

Nicholas didn't laugh, he barely blinked, and after a minute or so, I decided to get on with it. Standing tall, I nodded at the canvas but when I saw the brush wedged in the groove my lungs collapsed.

"What's this?" I asked, holding up the crooked twig. Joint at the end, was a feather. Thin and wispy, and speckled in streaks of silver and red.

"A brush," Nicholas replied.

"I meant, what is it made from?"

"Phoenix feathers. Is it not sufficient for the task?"

Unsure of how one tiny brush could cover an entire canvas, I uttered an indecipherable sound.

"A phoenix?" I questioned. Dunking the brush into a singed shade of hazelnut, I planned on beginning from the bottom and working my way up. Something I hadn't done before, but unprepared to meet his eyes just yet, I started with his boots.

"When a phoenix combusts, their feathers are collected and made into brushes." His smoky voice filled the spaces between us as I littered the sheet in tiny brushstrokes like the first bird tracks in snow. "Don't you think they're remarkable?"

"What are?"

"Phoenixes," Nicholas replied. "They shatter completely, resurrect themselves then become something stronger, something unbreakable. In art, creatures claim their feathers build an everlasting image."

Looking up, I caught his cheeks redden, and I wondered if I had misjudged him. By his excitement, it appeared Nicholas appreciated strength, a trait at first I was sure he lacked. Scrutinising the outline of his boots on the sheet, I wondered what else he might've been hiding.

"Do you… like art?"

"I like all sorts," Nicholas replied.

"I find that hard to believe."

"You find it hard to believe I like things?"

I glared at the sheet. He was doing it again, flustering me with that high and mighty attitude of his.

"Do you have any hobbies?" I tried.

"Hobbies?"

"I mean do you sing, read, write, paint?"

"I play."

"Play?"

"The piano."

Blotting the sheet, I wondered if he was forced to play as a child. I imagined a younger version of him bashing his claws against ivory keys, and bawling when he made a mistake.

"I know what you're thinking," he said suddenly.

"And what might that be?"

"Poor little rich boy, obsessed with himself without any understanding of the world."

Dunking the brush in a pot of grey water fixed in the easel, I swirled it around while my insides lurched with humiliation.

"Who collects them?" I muttered, wondering if I was that easy to read.

"Collects what?"

"Phoenix feathers, you said their feathers are collected, by whom?"

"Creatures," Nicholas replied.

"From what region?"

"The third."

"Are regions like cities, or countries?"

"They're like regions," Nicholas replied.

"How many creatures live in each region?"

He didn't answer. Peering up, I saw his lips had puckered into a half smile.

"You're inquisitive," he said.

"Is that a bad thing?"

Nicholas shook his head as I lathered the tip of the feather in a cherry violet.

"Wouldn't you be inquisitive if you were me? I mean, imagine stumbling into a world you knew nothing about. This huge place that shakes your entire belief system. Everything here is different, magical, captivating. Don't you wonder about the place I come from?"

From over the canvas, I saw his face had hardened. It was the same expression he wore the first time we met.

Anger mixed with fear, all tied together with the musty scent of charred stories. Pulling back my shoulders, I wondered what I'd said to offend him when he spoke with so much frost it caused the room to shiver.

"Why would I need to wonder about where you come from when I know it is barbaric."

"Barbaric?"

Nicholas stooped lower, the muscles in his forearms threatening to rip through his shirt.

I scratched my head. Nicholas had been borderline friendly before, and now I was practically getting was the death stare. And for what? Mentioning the place I came from? I thought better of prying. I would finish what I started, then leave.

With a little more force than before, I resumed shadowing the throne. All the while I questioned what Nicholas would really think if he knew about the place I came from. Not barbaric, but superficial – a generation obsessed with selfies, and filters, with everyone watching, but no one seeing.

I huffed, trying to get his portrait done with as quickly as possible when he spoke so unexpectedly, I dropped the brush.

"What did you make of Marianne?"

I shot him a look of contempt, before bending down to retrieve the stick. Now he wanted to talk? Did he not think I was barbaric like the place I came from?

"Marianne?"

"Our housekeeper, and a friend." Marianne must have been the woman who had brought me here. What was I meant to make of her without a head? Friendly, kind, a real conversation starter?

I offered a nod while massaging the knot in my shoulders. I wasn't even halfway through painting Nicholas, and already it felt as though I'd been working for days. My back ached, and my legs were getting a little shaky.

"Was she born that way?" I asked, marching about on the spot.

"What way?" Nicholas asked, lifting a brow as I wobbled around.

"I mean without a head, and her back, she seemed unbalanced."

His eyes slumped to the ground, but he must've seen me because when I motioned for him to sit up-right, he did.

"It was an accident," Nicholas replied. "The scars are from her wings, and her head… she still has her head in her quarters."

"She kept her head!"

Nicholas nodded meekly. "Why?"

"Wouldn't you, if you had an option?"

"I'm not sure, I can't say decapitation really crosses my mind on a daily basis."

Tipping back his head, Nicholas studied the chandelier with this glazed look in his eyes.

"So where are the rest of the creatures?"

"Which?"

"The Repsil, the Mithels."

"Candimore is tending to something in the valley."

"The valley?"

"A section in the fourth region. The trolls there are quite fond of him."

I clung to the brush with an image of the Repsil making my stomach hurt.

"They are?"

"Yes, I can't be sure of why. Perhaps it has something to do with the colour of his skin matching the marshland. He spends a great deal of time there. The trolls believe he makes them feel heard. He gives those lower in society a voice."

I gritted my teeth, reminding myself not to get piqued,

only when I brought the brush back to the sheet, I heard the words fly out from my mouth anyway.

"How can you speak about him like that?"

Nicholas's gaze bounced from the chandelier to me. For a second, he looked afraid.

"Like what?"

"Like he's not a monster. Like he didn't try to kill me. Like he—"

"He was ordered to carry out my instructions."

I stepped back as the ugly mess of the truth spilt out before us. The truth that my resentment was not directed at Candimore at all, but at Nicholas. Nicholas for having issued the commands, Nicholas for carrying such perverse intent.

"Candimore's heart is pure," Nicholas added.

"And you, Nicholas, what are you like inside?"

"I am content as I am."

"Are you?" Nicholas nodded, but everything about the way he looked at me told me he was lying.

"You don't seem it."

"You don t know me."

"Does anyone?"

"Only those I care for."

Tasting the bitterness in his tone, I spoke recklessly.

"I'm married." My voice hung in the air as I watched him, waiting to glimpse the damage my words had done, but nothing had changed. He was still staring at me with this vacant expression as though he was lost in something he didn't have the energy to find his way back from. "I have been with him, Daniel, for seven years. Married three."

A smile crept alongside his face. In the exuberance of the fire, his fangs glistened.

"Why are you telling me this?"

"I just thought it was necessary. The day at the lake you asked about my life, and I guess it's something I should have mentioned.

"Why?"

"Because we share a life."

"Do you?"

"Yes."

"Then why didn't you mention him before?"

I glowered at him with my face burning brighter than the fire. He wouldn't look away. He was challenging me, unravelling me, attempting to venture into places he didn't belong. In a fit of annoyance, I hid behind the canvas before he spoke three simple words that cut me wide open.

"Are you happy?"

"That's really none of your business," I scoffed. "And why would it be of any concern to you when you think I'm barbaric?"

"I didn't say you," Nicholas said. "I said the place you come from."

"Same thing."

"Well, are you happy?"

"Are you?"

"Not for a long time."

My lips parted. Wondering if I'd misheard him, I looked up and caught a flash of sadness litter his features. His eyes dulled, his cheeks sagged, and yet again I found myself questioning if I'd misjudged him. Had I mistaken his curiosity for arrogance? I sighed, wondering if I should tell him the truth, but how could I, when the truth was something I could barely admit to myself. No, I wasn't happy. No, I didn't share a life with the man who carved up my insides for fun.

Instead of admitting defeat, I continued painting while my mind wandered to the night Dan had found me in my studio. There was blood on his hands. My blood. He'd stood over me, insisting it was my fault. It was only a small cut, the size of an insect bite, but when he pulled me into the bathroom and I watched him mop up the gooey blood on my wrists, I knew he was lying.

"He hurt me," I whispered. My voice was too small for Nicholas to hear, but saying the words aloud was like an itch I'd finally scratched. I gnawed my lip, adding the red and emerald tints to the throne, the glossy tinge to his claws, the silky contours of his cheeks. There was silence for a long time. Throughout all of it, I felt his gaze running over my slightly crooked teeth and eyes that were too big for my face.

"Your name suits you, Raine," Nicholas said quietly.

My heart stuttered, but I didn't react. Getting on with the task at hand, I deliberated whether it was a compliment or an insult. In school, my name had been the source of many cruel chants. Raine the pain. Plain Raine. Raine, Raine go away, don't come back another day.

"You perplex me, Raine."

I lifted my head, and as our eyes met from a safe enough distance, I wondered why Nicholas kept looking at me as if he had one foot dangling off the border of a cliff. I smiled shakily. He smiled back. Dragging my attention back to the canvas, I began adding the small patches of hair on his cheek, understanding that Nicholas was not conventionally beautiful.

His eyes were much too damaged, his face was far too lined, and his chestnut hair fell across his face in a thunderstorm of knots, and tangles, that reeked of his lack of regard for mirrors, but there was something honest about him, and that surpassed any expectations of superficial beauty.

Hours passed, and after stepping back, and nursing my wrists, I studied his portrait half-heartedly. The whole thing emitted a sheen of kingliness; his palms against the armrests, his jaw lifted, his body erect like he was about to give orders for battle with the fire roaring on behind him.

My eyes caught bits I hadn't finished. The gems in the throne needed to be brighter, and the edges of the hearth were too sharp, but stepping back had somehow given Nicholas the indication I had finished, and when I looked back, I saw him striding over to me.

"Wait," I gasped, throwing my arms out to block the canvas. But Nicholas was already there. Hugging my chest, I backed away as he inspected my work with his brows sewn together. I reached just below his shoulders; I could smell him; earth and spring, as if the sun had made it its life's work to soak through his skin. I waited for him to say something, anything, but he was staring at the portrait with this expression I couldn't decipher, and it frightened me that I cared.

Taking a deep breath, he turned slowly when I cut in with far too much enthusiasm.

"So, will you tell me how to cross the lake now?"

"Yes," Nicholas answered. "Next time you come back, I will show you."

I focussed on a button midway up his shirt where dark hairs poked out from the places the material couldn't quite cover.

"Good," I said.

"Good," Nicholas replied, but the silence whispered something else.

***

"How long before you went back?" Pierce asks.

"Straight after."

"And when you went back did you feel accomplished? Lost?" The tea on the table has finished.

Watson collects the cups. Her spectacles judder on the crook of her nose as she stacks them, smiling. She thinks today has been a successful session, but it hasn't, because despite telling the truth about Nicholas, I still haven't mentioned what Dan did to me.

"Nothing," I tell them. "When I went back, I felt nothing."

CHAPTER TEN

I stare at the wall behind Watson and Pierce, ambushed by memories of the nightmare I had last night, Mia. It started innocently as most nightmares do. Then, like a glass of milk left out in the sun, it soured disastrously. I was driving the red BMW Dan and I saved for five Christmases ago, to where I couldn't tell you, but what I can tell you, is that you were there. I could just about make out your face in the rear-view mirror.

Honeyed skin, the rumour of brown eyes, a whisper of gold curls cascading around your tiny face, but like glimpsing a fish beneath glacial waters, every time I plunged my palms deep into the ocean, the image would stray.

I drove with my finger tapping the wheel as the world outside flickered by in a violent blur. I heard the rustling trees, ominous traffic, people rushing about in raincoats trying to get home as quickly as possible. You wore a pink net tutu. The kind I saw girls wearing when I was younger, and envied, and even though it was out of view, I sensed it scratching your knees as you thrashed the back of my seat.

"Mia, stop it, honey," I mumbled, but you continued to bash your little legs about until I was forced to use the voice Katie used with George. "Mia, I'm not going to ask you again."

Your kicking stopped, and as the rain beat down against the frantic wipers, I heard your voice.

"Sorry, Mummy." Your words were soft, sweet, with enough innocence to slice right through me, and before I could tell you I wasn't angry, a red glow from outside worked its way into the car, and everything blurred.

I squinted. My heart stung, something was wrong. Looking back to check you were alright, my stomach dropped. You were gone. Jamming down on the brakes, I glared at the fastened doors and windows, fighting to call your name but it was lodged in my throat like glue. Cold hands crushed my windpipe when I tried again.

Esme was there; I heard her raspy laughter. I choked, my lungs gasping for air, my face bathed in sweat, and just as I was about to rush off in search of you, the dead woman emerged in the passenger seat. She inclined her head, grinned. My heart stopped. There was a child in her arms, a bloody pink net tutu.

"Raine," I jump, then turn to Watson.

"No," I mumble.

"No, what?" she asks, and I wonder if I have answered a question she hasn't asked.

"No, I'm not talking about my childhood."

There is no tea today, only a mountain of paper.

"I'll tell you about Nicholas." Pierce and Watson exchange glances, because to them this information is irrelevant. They need to know logistics, not about the creature they assume I made up. They need reality or at least their version of it.

Why did I slaughter my husband? Did he provoke me?

179

Perhaps they can attribute my behaviour to something I was predestined for. Had I witnessed my father beat my mother? Did violence exist in my genetic makeup, or was it merely an observation of my environment?

In their hungry eyes, I see the question: *Why did this run-of-the-mill woman with no history of violence, really plunge the kitchen knife into her husband seven times, puncturing his aortic valve before watching him bleed to death?*

Watson sets down her pen. Her skin is dry, her lips chapped. I am aware she's met with my solicitor after the investigation has taken a turn. What did I expect after lying to the police?

"Raine," Pierce tries.

"He showed me how to cross the lake."

"Raine—"

"I promised I would tell her."

AUGUST 3rd 2018

Squinting at the tiny slit windows in the palace behind me, I wondered if Nicholas knew I was waiting. Before returning, I'd been afraid I would end up in the hall, but instead, I'd landed next to the spirit lake, and I was grateful I wouldn't have to trek through the iron folds of the palace to find him. Pacing backwards and forwards, I slumped down with my hands submerged beneath the wet strands of grass.

The sky was a cloudless blue. It was the kind of weather built for dreaming, but I couldn't relax. I was anxious Nicholas wouldn't uphold his end of the deal, and I'd already been waiting long enough for my mind to start reeling. What if he had second thoughts? What if what I painted wasn't good enough, or good at all?

My cheeks stung. The main thing was, I'd tried. I had worked until my wrists ached and my back throbbed, and despite the bits I hadn't finished, overall, it was something I was proud of. Still, that didn't mean Nicholas was. Chewing the inside of my cheek, I watched the sun bounce across the waves of the lake when I glimpsed a silhouette looming over me in the reflection.

My heart stirred as I peered closer, questioning if it was one of the spirits.

"Raine."

Nicholas's voice made me bolt upright.

"Hello, Nicholas," I mumbled, turning clumsily.

"Hello," Nicholas replied. He stood with his hands in his pockets and his muddy gaze flicking across his boot.

I held my breath, waiting for him to raise the point of why he'd come. Perhaps there was another hole I'd missed, or a bridge, or an underground passage somewhere, but when he spoke again, I felt the tips of my ears catch fire.

"Your painting is hanging in the dining room. I didn't get a chance to tell you I was impressed, as were the others in the palace." His nose twitched while the words fidgeted for room in his mouth. "You are a magnificent artist Raine."

"Thanks," I breathed, wondering if he'd told the creatures it was me who painted it. A barbaric human from a faraway world. Wasn't that against his regulations?

He liked it, a voice in my mind whispered.

Of course, he did, a sterner voice argued, *it was a portrait of himself, he would've liked it if a blind parrot had painted it.*

Folding my arms, I watched him with a lifetime of words stacking up in my throat, and even though I wanted to stay speaking to him about nothing and everything all day, I was under no illusion time was running out.

"Nicholas, will you please tell me how to cross the lake now?" I asked.

"Are you sure you want to leave?"

Yes, I wanted to reply. *Yes,* because leaving would give me the freedom to roam Wanderlust unguarded, to start my life over, and become a part of something greater, but the word was held back by something that troubled me more than I cared to admit. If I left then, I wouldn't see Nicholas again.

Watching him fumble round in his pockets, I knew I had to leave; it was ridiculous for me to have even cared. I'd spent two days with him– two days wasn't enough for someone to care, but deep down I knew that I did.

"Yes," I replied, though whatever angst I wanted to see mark his face, was veiled by a shrug of his shoulders.

"Okay," he replied.

"Okay?"

"Let's go."

My face dropped as he headed towards the palace.

"We should leave before it gets dark."

"I'm sorry we?" I gasped, chasing after him. "What do you mean by we?"

"You said you wanted to leave the first region, and I promised I would show you a way, remember?"

"You didn't mention you were coming."

"You didn't ask."

"I didn't think it was an option."

"Are you disappointed?" Nicholas swerved around to face me. Taking in his stubble-ridden jaw, I swear I saw him smile.

"No, I just…" I blinked, then jutted my head at the purple canister he'd pulled out from his pocket. "What's that?"

"Our transport," Nicholas answered.

"I'm sorry, our transport?" Nicholas nodded, and when the initial relief wore off that he was about to accompany me on my venture, all that was left was the sore reality of it. Nicholas was going out of his way to help me, a human he had insisted had no place here.

"Nicholas," I sighed, hating myself for the Get Out Of Jail Free card I was about to hand him. "If you have things to do here, kingly things. I'm sure I can go alone." I looked away, certain it wasn't what I wanted. Still, even if I didn't know how to use the canister, I assured myself I could do it. I had done plenty of things alone, travelling across a lake in another realm couldn't be too difficult.

"Not really," Nicholas replied.

"Nothing?" I asked. "You don't have anything better to do? No trolls to prosecute, no dragons to slay, no pixies to capture?" Judging by the warmth in his eyes, I was pretty sure he was fighting a smile now.

"Not that I can think of."

I nodded at my pumps, waiting for him to bestow upon me the details of our expedition as he twisted off the canister lid, and when I realised what was inside, my brows soared up to the sky.

"Bubbles!" I exclaimed, staring at the stick. "We travel by bubbles?"

"If you know what they are, why do you seem so surprised?"

"I didn't…" I ran my fingers through my hair, staring at the liquid juddering inside of the hole. "I know what bubbles are. But the ones I'm familiar with aren't used for travel."

Nicholas looked as though he wanted to say something. I narrowed my eyes as he she shook the unspoken words away. Then, in a voice much more forceful than I'd anticipated, he shouted,

"Ready?"

I flinched, feeling as if I should mirror his tone.

"Yes!" I shouted back.

Confusion skipped across his face, and in an effort to

stop myself from embarrassing myself further, I sealed my lips shut tight then watched as he held the stick to his lips and blew.

Thick veins bulged in his neck, and the buttons on his shirt looked close to popping off, but the liquid inside the hole barely wavered. I tilted my head as he blew again, harder this time, puffing out his chest and squaring up his shoulders until a gargantuan bubble erupted from the hole.

I fumbled back, eying the translucent ball in disbelief. It was like one of those gimmicks struggling street artists use to con money out of families when they've run out of ideas. Nearly ten-foot-tall, and about eight-foot-wide, I inspected the rainbow of colours pouring from its curve, mystified as to how this could pass as transport when Nicholas pulled me forwards by my wrist.

"Oh, gosh," I muttered.

A thunderous plunk rung in my ears as I peered around, stunned. We were inside the muggy bubble. Not only that, we were lifting higher, bustling through the sky, and jostling overhead of the spirit lake. Nicholas had already taken his seat opposite me, and before I could ask how it was feasible to sit upon the surface of something so fragile, we blew higher.

"Isn't this dangerous?" I asked loudly.

Nicholas focussed on me with his lips creased.

"Relax Raine," he instructed, but the bubble was taking us way up past the clouds, and relaxing seemed impossible, more than impossible, it became inconceivable. My face pricked with sweat as I gulped in hot sticky air, commanding myself to sit but I was petrified the second I did – the lining would tear and we would plummet to our deaths.

My legs were rigid. Everything was too bright; the sky, the breaks from the clouds, the glints from the bubbles lining, the glimmer of Nicholas's teeth, and all at once nausea was swirling through my gut like a hurricane.

"Relax," Nicholas repeated. His voice only made it worse. My hands began shaking, my arms too, soon my entire body was convulsing. Ahead of us, was a mountain cluttered in glittering rocks, but I couldn't take it in, all I could do was listen to the unsteady hammer of my heart.

"We could both die!" I yelled.

Beneath the bubble was an empty space of land, and all too speedily I realised the palace resided on the highest point of Wanderlust, and the only way to go now would be down.

"Oh, God!" My stomach churned as we swooped lower.

Squeezing my eyes shut tight, I clamped down hard on my lips. The whole ordeal was like a roller-coaster ride, only there were no seatbelts, and no stern-faced youths assuring you you'd be fine.

"Raine, if I promise you our transport is safe, will you try to sit?"

I wanted to, but I couldn't stop shaking.

"Are you afraid of heights?"

I waggled my head because I'd flown on planes before. I wasn't like those passengers who had to glug down a litre of scotch before departure, but this was different. Picking up a rapid speed, the bubble dipped lower.

"I want to get down."

"Breathe," Nicholas said.

"Now, Nicholas. I want to get down now!"

"Raine," Nicholas called in a voice so stern I looked up. "Do you trust me?"

I shocked myself by nodding.

"Then breathe."

"But what if we fall?"

"So, what if we do? Are you really going to waste the

last few seconds of your life scared of possibilities? No," Nicholas answered before I could scream *yes*. "So, breathe."

I threw him a look of resentment before obliging myself to remember what the yoga teacher with toothpick calves had taught me in class, years ago.

"Deep breaths," she'd sung in her drawn-out melodic voice, but the air refused to enter my lungs, and my face felt like it had been brushed under the armpit of the sun.

"Breathe," Nicholas whispered. His voice crashed around me in reckless torrents. "Breathe."

I tried it again. Shallow at first, then vigorously, unfathomably, and when I opened my eyes, I saw him standing so close to me I could see his pulse picking away at his throat.

I don't think he meant to startle me. If anything, he looked as taken aback as me. Stumbling back, I screamed. His hands went up as a warning, his eyes stretched, but it was too late, I'd already tumbled backwards with my scream looming in the atmosphere.

Half expecting to find myself flailing through the sky, I shuddered, but I was still inside of the bubble. Nicholas, looking a little shame-faced, hunkered down opposite me.

"I apologise," he said after a moment. "I should have warned you, but I assumed you knew about bubbles."

"The bubbles I know aren't used for travel," I told him. "They pop!"

"Then what are they used for?"

Dizzy, I didn't answer. Instead, I peered down, taking in a fuzzy polaroid image of clear-cut segments of red and blue and marigold shaped like a star. In the centre was a circular patch of snowy grass I imagined was the first region. Waiting for my heart to stop pounding, I watched Nicholas pull a black cape out from his pocket.

"What's the cape for?"

"So I won't be recognised," Nicholas replied, throwing it over his head.

"In the bubble?"

"At the market." So, we were going to a market.

I poked the spongy layer beneath me, wondering what this market would look like when I noticed Nicholas rubbing the face of his ring.

"I like your ring," I said stupidly.

"It's a reminder."

"A reminder of what?"

No answer.

Sighing loud enough to hint at my annoyance, I wiped my damp brow. Did Nicholas expect to spend this entire journey in silence? If he did, what was the point of coming in the first place?

"Do you leave the palace much?"

Nicholas shook his head at his knees.

"Why?"

"Just."

"There must be a reason."

Nicholas offered a grunt before rolling up his sleeves.

Catching sight of his wrists, my forehead puckered. He wasn't identified. I'd assumed all of the creatures in Wanderlust had been maimed, but there was nothing on Nicholas's veiny wrists but a smattering of fine hair.

"So," I asked, staring at his wrist. "Are you going to tell me why you don't leave the palace?"

"It's complicated," Nicholas mumbled.

"Complicated how?"

Nicholas exhaled, and when he met my stare, I realised his eyes were the same shade as earl grey tea in the light.

"Because, whenever I venture outside of the first region I'm treated by a title I don't deserve. As a king, I'm expected to be courageous and bold and striking."

"And you don't think you are any of those things?"

"It doesn't matter," he said. "The world decides who you are before you have a chance to prove yourself."

"That sounds a little self-defeatist," I said under my breath. "What happened to forget the world?"

"It's different," Nicholas argued, but I couldn't see how, and by the look of it neither could he. "I have to set an example."

"And you think you're doing that by hiding out at the palace?"

"I'm not hiding."

"Then what are you doing?"

Nicholas opened his mouth when I told him:

"I think you're courageous." My face sweltered. I had no idea of why I said it; I didn't know Nicholas, not properly. He was a stranger who'd flung a cape over his head, most likely to avoid me asking questions, and here I was dishing out compliments as though we'd known each other years.

"You didn't let them hurt me in the palace," I continued, studying the thick wisps of clouds lolling past us. "And you're true to your word because you're taking me across the lake, despite the law banning humans from Wanderlust."

"It's not enough," Nicholas said.

"Well, to me it is."

Nicholas watched me undecidedly and before he could form a response, the bubble began shaking. Alarmed, I glanced around as we jerked, stopped, then dropped.

Oh God, I'd never believed in God, but there I was praying to Him as I dug my fingers into my thighs. Deep breaths, I told myself, deep breaths, but my insides were somersaulting, and all I could do to stop nausea swirling round in my gut was to clamp down on my lips until I tasted blood. I couldn't open my eyes, even when the bubble came to a violent standstill on what I hoped was the ground.

Nicholas cleared his throat. Taking an unsteady breath, I unglued my eyes, and when I saw what Nicholas had clasped in his hands, the universe thinned to dust. A knife. Nicholas was holding a large kitchen knife.

Well done, Raine. Great job.

Shuffling backwards, I tried to fend him off. Only Nicholas didn't advance towards me as I'd expected. If anything, he just looked confused, and when he grasped what I was thinking, he shook his head quickly.

"The bubble will only burst when it's on the ground," he told me.

I crinkled my nose, wishing he'd mentioned that earlier. "Ready?" Nicholas asked.

I was nowhere near ready. I'd just fallen what I imagined was millions of feet and assumed I'd only survived the drop to be butchered on the ground. Licking my lips, I peered through the sheer layer. All around us bubbles were lowering and popping, and crackling into the atmosphere like fireworks, but the more I strained my eyes to see outside, the more distorted the view became.

Nodding hesitantly, I dragged myself up as Nicholas angled the blade.

"Ready?" he asked again.

I forced another nod as he smiled weakly, then lugged down the blade. Thudded with an almighty explosion, I struggled to gain footing after the blast, and when I lifted my head, I gasped. Surrounding me, were rows and columns of wooden stalls that seemed to go on for miles. Yellow and red and purple and white canopies hung overhead each of them, flapping in the gentle gusts of breeze.

I punched my sides, drinking in an abundance of creatures weaving in and out of the cluster of stalls. Some, chatting, others laughing, a few, marching around briskly. Inhaling the tangled scents of incense sticks, and freshly baked bread, I wandered forwards, trying to make out the faces of shoppers as the world rushed by in a chaotic blur.

"Follow me," Nicholas called, snapping me from my trance. "And stay close,"

"Nicholas, how did we stop at the right place?" I half shouted, chasing after his black cloak.

"There are different bubbles," Nicholas explained. "Each one will take you to a different region."

"So, there are different canisters for different places?" I asked, but my voice was lost in the commotion.

"Come on down folks, strongest mermaid hair known to Wanderlust," shouted a badger from a wooden stall. "Impossible to split."

Glancing at the twine clasped between his claws, I recognised it as the string that held me in place at the palace. Noticing my intrigue, the badger grinned, revealing teeth like yellow daggers.

"Fantastic prices!" Someone shouted as I hurried off under the ruffled pink sky.

"Goblin warts, get your goblin warts!" called a boy who couldn't be more than ten years old.

Entranced by the creatures' excitement, I bustled through the hungry crowd, knocking into a woman with a horn shooting up from the centre of her candy floss hair.

"I apologise," she whispered gently, scurrying off in a pink floor length gown.

"What are all of these things?" I asked, catching up with Nicholas.

"Creatures and produce in our world," he replied.

I quickened my pace, nearly tripping over the pebbles at my feet. Stopping to catch my breath, I peered at the wooden hut where I'd found myself. Assembled on a wonky shelf, behind an even wonkier trader, were hundreds of glass bottles labelled with coffee stained scribbles. Fairy dust, dragon tears, jelly legs, memory juice. Noting my wonder, the toothless trader grinned.

"Interested in any giggling drops, syrup? New bunch, made freshly by yours truly this morning."

Lifting a brow, I skimmed the crowd for Nicholas, hoping he wouldn't be too riled up when I caught up to him. Turning back, I saw the trader unscrewing the lid of a glass jar.

"What do they do?" I asked.

"Give you the giggles!" the creature exclaimed.

Inside of the glass jar were hundreds of beads. Plucking up a gummy red treat he held it on the tip of his callused finger.

"Well?"

"I don't have anything to pay you with," I told him.

"First one's on me," the trader winked. "Call it a sample, if you like it come back."

I bit my lip as he leant so far over the counter his nose was touching mine. The phrase 'never take candy from a stranger' came to mind when the trader held out his palm, gesturing for me to do the same.

Convinced the laughing drop couldn't be too dangerous if creatures were striding around with bags slung over their shoulders, I eyed the gummy red treat hesitantly as it tacked to my skin.

"Thanks," I said, backing away.

The trader shooed me off with a hand. Seconds later, I was rushing off in search of Nicholas. Sprinting through airy conversations, and groups of haggling creatures, I spotted him beside a few empty storefronts.

Pleased I'd managed to find him, I grinned, only when I caught his face from under his hood, my smile slipped.

"Stop disappearing," he snapped, hunching lower so that his face was inches from mine. "Do you know how dangerous it is for you to wander these markets alone?"

"Well actually, I don't."

Nicholas's face blanched, and I couldn't tell if he was angry, or embarrassed.

"This is all new to me," I said with a little less venom. "Can't you let me enjoy it?"

"This place is dangerous," Nicholas insisted.

"Then why bring me here?"

"I wanted to show you something."

"What?"

Nicholas examined the land behind me as if it were about to start raining bullets.

"It doesn't look very dangerous."

"Well, it is," Nicholas said. "Especially when you know nothing about our customs."

"So, teach me." I stepped closer, but as soon as my foot hit the ground, Nicholas jerked backwards as if we were in the middle of some weird salsa dance. Releasing an exaggerated breath, I palmed my face trying to dampen my frustration, but it was difficult when we were surrounded by so much enchantment.

In the distance fruit stalls sold mangos so big they would've fed families for months. To the left of them were children with vast translucent wings. I shook my head, struck by an urge to grab Nicholas by his shoulders, tell him to take down his silly hood and enjoy the beauty surrounding us. Just then, I had an idea.

"Here," I said, uncoiling my palm to the sticky candy.

"Where did you get that?" Nicholas asked eying the laughing drop as if it were about to grow teeth and devour him.

"One of the market stalls."

"No, thank you."

"Nicholas," I pressed.

Nicholas sighed, and when his eyes met mine, a small jolt of lightning past through my chest.

"What kind of sweet?"

"Cherry," I lied.

Nicholas bit the inside of his cheek.

"If I have this, will you promise to stay out of trouble?"

I nodded as he examined the sticky candy, and before I had time question whether the sweet was safe, he plucked hold of it, brought it up to his lips, then swallowed.

"Come on then," he called, dashing into the hustle and bustle of the market.

Chasing after him, I held my breath, waiting for the sweet to take effect.

"The markets are low key now," Nicholas said. "Most of the stalls have packed away, but some stay open late into twilight. If it's still here, I'd like to show you one in particular."

"Which one?" Nicholas didn't answer, and after minutes of rushing after him under the golden glow of the world, I couldn't help feeling disappointed. I had given Nicholas the laughing drop in hopes of getting him to loosen up, and he hadn't even cracked a smile. Perhaps the sweet had some sort of placebo effect. Served me right for accepting it free of charge.

About to give up, I squinted across at the hazy skyline when Nicholas came to a sharp halt a few yards ahead of me.

"Nicholas?"

No answer.

Waiting for him to continue moving, panic ripped through me when he keeled over. Rushing over to him, I prayed this wasn't anything to do with the sweet, and when I saw his face, my stomach dropped. His lips were scrunched up, and his eyes glittered with tears.

"Nicholas," I whispered.

"Raine," Nicholas whimpered.

"I'm sorry. I'll get help." Sweat punctured my brow as I scanned the market for someone, anyone, but the closest creatures were about half a mile off. I clenched my jaw. His lips kept shaking, his shoulders too. I was desperate. I wondered if I should do CPR, then punched myself when I remembered I didn't know how to do CPR.

Fuck. This was all my fault.

I ran my fingers through my hair as he struggled to catch his breath, and just as I was about to dash off in search of help, Nicholas laughed. I widened my eyes. The sound was so simple it sliced through me like a knife through heated butter. He was laughing. Nicholas was laughing.

"Raine! What did—" his lips juddered as he clung to his sides. Pretty soon I was laughing too, gentle at first, then harder.

"A laughing drop," I managed between breaths.

"Did you take one too?"

"No, this is just – you just seem so..." I hugged my chest, fighting to catch my breath, but the air kept leaving my lungs too quickly, and when Nicholas puffed out his cheeks walrus-style, I laughed harder. Wiping my eye with a fist, I tried to recall the last time I'd laughed, but couldn't. It felt wonderful, like a much-needed embrace from an old friend.

"Raine—" Nicholas couldn't finish. He could barely stand. Seconds after, he gave up entirely and fell to his knees. Clearing my throat, I crouched down next to him as his wild hysteria faded to gentle cackles, then tired giggles. I slouched lower, winded. I was close enough to see his chiselled jaw, the fur surrounding his left eye, and it may have been the aftermath of the sweet or the hazed frenzy of the unexpected, but I was pretty sure Nicholas was smiling.

"Don't do that again," Nicholas ordered, but his face said something else.

"It was worth it," I told him.

"What was?"

"Getting you to laugh, it was nice."

His lips parted as he eyed me thoughtfully.

"And me," I added. "I can't remember the last time I actually laughed."

"Me neither," Nicholas admitted.

Tucking a strand of hair behind my ear, I noticed something glimmering in the distance. I squinted. Flecks of sand were glistening around us. Peering back at Nicholas, I saw his face fading.

My heart shivered. I was drifting back, but I couldn't, not then. I wasn't ready. I tried reaching out to him, calling his name, but all that came was a painful silence. I tried again, and again, until his name poured from my lips in turbulent streams, flooding my studio and empty home, but by then, it was too late, Mia.

My eyes had already adjusted to the inky darkness, the mirror, the cardboard boxes. I blinked furiously, hoisting myself up and pounding the glass with clenched fists.

"No. No. No," I kept saying. I didn't want to be there. I didn't feel safe. Someone was banging the door downstairs. Dan. Dan had left his keys. My shoulders sagged. I couldn't leave the mirror. I couldn't face him, not after everything. Falling to the floor, I shuddered. Moments later, I smelt it — that foul stench of rot. I heard her footsteps next, her hot lips pressed to my ear.

"You can still go back," Esme whispered.

***

"Raine," Pierce tries for the thirtieth time. "How was your relationship with your parents? Were you close?"

"They're both dead," I answer flatly. "Why can't you just ask properly?" I glance over their pages heaped with

pointless scribble. The room is sweltering and as my
eyes skim through the names; Nicholas, Esme, Dan,
Katie, I feel it's all too much. Paved inside of their
words, I see his face. I chew my lip; I can't breathe, I
hear his laugh – something broken inside of me twinges.
Before I can stop myself, I smack my head against the
desk.

Beneath the pain, I hear them trying to coax me out of
it. Had I done this before? It seems familiar. I hear
Watson call for assistance as I think of you, Mia, of
Nicholas. I hit my head harder when someone rushes
into the room – the table splinters beneath my skull.
Cold hands grip my shoulders. I feel it in my neck – the
sharp prick of a sedative.

CHAPTER ELEVEN

Last night I was held in the white room – a nonsensical name for the maximum-security cell where everything was yellow. Four walls, the ground, the ceiling, even the mattress posing as a bed was stained mustard. A room, so silent all you can do is face the truth jammed under all the self-hatred in your gut.

I stare at Watson and Pierce, wondering if they would survive in the white room. What demons would visit them at night? Whose face would they hope to glimpse behind the little steel frame in the door each morning?

They go through formalities.

Any side effects from the medication?

Headaches?

Visits?

Tremors?

Nausea?

Checklist conversations remind me of Dan. Two weeks after I started venturing into Wanderlust, he suggested I went to the doctors to get my head sorted. *"It will be good for us both,"* he said.

I, the dutiful, fickle, blind wife, obeyed as we drove under Snowy Bridge; a crumbling overpass we named after joking years ago that the scattered petals from the flowers above were snow.

We always pointed it out, laughing idiotically as we sped through the dingy tunnel. It was dull really, unimaginable and drab, but it was our joke. So, I watched him, searching his wooden face for a flicker of anything, and I continued to watch him as we moved through the blizzard of petals in silence.

It went like this: The doctor asked questions, Dan answered all of them, listing my symptoms with this indifferent air about him; daydreaming, fatigue, a basic social disconnect. I remember peering around at the doctors bunged up office, decorated in medical certificates, and pictures of two smiling children, before staring at Dan's hand in mine.

Even then I knew it felt wrong, Mia. And it didn't matter how hard he clasped my fingers, or how many times he squeezed my palm; everything felt staged. Five minutes in the stuffy little office was all it took for my diagnosis.

"Depression!" the doctor exclaimed with a eureka grin. "Very common in women your age." He prescribed me a course of Prozac and told me to take them once a day until I felt *'normal'* again, only I did feel normal. Just not with Dan. No one could understand it. Not the Indian doctor with the creases buried in his face, or the heavily made-up receptionist gazing at the devoted husband who'd taken the day off work to hold his depressed wife's hand. No one.

It was after the visit to the doctors our ritual commenced. Each morning after Dan's interrogation, *"Do you feel dizzy? Nauseous? Tired?"* I would slip a tablet under my tongue. *"Are you okay? Are you sure?"* I'd nod, smile, usher him out of the house with the pill still crumbling in my mouth, and after listening out for the hammer of our front door as our car sped off into Dan's reality, I would spit out the pill and climb the stairs to mine.

"Were you afraid?" Pierce asks.

I stare at him with my head still heavy from the sedative, yesterday. A fresh cut to my scalp because of the silence.

"Yes," I answer. "When I went back that day, I was terrified."

AUGUST 7th 2018

Clamouring feet, and bustling arms, and feathers, and tails flurried past me in a whirl of motion. The market was ravenous. Creatures of all shapes and sizes, pushed, and shoved, and grunted, under the tired auburn glow of the world, and the scent of sweat and dirt hung low in the muggy air.

Trapped in the middle of the swarm, I questioned which direction was safest to move in. In all honesty, I'd come back hoping to take off where I'd left things with Nicolas, Mia, but I was alone, and admittedly, frightened I wouldn't see him again. Nicholas had told me he didn't venture outside of the palace, and so I had no idea why I thought I might see him casually striding through the crowd, looking for me.

I balled my hands into fists, about to head off through a jungle of stalls selling candles and parchment when a creature with the head of a badger barged into my shoulder. I widened my eyes as she tilted her furry black head and flashed me her pointy teeth.

"Come on!" she shouted. "We don't have time to stand around all day. There are deals to be made!"

"I'm sorry I—"

Not giving me an opportunity to finish, I stared after

her streaked white tail as she stomped off into the crowd. Deciding to move in the opposite direction, I headed south, zigzagging through hagglers dressed in prim frocks and finely tailored suits, and miles, and miles of heaving stalls, before pausing at a stand where hundreds of rings were stacked on honey-coloured shelves.

"See anything you like, syrup?" the trader called.

He had several missing teeth and wore a red velvet top hat that leant too much to the left, and when he brought his bony hands up to his face, I saw his spindly fingers smothered in rings with faces that moved.

Bewildered, I gazed at the polished expressions; scowling, and grinning, and sobbing in unison, before dragging my attention back to the trader. Like theirs, his face kept altering. His round eyes widened, then creased. His eyebrows shivered, then flew up so that they were submerged completely beneath the brim of his top hat.

"How much for a happiness ring?" asked a creature with bright green feathers.

"Ten pentons!" the trader exclaimed, bashing his palms together as the rings on his fingers yelped in pain.

"And for the sadness?"

"Twenty."

Wondering if the creature found the trader's one-man show as bizarre as I did, I stole a glance at her. If anything, she appeared bored.

"Twenty-five for the pair," she decided. Allowing no time for an argument, the creature dug deep in her navy purse and pulled out three gold coins. The trader peered at me hesitantly. I imagine he was weighing up the likelihood I might expect a similar deal.

"Twenty-eight?" he tried, but the creature had already thrust the coins in his face. With an overzealous nod, the trader pulled two rings from the back shelf and dropped them into a brown paper bag.

"Do they... change your mood?" I asked after the beaked creature had strode off without a thank you or goodbye.

"If you're asking if they work, the answer is yes," he beamed.

"But I don't understand, why someone would want to be sad?"

The creature's eyes flew open in alarm.

"You'd be surprised what emotions creatures can't get out!" he gasped. "Sadness, grief, loss, anger. Jealousy is easy. I can cut you a deal on jealousy if you like? How's nine pentons sound?" He was grinning again, a gesture so broad it crept up to his triangular ears.

"Surely it can't be healthy, forcing yourself to be jealous or sad?"

"I think you'll find forcing yourself to be happy is the most unnatural thing in the world!" the trader exclaimed, exploding backwards with his palms outstretched. "But creatures do that all the time. Painting on smiles, and living like they're not dying inside, forcing pleasantries with creatures they detest. How about anger or sadness? Sadness is very popular at the moment. Twenty-two for the pair?"

He tapped a blue line of rings on his index finger, and even though I wanted to ask more about his merchandise, without money – or pentons rather, all I could do was shake my head and head back into the crowd.

The trader shouted something after me, but fearful of drawing attention to the fact I didn't belong, I kept my head down, trudging deeper and deeper into the belly of the market. Not long after, I found myself in line at a stall where a tusked creature sold large feathered quills.

"Perhaps we can rewrite last night's shipping disaster," said a creature in front of me.

"If you can rewrite it in four words," replied another.

Shuffling forwards in a line, I debated what I would say when I reached the front when I noticed a figure in a long black cloak around fifty metres away. I narrowed my eyes. Whoever the stranger was – wasn't tall enough, or even broad enough to be Nicholas, but my feet had already taken on a mind of their own and soon they were whisking me through swarms of creatures, and conversations, and laughter.

It had been four days since I'd been able to journey back to Wanderlust, and in all of the time I spent prodding the mirror, I was almost certain I wouldn't see Nicholas again, but that didn't stop me from hoping. Panting as the stall, I saw it was darker there, as if the shadows had ventured long and far, before deciding this place was home.

Taking in the shape of the stranger's scrawny back, I was about to tap him on the shoulder when the trader at the booth hissed,

"What do you want?"

I turned, shaken.

He was bald, with a fat dimpled nose that spilt over too much of his face, and he squinted at me through eyes that resembled two rough scratches.

"I just... I..." The stranger I'd run towards spun around. Setting eyes on his face all of my words were snatched. I stumbled backwards, shaking my head. It wasn't Nicholas, but a part of me knew that already, Mia. Instead, the creature glowering at me had a face similar to a feline. Tight emerald eyes and ginger fur. Hissing, he stormed off, most likely because of my appearance.

"Just to look," I muttered. Bringing my attention back to the booth, I saw it was empty. I ruffled my brow. Had he packed up? Yards away stalls were bursting with life, and by the trader's optimism, I was sure most had just opened.

"I have nothing here that would concern you," the trader sneered.

"I was just curious—"

"Oh, were you now?" he smirked. "Well, I suggest you take your curiosity elsewhere."

Hunching lower, he jerked his leg under the stall. In that subtle gesture I understood whatever he was selling, was being hidden, and judging by the sparse onlookers, no one sought after the items or wanted to seem like they did.

"Now!" he growled so heatedly I knocked into someone behind me. Swinging around to apologise, my heart dipped.

"Bildred," the trader greeted.

The tubby mole inclined his head, his whiskers billowing in the gentle gusts of wind.

"Well, if we don't meet again, human," Bildred whispered, scuttling closer in the same white shirt he'd worn at the bar.

Immobilised by fear, I hugged my chest, hounded by memories of the mole's grubby home and that feeling of complete helplessness.

"You tricked me," I hissed, when I managed to find my voice.

"Tricked?" the mole gasped. "Never!"

"They were going to kill me."

"Kill? Heavens no!" Bildred tried taking a step closer when I flew out of the way, glowering at the creature who barely reached my chin. "I would never have allowed them to kill you," he said. "I was certain they would spare a remarkable treasure such as yourself."

"You had no idea what would've happened! If Nicholas hadn't—" Bildred gasped.

"His majesty spared you?"

I shook my head as he bounced on his stumpy little legs with all of the eagerness of a rambunctious toddler.

"Tell me about the palace. Was it grand? I expect it was marvellous." Seizing me by my arm, he hauled me towards a stall where creatures tried on top hats.

"Leave me alone," I barked, but my tone only seemed to excite him more.

Bildred's eyes sparkled with delight before I set off into the market in the hope I may shake him off.

"Raine," he called as I hurried on. "Need I remind you I know your little secret? Are you aware of the law here?"

The market was pulsing with so much life it was stifling, but I still heard his footsteps scuttling through pebbles.

"They will destroy you."

Understanding Bildred wouldn't leave unless I showed some backbone, I twisted around furiously.

"They will do no such thing!" I shouted.

My shoulders trembled as I watched him plodding forwards and drinking shallow mouthfuls of air with his hefty paws dangling at his sides.

"Tell me about the palace," Bildred panted. "It has been such a long time … since I last visited. Did his majesty mention me? His reward was rather generous."

I narrowed my eyes at the flimsy trinket he pulled out from the collars of his shirt. It was an ugly thing; a green emerald fastened to something that looked like the end of a door chain.

"Nicholas gave that to you?"

"Not personally," Bildred answered. "But it was sent from him."

"Then who gave it to you!"

"Never mind that, human," Bildred whispered, smirking. "Why not tell me about the palace? I bet it was magnificent, were there Mithels there? There must have been Mithels, good gracious."

"Go away!" I hissed. The mole barely flinched.

Clapping a paw to his chin, he watched me thoughtfully.

"You're lying," he cried. "You escaped! What were you doing at the black magic stall? You're trying to harm our kingdom. I know it. His Majesty would never spare a human. Was it Siren eyes you wanted? I can tell you where to get some in exchange for a little information."

Scratching his chin with a claw, Bildred tilted his head, studying me the way a therapist might regard a patient, but I wasn't about to divulge anything to him. He disgusted me. Still, I knew if I ran off, he'd only chase after me again.

Deciding the only way to get rid of him would be to show just how little he frightened me, I made my most menacing face. Eyes heavy with disgust, I bent lower, inches from his cracked snout.

"What were you doing there?" I hissed.

The mole's eyes dipped, and when he spoke again, his lips puckered as if he'd just tasted something awful.

"You cannot be trusted here," he whispered.

"Nicholas trusted me enough to bring me here."

Intrigue grazed his face before it dulled to humour.

"Oh, did he? Then where is his majesty?"

My cheeks turned red as I scanned the dusty market. It's not like I should've been embarrassed Nicholas wasn't there, Mia. He'd told me he barely left the palace, and it wasn't as if we'd planned on meeting, only I was embarrassed, because amidst all of the magical objects, and creatures, and traders, the thing I'd been searching for most was the collision of our glances.

"Just as I suspected," the mole chuckled. "Your kind is full of lies. His Majesty no longer travels outside of the palace."

I eyeballed my pumps, certain I could've argued he did, and that it was only days ago, we'd laughed on the sandy floor until we cried, but understanding all the mole craved was a retaliation, I hurried off through the tight audience.

"Where are you going?" Bildred growled.

Knocking into a tubby creature with horns, I sprinted through the crowd with my face flaming. How could I have been so stupid to think Nicholas would be here? And why had I expected this place would be any different from the tavern?

"Raine!" Bildred shouted.

Hurrying on with my head heavy with disappointment, I was nearly free from the crowd when it happened.

"Human!" Bildred shouted. "A real human."

Peering over my shoulder, I saw Bildred pointing an overgrown claw in my direction while the audience watched, waiting.

"I'm not dangerous!" As soon as the words left my mouth, it was clear I'd made a grave error.

All at once, wide eyes, and open mouths, and shrieks, and whispers ripped through me like gunshots.

"It admitted to being human!"

"Is it real?"

"Someone grab it."

Bildred stood in the centre of the audience, his face bathed in so much self-importance I wanted to rip it off.

"It escaped from the palace," he informed the crowd. "His majesty planned on beheading it, we must carry out his demands."

My brain went to pieces as the circle around me tightened.

"No, I…"

My heart skyrocketed as I skimmed through the faces, searching for someone who might understand this was a mistake, but all I saw was a rancid mix of horror and excitement. The back of my neck prickled as I tried moving past them. Those closest parted like the Red Sea, while those who were further back, fought to gain a closer look. Before I knew it, I was being pushed and pulled in every direction. Swallowed by a throng of musty feathers and sharp claws and smooth trunks.

"Leave me alone!" I barked. "Leave me alone!"

Nudging myself free from the voracious crowd, I barged past a woman with paper thin wings and berry eyes, when a warm hand gripped my shoulders.

Following the palm upright, my legs turned to glue. It belonged to a creature almost double my height that bore similarities to a bear; only it didn't look anything like those friendly bears you'd read about as a child. No, the creature with chestnut fur and a lopsided face was colder, and in its tight black eyes, I glimpsed a hunger for my blood.

I tried shaking myself free when he flashed his teeth, sniffing me as if I was a meal past its sell-by date.

"I promise I don't mean any harm," I whimpered.

"A likely story, human," he grunted.

"No, really. I've been here before, I swear." Shrugging away my arm, I winced when a similar creature grasped my free shoulder. "Let me go," I ordered.

Their claws grazed the skin under my arms as they hauled me up.

"I wasn't doing anything wrong."

Rage bubbled up in my chest as my legs dangled above the cobbled ground.

"Nothing to see here folks," one shouted as I kicked and jolted, fighting to claw at their furry shoulders. "We will dispose of the creature appropriately."

The words charged through me.

Disposed of.

My gut churned as I raked through the eager faces, clapping, and wolf whistling, and elbowing creatures at their sides, fighting to work out what the bear creatures meant. Nicholas had warned me this place was dangerous, but how dangerous?

"Please, just let me go," I begged.

Neither would meet my eye.

"I'm just a normal woman, I've been here before."

About half a mile off, I glimpsed a small iron cage. Sweat obscured my vision as I gazed at the crate growing larger and larger beneath the pink ruffled sky. Minutes later, we reached it. The elongated creaking sound of the cage door gashed through my spine when the creatures tossed me inside like an old ragdoll.

I winced as my shoulders clattered against the rusted iron bars. Peering through them, I saw onlookers from all directions heading forwards. Bildred was closest. On reaching the cage, he leant against the bars, with his pink snout pushed between the gaps.

"See, human, you shouldn't underestimate me," he sneered.

Swallowing the fear choking me, I looked away. I didn't have time to be afraid of Bildred. I had to find a way out of this mess.

Think Raine, think.

My eyes swept through antlers, and hooves, and bonnets, before halting at a child with tall white ears, and buck teeth — a child. A child should have enough innocence intact, to help.

"Is it real?" the infant asked the creatures who had imprisoned me.

"Oh yes," one replied. "But don't get too close, we don't know what it's capable of."

"It's not doing anything!" it bawled.

With that, both creatures glanced in at me, then back at each other before the largest dipped off into the crowd.

"I do love a good show!" cried a bald man, in a magenta shawl.

Staring into his bottomless ebony eyes, I felt my heart chink little by little, and when the creature reappeared, it shattered completely. Clasped in his furry paws was a long wooden stick, and fastened to its end was a blade.

I widened my eyes, shuffling so far against the cage the iron bruised my spine.

"Please," I breathed.

The stick was gliding closer. Slithering through the bars while the crowd whispered hungrily. I shook my head as they waited. My skull pulsed as I glared at the spike. My eyes stung as I bit hard on my lips. And then, I felt it.

The first blow sliced my ribcage. I howled, clutching my side. Applause shattered through my skull. Blood lined the creases of my palm. Attempting to stand, I fell forward when the blade struck my knee. Harder this time, faster. In my thigh, my ribs, my shoulder blades. Laughter crashed around me, but I couldn't hear it above the pain.

I was screaming, but my pleas only seemed to spur on more hand-clapping. I tasted dirt, sweat, the salt from my tears. This wasn't happening. No, I was safe in my studio, nothing was real, but the pain screamed it was.

Choking on bile and snivelling, I realised how fickle I'd been. Nicholas had warned me the market was dangerous but never had I imagined anything as bad this. I thought he was being over cautious, dramatic. What did the creatures intend to do to me after? Not after, don't think about after.

Time fell over me. I couldn't be sure of how long. My body was numb. My nerves shot to shit, my temples pulsed. I was drowning in a sea of nothingness, and then came the silence. Crisp cotton sheets against tired flesh. Was I dead? I'd heard something before the silence. Something had caused the sound to break.

Wedging open my eyes, I winced as I fought to see past the ginger light. My head throbbed, my cheek was pressed against the earth, soaked in splotches of burgundy. The crowd was still there. Only etched into their faces I saw fear. My eyes scraped the bars, the faces, the masses of mutant bodies, then him. At first, I thought I imagined him; my heart craving all of the things I knew were bad for me.

In my disorientated state I'd become a diabetic begging for truckloads of sugar on my death bed, but when I focussed properly, his image didn't stray. His hands were pushed against the bars, his face was wild, and his eyes were so sad that inside of them I felt my own anguish. My head spun. Nicholas roared again and then came the darkness.

Opening my eyes, all I felt was pain. It pulsed through my head, my chest, my throat, even my lips burnt cavities in my face. Pressing them together, I was ambushed by memories of an apartment I'd rented when I was nineteen. This shoddy little flat where the lights always flickered, and the hot water was always tepid no matter how long I ran the tap. I loved that flat.

But the longer my heart pumped away in the darkness, the more I came to understand I wasn't there. I'd met Dan a few months after – moved in with him, became a *we*. My pulse raced. Each palpitation brought flashbacks of the market. The creatures. Bildred. The spear. Blood. Too much blood. Nicholas.

"Nicholas?" It was dark, and the stale air carried a subtle hint of vanilla.

"You're hurt," Nicholas whispered.

My heart stirred as I struggled to make out his face in the darkness, but trying to see him was making my head throb, and so I closed my eyes.

"You shouldn't sleep," Nicholas told me.

"Why not?"

"Because you've been sleeping for almost eleven hours."

That woke me up.

"What? Where am I?"

"The palace."

The palace? The muscles in my neck tightened as I fought to recall venturing back to the arctic fortress, but the last thing I remembered seeing was Nicholas, and that torrid look of desperation.

"Why can't I see you?" I asked. "Nicholas?"

Nicholas didn't answer, but I knew he was close because I could smell summer pressed against his collarbone.

"Would you prefer the light?" he asked after a moment.

"Wouldn't you?" I muttered, slightly irate we hadn't been sitting in the light all this time, but then I remembered I'd been sleeping, and I was grateful Nicholas hadn't seen me sprawled out with my mouth hanging open.

"Nicholas?"

A heartbeat past as I waited for him to stand and switch on a light, but instead, he took a deep gutful breath, and when he released the air battering his lungs, I widened my eyes as hundreds of candles flickered to life around us.

I flinched as each one crackled and fizzled, spitting light against the black walls that were so indistinguishable from the ground, that the only clue where one ended and the other began, were the silver cobwebs spluttering down from the ceiling.

Conscious of Nicholas sitting next to me, I scanned the room groggily. It seemed even the spiders that weaved skyscrapers against the walls had grown tired of the emptiness and fled. All but for the candles, and a wooden rocking chair set next to a window with curtains the colour of spilt wine, the place was bare.

Nicholas sat beside me with his knees tucked to his

chin and his gaze locked on his boots. Watching his gold eyes glimmer with apprehension, I wondered how long he'd been sitting in the dark with me.

He'd saved me. And no one had ever saved me. Not that it had ever been an issue. I mean, when had I ever needed rescuing from a market full of blood thirsty creatures?

Nicholas had saved me. I chewed my lip as his eyes drilled craters in his boots. I'd always believed placing your life in someone else's hands was clumsy work, Mia, but Nicholas had acted of his own accord, and that unspoken act of kindness was marking my soul in a way that was irreversible.

"Thank you," I said quietly.

Nicholas's jaw twitched, and his eyes elevated to mine.

"Thank you?" he muttered. "Why would you thank me when what happened was my fault?"

"Your fault?"

Nicholas jutted his head angrily, a vein in his head bulging.

"Nicholas, it was my choice to go back. If I'd—"

'No, Raine. It was my fault,' he hissed, and when he widened his eyes, I could've sworn they were swollen. "I took you to the market knowing full well how dangerous it was. Even if I hadn't, the attitude of the creatures is a reflection of me. What happened to you was my fault."

"Then why?" I asked, understanding in some way he was right. "If you're so ashamed of the law, why do you enforce it?"

Nicholas lowered his head, and when he spoke again, I heard a sharp blade, that didn't fit his face.

"Because your kind is barbaric."

"Barbaric?"

Nicholas didn't answer. He just sat there staring at his knees. I watched him with my heart smashing against my chest. How could he think I was barbaric after everything the creatures had done to me? And for no good reason? If anyone was barbaric, it was them. My eyes pooled with tears while the candles circling us flickered.

"Look at me," I demanded.

He didn't. Instead, he clenched his jaw so tight I imagined his teeth crumbling to dust.

"Look at me," I said louder — still nothing. I glanced at the door behind us, certain if I hadn't been in so much pain, I would've stormed out. I was through with his inconsistencies. At times Nicholas regarded me with so much warmth I felt it pumping through my veins, and then he'd just take it back as though it was nothing– as though I was nothing.

"You're ignorant," I said.

The word hung in the air like a bad smell, but Nicholas still wouldn't look up.

"Don't you think you've spent enough time with me to know I'm not as barbaric as you claim humans are?"

My lips quivered as I waited for him to meet my eyes, even if it was for a second, I just wanted him to look at me. I glared at him, trying to work out why he'd saved me if he hated what I was? Why did he keep coming to my defence?

"You know me," I said quietly. "Not properly, but you know me enough to know I'm not this monster you keep painting me out to be. I need the truth, Nicholas. After everything, you at least owe me that."

Nicholas stole a look at me, his eyes wet with discomfort and his full lips pressed together. Still, no words came.

"Nicholas, tell me why you hate what I am," I pleaded, hating the desperation in my voice. I tried forcing my focus on him, but my eyes kept closing, and the heat of the candles were weighing heavily on my lids.

"Tell me."

I heard a plunk as they fluttered closed. A cloth dipped into the bowl, a gentle trickle when it was wrung. My body was drained, my mind a wreck, and just as I was about to surrender to the heavy blanket of sleep coming for me, softly, slowly, hungrily, Nicholas said something that made my eyes spring open.

"Can you lift your dress?"

My brows bumped together as I studied him hesitantly. The gesture made my head pulse, but I kept my brows pressed there while he inspected his hands.

"I need to clean the wounds," he said. "They may be infected."

Clutching the sheet on top of me, I faltered thinking of the mismatched underwear I'd thrown on this morning. Pink knickers and a frayed black bra. He couldn't see me in those, what would he think? Still, there was no desire in his tone; if anything, all I heard was reluctance.

"If I do, will you tell me the truth?"

"About what?"

"Everything," I bartered, despite my meagre position. "The reason you hate humans. The reason you are the way you are, the truth about why you came to the markets, everything Nicholas, I want to know everything."

His gaze slipped across my chest making cuts across my body pulse like hail against a tin roof, and just when I thought he was going to tell me to disinfect my own damn wounds, he nodded.

I didn't thank him or ask again. Focussing on the silvery cobwebs sewn against the walls, I tugged my dress over my head. When the material crusted off, I fell back, watching his stoic face.

I wondered what he was thinking. Was he repulsed by my translucent skin and the healed scars to my thigh from when I was sixteen? Or, did the body of a human fascinate him in ways he wouldn't admit to?

"Is it bad?"

Nicholas looked like he was about to answer.

"If it is don't tell me." I said, shaking my head so quickly my chest objected.

A gentle curve softened the creases around his eyes.

"Are you smiling because it's bad, and you want to distract me?"

"I'm not smiling," he said. He was, only slightly now.

"You are. You do that sometimes."

"Do what?"

"Let your guard down and allow yourself to be happy."

Nicholas's face pricked with alarm.

"Don't look so worried. I'm not going to tell anyone," I added.

Plucking up a white rag, he watched me dubiously before taking a deep breath.

"This might hurt," he said.

I rolled my aching shoulders, then winced as he pressed the cloth to my abdomen. It was cool, damp, and in seconds, I watched it transform from white to burgundy to black. Pushing my chin to my chest, I shuddered. My body looked as if it had been through a war, worse.

The biggest cut was below my ribs; a gummy wound the size of a finger. I held my breath, watching Nicholas dab at my frail skin as if he were tending to a task, and in the same moment I was about to ask if the wounds needed proper medical attention, he spoke in a voice that sounded a lot like someone who had a knife to their throat.

"I never told you about my mother," he whispered. "No one mentions her anymore."

Anxiety hung in the air as I watched him struggling to spit out words that had become boulders in his throat.

"Her name was Mia. She was a great leader, kind,

thoughtful," he squeezed his eyes together, and when he opened them, he seemed incredibly tired. "She was a human."

"But that makes you—"

"Half Clevil half human."

Nicholas hunted my face for an ounce of shock, and I gave it to him full throttle because in all of the time he hated what I was, he had hated a part of himself.

"How?"

Sweat punctured the skin above his brow as he shook his head at his hands.

"A long time ago she stumbled upon our world by chance. One night, my father found her at the spirit lake. She was beaten, badly. Her eyes were black, and her jaw, bloody. She told my father, her husband had attacked her. A brute with an iron fist, who viewed her as an object he could defile and destroy."

Nicholas paused as the cloth trickled down my thigh. Yellow pus seeped out from a small incision. Signalling I part my legs, I wedged them open then winced as his palm grazed my inner thigh.

"So what happened?"

Nicholas jumped at the sound of my voice.

"To my mother?"

I nodded as he stooped lower, his face built of steel.

"Both my father, and mother, became close," he replied. "For hours they'd speak about their worlds. Then, like you, she would disappear, and when she returned, she'd be battered beyond recognition."

Watching his eyes fill with tears, I could tell this was a story he'd held inside for decades. For a moment, I wanted to reach out and steady his trembling lips, but instead, I closed my eyes understanding silence is sometimes kinder.

"After months of venturing into Wanderlust, my mother confessed the truth to her husband," Nicholas continued. "He didn't believe her, but who would? Though she hadn't expected him to…"

"To what?" unsealing my eyes, I studied Nicholas as he scowled at the ring on his little finger. "Nicholas?"

"He beat her within an inch of her life," Nicholas breathed. "He had her committed to an asylum. A hole filled with screams, where she was strapped to a bed and force-fed pills and potions."

I bobbed my head. This must've been the reason Nicholas detested humans, because of the heinous acts they had committed against his mother, not because they were a danger to the Kingdom.

"So, what happened after?"

Nicholas's eyes glazed over as he swallowed.

"She wouldn't stop telling the creatures in your world about Wanderlust," he muttered. "My father begged her to stop, but she wanted to share the beauty of our world with them. Eventually, they administered electrical shocks to her brain. And as the months passed, the shocks grew more formidable, more barbaric, incinerating her thoughts until there was nothing left of her in your world."

"ECT?"

Nicholas wasn't listening. His head was bent, and his eyes were set on his bloody hands. I chewed my lip, silencing the hunger I had to tell him I was sorry for what happened to his mother, and that not everyone was the beast he thought them to be because I believed a part of him, a part he was still trying to grapple with, already knew.

Rubbing my eyes, I struggled to sit up when Nicholas shrunk back against the wall, his spine propped up by the shredded wallpaper.

"What is it?" I asked.

"You have no idea, do you?"

"Idea of what?" my jaw came unhinged as he watched

me the way a dying man might watch the world. "Nicholas?"

He shook his head, but I wouldn't give into his silence, not this time.

"What happened to your mother?"

"She stayed," Nicholas answered. "But at times she'd drift back to your world, and when she returned, she'd be different."

"Different how?"

"Empty."

"Did she stay in Wanderlust in the end?"

Catching the hope in my tone, Nicholas flared his nostrils.

"You seriously want to stay here after what happened to you today?"

I flinched, struck by the lightning in his tone.

"Is this a game to you Raine?"

His eyes tightened, and all I could do was shake my head like a red-faced child who had given the wrong answer in class.

"Do you have any idea of what you're doing to me?"

"No, I—"

"Do you?"

I closed my eyes, my head pounding so hard I thought it would shatter right there on the scarred floorboards, while a voice inside of it demanded I left this place, because after a lifetime of nothing, the way I felt then was too much.

"How do you expect me to know anything if you don't tell me?" I muttered, opening my eyes. "How can I understand anything, when you act like this? When you can't even be honest with me. One minute you're normal, the next you're disgusted by what I am and where I come from."

Nicholas stared at me as if I'd slapped him.

"Why did you come to the market Nicholas?"

"I didn't know you would—"

"You're lying!"

He shook his head with the light from the candles glittering in his eyes.

"Why do you keep showing up and asking me to do all of these things? The painting, accompanying me to the market, why do those things when you're going to act like this?"

"I don't—"

"Tell me! You need to tell me, Nicholas, because none of this is fair. You can't just ask me to stay, then treat me like I'm a burden."

"You're not a burden," he said.

"Then why treat me this way?"

Nicholas watched me regretfully. It was only then, I noticed my blood on his shirt. On the verge of pushing for an answer, I stopped when he stood much too evenly.

I peered at him towering above me, this creature from an alternate world draped in secrets like skin; I wanted nothing more than to unravel him, to have him soak me in the truth like gasoline and set me alight, but the feeling was unrequited. And I wouldn't beg for understanding like I had in the past with Dan, because the more you fight to understand someone I'd learnt, the more you lose yourself.

"I need to bandage the wound," Nicholas said.

"Fine," I sniffed, falling back and studying the ceiling as he lugged open the door.

Listening to his hefty footsteps disappearing down the corridor, I promised myself this would be the last time I ventured into Wanderlust. Nicholas was right; this place *was* too dangerous. What they did to me at the market was more than proof of that. I could've died. It was much better to go back to my empty life and play it safe.

Safe, the word was a life sentence.

Sleep was coming for me, and Nicholas still hadn't returned. I thumped my sides, listening for the hesitant patter of his footsteps, but instead, I heard the melody from a piano. The notes began timid, tangling themselves up in the dust swept air and painting the frosty chambers beyond me with a whisper of sorrow.

Nicholas was playing.

I blinked, waiting for the symphony to come to a halt, but it grew steadier, fiercer, each note stuffing the world with intrinsic vibrations that tunnelled deep in my chest and disturbed something in my core.

I clenched my eyes shut, listening, just listening. Had I ever truly listened to anything this intently? He didn't play with his hands, I realised. He played with his soul. It was a piece of art that couldn't come from a sheet of paper, but a place of sunken dreams that still carried the unyielding desire to rise.

Drifting off, I heard every secret he carried inside of him, gasping and coming up for air, and it made me question how leaving suddenly felt a lot like running away.

***

"What happened didn't frighten you?" Watson asks.

I stare at her blankly, this woman who might've been happy, but just missed it, like a train roaring off into the distance after you run after a cloud of smoke.

"Do you think, maybe, you wanted to believe these things would harm you?" Pierce asks. "Perhaps you were punishing yourself for something unconscious?"

"I know you don't believe me."

"No one said that, Raine. All we're saying is that the mind is a complex thing. Sometimes we see things, feel things, even taste things that aren't there."

Before Pierce can cajole me further, I stand and lift my shirt, showing them the scars from the market.

Pierce looks away, embarrassed, Watson's eyes are fixed on my abdomen.

"You're saying Dan didn't do this?" she asks.

I don't answer.

"Raine in your report to the police you said Dan inflicted these marks."

Silence.

"Raine, the forensic reports already—"

"It was her fault," I tell them. "She made me kill him."

CHAPTER TWELVE

"What was your relationship like with your parents?" Pierce asks.

"Tell me about your wife," I mutter for the third time.

His lips part as he pushes back in his chair, obviously trying to work out how he can put this off a little longer, but too many men found solace in running, and I wasn't about to hand Pierce a hall pass.

"Raine, we have a wide basis for you to cover and limited time for us to—"

"He promised he'd tell me," I inform Watson.

Throwing back her shoulders, she glowers at Pierce, and before a single word can pass through her pristine lips, Pierce forces a smile.

"Margo," he sighs. "Will you give us a minute?" Raising a brow, he juts his head at the door.

I hold my breath, waiting for Watson to retaliate, only instead of telling Pierce to stick his suggestion where the sun doesn't shine, she heads for the door. My heart sinks, and in her defeat, I realise it's not Watson in charge of my sessions, but Pierce.

"If there's anything you need Raine, I'll be outside,"

Watson says, and then she's gone, leaving nothing but the sounds of her stiletto heels smacking the disinfected corridors to puncture the silence.

Turning to the window, I watch the rain slink down the glass – the world beyond it, a blurry pool of tears.

"If I tell you what happened with my wife, will you promise to cooperate?" Pierce questions.

Despite my better judgement, I nod.

"I mean it, Raine. We need to know everything, times, dates. Anything you can remember. Yesterday you told us someone else had harmed you, is that true?"

"You first."

"Raine."

I remain quiet, and when he gathers that my silence is a nut that can only be cracked with the mallet of his confessions, he rises and hobbles over to the window.

Standing, I realise he is smaller than I first thought; his lint smothered blazer, baggy around his chest, his skin, pallid in the light. He stays there a moment; his eyes fixed on the long gravelly driveway and the bulging grey sky.

"If I tell you what happened, you need to cooperate. No more half-answers, no more silence. We need the truth."

I raise a brow as he peers over his shoulder. For a moment it looks as if he might sit back down, a big red ethics sign flashes over my head, but before practicality can get the better of him, he turns to the window and sighs.

"My wife's name was Gabriella," he says unevenly. "She was beautiful, really beautiful. Not this filtered Instagram crap we scroll through tirelessly every morning, Gabby, she had this energy inside her, this thirst for life, this constant look of fearlessness in her eyes that took everything not to fall into, and she chose me."

He runs his fingers through what's left of his hair, a man swallowed twice by life then spat out because he didn't taste right.

"She could've had anyone, and she picked me, this dumpy little kid who wore trousers that came just below his chin. The first time I saw her she was running to a physics class. She smiled, just a smile, thinking back now it's so simple the things that crack your world wide open, and after, you have no idea of how to repair it. We married seventeen months after we met, June 2007," he tells the window.

"Our friends told us we were too young. Her parents said I wasn't serious enough, I wouldn't hold down a proper job, a real job, but fuck, I would've given the skin off my bones to see that girl smile. For a while we were as happy as two kids in love could be. Two years later came Christian. Our boy, seven pounds and eight ounces of him. I was determined to teach Chris all of the things I wished my dad had taught me... how to speak to girls, how to shoot a basket, how to ride a bike." He lowers his voice; his hot breath punches the glass.

"We moved to Leeds when Chris was four. Gabby was working for an environmental company. Every morning she'd get up at five, it wasn't until after eleven she'd get home. By then we were too tired to talk, to fuck, to do anything. And I... I did nothing," he falters, his words jumbled up as if he's reading a page from someone else's life.

"It was fine at first, everything was fine. I was supportive, I had to be, we were married, but I couldn't find work, and I guess it made me feel inadequate or emasculated.... shit, I don't know." He rubs his forehead, then turns to me with eyes so dark they shadow his entire face. "Chris was six when it happened."

"What happened?"

Pierce shakes his head then shuffles back to the table. Taking his seat, he clasps his palms as if we're about to embark on some million-pound business venture. Then it hits me, to him this is a business venture. His scars, for mine. Cards to my chest, I feel the words stacking up in my throat like bricks.

"If I tell you the truth, will you tell me about Gabby and Christian?"

His chest gives out as he nods.

"You have to promise not to tell anyone."

"I promise," he says carefully. "If it's something you don't want to be mentioned, I'll keep it between us." Peirce holds a hand to his heart, but I wonder what a hollow man has left to swear upon.

"Raine?"

Shaking my head at the table, I feel the truth bubbling up in my throat, everything I know they will find out anyway Mia, it's only a matter of time.

"I'm pregnant."

My confession irons him. His shoulders fly up to his ears as he grabs his pen.

"Dan's?"

"No, she's not."

"She?"

I force a nod.

"Well, whose is she?"

I don't answer, can't, and as the seconds tick by, my eyes slip to the wall behind him.

Index finger down, little finger up, both thumbs down,

"Why didn't you tell anyone?"

"Because she'll be taken."

"Why do you think that?"

"Why?" I scoff, gesturing to the room with scarred hands. "Look at where I am. Of course, they'll take her. If I'm not convicted of murdering my husband, do you honestly believe social services will allow someone on trial for murder to raise a child? No," I answer before he can. "But I promised him I would keep her safe."

"Promised who?"

Making my hands into a claw, I feel my soul lose weight.

"Raine, what do you expect will happen after she is born?" I hear the click of a pen. But I can't look up; I can't look away from my hands. Hands that will never learn the constellations woven into the curve of your spine, or brush away strands of your hair after your salty tears, Mia.

"I will be in prison. Or here, based on whatever the judge decides, or a jury that doesn't know me. And Mia, Mia, will be given to someone you think can teach her all of the things I'm incapable of teaching her because I'm insane."

"Raine, the investigation is still ongoing, the evidence gathered isn't enough to—"

"Do you think they'll care?" Blood rushes to my face as I meet his glassy stare. "I was arrested in a pool of my husband's blood. I told them it was my fault because it was, I don't want to get out, I can't—" I wipe my nose with my sleeve.

"Do you think another family may offer your child something you can't?"

"I think…" my voice chinks. "I think…" I swallow hard, forcing myself to spit out words I have gone over countless times, Mia. Every morning under the watchful gaze of wardens as I swallow my pills, right up until I lay my head against my stiff pillow at night. If I can't keep you safe, I pray the parents you find a home with will.

I pray they will love you fiercely and read you stories leaving you stuffed full of magic. I pray they will educate you on the importance of being a strong woman who stands up for what she believes in. I pray they will dance with you, even if they can't dance, and bicker with you because they want what's best for you. And when boys play ruthless games with hearts, I pray they will cradle you in their arms and smell summer on your skin and tell you, you are so much more.

"She'll be safe."

"Would she not be safe with you?"

I shrug as he leans in close. His cologne fills the spaces between us with the scent of a tired man who tries too hard, and before he can wheedle out any more home truths, the door clicks open, and in walks Watson.

"What about your childhood?" Pierce asks as if we were midway through the conversation. "Did you feel safe growing up?"

Taken aback by his tactics, my mouth cracks as Watson slumps down in her seat with the smell of smoke emanating from her blazer.

"No."

"That must have been difficult." His eyes meet mine. Eyes that are still wholesome, but somehow darker. "Why?"

"I felt like I was always running."

"From?"

"What are most of us running from?"

He stares back blankly.

"Life," I breathe.

SUMMER 2004

We were thirteen, desperately trying to shake free the wafer-thin blanket of youth, without any real inclination of what adversities adulthood carried.

"Quick Rai," Lucile gasped, hauling me down the sunny street. "Follow me, and don't ask any questions." We ran faster. Diving past the bakery where the thick perfume of bread gusted after us, we raced by Mr Pardeep's sweet shop who waved from inside, but there was no time to return the gesture because already we'd shot off down a gangly side street.

Curious about where she Lucile taking me, I glanced over at her. It wouldn't have been the first time I was dragged into one of her escapades. There was the time we snuck cigarettes from her dad's stash, smoked half, then flushed the rest down the toilet and ate a multipack of polos. The night we'd snuck out and might've gotten into a bar if it hadn't been for the burly man standing outside.

I didn't mind; if anything, it made me feel cooler. Veering off through the town centre, we headed down a dingy alley, past two men dressed in tracksuit bottoms, and when her pace slackened, I knew where we were going; Manor Farm woods. The place older kids who wore more makeup than beauticians sold in a week went to make out.

I huffed as she tugged me through thick sheets of grass that grew taller, and angrier until we were completely submerged in the emerald woodland where we stopped at our den; a rotting canoe, covered in thick olive decay that emitted the scent of moss and life.

"Ready?" Lucile asked. Leaping into the boat, she pulled away a patchwork blanket, leaving me to gawp at the items sprawled across the seat; plastic cups, crisps, chocolates, sweets that turned your tongue purple.

About to ask how Lucile had managed to afford the feast, my face dropped when I saw a bottle of vodka in the centre.

"Where did you get that?" I choked.

"Nicked it from Mum and Dad's cupboard," Lucile said. "You haven't heard the best bit yet!" Something told me I didn't want to. I was already convinced Lucile's parents would be searching for us when they noticed the bottle was missing, and who would they suspect but their wayward daughter, and her weird gawky friend?

"Aren't they going to notice it's gone?"

"They're not going to think it was me, will they? Listen, guess who I ran into on the way to yours. Jake!" she exclaimed, waiting for my excitement to flood like hers, but all I could do was stare at the bottle with my stomach churning.

"He asked if I knew a place we could hang out, and I said here," she said, seizing the sweet packet and tipping half the contents down her throat. "I told him we had drinks. Jake is coming here! Can you believe it?"

The truth was, I couldn't believe it, Mia. Jake was the coolest boy in school. An outsider, with a cigarette smile and hooded eyes. He didn't even hang out with kids from school. He hung out with the older crowd, boys who worked in bars and swanned about with hazy eyes. What would he want with us? *Not us*, a voice in my head hissed, *Lucile*, and it wasn't completely unbelievable.

Lucile was popular, smart, with huge doughy blue eyes and long glossy hair, cultivated by a silvery laugh that resonated in your ears long after she'd left, but Jake was different. There were stories about him hotwiring cars and dating teachers, and living with his uncle who encouraged him to have beer for breakfast.

"Luce, he's nearly sixteen. Why would he want to hang out with us?"

"He said he's coming, didn't he?" Lucile snapped, rummaging through the boat, and when she found what she'd been looking for, my heart crumpled. Clasped in her hands were two pink skirts that could've easily passed for a four-year-old's hand me downs. "I've only got one top," she said, whipping off her shirt and replacing it with a hot pink tube top.

"So you'll have to make do with the one you're

wearing, but roll it up or something."

I hugged my chest before she tossed me the skirt and ran a disapproving gaze over my baggy shirt and tattered jeans.

"You better get changed," she ordered. "Jake is bringing his mate, so you have to look hot, and no offence, but no one is going to take a second look at you wearing that."

I sighed. There was no point in arguing with Lucile. Arguing only prolonged the inevitable. Nodding begrudgingly, I headed behind a tree to get changed.

Stripping down to my underwear, I scrutinised my pasty knees before stepping into the skirt, and when I re-emerged, toothpick legs, and flat chest in tow, Lucile wolf whistled then grabbed the bottle of vodka.

"Let's get this party started!" she cheered, but in her exuberance, it seemed she'd forgotten to bring anything to mix with the vodka. We contemplated venturing to Mr Pardeep's shop, but adamant about not missing Jake, Lucile demanded we stayed exactly where we were. And so, after pacing backwards and forwards, and sitting in the damp canoe whilst unsuccessfully trying to cover my veiny legs, we decided, well, Lucile decided, we'd drink it straight.

"I don't think this is a good idea," I admitted when she handed me a half-filled plastic cup. "It smells like one of those paint thinners decorators use."

"Just pretend it's water," Lucile ordered.

"But Luce..."

"But Luce, nothing. Stop being a baby Rai."

Dread coated my tongue as she held the cup to her lips and gestured for me to do the same.

"On three," she instructed. "One…two..." Lucile grinned, an expression that would become the foundation of so many of our disastrous adventures. "Three."

In no time at all we tipped back our heads, allowing the burning liquid to slip down our throats. Staring up at the fuzzy lilac sky, I spluttered, choked, and when I saw Lucile's face scrunched up like the cup in her hands, I couldn't help laugh.

"Again," she wheezed.

We drank more, and after the third cup, grew accustomed to the burning and laughter. We fell over a few times. I scraped my knee, Lucile bumped her head. Immune to pain, we raced through the hazy trees and leaves with a stolen sense of freedom like wild animals. The world became a magical fortress, and it belonged to us.

We hadn't even noticed the sky shift from auburn to indigo, or the birds grow bored with our pantomime and leave to rest up with their offspring.

"Shh," Lucile whispered when we heard voices, hours later. Attempting to pick up the sound, I strained my ears as she hopped out of the boat and staggered over to a tree, ushering me to get down.

"Lucile?" called a voice.

My stomach turned as I stooped lower.

"I told you they were no shows," said another.

"This is where she told me to meet her."

There was a crackle; a snapped twig, or a trodden wrapper. I knew they were close because I could smell Jake's aftershave permeating the stuffy night air.

Over the edge of the boat, I saw Jake. Glancing around impatiently in a sleeveless leather jacket, he had his hair gelled back, and a faint smatter of stubble dusting his chin. Beside him, his friend clung to an oversized rucksack and wore a t-shirt that read: 'what up.' He was taller than Jake and looked like someone who should wear glasses but didn't.

As both boys advanced towards the boat, I bent lower, and before panic set in they might see me squatting down like a half-dressed toddler, Lucile dove out and screamed a shrill sound that shook the woodland by its shoulders.

The boys tumbled to the floor.

"Told you they were kids," the friend muttered, springing up and patting down his jeans.

"They're pissed," Jake said. His voice was smooth, composed, skimming the indigo shadows with a whisper of danger.

His friend whistled then snatched the bottle from the boat. Taking a long hard swig, he wiped his mouth with the back of his hand then studied me the way one might regard a bike with a broken wheel.

"Who's this?" he asked Lucile.

"Raine," Lucile replied.

"Raine," Jake echoed.

I sat there awkward as I was, wondering if I should say something, maybe hi, or ask if they wanted to sit. Mulling it over I decided on a half-smile, then regretted it when Lucile threw me a look that said be cool, but being cool made me look even less cool.

"You Toby's cousin?" the friend asked.

I shook my head.

"You in our year at school?"

I shook my head again.

After giving me the once over, his eyes lit up.

"I know who she is!" he gasped, turning to Jake. "She's the kid whose dad hanged himself."

Vodka lurched through my gut as both boys gawped at me.

My father's suicide had been no secret in our small town, but it was rare for someone to mention it outright. It had been nine months, and still, everyone remembered. Teachers let me off with trivial things; being late to class, missing deadlines, fatigue. Most of the girls I was friends with before, scattered into smaller groups I wasn't part of, and whenever they spoke to me — which wasn't often, it was always with a sympathetic edge that was crucifying.

Lucile was my only actual friend, and even though I knew she'd never have noticed me before my dad's death, I was sure our friendship was real.

"Listen," Jake said.

Peering up, I saw him sitting on the ground with his knees to his chest, and his eyes too dark for someone of fifteen.

"No sweat, my old man left when I was a kid. I know exactly how you feel."

"Thanks," I mumbled, resisting the urge to tell Jake he couldn't possibly know how I felt. Had he discovered his dad hanging from the living room ceiling by a light fixture he hadn't gotten around to fitting?

"So, you come out here a lot?" the friend asked, lighting a cigarette.

I heard the sharp crackle as he inhaled.

"Sometimes, when we want to party," Lucile said.

Jake's eyes were still fixed on me.

"So, you like to party huh?"

"Depends on who there is to party with."

"How about you?" Jake asked. "Do you like to party?"

I opened my mouth, but before I could form any sort of uncool response, he turned to Lucile, then spoke in a voice that was both hungry and gentle:

"Shall we sit?"

Lucile hunkered down next to Jake, and Jake's friend whose name I learnt was Bradley, sat next to me in the boat. Minutes later, kissing sounds littered the air like furious crickets. Lucile told me she'd kissed boys before, and that it was no big deal. There was Ronnie, the boy she met on holiday with her parents in Spain. Then Brandon, the boy with cornrows from maths class, but when she glanced at me all feral and wild-eyed midway through kissing Jake, I wondered if she'd kissed boys like this.

Bradley and I chatted about music, films, school, his dad's loser restaurant, cars, then more music. We talked until the sky turned navy, then black with white freckles, and I grew hazier from the cigarette smoke and the sloshy taste of beer.

"It's cool to have a girl I can talk to," Bradley said after too much silence.

"You think I'm cool?"

"Yeah, I like you." He wrapped his arm around me, and suddenly I was conscious of the dead weight on my shoulder.

I squinted at him in the darkness. I didn't find him attractive. His skin was rough, and there was an American twang to his voice that seemed practised, but I started to wonder if he wasn't that bad after all. He liked me, and no one ever really liked me, felt sorry for me maybe, but never actually liked me.

The words played in my mind, until they were a rhythmic blur, clanging together like the discarded beer cans floating in the gentle raps of wind when I felt his hand slide. Like a snake, it slithered across my left shoulder, then to my chest. Without thinking, I leapt up.

"What's up?" he gasped.

"You just tried to... to..."

"So!" he laughed. "What's the big deal? I told you, I liked you."

I smelt him then, cheap cologne, sweat and beer. My stomach gurgled as I fumbled out of the boat, nearly tripping over Lucile and Jake on the floor.

"What's going on?" Jake slurred.

"I thought you said these girls were a sure thing."

"Mine is."

My skin prickled.

"I just don't want to do that," I mumbled.

"You frigid girls think you're so special."

My cheeks blistered as I glared at his twisted face in the bluing darkness. He scowled at me. Lips puckered, eyes unbearably cold.

"Can't we talk instead?" I tried.

"Talk?" Bradley scoffed. "You're a loser. Who'd really want to talk to you?"

I stumbled backwards, glaring at him in the darkness, certain of what was coming – even before he said it.

"It's no wonder why your dad hanged himself."

I jerked back as they laughed. Hugging my sides, I was throttled by an urge to shout, to scream, to pound my fists against their stupid faces, and tell Jake he wasn't all that cool, and tell Bradley he was wrong about everything. But all I could do was stand there with my skin blazing, trying with all of my might to block the sounds of their cutting laughter. And just as I was about to run, I heard Jake cry out in pain.

"Shut up, both of you."

Unsealing my eyes, I saw Lucile's blonde hair glowing brighter as she swam towards me like a firefly in the night.

"She just punched me," Jake wheezed.

Bradley laughed louder while Lucile steered me away by my arm.

"Ignore them," she whispered.

"Fine, piss off," one slurred.

"Did you really punch him?"

"Yeah," Lucile breathed. "He was a rubbish kisser anyway."

I hung my head as she led me through the cobwebbed passage, wrestling the urge I had to tell her she could go back or to apologise for ruining the night, but mostly, I wanted to thank her for doing something I couldn't.

I knew Lucile would overwrite the incident in a

heartbeat. She would've much preferred for me to have not said anything, but as we stumbled out of the woods, under the fluorescent crowd of street lights, I felt the words were too mighty to swallow.

"Thanks, Luce."

Lucile smiled then handed me a warm beer can, and it was in that moment, under the neon chunk of the night, an understanding passed between us, that Lucile was more than a friend. She was my sister.

It took around half an hour before we were creeping down Lucile's ghostly street with the manicured houses, and watchful gnomes that were never stolen before we reached her prim white door.

"I hope they're asleep," she whispered, but before we could even reach her pathway, the curtain twitched, the door swung open, and out-ran Lucile's roundly mother, white-faced and barefoot.

"Frank she's here!" she cried, grabbing Lucile by the shoulders. "She was with Raine."

"Is she okay?" shouted a voice from inside.

Lucile's mother didn't answer. She was too busy staring at Lucile and tucking strands of her hair behind her ears. Gathering we were fine, Lucile's mother folded her arms across her red nightgown.

"Do you have any idea of the time young lady?"

"Well, actually I don't," Lucile muttered.

My stomach flipped. Backing away, I expected Mrs Fleetwood to throttle us.

"It's nearly three am! Do you know what can happen to girls at three am – alone? No, I don't expect you do, and you." Skimming my bare legs, her gaze ran up to my face. "I expect your mother is worried sick! I called your house and got no response?"

"I'm sorry Mrs Fleetwood the phone line—"

She didn't let me finish.

"I can smell beer on your breath," she hissed. "You've been drinking, upstairs now," she said to Lucile.

"But Mum…"

"Frank, will you drive Raine home?"

"Mum please can she just—"

"Mum please nothing."

Her mother's face fizzled a whiter shade of pale, but Lucile wasn't taking the hint.

"Can't she stay? We don't have school in the morning."

"After everything, I expect Raine's mother would like to see her, not knowing where her daughter has been, Frank!"

Lucile opened her mouth when her thin father bounded out of the hallway. Dressed in a tartan gown and house slippers, he adjusted his wide-rimmed glasses then flashed me a battered smile.

"Hello darlings," he tittered, stumbling down the drive to the car.

"Can I at least go with Dad?" Lucile whined, but after her mother's forbidding expression, she offered me a last apologetic glance, before stomping inside and taking care to slam the door behind her.

Heading to the car, I studied the pavement wishing I could've stayed the night. I would fall asleep next to Lucile in her plush double bed then wake up to a full English breakfast she'd barely touch. Pulling open the back door of the beat-up Volkswagen, I was all set to jump in when I saw a figure in the reflection of the window. Someone was standing behind me.

Tensing up, I spun around. Mrs Fleetwood held out one of Lucile's jackets, a stale green cast off Lucile claimed was 'so last season.'

"It's cold," she said, offering me the jacket.

"I'm fine, really," I told her.

But she continued thrusting it in my face, the coconut

lotion on her hands pounding the air until I accepted.

"Mrs Fleetwood, I'm really sorry," I muttered, shrugging on the jacket, but she didn't scold me as I'd expected. Instead, she kissed my cheek, and before I could ask if it was okay to spend the night, she waddled back inside, leaving me to watch the orange lights inside blink off one by one.

We drove without conversation, just the sound of the car radio as the streets outside grew more and more unadorned.

"Here you go, poppet," Mr Fleetwood said, pulling up outside my house.

Sensing there was something he wanted to say, I glanced up, hopeful. Maybe he'd tell me it wouldn't be so bad, or ask if I was okay, or ask me to stay;

please ask me to stay.

Mr Fleetwood sighed, my heart stung, and before he had a chance to offer a pitiful solution to a problem he'd never understand, I piled out of the car. Racing to the front door, I pulled the key out from beneath the flowerless flowerpots and jammed it in the lock.

Fumbling, I tried again. And when the door clicked open, I inched inside, knowing what I'd see, even before I flicked the light switch. Still, there was always some hope; maybe today would be different. It never was.

When the light fizzed to life, I saw her curled against the uncarpeted ground, clinging to an empty bottle with her head over her knees. The room smelt of old milk and piss, and her violet nightdress hung from her shoulder, exposing her left breast.

I coughed, the sound loud enough to make her glance up.

"I'm sorry, Mum."

She wasn't looking at me, not properly, not in a long time. Her lank hair spilt further over her face. A face once beautiful, now lined with crooks and dents, housing eyes that were deepest pools of black. By the twisted hand of biology, she was my mother, but by definition, she was something much different.

"Turn off the fucking light," she slurred.

I shrunk against the wall, pulling off Lucile's coat.

"Did you hear me? I said turn off the fucking light."

"Mum, I—"

"You're a little whore. You know that?"

My heart dipped as her eyes rolled back in her head.

"Been out with your boyfriend?"

In an attempt to cover up, I hugged my chest, staring at her blotchy face, swollen from months of alcohol.

"I bet you had fun, fucking him and leaving me here alone."

I closed my eyes with all of the things I wanted to say pounding away at my skull like a rusty mallet.

No, I don't have a boyfriend. No, I didn't fuck him. No, I didn't have fun. No, I didn't want to leave this morning, but you threw me out with no explanation of why, and if I had a choice, I'd much rather sit here with you all day and have you look at me the way you used to. Please, look at me.

I clenched my hands into fists until my nails carved at my palms. There was no point speaking to her now. The best thing to do would be to leave her until she sobered up.

"Where the fuck are you going?" she hissed as I crept through the living room. "You think your dad would be proud of you?"

I swallowed hard, urging myself to keep moving, to not sweep up the smashed vase on the floor, or grab my school folder with spill marks staining the cover.

"You know it was your fault."

Making it to the stairway, I hid at the bottom, rocking backwards and forwards, demanding my ears to do anything but listen.

"Lies," I whispered. "All lies."

Sitting there, I thought about the bottle she clung to. White fingers squeezing the neck so hard I believed it would shatter. I wanted her to hold me like that, even if I were made of glass. I just wanted her to hold me. It was pathetic, but she hadn't held me in so long.

I clung tighter to my knees, visualising what would happen in the morning. The hangover would kick in and she'd forget the insults from the night before.

"*Where're my fucking painkillers,*" she'd mutter, with an empty packet tucked in the pocket of her nightgown. *"Where the fuck are they?"*

She wouldn't ask where I'd been, or who I'd been out with, or if I'd eaten in the past two weeks, then she'd start all over. Drink from midday till dark, slurring I was a waste of space, a mistake; she wished she'd gotten rid of me, the insults growing sharper and colder as the sky outside grew darker.

I stared at the muddy carpet feeling like that was it. At thirteen, I believed I was done with the world. I considered packing a bag and leaving, an idea I had on evenings much worse than this. Nights strange men locked me outside, and I heard my mother laughing, then crying through the walls.

But I didn't leave because it always came down to the same exasperating fact, Mum needed me. If I left, who'd make sure she didn't drink herself to death? Who would force her to eat? Studying my clenched fists, I reminded myself I wasn't staying for this version of her, I stayed for the woman who got lost somewhere before my dad died.

The woman who smelt of lavender and honey before breakfast, who had a laugh that could light up the world at night. I remembered her vaguely, the way her husky voice wrapped itself around my uncertainties gently reminding me I was enough. Days she'd pick me up from school with this magical expression that carried so much warmth, I thought my soul would erupt.

'How much do I love you?' She'd sing as I bounced alongside her.

I missed her. It started after my dad hanged himself. It was sick really, that in his death I found some solace, thinking it would be just us; no smashed-up kitchen, no walking on eggshells, no one to grab me by my hair when my knife scraped too loudly against the plate. I wouldn't see my mom decorated in bruises and bust lips.

With him gone, she began drinking. A few glasses of wine first, then enough to sedate her, then to forget. It became an ugly day to day occurrence where I had to be strong, but invisible, and there was no one there to whisper it would be okay or to look at me with magic in their eyes. I stayed on the stairs for hours that night Mia, waiting, praying, wishing for a place better than the world I came from, and to be honest, I don't think I ever stopped.

***

"And then I drew."

"What did you draw?"

I rub the base of my neck as they ogle me.

It was around that time I changed. I went in search of fires, wanting to burn, to be apprehended, to be stopped, to be seen. My mother died three years later. Left with guilt for all the terrible things I'd done in those three years, I tried to forget, but I couldn't.

I met Dan five years after. I was twenty-one and pretending to be someone better.

"I suppose it's a silly question asking if you remember what you drew fifteen years ago," Watson says, but I do remember, Mia.

"How often did your mother behave that way towards you?" Pierce asks.

I stare at the table.

"How long after your father passed away?"

"He didn't pass away," I correct. "He hanged himself."

"How long after?"

"A few months."

They continue speaking as I think back to what I drew that night. I still have it in the house I shared with Dan, tucked safely in my studio. I drew a palace. A huge crystal fortress, made of impenetrable glass, and outside of it stood a man, who was not a man, a creature with roses in his mouth, and thorns for his fingers. I glance at Pierce rubbing the space on his ring finger.

Everything crumbles eventually, Mia. All we need is a little patience.

CHAPTER THIRTEEN

Watson tells me Pierce has a meeting and won't be joining us today. Slouching lower in my seat I try assuring myself that Pierce wouldn't tell anyone about you. He promised. Still, despite all my rationalisations it didn't stop my imagination from unleashing havoc in my mind last night. And all because of one stupid slip. I hadn't been able to sleep. Every time I'd closed my eyes, images filled my head of creatures dressed in white coats, cradling silver tools dripping with blood.

My blood.

I couldn't see their eyes. Only smooth pink skin where their eyes should be. I felt my legs being held down as they chanted words obscured by surgical masks. I knew what they were doing, even before it happened, but I couldn't move, couldn't scream. The wold was a stone coffin. Earth was being scattered on the wooden casket. And then, I felt it, the weightlessness of my womb as you were snatched.

"What meeting?" I peer under Watson's brittle blanket of hair as she tuts at a page carpeted in red circles.

"Doctor Pierce is a busy man, I guess he enjoys the limelight." The words slip from her mouth like a bar of soap between fingers, and before she can take it back, I lurch forward.

"What do you mean he enjoys the limelight? did he..."

"Did he what?" she asks, raising a brow.

"Nothing," I lie. "What do you do outside of here?"

"Outside of here," she hesitates. "Outside of here, my life mainly revolves around Liam."

"Did you always want children?"

"Raine," She pleads, her eyes amplifying, but I stand my ground.

"Did you?"

"No. We need to get on now. We still have a wide basis for you to cover. Yesterday you talked about your mother, how would you describe your relationship with her after she got sick?"

Her pen drums the table as I study the dark circles swallowing her eyes. Something is troubling her, and I need to know what. The pens drums louder, a crescendo filling the room.

"What about your father?"

"Why?"

"Because a person's childhood shapes who they are. Evidence suggests early social interactions can structure a personality, the way we think, the way we act, the beliefs we hold."

"So, you think because my father hanged himself, I wanted to do the same?"

"No, I—"

"Or my mother drinking herself to death, you think that's ingrained in me?"

I stare back brazenly, exhausted by wilfully accepting the labels she and Pierce constantly tacked to me. I rarely drank, I hadn't contemplated suicide even after I was buried head first in the most bloodcurdling pit. I just kept going, stumbling forward until I found a trickle of light. All of the pain, and destruction, and beauty, I'd discovered at the end, every morsel of gold dust and bullshit was not a result of my parents or my husband. It was me, all of it was me.

"Raine, there is a biological link between—"

"Bullshit." I slam my fists hard enough into the table, to make her flinch. "None of that matters."

"So, what does matter?"

Nothing, I want to tell her. Not a damn thing.

"I need you to feel the way I feel."

"And how do you feel?"

Lost, scared, terrified.

I close my eyes. The air is too hot.

"Tell me about Liam."

"Raine, we have your father's mental health record. We know he was unwell. There are ways to manage symptoms. Hearing voices, seeing—"

"Tell me!"

A moment passes before she lets out a sound impersonating a laugh, and just when I think she is about to call security, she does something that surprises me.

"He's twelve," she answers.

I peer up at Watson studying the table with her chin to her chest.

"He's a good boy. Really good, like if he sees someone struggling the first thing he'll do is offer help, even if he isn't able to give it. He's kind. I know most mothers say that but that boy makes me so proud, I feel unworthy."

"Why?"

As her eyes elevate to mine, I glimpse a fragility that hadn't been there before.

"I don't know. I guess, when we mess up so many times and we're handed something precious, we convince ourselves we're only going to ruin it."

I nod, confident she'd never messed up once in her textbook life. Murdering someone, that was messing up.

"And Liam's dad?"

"He's not around."

"Why?"

Her face alters, a girl unfurling into a scorned woman.

"How were you in the next few days with Dan?"

I won't give up, not now.

"I want to know about Liam's father."

"And I've told you before I don't feel comfortable discussing my personal life with you, Raine. It's unprofessional and unethical if Elliot wants to do that then let it fall on his—"

"So it's fine for me to discuss my personal life with you?"

Watson pushes back in her seat, observing me as if I were a caged animal that had escaped through the door she left open. "You keep asking me all of these pointless questions about my life, my family, when all you want is to know is why I killed my husband."

"Raine, calm down."

But I can't calm down; I won't.

"Am I wrong?"

Her eyes shimmer and her mouth keeps opening and closing, but her justifications don't arrive quickly enough.

"You're only asking things relevant to your diagnosis. You don't give a shit about me. It's all based on your perception of what's real and what's not, and I don't understand."

"What don't you understand?"

Pressing my lips into a painful line, I watch her through sober eyes. Naked and unfamiliar, as if we were two strangers sitting across from each other on a crowded train, glancing up from a novel at the final stop.

"What gives you the right to play God, and tell me what's wrong with me?" My throat closes up as every muscle in Watson's face collapses. For a moment, her face is just skin.

"All I can do is try," she mutters.

I nod, and this time I have to look away because something in her eyes tells me it's the truth.

"Was there any overlap when you were seeing these things?"

Seconds pass.

Watson glances at her wristwatch then sets down her pen, but something inside of me almost wants to try, for her.

"She was at my house," I mumble. "I wanted her to leave, but she wouldn't listen."

Watson's eyes spark with confusion as she picks up her pen.

"Who was at your house?"

"Esme."

AUGUST 28th 2018

The sky was a black sheet. Wrapped in my patchwork quilt, I clung to a coffee mug that had long since stuck to my palms. I stared up, hungry for the stars, but all I received instead was the wind. An insatiable beast scraping away at my ears and tearing bloody gashes at my cheeks.

It was cold for August. A precursor of the months to come. I could hear Dan belting out the chorus to a song on the radio inside.

"And you give yourself away, and you give…" The sky seemed too dark, like all of the lights in the world had gone out, and the universe was stuck on pause. I huddled tighter in the blanket, struggling to ignore the smell of pasta slipping out from the cracks in the door, bathing the night in the odour of dreaded predictability.

"How was your day?" Dan would ask.

"Fine, yours?" I'd reply.

"Good."

"Good."

"How's dinner?"

"Fine."

Knives and forks clattering against the plates like thunder.

Staring at the rose bushes tangled against the off-white picket fence, I bit my lower lip, thinking of those old gold plastic afternoons when Dan would hack away at the thorns. I'd watch him almost longingly in those days. I remembered the way he'd wield the axe high above his head, his shirt soaked through, his skin gleaming as he turned to where I sat on the porch, sipping cloudy lemonade and sketching in my A4 leather sketchbook.

He'd give me this grin.

This warm burst of hunger I wasn't sure I could grasp, even then. It was in those minuscule seconds everything was clear. Too clear. I wanted to be happy; I wanted it so desperately I convinced myself I was. Practising it in the smile I returned, and the casual wave of my hand. And when Dan turned, satisfied, I knew something was missing. Something that left a hole in my chest the size of an ocean.

The truth was, I settled, Mia. And even back then I recognised I was performing the subtlest form of suicide.

"Babe, do you want goats' cheese?"

I jumped, trying to remember why I'd gone outside. I needed air, or space, or time, or something. I needed something, but I couldn't remember what.

"Babe, cheese?"

I glared at the tin shed at the back of the garden with a space in my chest I couldn't fill. It had been weeks since I'd travelled back to Wanderlust. Weeks draped in cordial conversations, and silent dining all the while I'd tried desperately to forget what had happened at the market, but I couldn't.

I'd gone up to my studio countless times, inspecting the mirror with minutes curdling to hours, and day sifting to night, but Nicholas's touch was buried so deep in my skin, I felt it tearing me apart from the inside out. Nicholas who was half-human. How was that possible? How was any of what had happened in the past few weeks possible?

I nestled deeper in the blanket as the radio hosts gave an update on traffic from inside.

'And the M42 northbound is blocked off due to a vehicle...'

After what happened at the market, I couldn't risk venturing back to Wanderlust, but that meant I wouldn't see Nicholas again. I ran my fingers through my hair, questioning if he'd care if he never saw me again. He watched me like he would, and after weeks, I still couldn't get that concentrated expression to wash from my mind. That look that whispered a thousand things his lips just weren't ready to say.

The wind ate away at my earlobes as I clung to the mug until my fingers were ready to snap. The night I made it back from Wanderlust, Dan found me in my studio. Driving me to the emergency room, I remember him barking questions that came out in a hysterical puddle of nonsense:

'Why did you do it? How did you manage to puncture your ribs, your legs, your thighs and with what? Where was the knife? Where Rainey, where?'

I couldn't answer, and Dan couldn't ask the question blistering his lips. *"Did you try to kill yourself because of me?"*

"He can't even remember you're allergic to goat's

cheese." I flinched then splattered cold coffee down my legs.

I didn't have to look up to know it was Esme. The pungent scent of rot lifting from her skin told me it was her. Clenching my jaw I tried to dismiss her, but the smell grew stronger and stronger, eroding my sinuses and scraping my throat, until I had no choice but to look up, and when I did, the world beyond her dissolved.

"You can't be here," I hissed.

"Of course, I can," Esme wheezed, looming over me with a piece of flesh hanging from her chin. "I'm here, so it's possible. Everything is possible if you have enough belief."

"You need to leave." Even as I said it, I knew it was pointless, Mia. Esme wasn't going to listen, when had she ever listened? "Please."

"Babe, cheese?"

Dan's voice made me jump.

"No... No, thank you," I shouted back.

"Quite handsome, isn't he?" Esme teased, glancing at the man pretending to be my husband from the window. The creases around her neck spread up her skull as she twisted her head, gawking at him.

'What are you doing here?" I asked quietly.

"I came to make sure you were well," Esme said.

Crouching next to me, she watched me with the spaces in her eyes tightening.

"I saw what happened at the market. So tragic, such brutality. I wanted to intervene, and I would've had someone else not have played the hero."

"You were there?"

"Of course!" Esme exclaimed. "I've told you I see everything, syrup. He carried you right the way through the crowd, took you back to the palace in the bubble. Oh, if you could've seen his face! So worried! He prowled the market in search of you for hours, he even threw that Bildred down to the floor, caused quite the ruckus."

My throat constricted as the grin she wore spread up to her empty eyes.

"I wonder what Daniel would say if he knew about all the time you're spending with a certain someone?"

I shrugged as she tilted her head, a scrap of skin from her chin flapped on its side.

"Such a shame when love dies," Esme wheezed. "Or perhaps, it was never there to begin with. What do you think?"

I lifted my chin, reminding myself not to get riled up, but something about Esme enraged me more than I cared to admit, and when she threw back her head and laughed a flat, parched sound, I decided I'd had enough.

"Tell me what you're doing here," I demanded.

"My, my we are full of anger, aren't we?" Esme giggled.

"Tell me the truth."

"Oh, the truth! Why didn't you mention that before?"

My mouth wandered into a grimace as she stroked her blistered neck with a fingernail.

"The truth is I had to be certain you would return to Wanderlust," she said. "After your last visit, I was afraid you'd be somewhat… put off. I've tried calling out to you. I admit my words may have been somewhat scathing. But the truth always is, don't you agree?"

"You think that was the truth? You told me I made Dan sick, that this was all my fault."

"As I said, the truth may have been scathing," Esme nodded, her silver hair thrashing the arm of my chair.

I looked away. I didn't have to discuss Dan with Esme; our relationship – or lack of it – was none of her business, but I knew what was.

"Why do you want me to go back?" I asked.

"Because, you are vital to Wanderlust," Esme insisted.

"Tell me how."

"Patience, Raine."

But I was through with patience. I'd been compliant, and calm, and guarded, and as a result, I was ruined. Before Esme could offer any more futile commands, I slammed my coffee mug into the concrete.

"Who are you?" I shouted. A searing pain shot up my wrist as I stared into the abyss of her eyes. "You're bartering with me, and I don't even know who you are!"

The wind howled louder, smacking my flushed cheeks and making Esme's hair waft around us in a silver thunderstorm.

"Tell me why I can't say your name, or why of all the people in the world it's only me that can travel to Wanderlust." My eyes trembled as a trickle of blood ran down my fingers. "Tell me, or I won't go back."

"Oh, but you will, Raine. You will!" Esme exclaimed. "Your curiosity is devouring you. Can't you see that without Wanderlust you'd be nothing?"

Focussing on the tips of her needle teeth, I struggled to keep my chin from shaking.

"Why not enjoy the madness flowing through your mind and allow yourself to be something greater than this? Is this really all you wanted as a child? Did you not dream of a life greater than your mother's?"

At the mention of my mother, my soul grew heavy.

"I see the pity in his eyes when he looks at you, Raine. I feel the ache in his heart when he wishes he could take back his proposal."

I watched Dan in the window. He was smiling at his phone. I hated that smile; it was the gesture that reinforced the truth that Dan was a liar. Someone who went around starting fires, and ran off, ignoring the screams for help behind him.

"Be someone greater," Esme whispered. "There is an

evil in our kingdom you do not know of, but it is you written in the stars, that you, Raine, are destined for excellence."

"How?"

Esme sighed, and for the first time, I witnessed a wave of sadness sully her features.

"Given the way I appear, I understand it may be hard to trust me," she said. "Creatures in Wanderlust called me a monster, a freak." Her black lips twitched, and if her eyes were more than empty spaces, I was certain they'd be swimming with tears. "But regardless of the way I appear, my heart is pure, and if you should find it in yourself to trust me, you will achieve greatness."

"You need to understand…"

"Babe?" Dan called.

My heart stopped as I shot up in my chair, imploring Esme to disappear with my eyes.

"Who are you talking to?"

My eyes skated to the door as the brass handle turned. My jaw dropped. What would Dan say when he saw Esme? Would he be afraid?

Just disappear I thought, *just go.*

Instead, Esme leapt back, muttering words I couldn't hear above my heart.

My lips cracked as the door clicked open and outstepped Dan, wearing a smile sharper than a knife.

"Dan." I froze as he strode towards me with a dishcloth writhing between his fingers.

"Dan what?" he asked, arching a brow.

Clapping her chalky hands together, Esme released a hoarse laugh as I stared at Dan, waiting for him to ask who the hell she was, but Dan wasn't looking at Esme, he was staring at me.

"He can't see me," she wheezed.

"What?" I whispered, blood surging through my cheeks.

"Are you okay, Rainey? You look like you've seen a ghost."

'You can't…" I paused, glancing at Esme who was nodding behind Dan.

"I can't what?"

I couldn't answer, and the longer I retreated into silence, the rougher Dan's voice became.

"Raine, you're starting to freak me out."

"Do you think he cares?" Esme asked.

"Yes," I said without thinking.

"Yes?" Dan questioned, tilting his head.

"I mean, yeah. I'm fine. I'm just hungry."

"Liar," Esme teased. "He thinks you're mad. Barking, wonderfully bonkers!"

I tried keeping my focus on Dan, but my eyes kept straying to Esme. She was hobbling closer. Her staff clinking against the concrete.

CLICK. CLICK. CLICK.

I wondered if Dan could hear her cane. How could he not see her? Did that mean Esme was a figment of my imagination? I forced my focus on Dan. He was sporting his deadline look. Panicked eyes plastered above a neutral smile for reassurance. I wondered how he saw me; bedridden and unwashed.

"You make him sick," Esme growled.

"Stop it," I mumbled.

"Stop what?" Dan asked.

I shook my head then huddled tighter in the blanket.

"He's fantasising about how glorious it would've been to have never asked to marry you," Esme announced.

I inspected my nails, forcing myself not to give Esme a reaction.

"Dinner will be ready in ten," Dan sighed.

"Great! What are we having?" Esme exclaimed.

"But listen." His tone wavered, and his deadline gaze faltered as it often did when he couldn't find the right words for the page. "I need to get back to the office for a few hours. There's this thing I need to sort, but you can eat without me if you're hungry?"

Clamping down on my lips, I fought the urge I had to scream I knew exactly where he was going.

"You don't belong here," Esme whispered. "He can't even stand to be around you, look."

Nodding hesitantly, I managed a shaky smile, but Dan didn't seem convinced.

"Are you sure you're okay, Raine? I mean, are those tablets working? If not, we can change them."

"Seriously Dan, I'm okay," I said, more forcefully than intended.

Dan nodded, before taking hold of my hand.

"Jesus, you're cold," he whispered.

I winced, about to take back my hand when I glimpsed the old Dan hiding behind this stranger. My friend. The man who would call in sick to work, and watch old movies with me in bed. The man who confessed that when he was eight, he stole a packet of crisps from his newsagents and was still racked with guilt. Now, so chock full of sins he didn't even care. How could he not care?

Staring at him, I'd never been more certain I didn't love him, Mia, not after everything he'd done. But what about before? Hadn't I loved him then? I wanted to love him, I knew that much, and he'd just tossed it in a cheap plastic bag and left it out for the bin men.

"Babe, I'm really going to have to get going," Dan said.

With that, he dropped my palm and headed for the door.

"Try to stay up for me?"

Esme laughed at the forced monologue we had grown accustomed to reciting in a bid to convince ourselves we weren't wasting our lives, but my God, we were wasted. I heard the door creak as I bit down hard on my lips, listening, waiting.

I sensed him lingering in the doorway. I know he wanted to tell me then, not for me, but his conscience, and so, I tempted fate. I thought maybe if he told me the truth, despite losing my husband, I might still be able to keep my friend.

"Don't go," I whispered.

My eyes throbbed as the wind blew harder, the smell of pasta wandered out from a house impersonating a home, and before I could tell Dan I knew everything, the door slammed shut.

My chest caved in as I waited, hoping he might still be there, hoping he was about to confess to everything so we could end this amicably and move on because seven years is a hell of a long time to disregard someone's entire being.

I waited, and when the car engine roared to life in the street beyond me it was clear we were over. Nodding at the smashed mug at my feet, I headed for the door. Esme was still speaking, but I didn't turn to her. Flinging myself through the kitchen door, I climbed the steps furiously before pulling down the cord to my studio steps.

After making my way to the top, I didn't even bother switching on the light. I just kept going. My knees jerked against scattered canvasses, and strewn paints, and labelled boxes, and forgotten clothes I didn't give a shit about until I was facing the mirror.

Holding out my hand I prodded the glass, waiting for that miraculous abandon to wash over me. Then, as if by magic, or the relentless waves of insanity I'd been courting for months, I saw I was back in the room I'd been in with Nicholas.

My legs quaked as I swivelled around, inspecting the place. It was dark, but I recognised it by the scent of the candles. Each one dripped with hot breaths of vanilla and cinnamon. Only I didn't blow on to the candles, or call out to anyone, because there was no one I wanted, and nothing I desired more at that moment than to disappear.

Fumbling through the door, I found myself in a long red hallway leading to the spiral staircase. Racing down the steps, I shoved open the entrance door. It was raining. Heavy emerald drops pelted my hot flesh as I darted down the steps, my insides ripping and my lungs gasping. Focussing on the lake glittering under the blood red moon, I forced myself to keep it together.

Only when I reached the lake, I lost all rights to my body. Falling to my knees, I buried my face deep in the pale shards of grass, and I howled. The sound was deep and rippled with angst, and pain, and grief. Not just for Dan, but for the past I ran from, and the future that shrewdly brushed my lips.

I howled until my face was bloodied with the tears of the earth, and the forgotten dreams of a child, and when I felt there was nothing left inside of me, I lifted my head and scowled at the lake.

The sight before me was beautiful, but I couldn't take pleasure in it. Why was I so engrossed in my pain that I couldn't stop for a second and appreciate the magnitude of the beauty surrounding me? Tearing off my ring, I flung it into the water then cried harder, breaking and falling apart until I heard footsteps.

Too exhausted to turn, or wipe the mud from my cheeks, I glared at the star-filled the sky with an image of my wedding day thundering away in my mind. I hadn't even been happy then. Had I ever been happy? Dan was right. I was a mess.

The footsteps behind me grew louder. Focusing on the lake, I saw Nicholas looming over me in its reflection. Nicholas, who'd left me on the night I'd needed him most. Nicholas, who was half human. Nicholas, who I craved to understand just as much as I craved to understand myself.

"Before you say anything about me not belonging here, I don't care," I muttered angrily. "Because I don't belong where I come from either. I don't want to go back. I can't—"

I trembled, clawing at my knees while the truth dismembered me.

"I'm a mess. I can't even remember being happy. I can't– I can't remember how it feels. When I was fifteen my mom got sick," I muttered, wiping my eyes with a fist.

I didn't know if Nicholas was listening, or if he would even care, all I knew was that I was through with telling myself I was fine because, in all honesty, I hadn't been fine since I was a child, Mia.

"Cancer. Stage C." I whispered. "I didn't know what it meant then, no one told me. Obviously, I know now it meant she had eleven months maximum."

I frowned at the lake as Nicholas perched next to me.

"She had three months," I muttered. "Growing up, I'd seen her drunk, but this… this was different." I hesitated remembering my mother's pale face in that hospital bed. She seemed so small. I wanted to go to her, to hold her, to tell her it was okay, but I was still so angry.

"The night the hospital called I was with a boy. I told him she deserved to die alone, but I didn't think— parents don't— I kept thinking God couldn't take them both—"

I screwed up my face, tasting warm metallic rain.

"She died," I said. "And I kept waiting for someone to call and tell me they'd made a mistake, but no one did…"

I shook my head as the memory of the day I went to collect my mother's things blared through my mind.

I'd sat in one of those cold green hospital chairs watching a family opposite me. A mother in her late forties, two children, both girls, their father. All with their heads bent and their eyes glued to the floor. After speaking to a doctor, I watched them collapse into each other's arms.

The mother ran her fingers through the older girl's hair. The father whispered something into the younger girl's ear. Something I couldn't hear, but I wanted to; I wanted to hear his words so desperately that for a second, I pretended I belonged to that family.

For hours, I watched couples walking in and out of waiting rooms, strangers, and doctors, and nurses, and gurneys blurring into a fuzzy dream, all the while I wondered where I would go. Who I would become.

I didn't want to be the messed up little girl who sought comfort in the arms of others, nor did I want to be alone. I wanted my mom, but she was gone, and I was more alone then, than ever before.

Five years later, I met Dan. After our first date in a restaurant, I still can't pronounce the name of, I really believed I could be someone else. Dan didn't know about my past. I liked that, without knowing I was broken he wouldn't try to fix me, and he couldn't be disappointed at my inability to be fixed.

For him, I became better. I masked the filthy pandemonium inside of me. I lived cautiously I made good decisions. I didn't heal.

"I'm a mess."

Tears lashed down my cheeks, streaming my face until the world became a mess of blurry ink and purple rivers.

"I can't even confront the man I'm married to, I can't—"

Burying my head in my knees, I shuddered as the world crumbled around me.

"Today was the anniversary of my mother's death," I

sobbed. It was the reason I'd gone outside. Dan was talking about meetings and football. He didn't even remember. Every year he'd bug me with questions, before sneaking out, then returning with a bouquet of lilies and a bottle of scotch.

'To life,' he'd toast, but today he hadn't even mentioned it.

"Sometimes it gets hard, pretending I'm okay when I'm not, plastering on a smile despite feeling so fucking broken I could scream, and sometimes I just want someone to tell me it's going to be okay. Even if it's not. I just need—"

I broke off when Nicholas moved closer.

Swallowing the spike in my throat, I stared at his outline in the lake. He sat right next to me. His face just as grief-stricken, and pale as mine.

Clearing my throat to apologise, I froze when he whispered,

"It's going to be okay, Raine."

My lip curled downwards.

Hearing him say those words did something to me, Mia. They carried the magnitude to bulldoze the stone walls I had single-handedly built around my heart, and for the most part, I was glad.

"It really is," he added.

Before I could stop myself, I pressed my head into the horizon of his chest, sobbing. I didn't care if Nicholas pulled away, or if he thought I was weak. I didn't care for all of the things I was afraid of with Dan. I just wanted to take down the mask that had become so heavy in my hands, and not have him turn away.

***

"I can't cry anymore," I tell Watson. "I never used to cry much. I believed tears were a sign of weakness.

When I was younger, my dad would tell me winners don't cry, but I always wondered what prize there was after you'd lost everything."

Pulling a folder out from her bag, she squints at a piece of paper.

"It's most likely to do with your medication. You're on risperidone. You have some of the side effects already… dry mouth, a rash—"

"How do you know that?"

Her eyes swoop up to mine.

"You told us," she says slowly. "It's likely you won't remember. Your thinking is a little scattered. This is why you need to tell us everything. You've done well today. You have a meeting with your solicitor tomorrow. Perhaps you can use this as a starting point for what to tell her?"

I shake my head, my words lost as I stare at the wall, wondering how much of the truth they already know, and how much I can take back before they learn what actually happened that night.

CHAPTER FOURTEEN

Glancing through the criss-cross window, my heart plummets when I see my solicitor, Shelly Peters, glaring at me with too many of her coffee stained teeth sticking out from her shrivelled lips.

"You lied again," she explodes before I make it through the door.

"I—"

"Don't," she holds up a hand.

Falling into my seat, all I can think of is how much she resembles a wrinkled-up paper bag. All creases and frump, compressing nothing but hot air.

"Forensics came back." She sits up straighter. The bounce of her shoulders doing nothing to iron out her wrinkled navy suit. "He didn't attack you that night did he Raine?"

My lips part as she studies me knowingly.

"You came in with a dislocated jaw and a chipped tooth."

I run my tongue against the place it split.

"Traces of your blood were found on your fist, and considerable bruising to your knuckles."

Rubbing my knuckles under the table, I watch her hands work themselves over stacks of mud-coloured folders on the desk before her eyes flick to mine.

"And there was nothing in the coroner's report to suggest Dan hurt you that night."

My heart stops and the walls are closing in on me.

"He did hurt me," I mumble, but Peters knows it's a lie. They all know it's a lie.

Everything is collapsing, and I can't find the right words to stop my face from reddening.

"Physically?"

No answer.

"Raine, it was clear someone had been harming you for a long time. There were the hospital reports dating back to September. Even before that there were wounds that looked like they'd been there for five months minimum. Was that person Dan?"

A direct question. Yes or no. No running.

"Yes."

Peters rolls her eyes. Pulling a photograph out from a folder, she thrusts it in my face. Despite staring past it, I see the woman draped in blood with death soaked into her eyes. I remember the flashbulbs exploding as I stood in the bright white cubicle. The helplessness when they swabbed my mouth, the uncertainty when the cell door slammed shut behind me. The silence that followed, the boisterous question it brought.

Was I doing the right thing?

"He didn't hurt you that night, did he, Raine?"

I can't breathe.

"I need the truth if you want me to defend you."

He did hurt me, I want to tell her. He hurt me in more ways than anyone could imagine because I trusted him, and he violated that trust.

"Raine, the police know you're lying. When this goes to trial, there's no way we can act on battered woman syndrome. The prosecution will argue you did this to yourself in a fit of desperation, which would mean you were acting rationally that night, making our whole plea of diminished responsibility turn to shit. Is that the night you found out?"

I shake my head.

"Last week when the police questioned you, you told them you found out months before."

"I did."

"When?"

No answer.

"Raine, I need a date. I need something to piece all this together. What he did to you was horrible, but things like this happen every day, and with the way it's looking, no one will believe you killed Dan in self-defence, they'll think it was because you were jealous."

I scowl at my reflection in the sweaty window. The sky outside is the colour of sour milk. A dull yellow, masquerading as white.

"When did you find out?"

"After lunch." My voice is unfamiliar. Broken and disjointed it ploughs through the air with wet repulsion. My lips move, my chest gives out, and the vision of my middle-aged solicitor clouds over as I think back to the day I started telling Pierce and Watson about but hadn't finished.

"It was after I had lunch with Lucile and Katie," I tell her. "I was driving home, and something, something just felt wrong."

JUNE 17th 2018

I drove down the pastel street lightheaded and panicked, regretting with each elongated mile having taken the car. My temples throbbed and all of my joints felt as if they'd been snatched from an old age pensioner. I was tired; I was always tired. Roads swayed as I zigzagged and swerved, convinced I had to tell Dan the truth.

Confessing all of my niggling insecurities to Lucile over lunch only made it clearer I should have told Dan sooner. I rolled my eyes at the washed-out road. It was probably nothing. We'd go to the doctors and Dan would whisper it was okay while I listed my symptoms. Fatigue, loss of appetite, withdrawal. The doctor would tell me there was a virus going around and prescribe me a course of antibiotics – just a virus.

Swallowing the ball of self-pity choking me, I spotted a red kite dancing against the pale sheet of blue. It pirouetted, jived, lost almost – the string, invisible. I was still staring when I smacked hard against the breaks and screamed. Glaring at my knuckles as they clung to the steering wheel, I tried catching my breath before eying the fence I'd narrowly escaped crashing into.

I'd only taken my eye off the road for a second. One second, and now I was a second from being road kill. Clinging to the gear stick, I clenched my jaw, reversing into the wayward road in an attempt to find my way home, wherever that was.

After parking the car, I fumbled through the front door. "Dan?" My voice bounced against the kitchens freshly painted beige walls, and the calendar that read May, because I'd forgotten to flip it to June. The TV was still on. An old Western movie flickered, giving the room a fuzzy blue glow. Seizing the remote, I switched it off.

The house still smelt of Dan. That sharp tang of fireball fused with the bleach he'd used to scrub the floor. I stared at a mug left on the table. Half filled with watery brown slush. I cradled it, still warm. Dan must have left for work.

Giving the living room a once over, I headed into the kitchen with the mug in tow. Stopping at the sink, I ran the tap, going over how the conversation would play out when he came home from work.

'*Dan, lately I've not been feeling myself.*'

My cheeks flamed when I imagined the look of embarrassment he'd fail to conceal. The schoolboy squirm of his lips, the way he'd brush over it and suggest a drink – anything to avoid the subject of real-life human emotion. The water singed my fingers but I kept my hands routed there as I studied the world outside.

The rose bushes tangled against the off-white fence, the tin shed fifteen metres away, the cars gently lolling by the cracks in the fence. Dan was never good with emotion. There were so many times I wanted to open up to him about my past, but every time I began the conversation 'when I was younger…' He'd always hit me with that schoolboy look, terrified I might shatter the illusion I wasn't the cardboard cut-out wife he was paying for in pennies.

Pressing my thumb against the place his mouth had rested, a thought struck me. It was a Sunday. Dan didn't work on Sundays. He claimed it was the day of rest. Though, I couldn't really see how there was anything peaceful about watching football all day and getting drunker as the sky grew darker.

I pulled my phone from my pocket. No calls. Tapping the screen, I decided to do the only thing I could when I was stressed. I would paint. Leaving the kitchen, I climbed the stairs, when the strangest sensation came over me, Mia. It felt as if someone was rubbing my heart between their forefinger and thumb.

Clutching my chest, I crept over to the bedroom door then pushed it open.

"Dan?" Buttery light blinded me. I squinted around. The dresser was still littered in jewellery, and makeup, and a post-it note reminding me I'd forgotten the milk.

Fuck. I rubbed my eyes. I was just tired; I needed rest. I'd paint later. Slinking through the room, I stopped at our bed. Studying the navy bed sheets and mismatched lilac pillows, I grabbed my chest.

My heart ached.

Something was wrong.

With the carroty glow from outside weighing down my lids, I fell against the lumpy mattress, waiting, but for what I had no idea.

I don't remember dreaming, but when I opened my eyes, the sky from the gaps in the blinds spilt a deep purple. I blinked. The door was still open. A splinter of yellow light sprayed in through the break and hit the wardrobe. About to go back to sleep, I jolted upright in bed when I heard running water.

Dan had come home.

I cringed, wondering if he'd seen me vegged out in bed mid-afternoon, yet another reminder I was failing at life. Taking a shaky breath, I decided now was a good as time as any to get this conversation over and done with. Ungluing myself from the sheets I crept out into the hallway still dressed in the clothes I'd worn for lunch.

I didn't call out to Dan, even now, I'm not sure why Mia. Shuffling through the shadows, I became a homeless apparition, heading towards the ginger light pouring from the creases of the bathroom door and illuminating Dan's suit crumpled up on the floor.

Bending down to untangle his shirt from his trousers, I was on the brink of throwing them in the wash basket in the bedroom when I saw something on his collar.

I wrinkled my brow at the red blemish.

A mark so minuscule that had the light not have been filtering in from under the cracks of the door, I might've missed it. I looked closer. A lipstick mark the size of a thumbprint, trailing alongside the place his collarbone would rest.

Studying the stain, I rubbed it between my fingers trying to work out what else it might've been, and when I recognised it was definitely lipstick, my gut wilted.

How could Dan have gotten lipstick on his collar?

Was he having an affair? The idea seemed so absurd I wanted to laugh; only the sound wouldn't come. Pushing against the wall, I listened to the water crashing against Dan's skin to the white tiled floor, before I brought the shirt up to my face and inhaled the cotton. I smelt him, that musky jawbreaker scent and sweat, but beneath that was something else – a floral perfume,

her.

I pressed the shirt to my face, convinced this was all in my head. What I needed were facts. The lipstick could've been anything, and the perfume might've been mine. Pulling his phone out from his trouser pocket, I unlocked it. His pin was his birthday. In moments, a black and white image of him sitting with his chin tipped forward, watched me disapprovingly.

I rolled my eyes.

I didn't know what I was looking for. A video of him fucking someone? A picture of them together? My stomach churned as I checked his camera folder. Nothing. His videos. Nothing. I scrolled down a stream of messages from Steven, a client at work. Steven would know what was going on. Dan went on about him all the time.

'You need to meet Steven, Raine. The guy's a legend, downed a whole bottle of tequila before a conference call.' 'Steven's girlfriend says Malta is good this time of year.' 'Steven asked if we wanted to go out to dinner tonight, but if you're not up for it, we can stay in.'

Steven. Steven. Steven.

Steven would know.

I stared at his name, but something wouldn't let me

click on Steven's message, because if I looked it would be real, and I'd have to leave. I couldn't just stay here pretending everything was hunkey dorey. But where would I go? What did people in situations like this do? Did they leave amid the heat, or did they try to work it out and move forward? If Dan was callous enough to lie to me every day, I didn't want to move forward.

My pulse hammered my throat as I clung to Dan's phone with my face burning. All this time I believed the reason our marriage was failing was because of me. I believed I was too drab and boring. I wasn't pretty enough, smart enough; I wasn't educated like him. I wasn't the fun bubbly girl who lit up a room at dinner parties; I was the strange woman who spent too much time staring at the door and daydreaming of a spectrum of colours.

I thought it was my fault.

I stared at his phone while my mind drowned under useless plans. I could stay with Katie, but she'd only insist I gave it another go because my cheating husband really did love me, and people had affairs all the time. Rob the banker had one just the other week, and she had one the month before, and everyone sleeps with everyone because no one sees anything but the pretty masks we paint in place of our faces.

I thought it was me.

Cold air sliced my lungs as I stared up at the ceiling. I couldn't stay in Katie's quaint little home, the idea of Rob tottering around, handing out tepid mugs of tea like plasters was enough to drive me mad. The screen dimmed. I jabbed it angrily. If Dan was cheating, he'd done me a favour. He had terminated a relationship that was doomed from the start, but I'd tried so hard to love him. All of those years wasted trying, and all for what?

I ground my jaw.

If he was having an affair, I'd stay with Lucile. She'd

know what to do. She wouldn't sugar coat anything and tell me it was okay for Dan to cheat because it wasn't. She wouldn't tell me to give it another go because he didn't deserve it.

My face perspired as I forced my fingers to click through his sent messages to Steven.

Can't wait to see you tonight.

I scrunched up my face reading it then re-reading it before checking the next message.

Miss you already.

My lip quivered as I scrolled down.

Tomorrow night if I can get away.

Was Dan gay? Taking a shallow breath, I checked his inbox.

Had so much fun, can't wait to feel you again x

Received twenty minutes ago. The air was thick; beneath it, I heard Dan's gravelly laugh when I sang to myself as I painted. I felt the way he held me as though I was made of glass. I tasted him, honeyed cigarettes with a splash of whiskey.

Bastard. Bastard. Bastard.

Clawing my cheeks, I searched the wreck of my mind for a warning sign Dan might've been gay. What would suffice as evidence? A pink feather boa hiding in the closet? Dan couldn't be gay. Then again, I'd read stories of women being married for forty years or so, without the tiniest inclination their spouse was batting for the other team.

I thumped the back of my head against the wall, wishing I'd met Steven. Maybe if I'd seen them together I would've glimpsed a glimmer of something, but what about the lipstick on his collar, what about the perfume? Then it hit me.

Sweat blistered the back of my neck as I thought back to the night I'd agreed to go out for drinks with them both. I'd seen this look cross Dan's face; only I couldn't work out what it was. So wrapped up in my insecurities I'd simply accepted that when Steven cancelled because of a stomach bug, it was the truth.

My lower lip trembled as I thought back to all those times Dan's face fell when Steven called.

'You alright mate?' he'd sing, watching me with that look, only I didn't understand then, that the look had been fear because Steven was a cover up for her.

The world clouded over as I stood outside the bathroom door, shaking with so much fury it surpassed red and ran a deep soul-shatteringly grey.

Glaring at the steam spilling out from under the door, I pushed my palms to my cheeks wondering how long he'd kept it up. Who was she? Did she know he was married? Had taken off his wedding band when he fucked her? Did he fuck her? Or was it something that stirred his soul in a way I couldn't?

I dropped his shirt, my head spinning under questions my mind was too exhausted to grapple with.

Where had he met her? A bar? Work? Was she a writer like him? A client?

Taking an uneven breath, I decided to tackle the problem head-on. I would call her, and when Dan jumped out of the shower with a lopsided grin, I would calmly tell him I knew everything, and that I was leaving.

Steadying my hands, I clicked through his contacts, but when I came across the number, my heart skated out of place.

"Raine?"

I shook my head, backing away through the hallway with that same feeling splintering through me from earlier, only I recognised it as betrayal, because the number was Lucile's.

***

"Katie knew, too."

"How do—"

"The morning after I found out, I called her. She was in the middle of cooking George's breakfast, I just needed someone to speak to, I was so lost, so—" I break off then clear my throat. "She told me she'd run into Lucile at the grocers the night before."

"Perhaps, she did."

"Yeah, and perhaps the only reason we don't see Santa Claus is that he really does know when we're awake."

"Raine—"

"She knew," I tell her. "And the most pathetic thing is that Dan didn't even love her."

"Then why did he do it?"

"Boredom, sex, anger." I shrug, staring past her at the clock.

Twenty minutes before I can escape.

"Okay, so let's go through the basics. Your husband was having an affair with your best friend for eight months?"

I nod, my stomach tightening.

"And you found out when?"

"Four months before it happened."

"It, being the night you claim you killed him."

"I did kill him," I remind her.

"Right, but you can't remember doing it." Disbelief crosses her face as I think back to the night I found out about Dan and Lucile.

It was one week before I discovered Wanderlust. The night Esme first appeared in my home, I was ready to leave. It took me some time, but I was ready, and had I not have moved through the mirror, I would've, but then things got harder. I met Nicholas, and I was afraid if I left then, I wouldn't be able to go back.

"How long had you and Lucile been friends?"

"Fifteen years." As the words blister my lips, I think back to all the times we'd chanted it, drunk on tequila and cheap wine. *Fifteen years* we would hiccup to one another, *fifteen years*.

Bitch. Bitch. Bitch.

"Had she always liked him?"

I roll my shoulders, because in all honesty, I had no idea if Lucile had always lusted after my husband, or if she decided to fuck him on the off chance because she was bored.

"And all this developed while she was employed as his secretary?"

I hide a smirk because I guess in some way, I was responsible. After all, I was the one who encouraged Dan to hire her. Lucile had been two months late on rent, and she joked she might have to take up escorting as an occupation. I'd laughed it off, but when I saw that glint in her eyes when she started going over how much money girls made each night, I suggested Gold Fires Publishing.

Lucile had basic admin experience, and Dan was overburdened with work. Seeing it as an opportunity for them both, I was beside myself wondering why I hadn't suggested it sooner. The only problem was, Dan didn't want to hire her. He refused outright, telling me he wouldn't employ someone so irresponsible, predicting all sorts of rubbish.

'She'll come in pissed, or fuck half the staff on the copy machine.'

I hated it when he spoke about her like that, hated him for not having the tiniest ounce of faith in her, then one day it was he who fucked her on the copy machine.

"Raine."

Eleven forty-five.

"I don't know if she always liked him."

"And you didn't say anything about the affair on the night you were arrested because?" Peters waits for an answer, and when no words arrive, she exhales, hitting me with a whiff of the coffee she'd wolfed down three hours earlier. "In Lucile's initial statement to the police, she claims she went to your home at 9.45pm and found you lying next to Dan in a pool of his blood, whispering to someone who wasn't there. Is that true?"

I nod.

"And that the reason she went there was because of a phone call you made from Dan's phone telling her you were in trouble?"

Again, I nod.

"This is the part I don't get. Why of all the people, would you call Lucile?"

"I didn't have anyone else."

"No one? Not a neighbour, or someone you used to work with? You didn't have anyone to could confide in?"

I shake my head with an itch in my heart I'm dying to scratch.

"Okay, so you asked for help from the person your husband was cheating on you with?"

I gnaw my lip, tasting the lie. My hands tremble under the desk, hands butchered moments before that phone call was made. I remember it clearly, but I can't tell Peters, I can't tell anyone but you, Mia. Dan and I were in my studio. I remember begging him to stop, pleading with him not to do it, but he wouldn't listen. Why didn't he listen?

He should've listened.

"In Lucile's initial statement she claimed she knew about the abuse, so if that was the case why did she continue having an affair with him?"

"Ask her."

I don't have to look up to know Peter's eyes have hardened.

"I'm asking you!" she retorts. "I'm defending you, and for what reason, I have absolutely no idea. Neither of you mentioned the affair until after it was brought to the officers' attention by Dan's colleague at Gold Fires."

She narrows her eyes in an effort to remember her name.

"Gillian, Gillian."

Her stubby fingers leaf through pages on the desk. Finding it, she bashes her hands against the table.

"Gillian Carpenter. The woman who told the police you made a scene at Dan's book launch when you thought Lucile and Dan were having an affair."

"They were," I point out.

"That's not the point. If Gillian hadn't spoken to the police, they wouldn't have interviewed Lucile's neighbours. Neighbours who identified Dan as the man who was regularly spotted at her flat."

She searches my face for a spark of discomfort. Giving her nothing, she lowers her gaze; a hunter dropping her rifle.

"I get why Lucile wouldn't want the police to know about the affair, Raine. Guilt, shame, Christ, even the idea of being implicated, but why wouldn't you?"

"It was my fault."

"Then why can't you tell me exactly what happened? You say the altercation began in your attic, but you can't remember why or what you were arguing about. You claim you called Lucile from Dan's phone because you needed help, evidence which is backed up by her phone record, but you can't remember anything after that, just that you woke up in his blood."

Rummaging through my steely persona for a glint of emotion. she glares at me.

"Is all that true?"

I nod.

"Then why don't I believe you?"

"You don't have to." Lifting my head, all I see is a middle-aged woman watching me pityingly.

Falling back in her seat, she rubs her eyes with both

hands.

"The night I was appointed to you, you told me the only reason you admitted to Dan's murder was because you were in shock," she reminds me. "You can't keep changing your mind. This isn't a game, Raine."

"You think I don't know that?"

"I think you're pretending not to care when really you're terrified."

"Of?"

"Losing."

"What if I've already lost?"

That brief proclamation is all it takes for Peters pity to flare up into rage.

"Why am I even here?" she cries. "Why am I even bothering to help you when you can't even be bothered to help yourself?"

I open my mouth to tell her it's because she's paid to when she smashes her fist on the table.

"Did you kill Dan because you were jealous?"

I shake my head.

"Then why did you do it?"

I duck, trying to stray from the truth, but my mind has already wandered back to that night. I see the fear in his eyes when he looked up at me, the desperation tangled in his gaping mouth. Blood oozing from the corner of his lips, and that question his eyes bought, that question I can never seem to shake.

After everything, how could you do this to me?

"I can't remember."

"Well try to," Peters hisses. "Because when your case does make it to trial, the prosecution will tear you apart. They'll mock you about the place you claimed you were going to, and paint you out as this jealous monster who stabbed her husband seven times because he was fucking her prettier friend."

I swallow, stung.

"Before the judge ordered your evaluation, why did you behave that way at your hearing? Was it because you believed the mental health facility would be better than prison?"

Biting the inside of my cheek, I shake my head.

"Then what was it?"

Focussing on the melting window, I urge my mind to stay in the box room, but Peters's husky voice is pulling me under, taking me back.

"Raine, what happened when you appeared before the magistrates?"

TICK. TICK. TICK.

"I heard you whispering to someone."

Clawing the bald patches on my scalp, I shudder as the memory rushes through my mind.

It was a few weeks ago; Peters was whispering something as the dark-skinned judge ran a disapproving look over me. For days, I'd told myself what I had to do. The plan, I had to stick to the plan, but then something changed. It was the first time I'd questioned the implications of what I was doing, and before I could tell Peters I needed to speak to her outside, I heard Esme.

"It was your fault he died, Raine," she hissed.

I flinched, reminding myself everything that happened in Wanderlust was over.

"Leave me alone," I whispered.

"You killed him."

"Shut up," I hissed. I smelt burning, that sharp whiff of melting flesh as I fought to make out the judge's voice.

"All those you have cared for have lost their lives at your hands, Raine," Esme hissed.

Grabbing hold of my face, I fought to untangle myself from her lies, but I couldn't Mia, because she was right.

And I knew that if I told the truth, you wouldn't stand a chance.

It was in that scathing moment I let go. I'd pounded my head against the desk and screamed until there was nothing left of me but a ball of atrophied energy, because I didn't want to give you up, nor could I risk hurting you as I'd hurt him.

It was the reason the judge ordered my evaluation. She had called for silence, but I wouldn't stop. Couldn't.

I blink away the memory, as Peters pulls a page out from her folder.

"A new witness came forward this morning."

"Who?"

"Your neighbour, Mr Thompson."

My heart scrambles as I glare at her.

"Wouldn't they have spoken to him first?"

"They were unable to reach him. Neighbours are the first to be interviewed, but after you confessed that night, they thought it was a done deal."

"And isn't it?"

She shakes her head, her lip sandwiched between her crooked teeth.

"Not when their main witness has been discredited. After lying about the affair, Lucile's statement can't be used in court."

"Why not?"

"She's an unreliable source."

"But I confessed."

"Under duress. And there are still questions that need answering before they can build a steady case against you."

"Questions like what?"

"Like Dan's phone going missing that night. Forensics, the clothes you were wearing, they were soaked in blood so they can't determine whether you issued the blow, but blood in the kitchen suggests if you did attack him, you left after."

"I did," I say without thinking.

"You told me you couldn't remember."

"I'm tired," I mutter hoping to shake off her questioning, but Peters is like a cannibal let loose in a strip club.

"Raine—"

"What happens if there isn't enough evidence?"

She watches me hesitantly, before lowering her voice.

"If your psychiatrists' report states you are mentally stable, you'll be released until the police can find something concrete."

"They can't." From the corner of my eye, I glimpse a light flick on in her brain.

"Who are you protecting Raine?"

I don't answer.

Jumping up, I shuffle over to the door where the warden is waiting with your name stitched against my lips Mia, because on the night Dan died, all I was doing was protecting you.

CHAPTER FIFTEEN

"How was your meeting with your solicitor, yesterday?" Pierce asks.

I stare back blankly, wondering how he expects me to divulge anything when he is so pent up on staying tight-lipped. After my meeting, I'd promised myself two things, Mia. The first, was that if Mr Thompson from next door had seen anything, I wouldn't argue or claim it was untrue. I'd simply let it play out as it was meant to because someone I once trusted told me that whatever was meant to happen, would happen anyway.

And the second, is not to utter a word in my evaluations unless Pierce bled the slightest bit like me.

"When are you going to tell me about your wife?"

"Yes, Elliot," Watson exhales. "When are you going to tell her?"

Pierce tugs the collar of his washed-out blue shirt.

"Did you have any headaches when you were going to these places?"

"When are—"

"In your last session with Doctor Watson, you claimed

you went back to Wanderlust?"

I stare at the perspiration glistening on his temples before turning to Watson.

"I didn't leave," I tell her.

AUGUST 29th 2018

I woke up with the earth smothering my face, and clumps of mud hanging from my hair. Jolting upright, I rubbed my eyes while my mind adjusted to the events of last night. I couldn't remember falling asleep, nor could I remember Nicholas leaving. Dragging my fingers through the tangle of my hair, I squeezed my eyes shut tight with the conversation from yesterday clanging about in my mind like the rusty wheels of an oncoming train.

My parents are dead, my husband doesn't love me, everything about me is basically pathetic.

I groaned.

I'd said too much, and Nicholas had barely even responded. What was I thinking? Lightheaded and in desperate need of caffeine, I peeked over my shoulder at the palace. Sunlight glinted from the glass panels, and as my eyes swept over the steps, my heart dipped. Marianne was waving me over. Why?

I chewed my lip. Was it too late to turn back? She thrust her arms frantically now that she knew I could see her. I exhaled, then, against every instinct urging me not to, I pulled myself up and started climbing the grassy mountain.

Keeping my head bent, I hoped my eyes weren't still swollen from the night before. Wiping them self-consciously I continued advancing towards the steps with the morning sun thumping away at my stale skin and my head heavy with doubt.

It was only after I reached the peak of the steps, I

realised Marianne would probably take me to see Nicholas, and I was in no fit state to be in the company of anyone, never mind Nicholas. Smoothing out the wrinkles in my muddy T-shirt, I was about to tell her I was fine staying put when she grabbed hold of my wrist.

I flinched as she pulled me inside. Half expecting Nicholas to pop out from somewhere and tell me he had enough to handle in the Kingdom, never mind my emotional burden, I raked over the place guardedly. The hall was just as ghostly as the woman tugging me forwards.

Exiting the hall, Marianne led me through the candlelit corridor, and up a narrow flight of steps I'd hadn't climbed. Beyond the staircase was a red velvet corridor. I narrowed my eyes at huge bay windows overlooking the spirit lake, before hurrying behind Marianne.

Halting outside of a large blue door at the end, her bloody shoulders turned to me as she pushed it open then waltzed inside. Following her, I gasped.

Surrounding me was a dazzling chamber wrapped in deep mahogany bookshelves stretching so high, and so far, that their ends were out of sight. Padding into the belly of the library, I threw back my head, staring up at a tight corkscrew staircase winding up to a bright skylight window where sunlight poured through the porthole, highlighting an identical floor above us.

I spun around, ogling the place breathlessly, inhaling the rich perfume of ink, and philosophies, and dusty tales when a mighty clanking sound snapped me out from my trance. Scanning the hall, I heard it coming from Marianne. She'd stopped a few yards away from me, facing a bookshelf.

Inching past hardbacks swathed in leather and fine embroidery, I screwed up my face as she ran a finger alongside the spine of a book. A titanic whoosh of smoke burst from the shelf ahead of me, and when the smoke began to clear, the books began disintegrating.

"What is—"

Revving up her shoulders, Marianne wiggled her behind then flew neck first into the bookcase, then disappeared. I flinched as her fingers sprung out from the buttery break, indicating for me to follow.

Studying her short fingernails, I stepped back, certain wherever this passage led, was bound to bring me face to face with Nicholas. I hung my head with all of the reasons he might've wanted to see me trampling over my heart: To tell me to leave, to tell me he was sorry about my past but he didn't have time for any more sob stories.

Thumping a grubby fist against my thigh, I shook my head. If Nicholas had asked Marianne to bring me here to end whatever nonsense we had between us, it was better to know now. Squaring up my shoulders, I took a blind leap of faith, and after making it inside, I released a desperate whimper.

The passage led to a hall that was colossal, bursting with light from the floor to ceiling windows to my right. Squinting around, I softened from the warmth flooding in from the glass. Lined up ahead of me, twisting up to a thick archway coated in onyx were a jungle of thick gold pillars.

I hugged my chest. The patter of Marianne's footsteps broke the silence as she headed towards a long mahogany table in front of the window with a view of the lake. I bit my lip when she took her seat facing four creatures. Creatures I wasn't able to make out with the gold light streaming in from the glass.

Tilting my head, I looked closer, squinting.

"Breakfast," Nicholas called in a voice that reduced me to dust.

Breakfast? Nicholas had invited me here to have breakfast? Palming my forehead, I wondered what had prompted this invitation. And why couldn't he have collected me himself?

Tempted to make a run for it, I turned to the gap I'd come from. The back of my neck moistened. The hole had closed up. In its place, was a magnolia wall. The only other door was on the other side of the hall, and that meant I'd have to slip past the creatures.

Chewing my lip, I lugged myself forwards. The hot aroma of silky blueberry muffins filled the trenched of my stomach as I pressed myself to keep moving, and play it cool. No mentioning what happened last night. No making a fool of myself.

Making it halfway, I stopped, questioning what good could come from having breakfast with Nicholas, especially after yesterday, especially in the company of others, especially caked in mud. Someone cleared their throat. The sound just loud enough to kick my legs into gear.

Driving myself to go the rest of the way, I sunk into the seat next to Marianne. Nicholas faced me. Unable to meet his eye just yet, I peered to his left, where Candimore sat with his reedy little elbows stapled to the table. Offering my warmest smile, my forehead sagged when he flared his nostrils then turned so briskly, I imagined it stung his neck.

Curbing my disappointment, I turned to the creature next to him. Speckled grey skin and a long hoary trunk smothered his face. Noting my disbelief, the elephant man bobbed his head, making two huge ears flap over his face like a wrinkled canopy.

Stunned, I turned to Nicholas's right, where a creature with the head of a fox watched me through slanted amber eyes. Jiggling his head, he ran his claws through untidy puffs of red fur on his neck before I turned to the final creature at the end and gasped.

"It's you," I whispered.

"It is," Morgana smiled. "It's a pleasure to see you again, Raine."

"Likewise," I muttered, questioning what she was doing there, then what I was doing there. Clawing my palms, I wondered if I should ask when Morgana she gestured to the fox with a grey paw.

"I believe you haven't been introduced to Theodore, Thistleturf, Three."

"Pleasure to make your acquaintance," the fox exclaimed, raising a wet nose.

"And over there is Petegril, Noseback, Five," she said.

"Delighted, really," the trunked creature giggled in a voice that sounded like he was getting over a cold.

"And of course, you have already met Candimore Repsil, Two, and Marianne, Flemgril, Six."

I bobbed my head at the panel, wishing Nicholas would speak. Had he expected me to come to breakfast looking this dreadful? Perhaps he'd wanted me to decline. Still not quite prepared to see any glimmer of truth in his eyes, I studied the table.

Placed on a white tablecloth, were hundreds of silver bowls containing mountains of fruit that appeared to be the wrong colour and size. I widened my eyes at apples the colour of midnight, wine coloured bananas, indigo strawberries, before realising I hadn't introduced myself.

"I am—"

"We know who you are, Raine," Theodore interrupted. "King Nicholas has told us all about you."

"He has?" From the corner of my eye, I saw Nicholas drop his head.

"Are you hungry?" Morgana asked.

"Slightly." My cheeks coloured when I gathered they'd probably heard my stomach growling.

"Well then," Morgana sang. "You must dig in."

I nodded, ready to gorge on the mountain of mutant fruits when Marianne snatched the plate in front of me and ushered me to stay sitting with her bloody shoulders.

"Do tell us, Raine," Theodore said as Marianne piled up my plate. "What is your kind like?"

"My kind?"

"Humans!" Petegril exclaimed.

I was about to tell them humans were pretty much the same as them when Theodore asked:

"What do they do?"

"What do you do?" Petegril inquired.

"Where I come from people have jobs," I replied, not quite sure of who to address. "And I guess I paint."

"You paint."

"She does."

"I do," I said into the ping pong of voices, before mouthing my thanks to Marianne as she handed me a plate cluttered in a rainbow of fruits.

"Ah yes, I have seen your work, simply magnificent," Theodore kissed his fingers.

Glancing up to thank him, I saw him staring at something behind me. Pretty soon all of the creatures were looking. Even Marianne had swerved around. Following their stance, I felt nostalgia flutter through my gut like a crippled butterfly.

Cemented into the golden waves of the wall, was the portrait I'd painted of Nicholas. It was tiny in the distance. A Polaroid snapshot of the past. It seemed so long ago I'd painted it. Since then, nothing and everything had changed. I wondered how often he used the dining hall. Then, if there was a reason he'd chosen to place it there.

"Are all of the creatures in your world monstrous?" Theodore asked.

"Monstrous?" I questioned, turning back.

Theodore nodded.

"There's good and bad in everyone I guess."

"Quite right, quite right," he agreed. "And is it true you have creatures strapped up for transport?"

"Strapped up?"

From down the table, I saw Petegril miming a carriage action, and I realised all of their assumptions about humans must have come from Nicholas's mother. A woman with a grudge against the very thing she was. A woman from another era. Which era? How old did that make Nicholas?

I rubbed the mud on my wrist before taking a sip from the goblet Marianne had placed in front of me. The liquid was hot, smooth and it rippled through my nerves with the same sort of bounty as caffeine. Supping, and gulping, and trying my best not to spill any of the sweet potion onto the dainty white tablecloth, my ears gradually adjusted to the honeyed conversation pouring alongside me.

"If they don't use bubbles, how do they travel?" Theodore asked.

"They fly!" Petegril exclaimed.

"How do they fly when they don't have wings?"

"I heard some do."

I blinked, a little brighter.

"Well, actually we drive cars," I told them.

Petegril and Theodore stared back blankly.

"Cars?" Theodore asked.

"Cars?" repeated Petegril.

"Cars," they chanted.

Morgana shook her head apologetically.

"Or buses, or trains. They're vehicles. We drive them."

"Drive? You mean you don't use bubbles?"

I shook my head.

"Are cars satisfactory for flying?"

"Cars don't fly, they are driven… on roads."

"But how can you assure you won't cause damage to the creatures on paths?"

"Road safety?" I offered.

Both were stunned to silence as I picked up what appeared to be a sapphire apple. Biting hard into the syrupy centre, an unintentional moan burst from my lips. Slapping my hands across my mouth, my cheeks flamed as they gawped at me.

"Is there a problem?" Theodore asked.

"This… this, doesn't taste like an apple," I managed, sweating even more now I knew Nicholas was watching.

"An apple?" Theodore whispered. "That's because it's spiced custard soup."

Morgana nodded for me to take another bite, and after a moment of hesitation, I did. The apple – or soup rather – was rich and thick and creamy and slapped my taste buds with the realisation they'd been asleep for the past twenty-seven years, and after demolishing the odd treat, I picked up another, a little lighter.

"If you don't mind," I asked, dabbing the corner of my mouth with a napkin. "I would like to know more about your kingdom."

"What would you like to know?" Morgana asked.

"Well, what do you all do?"

"I am head of authorities," Theodore declared.

"And I am in charge of welfare in the first to the fifth region," Morgana told me.

"And there are eight regions?"

Morgana nodded.

"Are you head of all authorities?" I asked Theodore.

"Unfortunately not," he answered. "At this present moment, I am head of authorities of the sixth region. Though, at some point, I would like to be considered." His yellowish-brown eyes slipped to Nicholas who still hadn't looked up from his empty plate.

"And what do you do?" I asked Petegril while he studied a burgundy plum in his palms as if it were about to evaporate. Silence stampeded around us, and when

Petegril gathered I was addressing him, his entire trunk quivered.

"Oh," he gasped, slamming the plum into the table. "I… I run a small market stall, collecting and distributing unicorn tears."

"Fascinating," I breathed.

"It thinks that is fascinating," Candimore sneered. The insult made Petegril's face turn a shade darker than the plum.

"It is," I said, irritated by Candimore's remark. Hadn't he been taught to keep quiet if he had nothing nice to say? "How do you collect them?"

"We read them stories," Petegril replied.

"Stories? What kinds of stories?"

"Real ones, about love and death and betrayal."

"And they cry?"

"Oh yes, bucket loads. A good story has the power to evoke the deepest of emotions. Words in my opinion, are the most magical substance in existence. The right words can do all sorts of things you'd never expect. They can educate, and enchant, they can trick and beguile you, or they can simply remind you of moments you thought were dead and buried, and all that starts from something as simple as a drop of ink. If that's not magic, what is?"

I peeked across at Nicholas who still hadn't looked up. Lines around his furrowed brow deepened as he stooped lower. Was he annoyed at me for asking questions? If he was, why had he invited me here in the first place?

I thought better of prying, I'd enjoy the morning and remain unaffected by his bizarre silences.

"So how do you get the tears to change colour?" I asked Petegril.

"Ah, you see the greater the story, the better the quality of tears. A poorly written tale will result in a batch of cloudy green tears, whereas a truly magnificent tale will create the most delicious gold tears one could only dream of tasting. I have the privilege of sampling every batch that passes through the farm."

Bobbing my head, I watched Petegril pick up the plum he'd bashed into the table. Holding it to his trunk, he released an almighty sneeze then vanished.

I widened my eyes at the place he'd been sitting.

"Sorry!" came his voice.

I continued staring as the outline of his bulky chest materialised, his stippled grey face, his wrinkled ears. My forehead dampened. Petegril had disappeared, and now, slowly but surely, he was re-emerging.

"Hate it when that happens," he sniffed.

"It's his gift," Morgana said, detecting my concern.

"His gift?" I asked, ogling Petegril, spooning handfuls of oranges into his trunk. "Do all creatures have gifts?"

"Some," Morgana replied. "Others use magic."

"Magic?"

"Prohibited substances banned from Wanderlust."

"What are—"

"Fairy dust," Theodore interrupted.

"And dragons' blood," Petegril added. "Creatures inject it."

"Why?"

They gawped at me as if I was mad.

"The rush," Theodore exhaled.

"Creatures believes it brings immortality," Morgana explained.

"And can it?"

"On certain creatures, but for the remainder, the effects are weaker. They breathe fire, gain strength, but eventually, their energy levels deplete, and they age considerably."

I shook my head, still trying to digest the information.

"Magic is banned from Wanderlust," Morgana added.

"It is stolen from creatures in a vile fashion and sold on the black-market stall, but gifts, creatures are born with and encouraged to practice."

"Theodore can shapeshift," Petegril announced.

I stole a look at Theodore.

"Show her," Morgana said.

"Do I have to?" Theodore whined.

"Yes, show her!" Petegril exclaimed.

More than ready to tell Theodore it was fine, I stopped when he rolled his eyes, sucked a thumb, and less than a second later, I was staring back at a mirror image of myself.

Pressing my palms into the table, I hunched lower, staring at a woman with stretched brown eyes on a pale face. Theodore had even managed to highlight the mud on my neck.

"It's terribly embarrassing," he said in his voice.

"Freaky," I muttered, and before I had a chance to ask anything more about these gifts, Nicholas laughed.

I peered up warily. It was the first time I'd looked at Nicholas properly since last night. It felt as though he'd peeled back my skin. My face flamed as his gaze scoured mine. Gold eyes shimmering on a face just shy of home. I wanted to say something, anything, to thank him for inviting me to breakfast, or for listening to me last night, but I couldn't find the right words. I could never seem to find the right words. About to look away, I caught him mouth,

"Are you okay?"

I nodded shakily.

Nicholas smiled.

I smiled.

Catching the exchange, Candimore thumped his fist into the table.

"This is an abomination!" he shouted, glowering at me. "This thing does not belong here, and all of you all sit here humouring the idea it may be welcome, teaching it our customs and equipping it with knowledge it may use against us."

"Calm down, Candimore," Morgana said, but Candimore looked as if he was about to burst into flames.

"You should all be ashamed of yourself!"

Pushing back in my seat, I had half a mind to ask what his problem was, but I couldn't, not when the creatures had offered me their hospitality. In an effort not to appear rude, I decided to leave when Nicholas spoke in a voice a crumb louder than a whisper.

"It's you who should be ashamed of yourself Candimore," he said.

My gut knotted as I watched the veins in his forehead bulging while he frowned at the table.

"Raine is our guest, and I'd appreciate it if you treated her that way."

"Our guest?" Candimore sneered. "It is a human. It needs to leave."

"Why?" I mumbled, shocking myself.

"I'll tell you why," Candimore spat, scowling at me with his chin touching the table. Before a single word could make it to his bloodless lips, Nicholas cut in.

"Leave, Candimore."

Candimore's face fell as his eyes darted to Nicholas.

"But Master, you're making a mistake. You're satisfying your own perverse desires if you could just—"

"Now," Nicholas growled.

With that I witnessed all of the treacherous things Candimore wanted to say, sink to the pit of his stomach. Lowering my head, I waited for Candimore to hurl some insult at me, or to fly over the table and drag me outside. Instead, he marched off to a large white door at the end of the hall.

On reaching it, Candimore watched Nicholas from

over his shoulder. Only he didn't look at him with rage or embarrassment as I'd expected. Instead, all I glimpsed in his eyes was a deep unfathomable sadness.

"Be it on you whatever pain this creature inflicts," Candimore muttered.

The sun from the windows burnt my cheeks as the door slammed shut. Dipping my head, I struggled to work out what on Earth Candimore was talking about. I knew humans were banned from Wanderlust, but the attack seemed somewhat personal. I huffed, so immersed in my thoughts that when Nicholas called my name, I flinched, uttered a sound, then masked it with a cough.

"You said you wanted to learn more about Wanderlust," Nicholas continued. "Would you like to accompany me to the second region?"

"Right now?"

Nicholas nodded.

Confounded about how Nicholas had come about this idea, I hung my head. Also, there was the issue of me being barefoot and covered in mud. On the precipice of refusing, I caught Morgana's eye from across the table.

"Go," she mouthed.

I looked back at Nicholas.

His lips were pressed together, his eyes glittered with apprehension. He seemed more anxious than I'd ever seen him, and I knew I couldn't let him down, not in front of these creatures, not at all really.

"Okay," I muttered.

Leaping up from his seat, Nicholas left no room for me to point out I was barefoot as he headed for the door Candimore had disappeared behind.

"Wonderful to meet you, Raine."

"Do enjoy."

"Farewell for now," the creatures all said at once.

Mumbling my goodbyes, I raced after Nicholas,

expecting to see him on the other side of the corridor when I made it through the door. Barging through the entry, I paused when I saw him peeling off his suit jacket in a wide sunlit corridor.

"Here," Nicholas said, offering the jacket. "I thought you might like this."

"What for?"

Nicholas pulled a face at my muddy t-shirt.

"You can stay dressed in that if you like."

I blushed, allowing him to shrug it over my shoulders.

"Thanks," I said. The jacket was warm, heavy, and it smelt of spring, and before I had a chance to ask where Nicholas wanted to take me, he took hold of my wrist and started running.

"Why are we running?" I gasped.

"Because you might leave soon."

"And so, we have to run?"

"And so, we will have more time to explore."

I laughed. The sound came so unexpectedly; it made me laugh harder. I didn't know why I was laughing. What Nicholas said wasn't even remotely funny, but I guess it's the simple things that tickle your heart and leave you breathless, Mia. No forced puns or rehearsed lines, only an unexpected burst of wonder and suddenly the world is smiling.

I stole a look at him. He was the same but different. He still had that edge of seriousness, but the more time I spent with him, the more I felt that edge scuffed out, with the real him pouring from its fractures. I knew I liked him then. I'm not sure why, or how, or even when it had happened, just that being around him felt like going on an adventure even when we were standing completely still.

Moments later, he released my arm and jogged down the spiral staircase.

"Where are we going?" I asked, marching through the

entrance door as he gallivanted into the pastel field.

"You'll see," Nicholas called.

"Nicholas!" I shouted, but he was too far away to turn back.

Stopping a few yards from me, he dipped his head to the space where he held a canister. Hurrying down the steps, a part of me was afraid I might disappear. I had already stayed overnight, and even that was a push. Would he have cared?

Joining Nicholas's side, I forced a shaky smiled as he brought the stick to his lips. He blew, once, twice, and on the third attempt, I flew back in awe of the bubble that broke through the gap.

"Ready?" Nicholas called.

I forced my head up and down because I couldn't be anything but ready. In no time at all, I mirrored Nicholas as he darted forwards. Staggering sideways when a mighty plunking sound rung in my ears, I unglued my eyes then grinned.

We were inside.

I almost wanted to do a happy dance, but my nerves decided against it. In an endeavour to not appear as terrified as I was, I placed my hands against the warbling surface then shimmied forward until my back was pressed against the thin layer.

Nicholas had already taken his seat opposite me. His forehead was furrowed. His eyes, unfocussed, and as we rushed through a silver sheet of clouds, I worried he might be over what happened last night.

"Listen, Nicholas," I croaked, the sun scorching the back of my neck. "About last night, I was really upset. I'm not always like that. I'm really embarrassed by the whole thing if you could just—"

"Do you feel better?"

My lips puckered as his eyes met mine.

Despite spending the night beside the lake, the truth

was I did feel better, Mia. Last night was the first time I'd released all of the pain I had no idea I'd been carrying around for years. For the most part, I felt lighter.

"I guess so."

"Good," Nicholas replied.

"Good? How is it good? You barely even responded and—"

"Did you want me to?"

"Some reassurance would've been nice."

"I told you, you would be okay."

"And you seriously think that?"

"I know it."

"You don't think I'm vile?"

Nicholas's eyes flicked to mine in alarm.

"Vile?"

"Horrid, a mess, a wreck," I listed.

"I told you I think you're brave."

"And you still think that?"

"Why wouldn't I?"

I shook my head, trying to silence all of my niggling insecurities, but they were flooding my mind at a staggering speed until I was left with no choice but to spit them out.

"I don't know. I just assumed you'd think I was crazy."

Nicholas's face loosened as he inclined his head, staring at me with those earl grey tea eyes.

"You're not crazy Raine," he said. "There is no such thing as crazy. Some creatures are just a little more awake than others, you should—"

"I should what?"

Nicholas sighed, studying his hands.

"You should have a little more faith in yourself is all." His words came at me like a terrific punch to the heart. Judging by his face; I think he felt them connect too.

Dropping my gaze, I changed the subject.

"Were those your friends in the palace?"

"Colleagues," Nicholas grunted. "They were there for business."

"What kind of business?"

"Issues that need addressing in the kingdom."

"Issues such as?"

"Such as poverty in the sixth region, the growing distribution of fairy dust in the fourth, regions that require more safety, more land, more everything."

"So what's your role in all of this?"

"Well, I'm the king."

"No, I mean what do you do on a day to day basis?"

Looking up, I could tell he was embarrassed.

"Mainly I just have to be present," he said.

"And if you're not?"

"Well then, the world will fall to pieces." Registering my confusion, Nicholas shook his head at his knees. "Nothing," he admitted. "Nothing would happen, Raine."

I bit my lip, wondering why Nicholas was so hard on himself. He always seemed to be beating himself up for something. Watching him, I questioned if it was the right time to mention what had happened with Candimore when the bubble came to a sharp halt in the middle of nowhere.

"Here," Nicholas said.

The back of my neck moistened as I glanced at him, wide-eyed. Moments later, my heart plunged when we dipped through miles of clouds. I shuddered. The drop made my ears pop, and my head spin, and my heart roar. Peeking through the gaps of my fingers, I saw Nicholas slanting the tip of the blade.

Fighting to drag myself up, I stood uneasily as he angled the tip. A deafening explosion followed. The sound stung my ears, and when my eyes adjusted to the place where Nicholas had brought me, I shook my head in amazement.

We stood on the peak of a twinkling mountain, transcending high above the world and stretching out for miles. Blanketing the ground was a formation of tiny silver rocks. Shimmering flecks singed my toes as I threw back my head, staring at the sky that was the deepest shade of coral I'd ever seen.

"It's Stardust," Nicholas said.

From over my shoulder, I saw him watching me in the same way I was watching the world.

"Creatures believe it's the place dreams begin."

Hopping over to the edge of the cliff, I peered down. Thousands of miles below the misty hemisphere were clear cut sections shaped like a star. Grey, and yellow, and red, and indigo segments filling my chest with a sense that everything was possible.

My lips trembled as I took in the scene. For so long I'd speculated the meaning of true beauty, Mia. I'd painted pictures depicting lush forests, scenic landscapes, magical side streets. I'd worked for hours, adding delicate brushstrokes, and carefully placed shadows.

Though, as I gazed into the world, I understood true beauty wasn't something that couldn't be captured on a canvas. It had to be felt. I felt it then, I felt it so terrifically my heart was uncoiling like a tightly wound spring stretched at both sides.

"This is… this is breath-taking," I whispered. With the sun ripping through me, I slid off Nicholas's jacket then pointed to nowhere in particular. "Are those regions of the kingdom?" Swerving around, I saw him striding over to me. Moments later he buckled down with his knees dangling off the edge of the cliff.

"So, this is Wanderlust," I said, taking a seat next to him.

"The mountain is hundreds of thousands of years old," Nicholas explained. "It's the place it all began. They say the universe overheated, causing the brightest star in the galaxy to combust, and in its destruction, Wanderlust was created."

"Sort of like the Big Bang theory?"

Glancing sideways, I couldn't help laugh. If expressions were punctuation Nicholas's would be a question mark.

"So how does it work?"

Once more, Nicholas turned to me bewildered.

"You said it's the place dreams begin or is that just a myth?"

Nicholas's focus dipped to his knees.

"Legend claims that if a creature takes a handful of Stardust while focusing on the thing they desire most, after blowing, the dust scatters into the world and sprinkles everything with opportunity."

"Do you believe it?"

The question seemed to startle him. His lips puckered as he wrinkled his brow.

"I believe we control our own fate," he said.

"So, you don't believe in destiny, or divine intervention, or that everything happens for a reason?"

"I think…" Lifting his head, he inspected the sky distrustfully. "I think the choices in life we make are our own. The mistakes, the accomplishments, the ventures, every big decision belongs to us, and whatever happens after, is up to fate. We trust the universe not because we want to, but because we have to. It's a joint effort. If we want something, we must learn to give and not just take."

"Can I make a wish?"

When Nicholas looked at me all I saw was a man battered by hope.

"And what would you wish for?" he questioned.

I blushed because the first answer that sprang to mind was him. To stay in Wanderlust came next. To start

299

again. To forget the past and live like this. Absorbing treasures in a world next to someone who listened, and as the sand scorched my palms, and my cheeks raged, I realised Nicholas was knotted into every single one of my outlandish wishes.

Nicholas lifted a brow, and before he could push for an answer I was too embarrassed to give, I brought a fistful of dust to my mouth, watched him decisively, took a deep breath and blew.

I blew hard and fast, thinking of art, and the past, and Dan, and Nicholas, with every desire fluttering through my head like an uproarious kite against a crystal sky, and when I peeked back at Nicholas, I saw him watching the dots scatter into the world wistfully.

"Nicholas," I said gently. "If you had a wish what would it be?"

"Does it matter?"

"Why wouldn't it?"

"Because wishes are for people with hope, Raine."

"And you don't have hope?"

"It's not that I don't have hope. It's just that the thing I would wish for is something I can never take back."

"Which is?"

"Does it really matter?"

"Well actually, it does."

"Why?"

My jaw trembled as I eyeballed the shimmering flecks of dust, searching for an answer that wouldn't come.

"Why would you care to know about a past belonging to a monster?"

"Why would you call yourself that?"

"Because I am."

"How?"

"What makes you think I'm not?"

"Because I just don't see it!"

My heart tremored as Nicholas's face softened.

Watching his broken expression, I realised it would've been easier to believe he was a monster – convenient even. But I couldn't, not because I didn't want to, but because of the slips of kindness he'd shown me. He had saved me at the market, stood up for me at breakfast, and now he had taken me to this magical place after everything I'd confessed to last night, and he was still looking at me in that exact same way.

Nothing between us had changed. And for the first time in longer than I could remember, I was grateful.

"Regardless of whatever mistake you've made, believing you're a monster won't rectify it, Nicholas. It just makes you a coward," I told him. "You said you believe you control your own fate, so control this. Stop wasting your life existing in a way that stops you from living and enjoy what we have now."

"I did something bad," Nicholas muttered. "Something that can never be forgiven."

"Well then, start by forgiving yourself."

Nicholas opened his mouth when I raised a brow. Part of me expected him to look away, but instead, he stared right back at me. His gold eyes inflamed with thought, his strong jaw shivering.

"You make it seem so easy," he said.

"What?"

"Life," he replied.

And just as I was about to tell Nicholas my problem was exactly that, he allowed the truth to spill into five simple words.

"You make me happy, Raine."

My cheeks stung as I looked away, struggling to hide the truth that Nicholas made me happy too, happier than I'd been in a long time, maybe ever. I pursed my lips as the sun crashed against my shoulders, and my insides raged with uncertainty. Being around Nicholas, made me feel something I just couldn't feel with Dan.

Nicholas watched me with history, and Dan, well Dan could barely look me in the eye.

"Here," Nicholas said.

Tearing my focus from the sky, I saw Nicholas offering the canister we'd used moments before.

"If you decide to come back, this will take you to the palace. I want – need, to show you something, and then can you make up your mind as to whether or not I can be forgiven."

Taking hold of the cold metallic canister, I silenced the urge to ask Nicholas what he wanted to show me. I didn't want to know the truth, not yet anyway. All I wanted was to enjoy the silence a little longer. Gazing ahead at black dips in the earth, between great creases of blue and gold, I flinched when Nicholas did something that surprised me, Mia.

He took hold of my hand.

Peeking over my shoulder, I saw him staring ahead at the world with a muscle in his jaw twitching, and for the first time since meeting him, I was terrified. Not of his past, or mine, but of the future, because something between us changed at that moment. I felt it in the way he held my hand. I felt it in the way he watched the world, and I knew whatever happened after that day, my heart would never be the same.

***

"It didn't bother you that Dan was sleeping with your best friend?" Watson interrogates.

"It got easier. When Dan was with Lucile, he left me alone. I just wanted to be alone."

"Raine," Pierce sighs. "This person you keep mentioning, this creature, Nicholas, he wasn't real."

Gritting my teeth, I glare at him sitting there all fake smiles and diagnoses.

"Do you know how frustrating it is to feel so much,

and have people claim it wasn't real?"

"We're not saying it wasn't real to you Raine—"

"You're telling me it didn't happen!"

"In reality—"

"Reality?" I force an ugly laugh. "Doesn't everyone's reality differ?"

"Raine, was Dan ever violent to you?"

"He was real."

"Raine, we need total honesty. Was Daniel ever abusive?"

"When I went home, I still had the canister—"

"Raine—"

"I had the canister, and I knew it was real because he held my hand, and—"

"Raine, was Dan ever violent?"

"No!"

Silence falls between us, and I'm certain I hear Pierce curse.

"What happened the night Dan was murdered, Raine?"

I look up at their hesitant faces. Dan thought I was crazy too, he thought I was making it up, he shouldn't have tried stopping me. He would've still been alive if he hadn't tried stopping me.

"I told him about Nicholas."

CHAPTER SIXTEEN

Going through the door, my immediate thought is to take back what I said yesterday. I shouldn't have told them Dan never hurt me. I should've stuck to my story. If I wanted to pull this off, I had to stick to my story. Making my way into the tight box room, I am more than ready to rectify my mistakes when I see two officers sitting side by side.

The first, is a silver-haired woman with steel eyes and a nose shaped like a broken arm. The second, a much younger officer whose acne serves to make him look like a boy forever trapped in puberty. In the middle is Peters, who when I move closer, see is grinning from ear to ear.

"Raine," she sings in a voice one might use to address an old friend they weren't expecting.

"What is it?" I ask, getting straight to the point. A tactic which seems to be preferred by the female offer who doesn't waste time answering.

"As you may or may not be aware, your neighbour Mr Thompson came forward a few days ago," she informs me in a voice as silver as her face. "And his statement has given the police reason to believe you may not have been responsible for the attack on your husband."

I force another nod, though this one feels ragged.

"Recent evidence has come to light that could exonerate—"

"What evidence?"

They glance between themselves, but no one answers.

"What evidence?" I ask louder.

"We're not at liberty to discuss that with you at this present moment Ms Black," the male officer pipes in.

"You're not at liberty to discuss the evidence that may lead to my release?"

No one answers.

"I don't understand. You found me with him, he was…I was—" Peters raises a hand.

"Raine, you told the police you couldn't remember what happened," she reminds me.

"It's not right. I can't—"

"Ms Black, you can't be charged for a crime unless we have concrete evidence to suggest you were culpable…"

I bite my lip until I taste blood. They keep mentioning this evidence, but no one is divulging what Mr Thompson had told them.

"Nicholas wanted to show me something," I whisper.

"Raine," Peters laughs. "The officers have come to tell you something important."

"He should've told me sooner. If he really cared for me, he should've told me the truth."

"Raine—"

"I should never have gone back."

SEPTEMBER 3rd 2018

It took nine attempts of blowing into the stick before I

was tucked inside of the bubble. Staring down at the neat slices of reds, and golds, and indigos, I nursed my arm. Despite the stick appearing slight, it was hefty, and angling and blowing at the same time had proved strenuous. By the fourth attempt, I'd managed to get the liquid to quiver, but when the bubble burst through the stick, I'd wasted far too much time admiring it before it coasted off without me.

Knowing I had to act quickly, I'd blown hard and fast, and after a few more unsuccessful shots I'd leapt off after the bubble, then jigged in triumph when I saw I'd made it inside. Relaxing a little, I gazed at the heavy pink sky, shattered with breaks of golden red. It was silent without Nicholas. Even if he did spend most of his time wrapped in silence, his lack of company was palpable.

Wrinkling my brow, I tried to distract myself from the rowdy stillness, but every so often my mind would skate back to him. What did he want to show me? What could he have done that would make me believe he was a monster?

Forcing a shaky smile, I convinced myself nothing he could've done would be that bad, but the truth was far worse than I could've imagined, Mia. It took around fifteen minutes before the bubble began lowering to a familiar patch of land. Peeking through the bubbles sheer layer, I glimpsed the spirit lake, the palace, then Nicholas.

I chewed the inside of my cheek. He was sitting at the bottom of the stairs, looking the way I imagined an officer might, moments before delivering news to a mother that her children had perished in a house fire.

Gripping hold of the knife I'd stowed away from my kitchen, I stood then poked the bubble as it came to a halt on the ground. It slipped. My cheeks flamed, and when I tried again, I missed. I bit my lip. Nicholas was already lumbering forwards and I was still trapped inside the bubble.

Wiping my brow, I focussed on the spectrum of colours glistening from the bubble's curve. The last time Nicholas had popped the bubble, all he did was poke the shell. With my tongue compressed between my teeth, I jabbed the foamy layer furiously. This time the blade connected, and before I could lug it down, I was walloped by an almighty explosion.

"Sorry!" I gasped, stumbling out and nearly knocking Nicholas over.

Nicholas shrugged but didn't speak.

Standoffish as he always was, there was something different about him that day. I thought he might mention the bubbles that had arrived without me, or maybe congratulate me on getting to the palace in one piece, but when his eyes darted to the lake, I knew something between us was about to change.

Looking at him was like turning the last page of a cherished book, or taking the final sip from a treasured bottle of whiskey, and all I wanted was to hold on to the moment a little longer.

"How was your journey?" he asked the lake.

"Fine," I replied, handing him the canister.

"Are you ready?" he asked, shoving it inside of his trouser pocket.

Whacked by an urge to shout NO, my stomach turned. No, I wasn't ready. No, I didn't want this to be the end, because without him the world was much too silent. I wanted to refuse to follow him, to ask him to leave whatever monsters he had buried inside of his chest. But I knew if those monsters were bottled up for too long, they had a special way of tearing you apart from the inside out, and so for Nicholas's sake more than my own, I forced a nod.

Mumbling an inaudible grunt, Nicholas spun around, marching up the palace steps with the sound of his soles

hitting concrete, matching the rhythm of my heart —
Thump, thump, thump.

Seconds later we were trudging up the spiral staircase.
Following Nicholas, I hoped he might change his mind,
maybe suggest exploring the rest of the kingdom, or go
back to the mountain where we could spend the evening
littering the universe in Stardust, but instead he moved
briskly.

Veering past the bedroom I believed was his, we
headed north through the arctic passages and hallways,
clambering up flight after flight of stairs until we
reached a wide stone corridor in what I believed to be
the highest point of the palace.

Certain this was it, I took in a single red door at the
end. Its rust panels were buried under plump wooden
roses and vines that sprouted out wildly into the walls.
Nicholas stopped outside of the door. Creeping over to
him, I watched his fingers fumble over the iron bolted
lock.

Preparing myself for all sorts of wretched scenes taking
place beyond the timber, I held my breath, imagining
flogged bodies hanging from the ceiling, human hearts
rotting in glass cases, the flesh of decapitated animals
littering the ground like carpet.

I closed my eyes, the door unclicked. Unpeeling them,
I watched Nicholas inch into a shower of tepid white
and when he disappeared completely, I slinked inside
the room, then gasped. He'd brought me to a garden, a
sunny little paradise swathed in miles and miles of
flowers.

They were everywhere; piles shot up from the grey
cobbled ground. Others towered high in huge gold
flowerpots. Some stretched almost ten feet tall; the rest
were sprinkled across the floor in blankets of gold dust.
Hovering in the doorway, I stared up at the roofless
ceiling where sunlight poured through and set fire to a

tight emerald pond in the centre.

Astonished, I made my way into the heart of the garden. Shifting through the perfumed scent of fresh fields, and budding daisies, I halted next to Nicholas. With his eyes set on the cobbled floor, he clung to the frame of a rusted swing set with feral roses tangled against its spine.

"This place…" As soon as the words left my mouth, I heard something rustle. A glance over my shoulder told me we were alone, but the rustling soon grew louder, building itself up into to a wave of crumpled patter, until we were surrounded by what sounded like a thunderstorm of invisible locusts.

My lips parted as the swing chain creaked. I inclined my head when I heard a drawn-out screech, followed by a sigh, then a yawn, and when I understood what was happening, I threw a hand over my mouth.

The flowers were coming to life. Some appeared half picked; decapitated and shrivelled, others were in full bloom, turning their fat heads and groaning. They were whispering – each one, begging to be picked like a classroom full of eager children. I widened my eyes at Nicholas when a stray dahlia bashed its furry head against my leg.

"Pick me," it cried.

"What is this place?" I choked, skulking away from the writhing flower.

"A memory garden," Nicholas replied.

"A what?"

"A place used for storing memories. When a creature wishes to capture an event, they plant a seed reflecting the pastime, and when the seed has reached full growth, a flower will bloom."

"And then what?"

"And then, when the petal is plucked it will take you to the memory."

"Take you there, you mean you can actually see it?"

Nicholas nodded, and after catching my breath, it dawned on me that Nicholas hadn't brought me here to admire this alien garden, but to show me something he'd done.

My face fell as I scanned the thick vines springing out from the walls, twisting their plump green heads and climbing up to the sky.

"So, every flower holds a memory?"

Looking over my shoulder, I caught Nicholas nod.

"Every single one?"

He bobbed his head again.

"Who planted them all?"

"I planted a few," Nicholas replied. "Others from the palace contributed, the memories mainly belonged to my parents. My father planted the garden for my mother as a gift."

"That's quite a gift," I whistled.

For the first time that day Nicholas smiled.

"It's always been a garden," he told me as I wandered forward, examining the odd assortment of watering cans dangling from the cobbled walls. "Just not as big, or as extravagant, but with my mother being fascinated by it all, somehow it became this. She appreciated the gift of being able to revisit a memory. She did it often. I watch them, sometimes. Nights my father would tell her she looked beautiful, mornings they would walk beside the lake. And if ever any of us were feeling angry, or lost, she'd take us up to the garden, and tell us to pick one of the flowers to remind ourselves of the magic we still have."

"Your mother sounded like a wise woman," I told him.

"She was," Nicholas agreed.

Making my way past a lilac bush bursting with vivid plum buds, I crouched next to it when an indigo tulip waggled its head like a stray cat, hungry for affection. I shifted my attention to its black button eyes and wide toothless grin.

"So, if I were to pull this one say… what would happen?"

"You would be taken to the mind of the person who planted the memory," Nicholas replied.

"How will I leave?"

Peeking back, I saw Nicholas's eyes shimmer with mistrust.

"You return once it's over."

I bobbed my head, about to release the flower when it grinned.

"Go on," it whispered in a child-like voice. "I don't mind, really."

Stroking its tiny face, I held my breath as it bobbed its head eagerly.

"Come on," it goaded.

"But don't—" Nicholas started to say, but my curiosity already had gotten the better of me, and in no time at all, I tugged the petal.

Tumbling through a deep blue fog, I gasped, fighting to see through the mist, and when the universe came to a crashing halt, I stumbled forwards, lost. I was outside of the palace. Nicholas was gone, as was the garden. I was inside a memory, but whose memory?

I skimmed the place unhurriedly; the thick red hue sitting above the lake, the watery pink sky, the blinding mountain of white grass when the sound of laughter behind me made me lurch forwards. A loud crash followed. Spinning around, I set eyes on a woman in a lilac summer dress, racing down the palace steps with hair so black it was almost blue.

Her face was pale, delicate, and perched upon it were wide eyes that reminded me of toasted caramel fudge.

"Mia, you know he hates that," came a voice from inside. Mia? This was Nicholas's mother.

I palmed my face, wondering how I should introduce myself.

Hello there, I'm the human your son keeps trying to ban from Wanderlust, how do you do?

"Excuse me," I called.

Mia didn't look up.

"Excuse me," I called louder as she bolted towards the lake. Nothing, and unless Nicholas's mother was extremely hard of hearing, or incredibly rude, I think it was safe to say she couldn't see me. Releasing a shaky breath, I turned to the palace where Nicholas's father burst out from the doorway.

I smiled as he pounded down the steps. Like Nicholas, he had generous gold eyes, and upon his burly shoulders was a loose-fitting shirt. Though unlike Nicholas, his face was carpeted in rich mustard fur, and his thick mane was tied in a loose ponytail behind him.

Reaching the last of the steps, Nicholas's father broke into a sprint, and when he made it to Mia at the lake, I questioned what I should do. If I followed them, I'd be invading their privacy. This was a memory both had planted for themselves, not for some stranger to gawk at. But if I didn't, Nicholas would assume I'd seen it anyway, and the memory would be wasted.

Gnawing my lip, I sauntered towards them, taking care to tread quietly, despite knowing they couldn't hear me.

"Here, Casius," I heard Mia say from when I reached them. "Take his monocle. I'm sure Candimore will find many ways to occupy himself."

"Mia, you tease him too much," Casius sighed.

"He needs it," Mia said. "And sometimes you do too, always so serious, so restricted."

Casius frowned at the ring on his little finger; the same black trinket Nicholas wore religiously.

"You think I'm dull?"

"Well, at times I think you could stand to be a little

312

wilder."

"Wilder?"

"But," Mia smiled. "It's just as well, there needs to be one sensible parent."

Casius's face brightened.

"Morgana told me this morning."

"You're sure this time?"

Mia nodded, still smiling.

"We're having a boy."

Closing his eyes, Casius emitted a frail laugh.

Edging closer to the pair, I felt a sense of pride; understanding Nicholas had come from a place of love. He was wanted, cared for, planned. Only when I crouched down next to the pair, that pride withered to rage when I saw Mia's face.

Set below her lip was a purple-green bruise, and upon her left cheek was a raw patch of skin. Saddened, I watched her, but even if I hadn't seen her injuries, it was clear she'd witnessed her fair share of darkness. There was this blanket of otherness that slipped through her eyes and stirred something sombre inside of my chest if I looked close enough, and it pained me to admit, it was a look I'd often seen in Nicholas's eyes.

Mia and Casius continued speaking. Soon their words grew faint., and as the sight before me clouded, panic set when I thought of what might happen when I returned to the garden. Walloped by the silvery tunnel, I coughed, then narrowed my eyes when I saw Nicholas shaking me by my shoulders.

I glowered at him. Registering I was back from the memory, Nicholas sprang back, studying his palms as if he'd just gripped fire.

"I didn't tell you to pick that," he said under his breath. "I didn't tell you it was okay."

"Those were your parents," I said, following him.

Nicholas shot me a dubious glance over his shoulder.

"They looked so happy."

"They were," Nicholas sniffed.

"What happened to them?" Shimmying through a thread of marigolds, I moved past him, then stood on my toes to meet his eyes. Following his gaze, I caught sight of a collection of stone steps leading up to a platform in the corner of the garden where a glass vase sat alone. Inside of it, a stem clung to a single petal the colour of a dove's wing.

"What's that?" I asked.

"Nothing," Nicholas muttered.

"It doesn't look like nothing." I wrinkled my nose as he continued to stare at the petal as if it carried the prophecy of an apocalypse. "So are all these flowers different memories?"

"Each flower holds the same memory," Nicholas answered. "After the petal is plucked, the memory ceases to exist."

"So, when there are no more petals…"

"There are no more memories." Mulling it over, I realised this was an ample opportunity to learn, not only about Nicholas but about Wanderlust too.

"I want to see more," I decided.

"Why?"

"Well, this is a memory garden," I reminded him. "And besides, what other reason would you have to bring me here?'

"I wanted to show you something in particular."

"Well then, show me."

Nicholas's eyes rippled with fear before he hung his head.

"Why is my life such an interest to you, Raine?" he asked quietly.

"Who said this was about you?"

Appearing unconvinced, Nicholas glanced up.

"What is it about then?"

314

"Wanderlust," I shrugged, and before he could call me out on my fib, I held up a hand. "As you're not one for talking, don't you think showing me these memories would be easier than you having to say anything."

Nicholas's face twisted, and while his mind ticked away with the escape routes and pointless excuses, I watched his chest pulsing against his off-white shirt.

"If I say no, will you pick them anyway?"

"Probably," I admitted.

Shock danced across his face, and when I thought he was about to tell me to mind my own damn business, he regarded me as if I'd squirted lemon juice in his left eye.

"Fine," he agreed. "But I'm warning you, Raine, you may not like what you see."

Satisfied, I threw him a look that reeked of fearlessness, because back then I believed nothing Nicholas could do would've frightened me, Mia. I guess being happy does that to a person. It blinds you to the prospect of danger and colours everything in delicious pink fuzz that wraps its arms around you and promises everything is for keeps.

Trailing alongside an army of giggling rose bushes, I settled on a lavender orchid. Refusing to allow Nicholas time to change his mind, I tugged it hard. It took seconds, and when my focus came through, I found myself on stage in the same hall where I'd painted Nicholas, only the colours were all wrong

I served around, dazed. The walls were deep honey, with no traces of ice, and the roses carved against them were a dull quartz gold. My eyes shifted through hundreds of guests, chatting, and laughing, and toasting. Some with heads of animals; squirrels and foxes and badgers. Others appeared ordinary until I glimpsed a tail peeking out from the hind of a suit, or a thick horn sticking out from a scalp.

By their animation, I gathered the occasion was one of

celebration, but when I glimpsed Mia and Casius sitting in two jewelled thrones behind me, it was clear something was wrong. They were speaking to a beaked creature who wore pearls that spilt down to her exposed navel, but neither seemed focussed. Cassius's hand was pressed against Mia's shoulder, his grip creasing the fabric of her dull white gown as her eyes darted through guests.

"He's just wonderful," the beaked woman gushed, gazing down at a wicker bassinet.

Moving closer, I peeked at a child with huge eyes and thin wisps of fur sprouting from the corner of his skull.

"Nicholas," I mouthed.

Nicholas looked up. Gold eyes meeting mine, a bubble of saliva burst from his gums. He couldn't have been older than a few months at most. Tiny, and naked, and flushed, he noted me with wonder.

"Oh, yes," Casius replied, frowning through his light tone. "And more than a handful."

Up close, Mia and Casius looked much different from the couple I'd seen moments before. Mia's eyes sat above dark blankets, and Casius's grey suit matched the streaks of the fur on his chin.

It didn't take long before the bird creature floated down the steps. Following her through the crowd with my eyes, I spotted Candimore laughing with a woman with immense black wings. Straining my eyes to get a closer look at the creature, I trembled when the door to my right burst open. Swinging around, I saw a younger Morgana flying through the hall with eyes like pistols. Alongside her was a similar creature with luminous pupils and matted grey fur.

"Santos," Casius exclaimed, greeting Morgana's companion as they lurched up the steps.

"Ah, so this is the grand festivity," Santos sang.

Casius forced a laugh as Santos ambled over to the

bassinet.

"And this must be the little one, may I?" he peered at Mia who smiled weakly before retrieving the gurgling infant.

"Nicholas," she whispered, swaddling the baby in a peach blanket. "Your godparents would like to meet you."

My throat tightened.

Godparents? Morgana was Nicholas's godmother?

"How are you?" Morgana asked Mia.

Mia stiffened, and I'm certain if she were asked that question by anyone else, she would've laughed and admitted she was tired, though the sleepless nights were worth it, but when her eyes settled on her son in the arms of the wolf man, in a voice much paler than her face, she admitted:

"Terrible."

"When did you leave?"

"After Marianne delivered him," Mia replied. "I couldn't even hold him. Can you imagine that? A mother not being able to hold her own son. I kept thinking what if this time I can't come back. What if Nicholas were to grow up without a mother? Three weeks I was lost, three weeks in that retched…" She dropped her head. "I can't keep doing this. I don't care what they do to me, but Nicholas needs his mother. When I told them about   "

"We'll find a way to keep you here," Morgana said. "Things are different now, you have a son."

"Are they?" Mia barked. "Or are they worse?"

Morgana's eyes slumped to the floor as guests within earshot shuffled closer.

"Don't say such things," she muttered, but it was obvious she was thinking the same, and after a sobering silence she held out her arms to the child Santos was bouncing.

Handing him over, Morgana brought Nicholas up to her nose and inhaled the skin on his wrinkled forehead. In the time it took for the breath to leave her lungs, her eyes flew open in horror.

"What is it?" Mia demanded.

Morgana shook her head; her chin tucked to her chest.

"Morgana, what is it?"

Morgana peered up regretfully.

"He will make a grave mistake," she whispered.

The world began to blur, the crowd, the stage, the music. I was leaving, but I wasn't ready. Casius was saying something, Mia was shouting, but no matter how hard I forced my ears to pick up the sounds, they couldn't, and all too quickly I was overwhelmed by the inescapable sensation of drowning.

I choked, my vision blurred, my head whirled around in frenzied tides of colour. Blinking sluggishly, I saw I was back into the garden. Tottering backwards, I scanned the garden before my eyes settled on Nicholas, sitting at the bottom of the steps.

"Why are you sitting there?" I asked.

"I didn't want to overwhelm you," he mumbled.

"It's a bit late for that," I joked.

Nicholas didn't laugh.

"What's wrong?"

"Nothing," he said. But I knew something was, Mia, and the longer I watched his glassy eyes, and tremoring jaw, the more I understood all these memories were doing were pouring salt onto bloody wounds.

"Nicholas, if you want me to stop, it's okay," I told him.

"Is it?" Nicholas countered. "Or is it cowardly?"

I gawked at him.

"You know, sometimes you're infuriating," I snapped. "If you were going to act this way, why did you even suggest coming? Why not let me stay at the lake, or tell this big secret instead of going through the trouble of bringing me here to act like this?"

"I'm sorry," Nicholas muttered.

I could tell by his face he was, but that didn't excuse the way he was acting.

"You say that a lot."

"No, really, I am, Raine. It's just, this place these memories…" Nicholas sighed then rubbed his eyes with a fist. "It's a lot."

"Well, like I said I'll stop. We can go back to the lake or do something else. We don't have to—"

"I need you to see something."

"What?"

Nicholas shook his head, his lip caught between his fangs.

"Nicholas, what is it?"

He wouldn't answer, and after fighting to meet his eyes and losing catastrophically, I decided I'd had enough.

"Fine," I bit back with enough spite to make him flinch. "Don't tell me then, but sitting here feeling sorry for yourself isn't going to change anything."

Not bothering to wait for an answer, I strode off. I wasn't an impatient person, but this was beyond ludicrous, Nicholas had brought me here, and all for what? So I could dance alone with my confusion?

Marching alongside a trail of swaying daisies, I questioned how it was possible for Nicholas to change so dramatically in seconds. There was barely any middle ground with him. And just once, I'd like to sit beside him and have a conversation about something as trivial as the weather.

Sinking to my knees, I plucked the first thing I saw – a yellow petal with a mouth like a spinning bike wheel. Tugging it, I found myself in the entrance hall. Still a little heated from my disagreement with Nicholas, I peered around. The hall appeared the same as I knew it, the stained-glass ceiling, the spiral staircase, the glistening tangerine ground. The only addition to the room was a grey-haired woman facing the window and tracing patterns on the glass with her fingertips.

Watching Mia's papery neck fill with air, I noticed her features deepen with each guarded step I took. Her eyes were perched above dark rings, her skin was loose around her neck, and her wispy hair hung limp at her waist. Transfixed by the sadness bleeding through her vacant eyes, I crept forwards then stopped when the door behind us flung open.

Veering around, I saw Nicholas barging through the hall. His hair was wild and shaggy. His face, smooth and void of lines. He was the same, but different. Younger, with a hint of aggravated madness slipping through his tortured stare.

"If you want to leave Nicholas, go," Mia called. "But your father and I have warned you of the danger."

"And I've told you before I'm not a child," Nicholas yelled.

Appalled by his outrage, I glared at him as he stomped towards the door with his eyes stuck to the floor.

"You think because you're my mother you know everything, but you don't." His words poured through the silence with all of the naivety of a teenager's dumbfounded rage, and something about the way he glanced over at Mia, told me he heard it too.

"You can't tell me what to do," he said from the doorway.

"But I'm your mother." Mia's words came out a desperate plea, but Nicholas had already shoved himself through the door.

Mia trembled as the door slammed shut. Pushing her palms against the glass, she watched Nicholas plod downhill, and when I saw who he walked towards, my mouth went dry – a girl. Nicholas was heading towards a girl at the lake.

My pulse chipped away at my teeth as I peered closer, but no matter how hard I looked, I couldn't see her face.

"We must let him make his own decisions Mia," came a voice from behind me.

In the reflection of the window, I saw Casius ambling down the spiral staircase, less smoothly than I'd seen him move before.

"He is nearly seventeen and wise beyond his years."

"He's making a mistake Casius."

"Then let him make it, Mia. How else do you expect him to learn?"

Mia's eyes swam with tears. When Casius reached her, he took hold of her veiny hand and brought it to his lips. Watching his parents racked with fear, I almost wanted to drag Nicholas inside myself. I wanted to shout at the foul-mouthed little boy and tell him to be thankful that his parents loved him. Turning to the window, my heart shook with unwarranted jealousy when I watched him laughing with the dark-haired girl.

Who was she? And why hadn't he mentioned her before?

"Morgana told us what would happen," Mia breathed.

"She didn't say it was certain," Casius argued.

"She predicted this!"

Before Casius could debate the matter further, I began falling through a sea of washed out shades of grey. I was leaving the memory, and I promised myself that when I returned, I would ask Nicholas about Morgana, and the girl at the lake and I wouldn't stop until I got an answer. I pulled back my shoulders, ready. Only when I stepped through the watery darkness, I realised the memory wasn't over.

The place I'd found myself inside of was dark, and the only light crept in from a door to the left of me, fractured just enough to light up a room with gold panelled walls, and red satin wallpaper. I peered around in the shadows while the sound of snoring punctured the stuffy air. Inching towards the place the sound was coming from, I stopped at a bed the size of a swimming pool where Mia lay next to Casius.

She stared up at the ceiling with her lips pressed into a tight line. On the brink of stepping closer, I froze when the door creaked open. Detecting the sound, Mia snapped shut her eyes pretending to be asleep while Nicholas skulked through the room. Buckling down at Mia's bedside, I watched his shaky face as he studied his mother.

"I'm sorry," he whispered. "I didn't mean to hurt you."

Creeping closer to the boy, I wondered if this was the same day I'd seen, seconds ago. Nicholas wore the same boots, the same jacket, the same petulant stare, but scraped into it now, I saw remorse.

"I think… I think you were right," he said. "I'll listen now. I've told her."

I tried moving closer as the memory greyed. In the faint crack of light, I saw Nicholas's eyes sparkle with tears; I saw his guilt. I saw glimpses of the boy I see now, and I wondered what had happened to make him this closed off vessel, pounding his heart senseless each time it beat.

"Nicholas," I whispered.

A sharp whistle of air burst through my skull as I fell through a snowstorm of undefinable colours. Coming through the memory, I saw Nicholas sitting on the steps.

"What happened to your parents?" I asked quietly.

Sinking lower, Nicholas shook his head at his boots.

"They loved you," I told him, but he knew that already. I wanted to ask about the girl, his mother. Why

322

hadn't she wanted him to see her? Who was she? But my questions were purposeless because I knew all of the answers I was searching for lay within the petal behind him.

Marching towards it, I moved with all of the confidence of a wolf approaching a herd of sleeping sheep. Clambering past him on the first step, I told myself I was ready. I could do this. I took another step, understanding this was the real reason he'd brought me here, to show me the terrible thing he'd done.

I glared at the blossom with steely determination. I could nearly feel the white velvet bud between my fingers, its pollen dusting my nailbeds, but before I could make it up the final step Nicholas grabbed hold of my knee.

"Don't," he begged. "Please."

Glancing back, I saw an earthquake had taken hold of his lips, and in each of its tremors I understood how much regret lay in that petal.

"Nicholas," I sighed.

Nicholas stared back woefully, and even though every instinct I had was telling me to pluck the petal, I couldn't. Not because I was afraid of what I might see, but because of the way Nicholas looked at me then. Terror battered his eyes, for his past coming back to haunt him, and I knew I couldn't force him to unburden his demons unless he was ready to, as I had been at the lake.

Taking one last look at the flower, I squatted next to him. Then, in a moment of unthought out desperation, I took hold of his hand. A part of me expected him to flinch, or pull away, but instead he sat there with his fingers trembling between mine.

"I just—"

"You just what?" I asked.

He shook his head as I stroked the rough skin around

323

his knuckles, understanding what he needed more than anything at that moment was a friend.

"Let's not talk about it then," I said. "Let's talk about something else. Something light."

I waited, pretty sure I'd lost him to the monsters in his head when he replied,

"Okay."

"Okay," I mumbled, stunned.

Blowing out my cheeks, I searched my brain for a question. Any question.

"So, what did you want to be when you were a child?" I cringed immediately. It sounded so juvenile, *what did you want to be when you were a child?* I lowered my head, waiting for Nicholas to throw me some rubbish about him wanting to be a king because of course, a king couldn't be anything other than a king, but when he replied, I questioned if I'd heard him correctly.

"I'm sorry, did you just say you wanted to be—"

"A mermaid," Nicholas repeated.

"Don't you mean a merman?"

An unexpected burst of laughter escaped my throat when Nicholas shook his head.

"Why?" I asked.

"As a child, my parents would take me to the third region," Nicholas explained. "The land is scattered in huge caves where Mercreatures control the electromagnetic energy in Wanderlust. They join hands, plunge deep into the ocean and swim beneath the waves with power from their tails sending electrical signals above ground. The caves are exquisite, especially at night when the rocks crystalise."

"Sounds magical."

Nicholas bobbed his head. Scanning the garden I glimpsed a daffodil a few feet away, waggling its head and watching us sit side by side, speaking like real people.

"What about you?" Nicholas asked.

"Me?"

"What did you want to be when you were a child?"

"I'm not sure," I lied.

"There must've been something."

The back of my neck prickled when his fingers tightened around mine.

"I guess..." I paused, weighing up how much of the truth I could tell him without letting on I was a complete waste of space. "I guess, growing up I just wanted to be someone who made a difference," I admitted. "Someone who did things for others, someone I would've looked up to as a child, but as you can probably tell my life hasn't really amounted to much."

"What do you mean?"

I stole a look at Nicholas to check if he was joking. If anything, he just looked confused.

"Well," I said, lowering my voice. "A majority of my life has been wasted trying to be someone else, someone I don't even like. If I take a step back and look at things, I mean really look, I'd see a woman with no real friends, a husband who lied to her. Even if he hadn't, I would've still been stuck in a loveless marriage because it was comfortable." I cleared my throat, trying to quieten the hysteria in my tone.

"So, if you think I'm this brave, fascinating woman, I'm sorry to disappoint you because I'm far from it, in fact, I'm the opposite."

"You're wrong," Nicholas said.

My face fell as I turned to him, and it pained me that this time he didn't look away.

"You're an artist, Raine. You give the gift of beauty to those who have blinded themselves to the magic of the universe. You bestow the miracle of hope, and education, and prosperity to those who have given up, and you tell me your life hasn't amounted to much?"

Watching his eyes flood with conviction, I wondered who he thought I was, some sort of revolutionary artist with my work displayed in the Louvre? I was about to shatter his boyish illusion when he added,

"You're art."

My stomach plunged. I'm art? How? If I were art, I'd be a tiny red squiggle on a canvas kept in the back of a gallery to fill space. Something people would stroll past and give that little 'hmph' face to, but every time I was around Nicholas, I didn't feel like another painting on the wall. I felt like the whole damn gallery, and before I could brush off the compliment that was more than a compliment, I allowed myself to believe it.

"Thanks," I said.

"No problem," Nicholas replied, blushing.

We talked that day, Mia. Not just polite conversations to pass time. We exchanged what felt like more than words. Nicholas confessed he didn't have the vigour his father had when it came to ruling the kingdom. He was more like his mother; a woman who led with her heart and had hands that smelt of jasmine when they brushed away his tears as a child.

He admitted that most of the time he felt like a fraud and whenever he slept, which wasn't often, he never dreamt, but always woke with the taste of running in his mouth. I told him things too; stories from my childhood, about the silent sense of freedom I found whilst painting, and the truth that after venturing into Wanderlust I felt more myself than ever.

I'm not sure how long we sat there trading secrets, but I'm pretty sure I caught dusk arrive then skip off twice from the hole in the ceiling, and in the hours that coasted by, so did the iron barriers we fought hard to keep up.

"Next time you return," Nicholas said, untangling himself from my shoulder. "Will you do something for me?"

I nodded sleepily. After hours we still hadn't moved and I began to wonder if Nicholas had things to do. As a king, he didn't appear to have many responsibilities, or perhaps he did, and he was just putting them off for me. I would've liked to think he was putting things off for me.

"There will be a ball, and I wondered if you would join me?"

Jerking upright, I turned, accusingly.

"You mean like a date?"

"I mean like us," Nicholas replied.

Was there an us? I skimmed the sleeping garden bathed in a rainbow of colours, searching for an answer that wouldn't come. I knew what I should've told him. *I'm married to a man who doesn't love me, who probably never did. There's something I still don't know about you, and I'm terrified the moment I find out it will destroy me. There's a stillness that settles every time I'm around you, and I'm petrified the second I give into to it everything will shatter*, but despite all of the reasons I knew I should've said no, in the reflection of Nicholas's eyes I saw myself nodding.

***

The officers have left, taking with them their sour faces, and cardboard words, leaving me in the incapable palms of Peters.

"It wasn't a love story," I tell her again. "Because he didn't tell me the truth, and what does the truth cost? Nothing," I mutter before she can answer. "Not a damn thing."

Peters clenches her eyes together then falls back in her

seat.

"Come on, Raine, we have serious things to discuss, it's not normal to—"

"Normal?"

Peters stares at me. No words, no thoughts, just a shabby blank face.

"What the hell would you know about being normal? You get paid to tear people apart and discredit everything they believe in because a system tells you to. Do you think that's normal?"

Peters opens her mouth, but I won't let her speak.

"Is it normal to assume I'm sick because you don't understand what I'm telling you? It's a numbers game. If the world saw what I had, and you hadn't, it would be you being judged, not me."

"Okay," she says. "Let's forget about that. Right now, we need to talk about the investigation."

"You need to talk about the investigation!"

Her eyes harden, and it looks as if she's about to scream.

"No, Raine, you do," she says, lowering her voice. "And it's about time you started acting as if you gave a damn because all you're doing is wasting police time."

"It's my fault he's dead."

"Are you going to tell me how? Or are you going to throw me this I don't remember spiel?"

I grit my teeth, glaring at the clock.

"As the police have informed you, forensics have to come back and if the DNA found is a match, then based on your psychiatrists' decision, you're free to leave."

I blink away hot tears, staring at the wall.

"Maybe you can't remember what happened that night because you don't want to. Perhaps someone else was there, and with Dan's phone turning up..."

I palm my chin as she goes over all everything the

officers have already told me.

"If you didn't kill Dan then the real killer is still walking about scot-free, is that something you can live with? Think about your future. Think about your daughter—"

"What?"

Holding up her stubby palms, Peters widens her eyes.

"Raine—"

"Pierce told you?"

"He had to Raine. He had a legal obligation. You have a real chance of getting out of here now and raising your baby and being—"

"Don't you get it?" I shout, slamming my fists into the desk. "None of this matters because I can't keep her."

CHAPTER SEVENTEEN

Pierce sits alone looking as though he hasn't slept in years. Gazing at his self-pitying face, I almost wish Watson was here to distract me from his snivelling pleas.

"I had to do it, Raine," he keeps saying. "It was mandatory to your case. I don't know how they missed it with all of your checks. It just seems so..."

He rubs his flaky scalp before continuing with his excuses.

"Look, I owe you an apology. I led you to a point of safety, and I get that you feel betrayed, but you need to understand this is a safe place." He pauses, watching me with a flicker of desperation. "Will you speak if I tell you what happened between Gabby and me?"

Afraid one wrong move might be all it would take for him to clam up, I stiffen, but this time I glimpse an urgency in his eyes that hadn't been there before.

"I told you we were married," he confesses, not even bothering to wait for me to agree. "But I didn't tell you how miserable we were. Young love is almost impossible to hold on to, you have all of these expectations you'll live happily ever after, but it's bullshit."

He picks up a paper, lays it flat on the table, then looks up at me with his eyes brimming with fresh pain.

"When Chris was five, we moved to Leeds for Gabby's job. As I said, I couldn't find work, so we agreed I'd look after Chris when Gabby was at work. It was a bad move. A cock-up on my part more than hers. I started drinking. Just a glass of wine at dinner first. Then a bottle, and before I knew it, I'd be pissed by noon. I was a drunk, and I wasn't even good at that."

He sinks deeper into his seat; his lint flecked blazer consuming him.

"It was Chris's summer holidays. The kind of summer that made you feel boxed in, and it didn't help that the windows in our apartment never opened, and we had a completely superficial air con system. I remember Chris watching telly. Gabby would always go on at me for letting him sit there for hours. Take him to the park, she'd say. These are the things he'll remember as an adult, an adult," Pierce sniffs.

"She was right. When I look back on all of the things we argued about, everything she wanted, all I can think is, my God she was right."

He gnaws his bottom lip, his teeth puncturing his unkempt beard.

"I was drinking that morning, not heavily, but enough to pass out, and Chris... Chris was in his fire engine pyjamas. He loved fire engines, wanted to be a fireman."

He blinks at his hands, clears his throat.

"The last thought I had before I passed out, was that Chris's summer school slip needed signing. The deadline was soon, and if I didn't sign it, he wouldn't be able to go canoeing. Chris always wanted to go canoeing. He was talking about it the night before, guess what Daddy, we get to learn to steer the boats."

Shaking his head, he widens his eyes at his hands.

"What happened?" I ask.

"He died."

A bolt in my chest tightens.

"How?" I breathe.

"He found a bottle of bleach in the kitchen cupboard and drank it. Probably trying to be like his dad. I woke up to Gabby screaming. She was holding him, but his body was… limp. It was covered in all this sick and blood and mucus. I remember her clawing at her face; I could see pieces of her skin under her fingernails. She was howling, but the sounds were—"

Breaking off he scrunches the paper on the table into his rocky fist.

"Some things you can't forget. No matter how hard you try. You just can't."

I open my mouth as the scene unfolds in my head. Officers rushing into the tiny flat I imagined Gabby had decorated with smiling family photographs; the disappointment in the officers eyes when they saw Pierce, panicked, and disorientated in his bed, the whisky bottle next to him, his beautiful wife destroying her face and cradling her lifeless infant in her arms. An infant who will forever have a love of fire engines.

I wonder how Gabby looked at Pierce when they tried to pry her dead child from her arms. Did she ever look at him again? I hear her sobs, her screams, her agony. I hear the words that rip holes in Pierce's mind. Neglect, carelessness, abandonment.

Lowering my shoulders, I study Pierce furiously, questioning how somehow could disregard a gift some would give both arms and legs to acquire, but my rage is purposeless because for the first time I see Pierce for what he is;

a man already dead.

I slump lower into my seat, and whilst Pierce buries himself in his past, I decide to confront mine.

"It was the night of the ball."

His eyes graze mine, conscious but distant.

"It was the night I found out what Nicholas had been hiding."

"And how did that make you feel?" Pierce asks.

"Terrified."

SEPTEMBER 7th 2018

"Are we going to talk about it?" Dan asked, from the bedroom door. He was always standing next to doors. Perpetually ready to leave or enter, never really content with staying in the same place.

"I don't know, Dan, are we?"

Dan was referring to the medication he'd found unopened in the bedside dresser, but for a moment his eyes betrayed his uncertainty. He was afraid I was talking about Lucile. Afraid I'd found out. Afraid I might lash out and tell him I was leaving. Then, just as quickly as his fear surfaced, it disappeared. Of course, his mental wife had no idea about his infidelity with her best friend, how could she when she was mental?

"Raine..."

"It's fine, Dan. Go, have fun. I'm sure Steven will be pleased to see you."

The uncertainty on his face resurfaced, before dissipating into a dark smile.

"If you're sure?"

I nodded, because I was sure, Mia. I wanted Dan to go. I didn't care about him or Lucile – not much, anyway. I still harboured a degree of resentment for them betraying me, but not enough to stop me from lying. After all, wasn't I doing the same thing with

Nicholas?

I jerked my head at the door where he hesitated, and when he couldn't be bothered to work out what I was thinking he rolled his shoulders then left. Gathering what I had left of my courage, I listened to the car engine rumble to life outside the bedroom window, and when I was positive Dan had left, I raced into the hallway and tugged down my studio steps.

After climbing the stairs, I threw on a navy summer dress from a box labelled 'paints' before heading to the mirror. I was excited to see Nicholas again, I was excited to attend the ball. No longer did I waste time questioning if I was a crazy woman living in a world too sane, or a sane woman living in a world too crazy, all I could be certain of, was that I had to leave.

Pushing my hand to the glass, my gut trembled as the sight before me thinned; the brown boxes, the thin slit window, the pyramid of paints. Blinking, I saw I'd made it back to the memory garden. I grinned, adjusting to the sluggish sounds of waking flowers, before swerving round to the doorway where Marianne waited.

"Pick me," the flowers whispered as I shimmied past a row of groaning daisies. I wondered if I'd made it there in time for the ball. I hoped I had. Most times I found myself back in Wanderlust, I usually caught Nicholas at the right time, and if I hadn't, well then, he could fill me in on the events of the night. Nodding in agreement with myself, I took one last look at the rusted swing set before Marianne hauled me out into the corridor.

Seconds later, we were marching through tall stone corridors lit by floating pillar candles and racing down tightly coiled stairwells before halting outside of a door, tucked inside of a burgundy corridor. I glanced around uneasily. The ball couldn't have been taking place inside. For one, it was much too silent inside and out. Shifting from one foot to the other, I peered up as Marianne pushed open the door.

Slinking in behind her, my eyes flew open. It was a place I'd been inside of but hadn't. Nicholas's parents' bedroom, just as it had appeared in the memory. The four-poster bed, the Venetian headrest pushed against a ripe red wall, the velvet chaise sofa positioned at the end. Stumbling forwards while Marianne made herself comfortable on the bed, I gazed up at a silver domed ceiling where a mural of angels watched me drift towards windows I imagined were as great, if not greater than those in the entrance hall.

Pausing at the maroon curtains, I stroked the paisley patterns stitched across the edges when I caught sight of a mannequin shimmering ahead of me. Upon it was a gold floor-length gown, kissing the berry carpet in a waterfall of silk. I eyed the dress apprehensively. Was it intended for me? It was certainly much grander than the washed-out frock I'd come dressed in.

Ogling the slit running from the place my thigh would rest, I was about to tell Marianne I couldn't possibly accept such a grandiose gesture when a woman's voice made me flinch.

"Beautiful, isn't it?"

My hands flew up as I searched for the person who'd spoken, but there was no one there. Collecting my breath, I peeked back at Marianne as she jutted her shoulders at two large glass cases on top of an ebony dresser. Making my way towards the glass fixtures, I gazed at the light bouncing across their panels, and when I was close enough to see inside, my legs turned to paste.

"Marianne," I breathed.

The severed head smiled from inside the first case.

"I understand it must come as a shock for you to see me this way, but finally!" she exclaimed, her breath fogging up the glass.

My smile trembled as I took her in, bit by bloody bit. Her body matched her face. The soothing movements, the compassionate grip, the girlish posture, everything belonged to this face.

Deep brown eyes, and wide lips, fixed on a face sprinkled with honey freckles. Breaking my stare, I took in the glass case next to her where two titanic black wings fluttered, then ceased, like the final efforts of a dying crow.

"I'm sorry," I said, finally.

"What for?" Marianne chuckled.

I pursed my lips, about to apologise again when she bobbed her head at the dress.

"It's a gift," she said.

"A gift?"

"From Master Nicholas."

At the mention of Nicholas, I felt my palms dampen.

"He assumed you wouldn't want it, but after a bit of convincing, he agreed it would fit the occasion."

"Nicholas didn't want me to have it?"

"Not at all!" Marianne cried. "Master Nicholas was adamant you'd look splendid in whatever you came dressed in. I just thought this would be more suitable for the occasion."

"It just seems so..."

"Extravagant?"

"Exactly."

"Those were her exact words when I dressed her."

"Whose?"

"Queen Mia."

My lips came apart as I turned to her gingerly. A rustle sounded behind us. Looking over my shoulder, I saw Marianne's body shuffling over to us with her arms swinging about at her sides. On reaching the glass case, she yanked off the lid then placed it on a dressing table next to the podium.

"Thank heavens!" the head sighed, shaking her bronze locks and swatting me with a musty whiff of lavender. "It was a bit stuffy in there. Anyway, it was such a long time ago. I remember it vaguely," she said while her body held a finger to the space above her shoulders. "I was preparing Queen Mia for a dinner, or Nicholas's recital, perhaps. She was pouting as she often did, claiming she wouldn't feel comfortable in something so regal, oh but when it was on, she looked ravishing!"

Still taken aback I was speaking to a head, I folded my arms. More than that, this was Marianne's head, a woman I'd encountered countless times but had only just met properly. I felt like some sort of internal jigsaw had slotted into place, and before I could tell Marianne I'd probably feel more comfortable in the outfit I'd come dressed in, her face lit up with so much glee I found myself unable to refuse when she announced,

"Let's get you ready."

The following hour was spent with Marianne's body flustering around my hair, and face, and patting my cheeks with creams, and lotions, which left me panting in a snowstorm of jasmine. All the while she spoke in a honeyed voice, distracting me from the fact that I was in my underwear, covered in scars from the market.

In the time it took to dress me, I learnt that the ball took place once a year, with guests from all over the kingdom, attending. After, it was tradition for them to visit the spirit lake in hopes of glimpsing a loved one.

Gradually, Marianne moved on to other things; the palace, the first region, her life before the 'incident' as she branded whatever had happened to her.

"The bedroom was a gift from his parents," she told me, jerking the strings of the corset tighter and tighter until I had to wave my hand for her to stop. "I was walking beside the spirit lake one day, when King Casius called out to me from beneath the waves and told me the room was mine. I refused it outright, insisting I couldn't accept a gesture so grand. It was Master Nicholas who made me see sense. He told me he wouldn't have it any other way. Truth be told, I assumed he'd take it, considering the shack he spends his time in now."

Her lips wandered into a grimace before she stroked my cheek with her cold fingertips.

"You know, Raine, there are things you shouldn't judge him on– Nicholas, I mean. He is a good creature, a little lost, but good, so if you should see something unsettling or tragic tonight, keep in mind that your world is much different from ours."

"What will I see?" I asked.

Marianne's face paled.

"You're ready." She whispered.

Silencing my suspicions that Marianne may have been exaggerating, I studied the gold strappy sandals she'd lent me when a tingle shot up my spine. I was ready for a ball I knew next to nothing about. I knew the basics, but how would I behave? What would I talk about? Would I be left to chit chat amongst guests? If I was, would they regard me in the same manner they had at the market?

"About the ball," Before I could finish, Marianne tilted her head at a floor length mirror in the corner of the room.

Crossing the room, I gasped when I set eyes on my reflection. I barely recognised myself. My hair was pulled high, and for the first time in years, my cheeks had colour. Patting down my sides, I inspected the snug dress that hugged my hips and created the illusion of curves, before rushing back to the head.

Kissing her frozen cheek, I thanked her as her body lugged me off to the doorway.

"Goodbye," I called, despite three-quarters of her still being there.

"Have fun," Marianne shouted as the door slammed shut behind us.

"Have fun," I whispered as Marianne's body hauled me into the mile-long stretch of burgundy. Though as we marched on, I felt my fears re-emerge. What if my dress was too lavish? What if I did something stupid? I'd probably do something stupid. I scraped my palm, praying the night would follow smoothly. No awkward silences, no making a fool of myself.

We moved faster; striding through hallway after hallway, and tight stairwells that made my heart jump every time I trod on the dress thinking it might rip, right up until we reached an area of the palace I recognised – the spiral staircase.

Gripping hold of the rail, I told myself I could do this. Yes, I could do this! But before I could build myself up with any more sagging fortitude, Marianne unclasped my arm.

"Aren't you coming?" I whispered as she scurried off into the shadows. When she'd disappeared completely, my feet turned to stone. Peering down at the flurry of strangers, I bit my lip. Scattered amongst hushed laughter, I detected the symphony of a violin.

Taking a deep breath, I reminded myself I could do this. It was just a small gathering of creatures from an alternate universe, nothing major. Slinking down the stairway, I counted the glass steps in a bid to distract myself from my boisterous heart.

One… two… three…

The dress slapped my ankles, and the silk licked the frozen steps.

Four… five… six….

My chest tightened as I prepared myself for an evening spent trapped between creatures who'd probably be disgusted by me. What if Nicholas sat in his throne all night judging me based on how I interacted with them? What if he asked me to leave because I didn't behave the way he expected? Something changed between us had the last time I'd seen him. We had shared all of those wavering little truths that emerge only after you learn to trust someone. But what if that were to change in the company of others?

I blinked angrily.

Don't trip, stay composed, remember to breathe. How long hadn't I breathed?

My face was burning. God. Close to the bottom, I glanced up, then froze. Surrounding me were three, maybe four hundred creatures. Some with heads of animals, others appeared completely alien. Whiskers popped out from pinched noses, tails stuck out from the hinds of ball gowns, and the entrance was still heaving with guests on their way in.

Clinging to the melting rail, I was throttled by an urge to race back upstairs and take cover in Marianne's room. Realising I probably couldn't do this, I stared at the hall. By all rights it was bright, but it was an unnatural sort of bright. I had assumed there'd be sunlight flooding the tangerine ground, and bursting through the huge domed ceiling. But the curtains were drawn and the only light glittered from various white pillar candles dotted around the room.

Glancing through the creatures' baffled expressions as I lingered on the stairs, I was about to bolt when I noticed a movement in the congregation. I narrowed my eyes. Creatures began splitting and scattering to the edges of the room. From the break, I saw Nicholas. My heart dipped as he trudged towards me in a crisp white shirt. On his feet, the same hefty boots.

I liked his boots; I thought as he made his way over. They spoke of strength, and hardship, and endurance, all of the things that reminded me of him. Halfway there, he smiled. It was a shy sort of smile. A sort of, I'm glad to see you, this is as daunting for me as it is for you kind of smile, and as I watched him stride through the dusty orange light it was as if all of the guests disappeared, and for a second, it was just us.

Making my way to the bottom of the steps, I relaxed as he took hold of my hand then led me through the conversations, and music, and excavating eyes to the doorway where we were partially out of sight. Once there, he let go of my hand and stood with his back against the wall.

"Thank you," he said.

"What for?" I asked, conscious of the creatures nearby watching us parked in the doorway.

"For coming," Nicholas shrugged. "You didn't have to. I mean, I wouldn't if I had a choice."

"You wouldn't?"

Nicholas shook his head.

"Well, what would you do instead?"

"Run off."

I smiled, then lowered my voice.

"And where would you run off to?"

"The spirit lake, the third region, anywhere. The marshlands are frozen this time of year. I hear the goblins are quite the skaters." His eyes slipped across the guests, then back to me. "Do you think we could?"

"Could what?"

"Run off," Nicholas replied.

I furrowed my brow. Was this how he addressed all of his guests? Thank you for coming, seemed formal enough. Do you want to run off – did not. Scrutinising the thin strappy sandals pinching my feet, I waited for him to shake my hand and leave, to tell to me to have a wonderful night and enjoy the music and refreshments. Looking up, I saw he was still there, only now, he was smiling.

"What is it?" I asked. "What?" I repeated when he clawed a patch of fur under his eye.

"You...You look really nice," Nicholas said.

I pulled a face, wondering if he thought it was odd I was dressed in his mother's clothes. I certainly did.

"I think your judgement may be clouded by all of the excitement of the ball."

Shaking his head, Nicholas watched me closely, and as the creases around his eyes deepened, I couldn't help wonder what he was thinking. He always watched me like he was thinking something big. There was history in that stare. A vast galaxy of thoughts, and words, that were never spoken, and every time he watched me in that way a gentle thunder would always pass through my heart.

Feeling a little discomforted in the doorway, I inspected my chipped fingernails when Nicholas asked a question so simple, my shoulders snapped back.

"How was your day?"

"My day? You seriously want to know about my day?"

Nicholas bobbed his head while I went over all of the menial things I'd done with my day; washing the dishes, showering, making a sandwich I didn't eat. Standing there, grappling with my mundane existence, I began to question if Nicholas and I, were too different. Not just in worlds, but in status.

"I'll go first," he said.

I glanced up, curious.

"I woke up and had breakfast with Candimore and Marianne. I paced about the palace grounds for an hour or so, got dressed, and for the past few minutes I've been trying to work out whether that elf is stealing from me."

Following his gaze, I saw a small man with the top of a candlestick poking out from his trench coat. My lips parted as I watched him scanning the room impatiently.

"That might just be his spine," I joked.

"Her spine," Nicholas corrected.

I widened my eyes, about to ask how a pudgy little man with a beard could pass as a woman when I saw Nicholas fighting a smile, and I realised he was joking.

"I painted last night," I told him.

"Oh," Nicholas replied.

Just oh.

I nodded, inspecting the frayed laces of his boots with my cheeks burning.

"It was the first time I painted anything I thought was good in a long time."

"What you painted before was good."

On the precipice of arguing Nicholas was probably only saying that because it was a portrait of himself, I caught his eyes swell with pride. This radiant shimmer he didn't even seem to be aware of; and it was in that minute slip, I realised it didn't matter about his status, or my past, or even his. Around him, I felt like I could just be me, and that was okay.

"It was of the market…"

That was our beginning, Mia. In the doorway, chatting about our dreams, and mistakes and our day to day lives and laughing, really laughing, with the middle of the night merging into a colourful blur. I remember the apprehension in Nicholas's eyes when he asked me to dance. The relief that followed when I agreed. But the moments after; of fairies, and elves, and creatures with trunks, and beaks, waltzing round us in an animated cluster, were overshadowed by what took place after.

It happened when the ball was over. I'd slunk off into the shadows watching Nicholas bid farewell to guests at the entrance door, shaking hands and sending them stumbling out into the night. Only a handful of creatures remained at a lengthy mahogany table to the left of me. Amongst them were four Mithels, a tusked creature, a creature with the head of a rabbit, two goblins, Radalpho, and at his side, Candimore was announcing the commencement of the ritual.

The ritual?

At first, I thought he might've been referring to the tradition Marianne had mentioned where creatures joint at the lake, but when the entrance door slammed shut, I realised whatever this ritual was, was about to take place inside. Hanging about in the doorway, I watched Nicholas take his seat at the head of the table. Fighting to meet his eye, apprehension soaked my chest when Candimore bobbed his head at the seat next to Nicholas's.

Heart heaving, I raised a brow, examining Nicholas. He had his face in his palms, and his head was bent so that he was all shoulders. Something was wrong, not only because of Nicholas's posture but because of the sudden chill bruising the air. Nervous excitement littered the creatures whispers and hungry eyes, and I was certain something awful was about to transpire.

Fighting to quell my mistrust, I crept over to the table, though when I reached Nicholas, my mistrust buckled to fear.

"Nicholas," I whispered.

He wouldn't look up.

My brow dampened as I sank into the seat next to his, waiting for him to lift his head. He was afraid, but of what? Had I done something to offend him? I nudged him in the ribs.

"Nicholas?"

He recoiled, lowered his head.

About to ask him what was wrong, I jumped when a violent clatter cut the silence in half.

Swivelling around, I saw the entrance door had swung

open. From the break, came two figures. The first, a grey-haired baggy woman, dressed in what looked like a stained potato sack. Heart racing, I squinted as she yanked the second forward by an arm. A slender naked girl with two cracked horns sprouting from a dark head of hair.

"Nicholas?"

Still nothing.

As the pair drew nearer, I noticed chains shackled around the nude girl's ankles. My heart stuttered. Something was off. The sound of the chains hitting the cold marble floor sent huge chills crawling up and down my teeth as the creatures chattered breathlessly.

"Nicholas?"

Nicholas stooped lower, his face ashen and his eyes unfocussed. Punching my thigh, I watched as the baggy woman threw the girl the remainder of the distance then swung back around, heading out into the night.

"What's happening?" I asked Nicholas.

Focussing on his palms jittering in his lap, I was about to call his name again when the nude girl lifted a leg and climbed on top of the table.

"Nicholas?"

Nicholas ducked his head as the entrance door slammed shut, and before I could demand an explanation, a violin symphony erupted. My brows bumped together as the girl began dancing. Was this some sick form of entertainment? If it was, why was she tied up? I shook my head as she thrust her gaunt hips in rhythm with the music, and when she bent lower, I saw her eyes.

Two dark pupils the size of fists, bubbling with wonder, and lust, and temptation, and beneath them, I glimpsed a waterfall of sadness. A bolt in my chest tightened as the music roared louder. The girl twirled faster, her ribs heaving through her skin, below them were deep red welts.

Certain this wasn't right, I peered at Nicholas. Whoever this girl was must've been imprisoned. She had to have been brought here against her will. I wasn't about to stand for it. How could Nicholas condone such sadism? Prepared to demand he stop this madness, I heard his chair graze the ground.

Stumbling out of my seat, I saw him mount the table. He stood behind the girl. She was still dancing. Nicholas was rigid as stone. What was he doing? Her dark hair smacked his chest. She was a few inches shorter than me. My heart stammered as her tiny breasts bounded and the creatures wolf whistled.

I shook my head as Nicholas's chin quivered. I wanted to call his name, but my lips were too heavy. Everything was static. His fingers jittered, his ring shone as he lifted a hand. I knew something terrible was about to happen, Mia, but I couldn't stop it. I tried to, but all I could do was stand there, staring.

My eyes stung as Nicholas stepped closer, the table protested under his hefty boots. The girl turned to him. Her eyes wide, defenceless. Nicholas tilted his head, his face a mess of anger and fear, then in one swift movement one can never retract – he dove forwards and slashed her throat.

Those next few moments sort of felt like the nightmares you have when you're falling. You can never recall if you were pushed, or if you lost your footing somewhere alongside the mountain top you were spiralling down from. All you can think of is the pain before you hit. I was trapped in that bad dream; only unlike the dream, I didn't wake up before I hit the ground.

I flew back as the girl fell to her knees, and started convulsing on the table with her legs shuddering. I gasped, tasting blood. Bitter and metallic, and soaking my chest and hair as the creatures applauded. Nicholas was still on the table; only now he'd fallen beside the girl. Was he trying to save her? He had his arms around her shoulders. My eyes trembled as he brought her limp body to his lips.

Sweat blistered my brow as her eyes rolled back in her head, and before I could delude myself further, I watched him suck at the dark wound on her neck.

My gut twisted.

Everything was too hot. I gagged. The room was spinning, and I couldn't catch my breath.

"Raine," Nicholas whispered.

My stomach flipped as I focussed on the oily blood dripping onto the floor from the table. I couldn't lift my head. Everything was going slow and it hurt to breathe. I needed air, I was drowning and that smell of blood... I stumbled backwards. A chair clattered.

"Raine?"

I had to leave, but my feet wouldn't work. Swivelling around, I gazed at the door wobbling miles away, and before any of the monsters had a chance to stop me, I ran. Kicking off my heels, I sprinted through the hall, panting, and gasping, and breaking.

Making it to the door, I threw myself behind the gap, grateful for the heavy downpour pelting my hot flesh. I had to escape. I couldn't risk Nicholas coming after me. What if he did the same to me as he did to that girl? Who was she? And what reason did he have to slaughter her?

I gagged, my chest pulsing manically. How could I have gotten him so wrong? Was I really that desperate I'd mistaken kindness for safety? Unable to shake the questions, I sprinted down the steps, drenched in rain, and sweat, and tears, and blood, until I was wheezing at the lake.

I had to find a way back; I had to leave. Swinging

around to the palace, I saw a silhouette bounding towards me. Nicholas.

I froze.

He was calling my name, but it sounded different from his lips. Watching him rush towards me, I felt myself sinking deeper and deeper into the muddy earth.

"Raine," He whispered when he reached me.

I shook my head. There was blood on his chin and the front of his shirt was soaked a deep burgundy.

"Get away from me!" I screamed, pounding my fists against his bloody shirt. "Get away!"

Struggling to fend off the blows, Nicholas threw up his hands with a face that was just as terror struck as mine, but I didn't want his fear. I wanted him to fight back; I wanted his anger, his rage, anything but the fictitious warmth he was watching me with. I hated him. I hated him so much because I'd trusted him, and he'd just ruined it all.

"Tell me what I did," he said.

I threw my fists at him, shaking and gulping in air that refused to enter my lungs. How could he be confused about what he'd done when he murdered that girl in front of me? I trembled, hitting harder and harder until he shouted,

"Tell me!"

Shrinking back, I glared at him lit by the skeleton of the palace. Veins crawled up his neck as he struggled to catch his breath. He watched me indignantly, but I wasn't afraid of him, Mia. I was furious.

"What you did?" I barked into the torrential downpour. "What you did? Nicholas, you just murdered that girl. You killed her right in front—"

"That wasn't a girl. It was a Siren. They're destroyed before they can harm—"

"You harmed her!"

Rain drenched his hair, turning it the same colour as

the blood under his claws. Everything hurt and nothing made sense. Nicholas was a murderer, not only that, but I'd seen him drink her blood. It was sick. I was sick for ever trusting him.

His eyes twinkled with hurt, but I wouldn't let him revel in his misery, not this time, what I needed were answers.

"Why did you drink her blood?"

"Raine they disguise themselves as innocent creatures. They hold power to slaughter entire regions. They have no—"

"Tell me!"

Rain slinked down his chin as he ducked his head, and when he looked up, all I saw was shame.

"It makes me strong."

My heart sunk.

"How do you even know that?"

"I just do, Raine. For others it's lethal but for me—"

"For you what? It makes you strong, so you kill them?"

Nicholas's eyes trembled as he compressed his jaw.

"Please, just listen to me," he begged.

But I wouldn't, not after everything I'd seen. Swerving around, my eyes glazed over as I stared at the flushed burgundy ripples.

Nicholas sighed, the sound tore through my chest as I lowered my head, ambushed by memories of the night where I'd unburdened my soul to him at the lake. I thought I could trust him. I believed he was my friend. My cheeks smouldered as the rain lashed the lake.

I heard Nicholas step closer, and for a moment, I admit I found myself questioning if there was any truth in what he was saying, Mia. Morgana had mentioned Sirens were dangerous; that if they were permitted to live, they'd annihilate entire regions, but how could Nicholas have known that for certain? How could he play the role of God with so little remorse?

Torn between hearing him out and running, I screwed up my face, but when the image of the girl flashed in my mind, it all became clear. I didn't know if the decision I was about to make, was brave, or cowardly, Mia. All I knew was that after everything I'd seen, nothing between us would ever be the same.

"I can't see you anymore Nicholas."

"Raine—"

"No!" I barked, veering around to face him.

Hope punched his eyes, and for a moment all I wanted was to take away everything that hurt, but I couldn't because it was me standing there with a bruised heart, not him.

"I can't keep going around on this roller coaster with you," I muttered. "One minute I'm happy, and I feel like the whole damn world is on pause with you, and then something like this happens and I realise how insane I've been for trusting you, and the most pathetic thing is that I only feel this way with you and—"

"Raine—"

"I only feel this way with you," I said louder. "Not with my friends or my husband or anyone in my miserable little life, and the most pathetic thing is that I don't even know you."

"You do know me," Nicholas argued.

But I didn't, because standing in front of me was someone completely different from the creature my soul had learnt to rest alongside.

"Do I?"

Nicholas nodded.

"If I knew you, you would've told me this," I panted, wiping wet strands of hair from my eyes. "You've had so many opportunities, Nicholas, at the lake, the memory garden, we talked for hours and not once did you mention what you did to the Sirens. I've told you everything, about my parents, my husband cheating on me and—"

"Fine."

"Fine?"

Nicholas nodded.

The gesture turned everything inside of me to ice. Stepping back, I searched his face for a flicker of truth. All I saw was anger. It resonated in his lips, his eyes, even his skin was seething.

"Yes, fine," he repeated. "If you want to run, then run. Run back to your husband, and your barbaric little world and spend every moment numb, because it's easier."

"You think this is easy?"

"I think condemning me for things you don't understand is."

My lips parted as Nicholas watched me through eyes like rusty chainsaws.

"You want to know what a real monster is?"

Call it weak Mia, but I didn't, because after everything I'd seen that night, I knew my heart wouldn't survive encountering anymore of Nicholas's demons.

"Ask me about my parents."

"Nicholas, please."

I tried moving past him when he dove sideways, staring at me with this look about him as if he was about to burst out of his skin.

"You said you wanted to know everything."

"I don't care," I lied. "I just want to go."

"Ask me what happened to them."

"I don't—"

"Ask me."

"Nicholas."

"I killed them."

My lips split as I gazed at him, hoping I'd misunderstood.

"What?"

"Seventeen years ago, I was possessed by a Siren. She forced me—"

"Possessed? Possessed how?"

He stared back blankly while I grabbed hold of my head.

"I don't understand," I whispered. "I don't understand."

"Wha—"

"Everything!" Suddenly all of the timid angst swirling about in my chest had balled itself up into fury. "How is it possible for someone to be possessed!"

Nicholas sprung back. The world was spinning, and nothing made sense. Nothing.

"How is any of this possible? How am I supposed to believe anything you're telling me when it defies everything I've ever known? You're telling me you killed your parents. I saw you kill that girl. You're a monster Nicholas, you're…"

Cold sweat stuck to my forehead. I tried to pull myself together, but I couldn't because It was only hours ago, I'd fooled myself into believing I had a future with Nicholas, and now the only thing I could think of was escaping him. And the worst part was, I didn't even know if any of this was real – if he was real.

My heart lurched as I went over all of the opportunities Nicholas had to tell me the truth, but like Dan, Nicholas had fled from his mistakes. I couldn't trust anyone. I clenched my jaw shut tight, the sound of the waterfall drilling cavities in my skull.

"Is that why you took me to the memory garden? Because you wanted to show me what you'd done so that I would support you?"

Nicholas opened his mouth, but I wouldn't let him speak.

"Why did you take me there?"

"I didn't—"

"What, Nicholas? Are you going to answer or are you going to continue running from the truth like you're so good at?" I glowered at him, hating that when his eyes pooled with tears, my heart stung. "Come on, Nicholas. What? You were afraid I'd find out you have no conscience?"

"I have a conscience," he growled.

"Oh yeah, because good people just go around committing murders weekly."

"I'm not a person," Nicholas reminded me. "And it's not as though I didn't try and tell you I was a monster. I warned you to stay away. I warned you I did something bad, but you kept insisting I could change. You made me believe I could be better."

"If I'd known—"

"Then, what? You wouldn't have spent so much time trying to convince me I wasn't a monster?"

"I just—"

"What?"

I hung my head with an urge to scream, but all that rage had fizzled away, and in its place all that was left was a huge tank of sadness.

"You don't understand," Nicholas breathed. "But the problem isn't that you can't understand Raine, it's that you don't want to." Veins expanded in his skull as he shook his head at the sky. "We have something, and you're just running."

"I'm not running."

"Then what are you doing?"

I shook my head, but no words seemed to be enough. Were they ever enough?

"You feel something for me. I know you do, but instead of hearing me out about the biggest regret in my life, you stand here persecuting me."

"We're just too different. We—"

"You're lying!"

I flinched at the lightning in his tone then searched his face for traces of the monster I'd seen moments before, but all I saw was Nicholas. His lips sunk at the corners, and it took every ounce of strength I had left inside of me, not to go to him.

"Why are you making this so difficult?" I asked.

Nicholas looked at me then. He looked at me without anger, or frustration, or resentment, or fear, just two huge balls of fire burning right through me, and before I could walk away from all that my heart secretly craved, in a small voice he told me:

"Because I'm falling in love with you, Raine."

For a moment there was dead silence. The sound of the rain pelting the lake disappeared, the thumping of my heart disintegrated, the sound of his heavy breathing vanished, and we just stood there, two misfit souls begging to be understood.

Wiping my eyes with a fist, I shook my head.

"You can't," I told him, because after everything I'd seen that night, all I could think of him as was a monster, and monsters I was quite certain, didn't know how to love. "Goodbye, Nicholas." Before Nicholas had a chance to argue, I walked away, and with every step I took, I felt my heart break a little more.

***

"What do you think?" I ask.

Pierce jumps as though he hasn't been listening.

"I think everything that happened to you was very distressing, and to you it was real," he replies mechanically.

"I don't mean that. I mean what would you have done?"

"What would I have done?"

I nod, watching him squirm.

"I guess it would all come down to one question. Did you love him?"

I glance down at the table with my heart drumming a sad song.

"If you loved him, it really wouldn't matter what you did, because if you give in to that desire even for a second, logic is obliterated. That's the terrifying thing about love. You allow yourself to be completely defenceless, knowing the person may leave, or change, or be taken by life, but all of those doubts fail to exist in those moments because when you truly love someone, logic is nothing more than a backseat passenger."

Before I can stop myself, the truth slips from my lips like red berry kisses.

"I did," I tell him. "Still do."

CHAPTER EIGHTEEN

Pierce's eyes are bloodshot, and the stench of his skin tells stories of a sour brewery. I wonder if after our session yesterday, he'd stumbled into the nearest bar, then glugged down anything remotely alcoholic until he'd forgotten his name. Watson, on the other hand, appears revitalised. I assume that's where she was last session. Tanning herself, and buffing her nails for the hearing tomorrow.

One session left before they can pass their verdict on whether or not I am mentally stable enough to be released. One session left before the end.

"Raine, we need to talk about the night of Dan's book launch," Watson says, in a tone as varnished as her face.

"It's true," I mutter.

Her expression blanches as I glance at Pierce. Pierce the murderer. Pierce who I am trusting with nothing but blind faith.

"What's true?"

"Everything Gillian told the police I did that night. It's true."

"You mean Dan didn't—"

"Dan didn't attack me."

"But you—"

"I lied."

OCTOBER 1st 2018

After the ball, three dark and dismal weeks passed existing in what was, and always had been my uninhabited life. I stopped eating, speaking, I barely slept, and in all the time I wasted lying under my grubby blue bed sheets, I couldn't keep the emptiness from eating away at my heart. All I could do was pray for sleep. And when sleep did eventually arrive my nightmares were always filled with Nicholas.

I'd see the Siren with her slashed neck, blood soaking the white table cloth. Then him, hunched over her naked body, gorging on her insides. I'd scream, but my voice was always soundless, and just as I was about to run, Nicholas would swerve around with blood dripping from his lips.

'I'm falling in love with you,' he'd whisper.

I'd always wake up before I had a chance to flee, and each time I'd promise myself the same thing, I would never go back. Nicholas had been right all along. I didn't belong in Wanderlust. Perhaps what he'd done *was* for the good of the kingdom. Perhaps if the Sirens were permitted to live, they'd go on to slaughter entire regions. Perhaps if I'd grown up with that sick knowledge in place, I would've toasted like the others.

Only I hadn't, and so I couldn't support the twisted ritual, but the strangest thing of all was that I didn't believe Nicholas did either. He'd seemed appalled before the massacre. His face betrayed just how much he loathed what was about to commence. Still, the Siren's death lay heavily on his hands. Not only that, his parents' deaths too.

In spite of however much it sickened me to recall the events of that night, Mia, a large part of me couldn't help but feel sorry for Nicholas. He'd told me he'd been coerced into murdering his parents by some supernatural force. Had he been telling the truth? Had a Siren forced him to carry out the most heinous crime imaginable?

As time progressed, I began to understand Nicholas, not all of him, but fragments. I understood the guilt sewn into his face every time he glimpsed something beautiful. The shame in his eyes after every smile. The constant need for him to flee from happiness. Everything spawned from what he'd done to his parents.

Nicholas didn't allow himself to enjoy life, not because he was afraid of living, but because he believed he didn't deserve to. I admit I became a wasted version of myself after the ball, Mia. And it wasn't only what Nicholas had done that had broken me, it was what happened after.

After fleeing through the violent monsoon, I'd collapsed beneath the keen glare of the moon, only yards away from Nicholas. And after everything I'd seen, and everything I'd pushed myself to believe, the thing that destroyed me most was that he hadn't come after me.

Love. How could Nicholas have believed he loved me if he hadn't chased after me? You don't let someone you love, leave. Nicholas wasn't falling in love with me, I decided. I was something that fascinated him – an odd creature from a world he detested. His love for me was nothing more than rebellion. He barely knew me. I barely knew me.

Still, despite all of the justifications I force fed myself each night, I couldn't deny I'd never heard those words spoken with such raw sincerity. And every time I questioned what they meant, or whispered them when the emptiness became too sharp, I always saw his face.

The night I made it back, Dan said he found me in the garden with my fingers bloody from picking thorns. He told me I was talking about memories, but I couldn't remember any of that. What I do recall, is the way he carried me inside after. The way undressed me in the bathroom with his lips puckered as he bathed me.

'I need to support her,' He'd told the office when he called in sick to work, regarding me as if I were terminally ill, completely unaware it was his life that would end in a matter of days.

Dan did try helping, but looking at him was a constant reminder I'd chosen poorly my entire life. I'd picked steady options in fear of being hurt, and even that had blown up in my face. Dan was sleeping with my best friend, and the most gruelling thing of all was that it barely hurt.

Heartbreak became the mother of my indifference.

I was withering away. Fluttering into oblivion and laughing, but on the morning of Dan's book launch, something inside of me had shifted. Lying in bed and rubbing the space on my ring finger, I decided to do something I should've done a long time ago. I would confront Dan and Lucile. And I'd do it at the worst possible time – at the party celebrating the publication of his second novel.

Causing a scene would be the last thing Dan would've expected from his washed-out bumbling wife, and if on the off chance he would've wanted to work it out, I wouldn't let him. I'd pack a bag and leave. I was clueless as to where I'd go, or what I would take, just that I had to disappear.

With thirty minutes to spare, Dan stood next to the bedroom window when I announced I would join him.

"Fine," I said.

"Fine, what?" Dan asked, fiddling with his cuff links

and squinting at the buttons.

"I'll go."

Dan turned me with an expression belonging to a dog who'd just misplaced his tail.

"Only if you're sure."

"You need me," I answered too brightly. "If you need me, Dan, I'll be there."

Dan's eyes dripped with concern before he swerved back to the window, and in that timid gesture, my plan commenced.

The dress I bought months before, didn't fit. Black, knee length, and expensive, it highlighted my recent weight loss in all of the worst places. While Dan rushed around making calls and muttered about nothing, I put on a black chiffon scarf to cover the marks on my neck.

We took a taxi. The driver's eyes kept tracing Dan's expensive suit and my baggy dress in the rear-view mirror, probably trying to work out how we knew each other. Not entirely surprising considering we sat propped up against the windows, facing forward and not speaking.

"Try to be okay tonight, Rainey," Dan said as we piled out of the car.

I bobbed my head, wondering what Lucile would say when I confronted her. Would she act brassy and tell me it was my fault for neglecting my husband, or would she bawl a pointless apology? I played out all of the scenarios in my head as we reached the high-rise stone building, only when my eyes skipped across the steps, my heart stopped.

Staring at them brought back memories of Nicholas. Nicholas waiting for me at the palace. Nicholas looking over his shoulder and smiling. Nicholas, Nicholas, Nicholas. I tried shaking the image of his face, but it was already there, his fragile words eating away at my heart. *'Because I'm falling in love with you, Raine.'*

How, when he hadn't bothered to tell me the truth about the Siren until I found out for myself? Shaking the thought, I followed Dan inside. Marching past the reception, we headed through a set of double doors, and down a long mahogany corridor before halting outside of a door at the end.

"Ready?" Dan asked.

I nodded, but my nerves had gotten the better of me and I wondered if maybe, I should abandon the plan. It all seemed so farfetched now that I was there. I could pretend I had a stomach bug. Dan wouldn't care to check up on me; he'd be too busy getting pissed and lapping up forced praise from people he didn't like at the bar. All I had to do was pack a bag. What would I take? Nothing sprang to mind except my passport and bank card.

Pulling my best 'I'm going to throw up' face, I turned to Dan when I caught him plaster on the wide grin I'd seen him practising in the bathroom mirror earlier. Pushing through the door, he waltzed inside. With my arms enveloping my chest, I followed him into what looked like a lawyer's living room.

Everything was mahogany and impeccably polished. Slinking past a brown leather sofa, and a piano that was probably never played, I halted with my back against a floor to ceiling window. Skimming through washed out November guests impersonating Summer, I bit my lip, eyeballing Dan's work friends, people we'd met at parties, birthdays, work events, women with cropped haircuts nodding at men who spoke in voices two octaves too low, all of them crowding around a table stacked with Dan's books.

Watching them, I realised I didn't care about any of this. I didn't care about confronting Dan or shaming Lucile. All I wanted was to go back to Wanderlust. I wanted Nicholas. Where was he? Was he as distraught as me, or did he not care? Pushing my hand against the glass, I overlooked the grey courtyard. Keep it together, I reminded myself, but what for? What did I have left here? A cheating husband, and a dwindling art career?

"May I take your shawl madam?" asked a gaunt waiter. My stomach dipped as I tried to stand up straight, but I could barely breathe. Love? Love wasn't meant to hurt like this, but if it wasn't, what was this sensation stepping all over my heart? Fighting to keep my composure, a cold hand gripped my shoulder. Turning to tell the waiter I was fine, I almost lost my balance when I saw Lucile.

She grinned, her bright eyes exuding the same fuzzy joy mine should've, had she not have been fucking my husband.

"You must be so proud, Rai," Lucile gasped, pulling me into a one-armed embrace and clouting me with the same perfume I'd smelt on Dan's shirt months before. "How are you feeling? Dan's told me you're a little under the weather."

I watched her vigilantly; her glossy blonde hair framing her overly made-up face, thick lashes batting the air, a tight navy dress, and those eyes, those bright blue eyes, staring at me like the barrel of a gun.

"Is everything okay Rai?"

Nothing was okay. My best friend was sleeping with my husband. My life here was over, and all I could think of was a creature that no one knew existed. The words bitch, traitor, liar, went around in my mind like a spiked bicycle wheel as Lucile ran a hesitant gaze over my uncombed hair and baggy dress, and just as I was about to ask if she was pleased with herself, I glimpsed Dan marching towards us both.

Rushing through the obstacle course of handshaking, and back patting, he battled his way to the finish line of the two women he was screwing.

I saw it all when he reached us.

Those tell-tale signs I should've noticed sooner. The way Lucile's eyes lit up when Dan jammed his hands in his pockets, the way she stuck out her flat chest as he eyed the place proudly. Then Dan, unable to hide that stupid practised grin of his.

"Well, well Mr Hotshot," Lucile teased. "I told you everyone would come."

"You did," Dan agreed. "Now we just have to make sure it sells."

"Of course, it will. It's brilliant."

"Brilliant?" Dan fanned Lucile off with a hand before turning to his mental wife. "You okay, Raine?"

"Fine," I breathed. I could tell them now. The stage was set; the words were there.

'Of course, you think it's brilliant when you've been fucking him, Lucile.'

The words disintegrated when Dan wrapped an arm around my shoulder.

"Anyway, Daryl Miller from publishing is here," Lucile said with less cheer. "Apparently he wants to have a word."

"About what?"

"Something about the office in Paris."

"What about it?"

"Publishing malfunction." Lucile shrugged, and when Dan smirked, rage bubbled up inside of me. How stupid did they think I was? There they were, screaming sex with their eyes and they didn't even have the decency to stay away from each other for one measly day.

Shrugging off Dan's arm, I stumbled through the mob of suits to the bar.

"Raine," Dan called, but he didn't follow me, and I didn't have to look back to know he'd moved closer to Lucile.

Collapsing on the bar stool, I ordered a double gin and

tonic from an adolescent bartender who had more piercings then all of the people put together at a tattoo convention. Draining it, I ordered another, then another, because sometimes, the easiest thing to do when you miss someone whose name you don't have the balls to say aloud, Mia, is to get catastrophically wasted.

Only then can you speak it, slur it, tell any stranger who doesn't care about it, but what we must be cautious of is the ones we're around when our brain shuts down. I should've been careful that night, but I was broken, and broken people don't care for caution, all broken people want is to hurt.

On the fifth Hendricks, I felt my elbows moulding into the sticky bar. The room thickened. Bringing the glass to my lips, I jumped when someone squealed my name. Following the voice, I groaned when I saw Dan's bouncy agent, Gillian Carpenter the forty-year-old child, grinning at me in a duck-egg blue suit.

"It's going well," she said. "I mean, we all knew it would be a success, but with the uproar he's caused on social media, he's already got a ton of followers and the younger crowd love him."

"I bet they do," I mumbled.

Gillian swatted me off with a hand. Catching a whiff of her musky perfume, my stomach turned.

"Are you coming to the book signing next week? It's in London, that's the big one, then the week after its Cheshire, and Leeds—"

I closed my eyes. I didn't have time for pleasantries. I didn't want to be that woman. I wasn't that woman.

"We're hoping to go international. So much to do!"

She wouldn't stop speaking, the room was spinning and she wouldn't stop speaking.

"Leeds is sure to be a hit. We've mapped out—"

"Did you know?"

That shut her up.

"Know what?" Gillian questioned, regarding me as though I were a dreadful piece of art.

"About them," I spat, only mildly aware I was slurring. "The golden couple every — everyone must know."

Gillian's lips spread, exposing two lipstick stains on her front teeth.

"And no one thought I'd find out because I'm just this stupid… this stupid…"

The crowd started to look up. I caught sight of Dan speaking to his boss; a middle-aged man with terrible sideburns and chronic bad breath.

"You know, Raine," Gillian said, slowly. "Dan's told us you're not feeling too great." Leaning in close, she flinched when I grabbed hold of my head.

I exhaled, throttled by a sudden urge to rip out every single strand of my hair and to smash my fists into the empty-eyed strangers, but mostly, I wanted Nicholas.

"Let me get Dan. I'm sure he will know what to do."

"I just miss him," I heard myself saying.

"Well, he's right there. I'll get him."

"I miss him, and I can't go back, I hate this. I hate it." Fat tears leached out from my eyes, and strands of hair plinked out in my fists. "He should have told me the truth, and now I can't go back."

"Raine, I'll be right back. I'm going to get Dan. You're obviously drunk."

"Oh yeah," I snapped, opening my eyes to her terrified little face. "Because Dan can fix everything. Because Dan's a bloody hero."

I saw Dan moving towards us then. His eyes scraped the mess of me on the bar stool. Behind him, Lucile shook her head pityingly. Lucile, my best friend. She had betrayed me, and all for what? A man who practised his expression in the bathroom mirror?

"Rai," Dan called.

Bounding off of the stool, I dipped through the tight-lipped audience, then paused next to a canvas illustrating Dan's book. 'The Burning Man' it read. An image of the smug author next to it, with a stack of his books ready to be signed, and handed out, but the words inside were a lie. Everything was a lie.

Gritting my teeth, I shoved it hard, sending the mountain of red paperbacks scattering across the floor.

"Raine, what the fuck do you think you're doing?" Dan grabbed my arm, but after glimpsing the fury in my eyes, he released it then shrunk back. Everyone watched, all of them waited for the author's crazed wife to strike. Maybe he could put that in his next book. A sequel to the pyromaniac's mousy wife who knew nothing about the fires he was starting at night.

Dan whispered something, but I didn't stick around to listen. Racing out of the hall and into the corridor, I pushed myself to keep going before I bounded out through the entrance door. A taxi, I needed a taxi. I'd go home, pack a bag, and disappear. I had to disappear. Sprinting through the street, I knocked into strangers in anoraks eying me suspiciously from under their hoods, before I spotted a taxi on the far side of the road.

Rushing over it, I flung open the door.

"Where are you going, love?" the driver asked.

"Home," I exhaled. "I need to go home."

Throwing myself through the front door, I slumped against the living room wall, overwhelmed by plans of packing a bag and leaving, but if I left then, that would be the end of Nicholas. There'd be no chance of spotting him in a café months later, or a smoky bar at midnight when they called last orders. If I left, that really would be it.

And despite telling Nicholas I never wanted to see him again, the reality of it terrified me, Mia, because I think sometimes when we say those words aloud, all we're looking for is for someone to grab hold of us and tell us to stay.

I clawed my knees, ambushed by memories of how he'd watched me that night. He'd told me to go back to my life because it was easier, but nothing would ever be easy again with so much of him in my heart. Shaky from gin, I lugged myself up and stumbled through the kitchen, before climbing the stairs. With each unsteady footstep, I told myself I would pack a suitcase and leave. I'd start over; only after making it to the top, I found myself staring up at the cord to my studio steps.

Half-drunk and aching, I waited for some bountiful sign to come rushing down and tell me what to do, but there was nothing in the hallway but two fluctuating options. My head told me to leave because in the long run, it was probably the right thing to do. It was sensible, and pragmatic, and how could I justify staying with a man I didn't love, because I'd discovered a world beyond a mirror?

I nodded, leaving was the most level-headed thing to do, but my greedy little heart didn't care for sensibilities, and already it had tugged at the chain. My eyes watered as the dusty steps unfurled in front of me, whacking me with the scent of an adventure my heart was about to embark on alone.

Clambering upstairs, I stumbled through the hole in the floor, then felt around for the switch. Flicking it, my soul heaved with homesickness. Surrounding me were canvases swathed in vivid colours depicting a magical place I could never go back to. Images of a place in which I was certain I belonged, but not here. I didn't belong here.

I hugged my sides, overcome by an urge to say goodbye, to end things amicably, and tell Nicholas I was sorry it hadn't worked, because there were too many good memories for the night at the lake to have been the last one. I had to say goodbye. The cat meowed downstairs as I knocked into boxes and easels and blank canvases until I was facing the mirror.

I held my breath. My eyes carpeted the mess that I was in the reflection: bloodshot eyes, and a gaunt face cloaked by wet chestnut hair. Of course, Dan had chosen Lucile.

Lifting my chin, I pressed a hand to the glass fixture, waiting for that burst of white light so I could forget this madness. Nothing happened. My brow sagged as I jabbed my reflection desperately.

"Come on," I whispered. "Come on."

Nothing.

Swinging around, I studied my loft, musty from its abandonment and dried up paint. This couldn't be it.

"Please," I whispered. "Please, please, please."

Pressing my palms against the surface, I made myself small as the room shuddered, my legs buckled, my heart raged with uncertainty, and when I opened my eyes I saw I was back outside of the palace.

Relieved, I squinted across the barren land as the bloated sky bled, showering the spirit lake and the earth. It was night. Looming over the lake was a huge red moon. Pulling back my shoulders, I skulked towards the palace, clueless if Nicholas would be inside, or if he'd even want to see me, but I had to check.

Mounting the stairs, I pushed through the entrance door before forcing my way up the spiral staircase. The raindrops that had soaked into my hair smacked the glacial sheet beneath me as I climbed messily, clinging to the bannister like a lifeline, forcing my legs to keep moving until I was outside of his door.

My eyes trembled as I focussed on the blemished wooden surface, assuring myself I would leave if he wasn't inside, but what if he was? What would I say?

Pulse racing, I glared at my hand shaking in front of me. What if Nicholas told me what he said at the lake had been a mistake?

Taking a deep breath, I nudged open the door. Candles were strewn about on the floor; each one radiated small cotton breaths of vanilla and cinnamon. Pushing my head in further, I held my breath, skimming the place silently, and when I set eyes on Nicholas facing the window with the curtains pulled apart, my heart stopped.

He held on to the walls as if they were about to come tumbling down, and as he turned and met my eyes, for a moment, I felt as if they had.

"Raine, what are you doing here?" he asked.

I tried to answer, but all I could do was stand there with my lungs relishing in the simple fact that after weeks, they could finally breathe.

"Are you okay?" Nicholas asked.

I opened my mouth to tell him I was fine, but the truth was I wasn't fine, Mia. I was terrified, because for so long it felt like someone had pushed my head under cold water, and all it took to come up was seeing his face.

"Raine," Nicholas said softly, and it dawned on me then, that without him I'd never be okay again because nothing in this chaotically messed up world came close to the way I felt when he said my name.

"No," I whispered. My cheeks flamed, and before Nicholas could offer a reason why I shouldn't be there, I cut him off. "The night at the lake, you broke me," I told him, clinging to the doorframe with fingers that were about to snap.

"What you did was sick, and wrong, and unjustifiable, Nicholas. You hurt me, not only because of what I saw you do to the Siren, but because you didn't tell me the truth about your parents. You shouldn't have left me to find out like that." My voice shattered as Nicholas shrunk back, nodding at the scarred floorboards.

"Even if I were to put that aside, I'm never sure of where I stand with you. You're either hot or cold, you're up or down, you're like a one-man opera, and trying to work out your next move is exhausting." I glanced at his shadow draped across the burgundy curtains while my throat burnt with words that I knew would only haunt me if I didn't say them aloud.

"That being said, I should've told you the truth."

Nicholas's eyes rose from the floorboards, and for a moment I glimpsed a flicker of hope.

"That night you asked if I felt something for you, and I told you I didn't, but the truth is I think I feel more around you than I have in my entire life. Whether it's rage, or happiness, or exasperation, or something more, I always feel it, and I can't keep convincing myself I don't. You don't deserve that. I don't deserve that," I said, louder.

Nicholas opened his mouth, but I shook my head, unable to stop the words.

"You were there for me when my world fell apart, and I should've been there when yours did too."

"That's all you wanted to say?" Nicholas asked.

My cheeks turned red as he inclined his head waiting for an answer I was too afraid to give. I knew I had a choice then, Mia. Go back to my life, breathing a little and calling it living, or take the plunge into the great unknown, regardless of the injuries my heart may sustain after.

It was a choice I knew would change everything; all I needed was three seconds of dumb courage.

"I missed you."

A moment passed, thick, and swollen with truth, and hope, and words that were colours, and when Nicholas shook his head at the floor, the sky came crashing down and I was terrified my confession had come too late, because timing, in almost all cases is everything, Mia.

Relationships can rupture and die because we are too young to understand compromise, or they can fade to nothing because we are too cynical to believe in happy endings. But if Nicholas had meant what he said at the lake. If he was falling in love with me, well then timing should mean nothing.

"So?" I asked, unable to mask the anger in my tone. "Are you going to tell me to leave now?"

Nicholas began making his way over to me with his burly shoulders going up around his ears and his head bowed.

"Well?" I pressed angrily.

"Well, what?" Nicholas asked when he reached me.

"Are you going to tell me to go now?"

Nicholas pulled back his head. He watched me carefully, his gold eyes dusting mine, his face so close it hurt, and I knew if he told me to leave then, I wouldn't.

"Nicholas?"

Before I could push for the truth, Nicholas brought a palm to my chin and he kissed me.

My grip on the doorway loosened as I kissed him back. It was a kiss that tasted a lot like a lifetime of adventures, and somehow it made all of the broken pieces of my soul feel like they were coming back together.

"I missed you too, Raine," Nicholas whispered.

My lips curled downwards as I studied him seriously. "Really?"

"Really," Nicholas replied, smiling.

He kissed me again, slower this time. Pulling away, he cupped my cheeks in his palms, then lowered his head so that I could see the branches expanding in his gold irises.

"I meant what I said at the lake. I'm falling in love with

you, Raine."

Nicholas's jaw trembled as I watched him, stunned. Then, without warning, I heard myself speak words I finally understood.

"I'm falling in love with you too."

I won't bore you with the details of what happened after, Mia, needless to say; it was a night filled with fireworks, and a little fumbling, and moments where I found myself overcome by understanding that this was how love was meant to feel. Nicholas was a magical voyage I never wanted to come back from, he was a fresh start, but there was history there too, and when he watched me up close, his lips against mine, his chest bruising my skin, somehow everything just made sense.

We fell against the ragged floorboards after, and when Nicholas sat up, I worried he might leave. My lips puckered as he peered around hazily before throwing an off-white bed sheet across us both.

"Nicholas," I whispered as he settled back next to me.

Nicholas's eyes skipped to mine. His arm tensed up beneath my spine.

"You honestly think you're falling in love with me?" I held my breath, searching his eyes for a trick, but they were just as brazen as ever.

"I don't think, Raine. I know."

"How?"

"You want an explanation?"

I wanted a seven-thousand-word essay, but I settled on a nod.

"I just want to make sense of it."

Nicholas smiled; the gesture made the bristles on his cheeks creep up to his eyes.

"I don't think anyone can make sense of love, Raine. It just…" he furrowed his brow at the ceiling. "One day you meet someone, and something broken inside of you slots back into place, and suddenly you know."

"Know what?"

"That you would sacrifice anything in the world to make that creature happy. You learn their weaknesses and flaws, and you do anything in your power to remind them how wonderful they are. You're wonderful," Nicholas said, peering down at me in the crook of his arm. "Really wonderful. Just being around you reminds me what it's like to want to be better, not just for myself but for you too. I can't explain why, just that every time you laugh, or smile, I get this sense of pride that I know you. If that's not love, I'm not sure what is."

Pushing my face to his chest, I closed my eyes revelling in the fact that after so long I could finally touch him, and despite wanting to tell him I felt the same, I couldn't; not when there were so many other things I needed to know.

"What is it?" Nicholas asked.

I closed my eyes as the hairs on his chest tickled my cheek.

"Raine?"

I shook my head, certain that asking about his parents, or the Siren, couldn't come at a worse time. This was hardly pillow talk, but if there was ever going to be any future between for us, I had to at least try and make sense of his past.

"You want to know about my parents?"

My heart dipped. My first instinct was to shake my head again because the truth still felt like an anchor I wasn't ready to grapple with, but positive I had to get this over and done with, I nodded.

Nicholas sighed, and as I sidled closer to him, I listened to the story he had buried inside of him.

Nicholas told me it all started with a creature, who, like him, was not pure of blood. Her mother, a Siren, had died during labour, and her father, a great sorcerer, was executed for his indiscretions with the Siren. As a result, the child was castaway to the Valley Of Chosen Souls, where she spent her days living amongst the forest folk.

Nicholas explained he was just a boy when he met her. He believed she had no idea how to use her power. His parents disagreed, they'd frowned upon the friendship and assumed the Siren's thirst for power was greater than their companionship. Nicholas's view differed, he couldn't understand how both his parents were so pent up on status when his mother was a human.

Eventually, Nicholas began to slip away from the role of the prince. He ran off with the girl, and spent his days in the Valley Of Chosen Souls, growing madder with the world, and living as frugally as life would permit. And had the girl not asked him to do something monstrous, he might've abdicated his title completely.

"What did she ask you to do?"

When no answer came, I felt something wet on Nicholas's chest. A single bead glittered between the stray hairs on his torso. Nicholas was crying. My face twisted, and just as I was about to mop up the tear, I stopped, thinking it was probably kinder to pretend I hadn't seen it.

"I told her Wanderlust would be better with my parents gone," Nicholas breathed. "It was a passing comment, nothing more, I swear, but she pushed and pushed, urging me to slaughter them so that I could become King."

"She wanted you to kill your parents?"

Nicholas nodded.

"But that's messed up, how could she expect you to do something like that?"

"When I refused, she told me I was weak."

"So you did refuse?"

"Of course, Raine, what do you take me for?"

My cheeks coloured as Nicholas looked down, stung.

"So what happened after?" I asked, skirting away from the insult.

"She left," Nicholas replied. "At first it was difficult to reintegrate within the palace, but after a few months, I started to appreciate things I took for granted before. The sound of my mother's laugh, the way my father pottered around mumbling about nothing, just being around them..." A sad smile scuffed his lips as his eyes filled with tears.

"And then it happened," he whispered. "One night, I woke up and saw her standing over me, and it terrified me because I knew what she'd make me do, and I couldn't stop it, I tried to, but I couldn't, I couldn't…" The colour drained from his face. This time he didn't even bother fighting his tears.

"She possessed you?"

Nicholas nodded, the jolt of his head sent tears slipping down his cheeks and pooling up around his neck.

"I woke in the hall next to my father. His insides were torn from his stomach, and I couldn't… I couldn't put them back inside, and when I saw the blood on my hands, when I saw my mother's face…"

"Nicholas it wasn't your fault," I told him, but all I saw in his eyes was saddened disbelief.

"My parents warned me what she was capable of, Raine. Morgana predicted it. It was the prophecy you saw in the memory. I thought standing by the Siren was the right thing to do, but I was stupid, and weak—"

"Stop," I said.

When he did, I forced a smile.

"Stop," I said, kissing the tears on his cheek.

Nicholas closed his eyes as I nestled back into the curve of his arm, thinking of my own parents. At times I'd questioned if their deaths had been my fault too, mainly because when you have no one to teach you any different, the uncertainty stalking you is strong enough to creep inside of your head and fill in the blanks of your mind. But Nicholas had been coerced into physically carrying out the act himself. I wondered how he'd survived that night, then if he actually had.

Burrowing deeper under the sheet, my mind wandered to the Siren. Had she been punished? Or had she escaped and reaped havoc on some other unsuspecting creature? I decided not to ask right away, Nicholas had confessed to enough already, but as I lay there, fighting sleep, I thought of the Siren in the hall. Had he drunk her blood as some sort of revenge? If he had – could I seriously continue beside him whilst clubbing my conscious to death?

"So, the blood from the Siren…" I tiptoed, his chest stiffened. "Why did you drink it?"

"A Siren's blood is lethal when ingested," Nicholas answered.

"Lethal?"

"After what happened with my parents, I ventured into the Black Lands with a plan to end my life."

"You wanted to kill yourself?" I gasped, bringing myself up to face him.

Nicholas nodded.

"But I don't understand—"

"Raine, I had just killed my parents—"

"But you—"

"I had just killed my parents. I didn't believe I deserved to live, and a part of me still doesn't. I was lost and angry, and confused and so I found a Siren closest to its end—"

"And you murdered her?"

"All Sirens are disposed of," Nicholas replied.

"Like rubbish?"

"Like they are meant to be. A Siren's lifespan is nineteen years. On the eve of their eighteenth birthday, their power becomes complete, and their urge to kill strengthens. It has to be done." I shook my head, still trying to grapple with what he was telling me.

"So why didn't it work, if you wanted to... to..."

"To kill myself?"

I threw him a look of contempt, hating how he spoke of his life with such frivolousness, but understanding that openly admitting to how weak he'd been, in some way was braver than any war tale.

"Candimore found a Hen," Nicholas explained. "The older creatures who guard the Sirens. She claimed because I was half human, the blood had fused with mine, and in order to stay alive, I would have to keep ingesting it."

"That was the creature I saw in the hall," I thought aloud.

"The rituals came after," he continued. "We had asked for vials of blood, but the Hens argued the rituals would be more fitting. It was agreed in exchange for their help."

"You mean they wanted the rituals?"

My eyes bulged when Nicholas nodded.

"Why?"

"The Hens believed the Sirens should showcase their talents before they met their end."

"But that's sick!"

Nicholas dipped his head, and that was all it took for remorse to hit me like a ten-ton pickup truck. On the night of the ball, Nicholas had tried to explain all of this, and I hadn't stuck around to hear any of it. He was right; I had run off because it was easier. I was so used to disappointment; I hadn't even bothered fighting for happiness.

"I'm sorry," I said.

"It's fine," Nicholas replied.

But nothing was fine, Mia. Nicholas had cut himself

open, and I had left him bleeding when he needed me most.

"It's not," I told him.

A warm silence followed. Glancing up, I noticed his eyelids fluttering closed, and even though nothing would give me greater pleasure than to fall asleep next to Nicholas, I was worried the moment I did, I'd wake up in my world.

"Nicholas," I whispered.

Nicholas's eyes crept open, and when he saw me, he smiled.

"I don't want to go back," I told him.

"I don't want you to leave either," Nicholas replied, his smile slipping. "Waiting isn't easy either, Raine. Have you ever waited so long for something you're terrified will never arrive?"

I nodded uneasily.

"So what shall we do?"

Nicholas watched me thoughtfully; his eyes full of conviction, his face undisturbed.

"Take this," Nicholas said. Wrenching off his ring, he slipped it on to my index finger.

"I couldn't—"

"Please," Nicholas interrupted. "It's a gift. My father's father gave it to him, and he gave it to me."

"And you're giving it to me?"

Nicholas nodded.

"Why?"

"There are billions of creatures in existence, Raine," Nicholas said. "Some tread paths we'd never dream of treading, others appear vastly different to ourselves, despite our similarities. But there is one universal trait that binds every creature together, in your world, and in mine."

When I stared back blankly, he smiled a tired smile.

"Love," Nicholas said. "Whether it's the love of a

parent, or a friend, or a partner, if you are loved you can never truly be alone. I don't want you to leave," he continued. "If I could keep you here forever, I would, but I understand it can't be helped, and if ever you feel alone, I want you to look at this ring and remember there's always someone who cares for you. Whatever happens."

My insides stirred with something I didn't quite know what to do with, but instead of running from it like I had so many times before, I tried to understand it.

"You know this could all still change," I said, shifting closer to him so that my head was pressed against his chest.

"What could?"

"Us."

Saying the word out loud was like opening the first page of a book I'd been waiting to read forever.

"It won't," Nicholas said.

"Promise?"

"I promise," Nicholas replied.

I nodded, scrutinising the black crystals glistening on my finger, then Nicholas, falling asleep next to me.

Home, this is was home.

"Nicholas," I whispered.

"Yes, Raine,"

"What happens now?"

"We rest," he said.

"And then what?"

"And then, we will have tomorrow."

"Do you Promise?"

"I promise," he replied.

***

"In the statements from the witnesses at Dan's book launch they claim they saw you threaten Dan," Pierce tells me.

"Probably," I shrug.

"Raine."

I hated the way he said my name.

I hold my breath waiting for the anger to wash over me, but all that flows through my bones is a bitter hollowness.

"Your hearing is tomorrow, no more messing about. We need to get a handle on what was going on. In light of recent developments you're no longer a prime suspect, but if you don't cooperate, it's likely you'll remain a patient at Raven House. Tell the truth. Did you honestly think you were going to this place or—"

"I didn't think, anything. I went there. It happened."

"Just tell us—"

"Why would I tell you anything, when you're responsible for your son's death?"

Pierce's face plummets.

"He told you that?" Watson chokes.

I'm too busy glaring at Pierce to answer.

"Raine, this is important. What did—"

"He told me his son died because of him."

Watson stifles a laugh before turning to Pierce.

"For fuck's sake," she curses as he jumps out of his seat.

"What?" I mutter, gawking at Pierce.

"That's it, run like the last time."

"What's going on?"

"He hasn't got a son," Watson exclaims. "Never has, Raine. He's been lying to you."

A wall of ice shatters inside of me.

"And it's not the first time, is it, Elliot?" But Pierce has already pelted down the corridor.

"He lied?" I ask as the door slams shut.

"Yes, Raine, and all I can do is offer my deepest apologies. We're sent here to help, not fill your head with nonsense. It's against every ethical code to divulge anything about our personal lives to a patient, but to lie, and about something so—"

Taking off her glasses she rubs her eyes with a fist.

"He lied?"

"He has a track record of developing a rapport with a patient then gutting them. It's been speculated over a few times, but there's never been anything concrete to convict him on, or even have his license revoked. He did the same to a girl charged with the death of her new born, a few years back. She was assigned to Pierce for an evaluation. After diagnosing her with multiple personality disorder, Pierce promised she could trust him because he was a figment of her imagination."

Listening to the hate bubbling up in her throat, I realise this is the reason Watson kept her distance from Pierce, not because he was a fumbling man she had a past with, but because of his crimes against humanity.

"He completely messed that poor girl up. Gemma Bradshaw ended up confessing to a crime she didn't commit and was sentenced to life imprisonment."

Her name rang a bell, and when it connects, Watson bobs her head.

"Gemma Bradshaw the twenty-two-year-old mother falsely accused of suffocating her child who later hanged herself in prison."

I remember the story vaguely; a nurse came forward after Gemma's death and confessed to swaddling the baby too tightly. The mother had barely held the child. The nurse had only recently lost a child herself. The hospital was being sued for negligence.

The story was everywhere a few years back, but there had been no mention of Pierce. I rack my brain in an effort to glimpse his face in the news coverage, and when I hit a brick wall, Watson nods again.

"They never mentioned Pierce. The story centred

around the hospital, rather than the over ambitious psychiatrist who could've helped when Gemma told him she suspected it was the nurse who'd checked on the baby."

"Then why—"

"Why was he appointed this case?"

I nod stiffly.

"Pierce comes from a family with more money, than sense. His father threw a bit of cash around, and that was it, his name was kept out of the paper and Pierce continued to play doctor." Shaking her head, she pushes back in her chair. "All I can say is that I'm sorry, Raine. I should have fought harder to keep him off the case. I should've used my head."

Staring at the wall behind Watson, I wonder where Pierce has run off to, and how? How could he have run? He hadn't even bothered to stick around to argue.

I turn to Watson, understanding how wrong I'd gotten her, and now it's too late. My hearing is set for tomorrow and everything that seemed so straight forward, is now a tangled ball of lies.

"I'm sorry," she repeats.

"No," I tell her firmly. "I am."

And for the first time since entering that putrid little box room I understand all that's left now, is to fight.

CHAPTER NINTEEN

Peters is coaching me on what to say inside of a room intended for those final pep talks, but I'm not listening.

I watch her sagging face, the dark rings swallowing her eyes, her carroty lipstick smudged over her front tooth. She's been talking at me for nearly ten minutes and continued with no response. This is it; my hearing. The day that should've centred on the judge deciding whether or not I could plead diminished responsibility, to lessen the charges from murder to manslaughter.

Only after a cocktail of bitter ingredients was thrown into the empty glasses of the investigators, and an unforeseen witness came forward resulting in the charges being dropped, my hearing is to assess whether I am mentally stable enough for release.

I bite my lip as Peters runs through the procedure for the third time. She asks if I understand. I do understand; it's her who doesn't. I clench my jaw, examining the fine hairs on her forehead as she outlines the events that would play out in the hours to come.

Pierce will take the stand first, giving his jumped-up

medical opinion on the psychiatric disorder both he and Watson have decided I am suffering with.

He will summarise the condition, and the medication I am being forced to take, before making the ultimate prediction of whether it would be in the publics', and my own best interest to be released.

"A short recess will be called…"

I couldn't sleep last night, Mia. Every time I closed my eyes, anger gurgled up inside of me that no amount of reasoning could dampen, and all because Pierce had lied. He'd played the role of the awkward psychiatrist to get me to open up and trust the mess of a man he had meticulously constructed. As I lay in bed staring at the cracked ceiling, something inside of me had lifted.

I almost wanted to tell Peters what happened that night, not to assist in the investigation, or even to exonerate myself, but to show them I wouldn't be trampled like the year-old rubbish they view me as.

I clear my throat, trying to focus on Peter's voice.

Watson's report will follow next. Like Pierce, she will outline the reasons why I have been diagnosed with a mental disorder no one can actually be sure of and pumped full of pills to ensure I saw the world the way society expected me to. A shiny cut out version of the universe where everyone must obey, follow, and blink through the same vacant eyes.

Go to school, go to college, get a job, work hard, go to bed, wake up, repeat. Don't think too much or challenge authority. Don't question why the world centres on paper to survive, or why there are calluses on your soles from the perpetual routine. Don't focus on children dying of starvation in third world countries, while others throw around paper in bars on expensive bottles of nothing to impress people who don't give a shit about them.

Don't claim you see any real magic in the world, or

look too closely at the stars. Don't tell anyone you believe in something greater than this mechanical trance we deem everything, because if you do, you're crazy. If you do, you're not straight enough for the well-oiled system you were socialised to stay within the lines of.

Stay within the lines, close your eyes, quieten your soul, force your smile and repeat.

"And then the witness will read his statement."

Her words snap me from my thoughts.

"What witness?"

"Mr Thompson. Your neighbour? It was his statement—"

"I don't understand."

Peters releases an exaggerated breath.

"Why does he need to give his statement if it's not a trial?"

"The judge has requested for him to be present," Peters tells me. "Not only is he an eye witness, but he's lived next door to you for four years, and after speaking to him I'm certain any doubts the judge may have about your release will be dismissed. He had nothing but pleasant—"

"He can't."

"Raine."

I blink at the table. My insides whirl around in huge messy waves.

Index finger down, little finger up, both thumbs down.

I miss him. I always miss him, only now it feels like there's an army detonating their weapons in my chest.

"It was Mr Thompson's statement that made the investigation team pull their finger out of their arses. They assumed it was an open and shut case after your statement. It was only after Mr Thompson came forward they had to re-open the investigation. The police are still pissed at him for not coming forward sooner, but more than anything it was their mistake." Her eyes sweep over the door where black robes are already fluttering about in the corridor.

"With that in mind, he won't be charged for withholding information if he is willing to—"

"It doesn't matter."

"Raine, if someone else has been arrested it means you're in the clear. People make false confessions under duress all the time, if they release you, you can go home and forget—"

"Forget?"

"Maybe not forget but—"

"It's my fault he's dead, and you think I can just forget?"

"Raine, forensics paint a completely different picture. You keep telling us you can't remember what happened. When suffering from shock, things like this happen, but with the results of the blood splatter report, and the police finding Dan's phone there's nothing to—"

"I don't want to get out!"

The words snack her in the face, and for a second, I worry I may have gone too far.

"Carry on like this, and you won't," Peters hisses. "Falsely admitting to a crime under duress is one thing, but to lie openly under oath is a criminal offence. Raine, if someone has threatened you—"

I close my eyes. Eight forty-six. Fourteen minutes to go.

"Raine, you can't be held accountable if—"

"Stop," I whisper.

"I have the release papers drawn up, all we need is a signature from the judge, and you can be out of here as soon as this evening."

Straying from the mess around me, I think back to the morning I'd woken up in Wanderlust, but even that turned to shit. Everything I touched turned to shit.

"I woke up with Nicholas."

"Raine, we need to—"

"He told me he loved me, and I really believed him, because people can't just throw words like that around and not mean them—"

"Raine!"

"I really believed I could trust him."

OCTOBER 2nd 2018

I woke up with sunlight slinking through the gap in the red velvet curtains, and flecks of dust dancing in the air, and for the first time in longer than I could remember, waking up didn't feel like a chore. Nicholas's shoulder was cushioned against my head. His chest pushed to the small of my back. I blinked, then, as gently as I could manage, turned and saw he was still asleep.

My heart rattled. Torn between kissing him and running, I memorised the way the sun scuffed his hair, and his lips trembled every time the air entered his lungs, before shifting my attention to the window. The sky outside was the same colour as his skin – pale gold and swimming with promises.

Rubbing my eyes with a knuckle, I sighed. Last night Nicholas had unveiled his scars willingly. He'd told me the truth about his parents, and that after, he'd wanted to end his life. Something that took guts to say aloud, something you had to trust someone to even admit to.

But I knew too well, the truth only rears its head in the inky shadows of night when exhaustion forces us to take down our masks. But what happens in the harsh light of dawn? What would happen now? My cheeks flamed as I scanned the room for my clothes. I had to leave before he woke up. It would be inconvenient for us both; he probably had things to do. I had things to do, and not sticking around to see him look at me as though I was a mistake was one of them.

I spotted my dress a few inches from his head. Plucking it up, I blew out my cheeks. It was too damp to wear. Crap. Stroking the sodden material, I snatched up his shirt. Shrugging it on, I was hounded with memories from the night before – his lips against my neck, his claws running through my hair, his breath against my skin.

I blinked crossly, reminding myself how temporary affection could be. I learnt that first hand from Dan. Standing unevenly, I took a step towards the door when my stomach growled. I blushed hoping the noise wouldn't wake Nicholas, before debating whether it would've been rude for me to have made a quick pit stop at the dining hall.

I hadn't eaten in days, and the idea of that huge spread of delicacies made my stomach gurgle even louder. Squeezing my eyes shut tight, I decided against it. It was better to go without leaving any evidence. I couldn't risk Nicholas waking up and asking me what I was still doing there.

I nodded at the door then made the grave error of glancing back. Nicholas was still asleep. His arms, draped around his chest, his muddy hair stuck up around his ears. Lifting my hand, I studied the ring he'd given me. Last night, Nicholas had told me he loved me, but they were just words. People did that sometimes, said things they didn't mean. Dan did it all the time, but last night felt different.

I hung my head, questioning if I should leave some sort of note, maybe a goodbye or a thank you message. Would Nicholas have looked for me when he realised I was gone? If I didn't disintegrate immediately, where would I go? My chest resounded with doubt, and just as I was about to flee, his voice made me shudder.

"Leaving already?"

Peeking over my shoulder, I saw him smiling at me from the floorboards. His hazy eyes spilt the same warm hue the sun gives after a long day of shining. How could I not love him? How would I tell him?

"I was just going to…"

"To leave?"

"Well yeah," I mumbled, feeling a little discomforted in his shirt.

His face softened as he sidled over. After a moment of wavering, I crept back over to him then buckled down on the floor. My heart slid out of place when his chest grazed my cheek.

"I thought you wanted to stay," Nicholas said.

"I did — I mean I do."

"Then what's stopping you?"

The fear of actually being happy.

"Is this what you want?" I asked forcefully.

"You asked me that yesterday."

"You didn't answer."

When I came up for air, I saw him watching me with his eyes wet with thought.

"I told you I loved you."

"And that hasn't changed?"

"Why would it?"

Inspecting the cobwebs curving down from the ceiling, I shook my head. Everything seemed less mystical in daylight. The candles had gone out, leaving thick jellied puddles across the floorboards, and when I looked closely at the walls, I saw claw marks scabbed against the black paint.

"What is it you actually want?" I asked.

"What I want…"

I held my breath, my pulse clanging in pursuit of words that had the capacity to build or bulldoze everything.

"Is breakfast." Nicholas finished.

I arched a brow as he leapt up then scanned the room, naked.

"And then what?" I asked, averting my eyes from his sculpted behind.

"And then lunch and dinner."

Studying my fingernails, I wondered if he was going to mention what happened last night when I noticed him smiling.

"What?"

"You're wearing my shirt," Nicholas said.

My lips parted as my fingers fumbled over the buttons. "Sorry I—"

"Don't be," Nicholas said.

Crouching down, he tugged my dress up with a claw.

"But I'm not sure if this will fit me."

His eyes softened, and even though I wanted to laugh, I couldn't, because I was afraid if I got too comfortable then, the illusion might shatter.

"Come on," Nicholas said.

Wrapping the sheet we'd used as a blanket twice around his waist, he looked across at me, and when I caught the subtle tremor of his jaw I realised he was just as nervous as me.

"Fine," I muttered, grateful he wasn't as confident as he made out.

Seconds later, we were heading down the red velvet corridor. I kept glancing at him, wondering what he was thinking. Was he going over last night? If he was, did he think it was a mistake? He didn't look as though he thought it was a mistake. In fact, this was the most content I'd ever seen him. With his chin lifted, he had this spark in his eyes I hadn't seen before.

The hesitant patter of our footsteps filled the corridor as his shirt brushed up against my thighs. I chewed my lip, dreading dining with other guests because if I were to cross my legs and someone was to peep under the table at the same moment, they would be sure to get an eyeful.

It took a few minutes before we made it to the hall. Punched by the heat from the long oblong windows, we continued skulking on in silence. Taking my seat next to Nicholas's, my eyes expanded when I saw the spread of delicacies laid out across the table.

Golden bowls filled with mountains of fruits, and bread, and at their sides were jugs bubbling with the scent of home-made cakes and pastries. I scanned the feast keenly, and before my stomach could grow teeth and devour the food itself, Nicholas's voice made me tense up.

"What wrong?"

"Nothing," I lied, forcing a smile. "I'm fine. Everything's fine."

"You don't seem fine."

"How can you tell?"

"Because anyone who says they're fine more than once, definitely isn't."

Licking my lips, I fiddled with the ring he'd given me. Nicholas was right. I wasn't fine, Mia. I was happy, and sometimes when your heart receives all the love it's craved for years, instead of jumping for joy, you crumble under the realisation that not everything in this world is for keeps.

"It's just, all this," I said.

"You don't like the food?"

"It's not the food. It's just what happens when I leave? What happens if I can't come back? Your mother couldn't come back for weeks after she had you, and last night was..."

I paused, choosing my words carefully.

"Last night felt like the start of something real, and I'm afraid of what might happen when I leave."

"You can come back."

"It's not that easy. There are things I need to sort out, and a life I need to leave behind."

Nicholas watched me, his eyes heavy with concern, his breath wedged in his lungs.

"Raine, is this what you want?"

"Yes," I replied so quickly he smiled.

"Well then, let's enjoy it," Nicholas said. "You told me to stop wasting my life being afraid of what might happen if I let myself be happy, remember?"

I nodded as he hunched lower with his lips pressed together.

"I can't be sure if this will be our only morning together, or the first of many," Nicholas continued. "All I can be sure of is how I feel about you. I meant what I said last night. You make me happy, and I don't want whatever time we have together to be wasted tied up in what-ifs or maybes."

"So this, we could actually be something?"

"We already are," Nicholas replied.

I blushed, allowing my mind to wonder what it would be like to have breakfast with Nicholas every morning, stealing glances at him from across the table, falling asleep next to him every night. The idea made my heart swell twice the size of my chest.

Fixing my face to appear impassive, I turned to the portrait I'd painted on the back wall.

"You never needed that portrait, did you?" I asked.

"Not really."

My jaw hit the floor as I spun back swiftly.

"Then why did you ask me to paint it? I spent days practising, and working myself up and—"

"Exactly," Nicholas cut in. "At the lake, you told me you couldn't paint, and after speaking so fiercely about art, I thought you needed a push."

"So, you tricked me?"

"A little," Nicholas grinned. "Plus, I wanted something that reminded me of you before you left."

"You thought a portrait of yourself, would remind you of me?"

Nicholas's lip jerked, and when I pulled a face he laughed; a goofy unrestrained laugh that took me by complete surprise. From out of nowhere, I felt proud I could make him laugh that way.

"So..." I said, taking hold of a silver jug, and pouring a thick gold liquid into two glasses. "I guess we need a plan."

"A plan?"

"Of all the places in the kingdom we're going to see. If we're going to do this, I want to do it properly."

Seizing the glass I'd filled with a glittering substance that looked a lot like paint, Nicholas's brows came together as he searched my eyes for a flicker of doubt, and when I stared back daringly, he lifted his chin.

"Where would you like to start?"

It started with a plan. After borrowing something to wear from Marianne, we agreed to meet at the lake. I didn't have time to ask where we were going, or if I needed to bring anything with me, because seconds later, Marianne had burst into the hall then ushered me away.

Mumbling a wobbly goodbye to Nicholas I set off through the corridor, wondering if there was some place I could shower, or at the very least brush my teeth. Visions played of a bathtub the size of an ocean, set below rich copper shelves, stocked with magical creams and potions before Marianne halted outside of the bedroom that had belonged to Nicholas's parents.

Stumbling in after her as if doing the walk of shame, the sensation intensified when the head inside of the glass case raised a thin brow, raking over my bare legs and messy hair.

"How are you?" she asked a little too knowingly.

"Fine," I replied.

My cheeks flamed as her body sifted through a rainbow of fabrics from inside of a wardrobe behind me.

"Too grand, too long, too plain," Marianne sang as her fingers worked their way through the catalogue of ancient dresses. "We need something loose, something colourful, something comfortable, something ah!"

With a backless indigo summer dress clasped in her chalky palms, her body marched over to me.

"No, wait!" I gasped as she pulled Nicholas's shirt over my head.

"Not to worry," Marianne chirped. "I've seen it all before. I have parts like that myself. Are you excited?"

"Excited?" I repeated, mortified she'd seen me naked.

"About seeing the rest of the kingdom. It's a magnificent place. One can only dream of the wonders that rest beyond the lake."

I forced a smile as Marianne swung around with her arms outstretched and her dress flooding with air, but in spite of my excitement to venture out into the kingdom, Mia, I couldn't help think of the Siren Nicholas had been friends with. Then, of the rituals, he'd have to adhere to in order to stay alive.

"What is it?" Marianne asked.

I shook my head as her body swanned over to the bed. Taking her seat in the middle, she crossed her ankle and leant forward so that the marrow in her neck was exposed.

"Go on," she insisted.

But I wasn't even sure of where to begin, and the longer she waited, the more ridiculous I felt for even worrying about Nicholas's past.

"The Siren he was friends with," I tiptoed. "were

they… where they more than friends?"

"She loved him."

My gut twisted as I stared at her, stunned.

"He didn't return the feeling," Marianne added quickly. "I'm not sure Nicholas even knew."

"How?"

Marianne raised a brow in question.

"I mean, how could she have loved him when she forced him to do what he did?"

Her eyes flashed with understanding before they slipped to the dry blood on her neck.

"Well, like his father, Master Nicholas always strove to see the best in creatures. When he met the Siren, he treated her as she was, instead of the monster our world believed her to be. And after being regarded as an outsider for most of her life, it was only inevitable she'd fall prey to love. Only she loved Nicholas in a way that devoured all of the light inside of him. We all saw it. Candimore, his parents, Morgana. The more time Nicholas spent with the creature, the more short-tempered he became with the world."

Her eyes grew glassy as she swallowed.

"When Master Nicholas did eventually see sense, we all harboured some hope Morgana's prophecy would not transpire, but then of course it happened," she muttered. "That poor child, waking up in his parents' blood. He was trying to save them when Candimore found him. Trying to put back his father's intestines. We didn't know what the creatures would do when they found her. I certainly didn't support it, and the curse, the curse that—"

"Curse?"

A light flicked on Marianne's eyes as she peered at me tensely.

"Pardon me?"

"You mentioned a curse."

"I mention a lot of things."

"No, this in particular."

Marianne buttoned her lips so tightly her face became chalk.

"Marianne, what are you not telling me?"

"It's not my place to mention such things," she tittered.

"And if I were to ask Nicholas?"

With that, her focus bounced right back to me, and for a second, I was terrified. I'd never seen Marianne angry, but the way she looked at me then, was enough to send any nightmare I'd ever had, running in the opposite direction.

"Now listen to me, Raine, and listen carefully," she hissed. "All this talking about the past is a waste of time. It won't bring back the creatures that were slaughtered, nor will it change the future, so stop trying to resurrect things that are buried."

"But I just—"

"You want to understand," she interrupted. "But believe me, now is not the time."

"Then when is?"

"When Nicholas is ready."

I opened my mouth to argue when Marianne waggled her head at the door. Shamefaced, I skulked through the silence like a misbehaving child that had been sent to bed without supper, when she called my name.

"Yes?" I asked, turning to her from the doorway.

"I just…" Marianne sighed then shook her head at the ceiling. "Do you love him?"

My lips parted as I stepped back, uncertain of how my feelings towards Nicholas would concern her.

"That boy has been through enough heartache to last him a lifetime," she said before I could answer. "And I just wanted to make sure whatever he is sacrificing is for the right reasons."

Unable to offer any half-truths, I found myself nodding.

"Then let love destroy you," Marianne said. "Venture out into the kingdom and allow yourself to be cut open by the wonders you digest, Raine, because you, my dear, reek of a girl who is in love and is too afraid to admit it."

"I'll try."

"Now go. Stop wasting all of your time with a headless Flemgril. There are adventures to be had, shoo."

Thanking her again, I crept into the corridor with her words strumming around in my head like a rogue mariachi band.

Let love destroy me.

Nodding at the corridor, I trooped towards the end, and before I knew it I was hurdling through dusty stairwells, and sunny corridors, and huge bolted doors before I reached the spiral stairwell. Jogging down the steps, I saw the entrance door cracked open. A sliver of pink sky spilt in through the gap, tickling the hall in cerise fuzz.

Peering behind the entry, I caught sight of Nicholas pacing backwards and forwards on the steps. I wrinkled my brow. He was speaking to someone, but I couldn't see who.

"How are you?" he asked. "How are you?" he repeated in a lower tone.

Sticking my head behind the door, I saw he was alone.

"How are you?" he asked the space in front of him.

I grinned, wondering if I should wait for him to finish his one-man pantomime when he spoke in a voice so poised, I couldn't help laugh.

Swerving around to the doorway, Nicholas hung his head with his cheeks colouring.

"I'm fine," I told him. "Do you always talk to yourself?"

"I wasn't talking to myself," Nicholas mumbled.

"I'm sorry," I teased, extending a hand to the space next to him. "How do you do?"

Nicholas raised a brow. Taking in his scraggly hair and unkempt beard, I noticed there was an effortlessness about him that hadn't been there before.

"Are you ready?" Nicholas asked as I padded outside.

"Well, that depends on where you're taking me."

"To the third region."

"With the Mercreatures?"

"With everything," Nicholas replied.

Trotting down the steps, I stopped when Nicholas trod back, studying me with his head tilted.

"What is it?" I asked.

"You," he said.

"Me what?" I asked, in that Tarzan and Jane sort of way.

"You look nice."

My lips cracked as I watched him uncertainly. Is this what we were going to do now? Compliment each other? Did he actually think I looked nice? Or did he practice saying it before I walked outside? Maybe I should return the compliment and say something about his boots, or his shirt, definitely his boots.

"But," Nicholas said.

"But?" I repeated, waiting for the blow.

"You're not wearing any shoes."

Shoes! I'd forgotten to put on shoes, and when Nicholas studied me as if being barefoot was the most horrendous crime imaginable, I fought to keep a straight face.

"I'll manage," I told him.

"You're sure?"

"Positive."

"But you can barely tolerate being inside of a bubble, how will you manage without shoes?"

"I'll steal your boots,"

Nicholas watched me challengingly before he stepped closer so that his chin was above my head. I held my breath, staring at a button midway up his shirt. Was he going to kiss me? Even if he wasn't planning on kissing me, I wanted him to. I bit my lip, waiting for him to say something, anything, but he just stood there, silent as the soft breeze tangling itself between us.

Kiss me, I thought, *please kiss me.*

Peeking up at his bristled jaw, I reminded myself what Marianne had told me. I had to be fearless and let love destroy me. It was for that insane reason, when Nicholas opened his mouth, I squared up my shoulders, pounced forwards then planted a hefty kiss on his lips.

The gesture I imagine, came as much of a surprise to Nicholas, as it did to me, because the second as our lips connected, he stumbled back and gasped.

"Sorry!" I choked.

"Don't be," Nicholas laughed.

Beyond mortified, I looked away as he set off through the field. "Are you excited?" he called over his shoulder.

"Are you?" I asked, chasing after him with my cheeks stinging.

"More than you can imagine."

"Me too," I admitted.

Stopping in the centre of the field, Nicholas extracted a canister from his pocket. Studying it in his hands, he smiled a sly smile and before I could delude myself with any more blind hope, he stepped over to where I'd been watching him, took my face in his palms, and he kissed me right back.

"Let's go," he said.

***

Peters is pulling me down the corridor, telling me I can fall apart after my hearing, but all I can think of is

Nicholas.

"He took me to the third region and explained the hydroelectric energy used to power Wanderlust—"

"Raine," she mutters.

I have to finish; I have to tell you what happened, Mia.

"I slept on his floorboards, and I was happy, but I didn't tell him. He took me to the unicorn farms, and there were these huge white stallions that cried in barns."

I'm more than aware I sound insane, but I can't stop.

"He told me I made him happy, and if I did, I don't understand why he didn't tell me the truth. He had so many opportunities, and he just let me believe—"

"Raine," Peters jerks around when we reach the door.

Behind the gap I see the audience in their hoary wigs and black robes; their grey faces dusted with winter sunlight, the hunger in their dead eyes.

I blink forcefully, my head orbiting like two revolving doors. "I'm not one of your psychiatrists, right now you need to—"

"I need to tell her."

"Who?"

"My baby." The second the words leave my mouth, I realise it's the first time I have spoken them aloud. My baby; mine. A part of me, of him, of us. A child we created when there was an us. Us. That cruel little word that carried a revolution.

Wiping my nose with my sleeve, I work my hands through the dry tangle of my hair.

"Come on," Peters instructs, but I won't budge. "Jesus Christ," She stoops lower to meet my eyes. "Whatever happened outside of this case, forget it. Despite all of this stuff about the place you thought you were going to, you have a real chance of getting out. Now pull yourself together." Before I can argue Peters heads through the door with her gown ballooning at her feet.

I stare at her taking her seat in the bottom row of a long panel. She juts her head at the empty seat next to her, and as I step through the hushed voices, and exhuming stares, I swear all I hear is Nicholas's voice.

'*Are you excited?*' He'd asked me.

I was Mia, I really was.

CHAPTER TWENTY

"Whatever happened outside of that night, forget it," Peters had told me. Her words play on repeat as I state my name, and address, to a room full of strangers – only I can't forget, Mia, I promised Nicholas I wouldn't. I say his name in the back of my head while Peters outlines the reasons why the case has been dropped. Why the evidence put forward was too damning to dismiss. Why a new suspect has been apprehended.

Nicholas, Nicholas, Nicholas.

Collapsing in the seat next to me, Peters whispers for me to be quiet, but my heart won't let me. Clenching my jaw, I hear a sound like someone rubbing together their dry palms, and when I look up, I see Pierce striding over to the bench, cleanly shaven, and wearing a snug grey suit.

"State your name and address for the court," calls a thirty-something-year-old man behind me.

"Doctor Elliot Pierce."

My gut wilts as I listen to the crisp edge of his voice with no traces of the warm indecisiveness I'd believed he was built of.

"Address 915 Holmgreen Meadow."

It was all just an act, everything; the scruffy beard, the muddling persona, every squiggly flaw about him, created to get me to open up. He never had a wife or a child, never experienced pain or anguish; his only priority was himself.

Over my shoulder, I glance through the students eagerly observing the spectacle — the magistrates in their silver wigs. Watson, with her dull hair scraped into a messy bun, and her face devoid of its usual paint.

"Doctor Pierce," the clerk begins in a thick Northern accent. "You were appointed to Ms Black as one of her clinical psychologists on the date November 22nd to assess whether she was mentally competent during the time she was arrested, is that correct?"

"Correct." Pierce grins.

Why is he grinning?

"During which time the charges have been dropped, and the hearing today is to assess whether Ms Black is mentally stable enough for release."

"Correct."

I grit my teeth, wanting to be anywhere but here, wanting to be with Nicholas.

"Index finger down, little finger up, both thumbs down," I mutter.

"Shhh," Peters hisses.

"…A joint diagnosis of paranoid schizophrenia was concluded by my colleague, Doctor Margo Watson and I."

"Index finger down, little finger up, both thumbs down."

"…Paranoid schizophrenia is a sub-form of schizophrenia. The main symptoms include hallucinations, delusions, disorganised speech and catatonic…"

Nothing he is saying is true. He hadn't seen any of the

things I had; he hadn't met Nicholas, been lied to by him.

"… Three phases of schizophrenia. The first is prodromal. The phase in which the sufferer withdraws from work life and social interaction."

An image of Nicholas batters my lids as I cling to my skull.

Thirteen days, I managed to spend with him until my world took me back. Thirteen days. On that last night, he was playing the piano. I remember watching his claws crash upon the bare surface like rain, pattering, falling, pelting.

I remember knowing I loved him then. I'd told him freely, and it felt so good to be able to say it without wanting anything in return, just saying it so that he knew.

OCTOBER 5th 2018: The morning of the murder

Coming through the mirror, I was graced with the sort of feeling you get when you arrive home after a holiday from hell. That balmy sense of security that grazes your bones when you slip into your plush bed sheets after an unbearably long plane ride, turn out all the lights, and fall asleep surrounded by timeworn photographs, and coffee stained books that welcome you back like old friends.

It had been two days since I was able to return to Wanderlust. Both were filled with petulant little hours wasted prodding the mirror, falling back, then waiting. Prodding, falling, waiting. Prodding, falling, waiting. After being unable to return the first day, I feared what might happen if I didn't make it back at all.

Pacing about my studio, I'd gone over all of the ways I might be able to force my way back, summoning the strength I had to stand with my hand pressed against the mirror for hours. Lightheaded and devoid of sleep and sustenance, I waited and waited until that huge flood of white light whispered, I was home.

Pausing outside of Nicholas's door, I smoothed out the creases in my pearl summer dress, hoping I wasn't overdressed. The last time I'd seen him, he promised to take me to the blood river; a mighty stretch of land kissed by a shore that was the colour of violent nights. I had no idea what outfit would befit such a place. Probably jeans and a t-shirt I mused as I knocked on his door.

"Nicholas?"

After three hefty raps went unanswered, I stuck my head inside. The curtains were drawn, and the off-white sheet we used as a blanket was sprawled across the floor like an exhausted ghost. Wondering if I should try my luck elsewhere, I pulled a face. The spirit river, maybe, or the dining hall.

Hurrying down the corridor, my heart ballooned with wonder for how Nicholas would regard me after two days.

'*You took your time,*' I imagined he'd say. To which I'd muster up a playful,

'*Don't look too happy to see me.*'

Fighting a smile, I skipped down the steps, recalling the past thirteen days we'd spent together. It wasn't long, but it was enough time to awaken a childlike excitement inside of me; that tingly sensation you get before the world smudges you out and burdens you with fears of bills, and qualifications, and divorce settlements.

Nicholas and I had fallen into a routine. The kind that was full of the promise of what was to come. Every morning we'd wake from the light streaming in through the windows, and after breakfast he'd produce a rainbow of canisters.

'Which one?' he'd ask. 'Are you sure?' He'd question after I nodded, faltered and nodded again. Then off we went, venturing into the kingdom with nothing but an unburdening lust for life, and in that mighty accomplishment we were rich.

We'd managed to see a lot in those thirteen days. So far, we'd journeyed to the Unicorn farms in the fifth region where white stallions cried bucket loads of tears after being read stories. The Valley Of The Chosen Souls in the sixth region, where pudgy trolls with wild purple hair ran amongst us, laughing and plodding barefoot through miles of thick spindly trees.

I was as content as a fat cat that could eat no more, but I admit the idea of staying in Wanderlust threw me a little at first, Mia. On the first day, I questioned if Nicholas or I would feel suffocated with the amount of time we were spending together.

Both of us enjoyed our solitude. And so being alone never really felt lonely. But after a few hours spent exploring the kingdom beside him, I'd surprised myself, because my affection towards Nicholas had only grown, and when I wasn't with him, I found myself wanting to be.

"Nicholas?" I called on reaching the entrance hall.

My voice pirouetted into the silence, resounding alongside the stonewashed pillars and clattering against the mural. Heading through the crystal maze, I expected to run into Marianne, or Candimore on my way to the dining room, but all I came across was my distorted reflection in the glass walls.

Pushing open the dining room door, I glanced around expectedly. There were no goblets, or beakers, or mountains of fruit on the table, and most importantly, no Nicholas studying me from the seat in the middle. Where was everyone? In the past thirteen days, the palace had been overflowing with life, and now the place was a ghost town at best.

Traipsing through the rowdy silence, I stopped at Nicholas's portrait. The reflection of the lake poured through the windows, dancing across his high cheekbones and furrowed stare. I chewed my lip. Was he at the lake? It seemed plausible enough. About to head off, I jumped when someone laughed. The sound was shrill, and earthy, and wrapped the hall in a frosty blanket of unease, but after peering around, I saw I was alone.

I rubbed my eyes. I was imagining things. What else did I expect when I hadn't eaten or slept in days? Stroking Nicholas's ring, I prompted myself to practice some self-care when I noticed a gunky substance under my fingernails. My lips puckered as I brought my hand to my face, inspecting the powdered red stains.

"Thank you," a voice in my ear hissed.

Esme.

Veering around, I held my breath expecting to be faced with the dead woman, but yet again, I saw I was alone. I groaned. All of those sleepless nights must've been taking a toll on my health. With the weight of an oncoming headache burning bright between my temples, I rolled my eyes when a clanging sound echoed above me.

My lip twitched. The noise began softly. The gentle symphony of a wind chime gonging on a bored summers day before it grew louder, and louder, until all that echoed above me was the melody of two huge cymbals bashing into one another other wildly. Looking up, my jaw smacked the floor.

The ceiling was shaking, not only that – the pillars were shuddering too; the walls, the portrait I'd painted, everything from the ceiling down to the floor was juddering as it were midway through mourning the loss of a loved one.

Pinpricks of sweat blistered my brow as I skimmed the place frantically. Was I in the middle of an earthquake? Is that where Nicholas was? Hiding in some evacuation spot I didn't know about? Is that where everyone else was? Throwing my hands over my chest, I stumbled backwards when a cloud of smoke burst from the corner of the room. My eyes flew open as thick wafts of smoke filled the hall, carpeting everything in the pungent scent of burning. I coughed as the smoke grew thicker, puffing itself up like a fierce alley cat.

What the hell was going on? The walls continued juddering, and the ceiling quaked louder while I struggled to see through the smoke, and before I could spoon feed myself any nonsensical explanations as to how I was safe, the windows behind me shattered.

I winced. Hundreds of shards of glass slashed my arms and legs as I keeled over, dumfounded. The pain, similar to a thousand tiny kittens clawing at my legs. I had to get out. If I didn't, I was either going to die of smoke inhalation or be trampled by the ceiling.

Bolting through the pandemonium, I lurched forwards, praying I could leave through the entry to the library.

"Come on," I muttered, reaching what I hoped was the wall. "Come on!"

I groped the panel pathetically. My eyes stung, and my lungs gasped. I had to find Nicholas. I had to warn him about Esme. What would he say when he realised the reason she was destroying his home was because of me? It must've been Esme's doing. I'd heard her voice, her laugh. Forcing myself not to think about the repercussions of associating with Esme, I whacked my fists against the wall.

The fracture widened. Relief grazed my sweaty face as an entry formed, only when I managed to stumble through the break, any hope I harboured shattered at my feet. I stared at the place, mortified. All around me novels were flying down from high tiered shelves and ladders at their sides were coming apart from the bottom up.

The ceiling had cracked in the middle, and bits of brick rained down heedlessly, littering the floor in thick brown chunks. Creeping forwards, I was tackled by the realisation I should've mentioned Esme sooner. I'd spent thirteen days with Nicholas, and not once had she crossed my mind. But what would she gain from destroying the palace?

Mustering up whatever courage I had left to battle through the collapsing library, I made it into the hallway, promising myself that when I found Nicholas, this would all make sense. I rushed on, wheezing, and retching, and tripping over pieces of brick as I bolted down collapsing stairwells, and crumbling passages, and when I pushed open the door to the corridor where I'd painted Nicholas, somehow, everything stopped.

The walls quivered, then became still. The black smoke thinned, then cleared. And when it dissipated completely, I saw Marianne, Candimore, and Morgana, manning the ruby door with their arms enveloping their chests. By their expressions, I knew something had happened, something terrible. Taking a step backwards, I froze when Candimore peered up at me with his teeth bared.

"What's going on?" I asked, forcing my legs to go the rest of the way.

No one answered.

Marianne slumped to the floor.

My face paled as she rocked backwards and forwards with her hands around her knees.

"The palace was just collapsing," I told them. "I need to tell Nicholas, it's not safe for any of us." I waited for the shock to resonate on their faces, I waited for their anger, their fear, but all that followed was more silence.

"Where's Nicholas?"

"Don't pretend you don't know," Candimore snarled.

"I don't—"

"Candimore," Morgana scolded, narrowing her grey brows. "Nicholas told you she didn't know."

"Didn't know what?"

Both watched me carefully. Despite the chill bruising the air, my face was radiating heat.

"Didn't know what?" I barked, not caring whether I sounded cross. They were hiding something, and I needed to know what. Perhaps Nicholas had told them he didn't want to see me. But if that was the case, why couldn't he have told me himself?

The corridor shrank as I glared at them, half anger, half desperation, and when no answer came, I shouted loud enough to make Morgana flinch.

"What did he tell you?"

"You don't remember?" she whispered.

"Remember what?"

"The Siren Master Nicholas told you about. The creature responsible for his parents' death."

"What about her?"

Morgana took a deep breath while Candimore paced up and down with his eyes set on the floor.

"What about her?" I snapped.

Morgana looked back sadly.

"You know her," she said.

"But that's impossible. I couldn't…" I paused, mentally sifting through all of the creatures I'd met in Wanderlust, but the only Siren that sprang to mind was the creature I'd seen on the night of the ball, and I knew it couldn't have been her. "I'm sorry—"

"You can't say her name."

It took a second for me to register what she meant, and when it clicked, everything inside of me smouldered to ash. I stared at her imploringly. I had to have been mistaken, because the only creature whose name I couldn't say aloud was Esme's, and it couldn't have been her.

"We could have stopped it," Candimore was saying. "He knew."

One word jumped out at me.

KNEW.

"What do you mean he knew?"

I barely heard my voice.

"Where's Nicholas?"

Again, a whisper.

My throat was drying up, and the sound of Candimore's feet thwacking the corridor were ploughing right through me.

I clutched my chest. He wouldn't stop walking. Wouldn't answer.

THWACK, THWACK, THWACK.

"Candimore, where is Nicholas?"

My heart hammered as Candimore stopped. Studying me in the bluing shadows, he shook his head then uttered three words that ripped through me with more force than a wound from a submachine gun.

"Nicholas is dead."

Stifling an inaudible laugh, I turned to Morgana.

"Morgana?"

She wouldn't look up.

"Morgana!"

And when she shook her head at the floor, I lost all rights to my body. Bile lurched up my throat as I flung myself at the door, convinced Nicholas would be inside.

I rammed my knuckles into the wood in a feeble attempt to get it to open, but my muscles wouldn't work, nothing would work. Candimore was still speaking, but the only voice in my head was Nicholas's. He was promising me everything would be okay; all I had to do was get through the door.

Colds beads of sweat slithered down my temples as I tugged the lever furiously.

"No, no, no," I mumbled. "No, no, no!"

They were lying. They had to be lying.

"Raine—"

I wasn't listening. I had to get through the door. The sight before me swayed as I yanked the melting lever.

"Raine—"

The door clicked open.

On flinging myself behind the gap, something odd began to take place, Mia. A film reel started to flicker in my mind. A memory I'd tried to block for years. Only when the door slammed shut behind me, and I set eyes on Nicholas sprawled out in the middle of the floor, it seemed I no longer had the strength to keep that memory at bay, and suddenly I was twelve years old again.

I remembered rushing home from school with my red ladybird bag slung over my shoulder with a plan to ask my dad if I could go to the library to work on a project on the Second World War. We didn't own a computer, and it was the only other option, lest he wanted me to fail.

It seemed like a good enough excuse. And perhaps it wouldn't have even been such a big deal if Lucile hadn't said hi to me at lunch that day – Lucile rarely said hello to anyone, let alone me, and I knew she hung about at the juice bar opposite the library at around six.

Filling my lungs up of sharp autumn air, I'd dashed down our shabby street, then raced up our shabbier drive, before pushing open the front door, and when I saw him, I stopped, not fully grasping what I was seeing. It took a few seconds for my focus to come through, and to see the chair by his side. The same chair my mom would stand on to fix the light bulb in the kitchen.

Rot grazed my lungs as I pushed back in the doorway,

studying the skin around his neck. Purple, bruised. His tongue lolled out from the corners of his lips. Both eyes, red, bulging. My gaze crossed the rope around his neck, the same rope I'd seen him fooling around with the night before. Making knots then undoing them with his tongue compressed between his teeth. Is that what he'd been practising when he winked at me while I played with my Lissey doll?

Immobilised by fear, I stood there for what seemed like hours, watching my dad swaying back and forth, no thoughts, no feeling. It was the clatter of tins that had snapped me out of my trance, Mia. My mother had walked in from the supermarket only to find me gawking at my father's bloated corpse. What a strange girl she must've thought. Is that when she began detesting me?

It was when my mother's screams punctured the silence, I made a promise to myself, Mia. A promise that went on to change the course of my life. I promised I would never, ever, give my heart away. I vowed to keep it locked up, safe, chained from anyone and anything because handing a piece of yourself to someone who could leave is fickle.

Loving someone so much that in their absence you become nothing is nonsensical. I lived by that philosophy for years, reminding myself of it daily, practising it in every half-hearted choice I ever made. I married Dan because of it; turned down jobs my heart secretly craved because deep down, I was terrified of having anything worth losing.

Only when I staggered over to the stranger pretending to be Nicholas on the floor. When I couldn't feel, or think, or breathe, or do anything that living people do when I saw his unmoving face, I realised it was too late.

"Nicholas," I whispered, buckling down next to him.

I waited for him to jump up, laughing, but he wouldn't

413

get up. Why wouldn't he get up? My throat tightened as I glared at his face; this wasn't his face. Not the warm chiselled face I knew. His cheeks were sunken, and his skin belonged to someone who'd been left out in the rain too long. And his eyes, his eyes were still open. They were red, bulging, just like my dad's.

"Nicholas please." A sourness shot up in my throat as I shook him by his shoulders. He wouldn't move. Why wouldn't he move? And when I saw the blood on his chest, I clamped down hard on my lips to stop myself from screaming.

"Nicholas, get up!" My frantic wails filled the arctic hall as I fell against his bloody shirt.

What had happened, and how? I shuddered as the hot scent of blood rose from his abdomen, and just as I was about to force the creatures outside to get help, I heard her.

"Bravo Raine!" Grinding my teeth, I was certain that when I looked up, I would experience a different sort of rage. Wild, and unobstructed, and puncturing every crevice of my body until I was nothing more than a ball of used up energy. But what I didn't count on, was that when I saw Esme grinning at me from Nicholas's throne, I'd understand what it was like to have the desire to kill, not knowing then, I'd killed already.

***

"Doctor Pierce," the clerk continues. "In your professional opinion if released and kept under supervision, do you think Miss Black may be in danger to herself and others?"

Pierce screws his lips into a dishevelled smile.

"Yes. In my professional opinion based on the aggressive behaviour exhibited by Ms Black in the previous weeks, she'd require a minimum stay of up to three years in a secure mental health facility."

The clerk is about to say something when Pierce raises a hand.

"Can I also add, as I mentioned earlier to the police department, Ms Black is carrying her husband's child."

Flinging my hands over my stomach, I am pummelled by an urge to fly over the bench and smack my fists into his smug face.

"Don't react," Peters whispers.

"...and I believe due to her violent outbursts, it's in the child's best interest to be placed in care immediately."

I stare at him grinning. Grinning like Esme. Grinning like hate, and despite wanting this outcome all along, something snaps inside of me, and I decide to end this now.

CHAPTER TWENTY-ONE

"What happens now?" I mutter.

Peters studies her short-bitten fingernails. The guilt she exudes, makes me question if she already knew what Pierce would say.

"We have to wait for Doctor Watson to give her professional opinion."

"And if they don't agree?"

"It's up to the judge and psychiatric board."

"So, what you're saying is…"

"You still have a chance of getting out of here."

OCTOBER 5th 2018: The afternoon of the murder.

"He's just sleeping," I muttered, rocking backwards and forwards on the floor. "He's just sleeping."

"He's not!" Esme hooted, sauntering over to me from the stage.

"Nicholas get up! This isn't funny."

"No," Esme said. "It's side-splittingly hilarious."

I swear it took every ounce of strength I had left in me not to launch myself at her, Mia. Cradling my chest in my arms, I keeled over fighting to get the air to enter my lungs, and trying to make sense of all that was going on, but I couldn't. Nicholas couldn't be dead. It was only days ago we'd been making plans, and now…

Raising my head, my gut churned as I stared at his pale face. My chest was a blender, and my heart was trapped inside.

"I guess you're wondering why this happened," Esme questioned.

I couldn't answer. All I could do was stare at Nicholas's blue lips, waiting for them to twitch.

"Don't do this," I whispered. "Don't."

"He betrayed me," Esme went on.

I wasn't listening. I was trapped in a bad dream. The world was foggy and nothing made sense.

"Nicholas, get up," I cried, bashing my palms against the open wound on his chest. It was cold, wet, and when I gazed down at my bloody fists, my eyes blistered with hot tears.

"No," I breathed. "No. No. No."

"No, no, no," Esme mimicked, twirling around next to me with her arms above her head.

I cupped my face in palms. If this was real, how had Esme managed to break into the palace? And why wasn't anyone here to stop her? Why wasn't anyone here now? I wanted to scream. I was sinking, tumbling through the arctic floor, and I couldn't stop.

Esme was speaking, her words somewhere far off. She was insisting she and Nicholas had been friends, and that both of them had planned on murdering his parents; but that was a lie, this megalomaniac beast had taken a passing comment he'd made and held it against him.

"…and he lacked the integrity—"

"You think murdering his parents takes integrity?" I hissed. Lifting my head, I struggled to keep my jaw steady, and my eyes from pooling with tears. Esme dipped her head, her silver hair falling to one side and her scarred cheeks following.

"Are you honestly going to question me on the logistics of murder?" she growled. The hoarseness of her voice itching my skin. "Wasn't it you who stood by idly and watched as Nicholas massacred an innocent Siren? Slit her throat with the same claws he ran through your hair, feasted on her blood with the same lips he used to kiss you?" Esme's empty eyes danced over Nicholas, but she didn't deserve to look at him. She didn't even deserve to be alive.

"Nicholas shared that view once."

"Don't," I breathed. "Don't say his name."

Esme smirked then crouched lower so that the ends of her hair brushed up against my shoulders.

"Nicholas and I," she sang, taking care to enunciate his name. "Planned on setting the Sirens free. Only he was afraid of what his dear sweet parents would think. Fear does strange things to a creature, Raine. It messes with your mind, and forces you to speak words you don't mean. He told me he couldn't see me again. He claimed if the Sirens were set free, they'd destroy Wanderlust."

"And would they?"

"Probably," Esme shrugged. "But that's neither here nor there. We can never truly be certain of the future. I mean, take this for example, I guarantee this morning you had no idea your afternoon would consist of holding hands with a corpse."

My face paled as I focussed on Nicholas's bloody shirt. A button midway was open. Dark hairs poked through the fracture. Beneath that, oily burgundy ink.

"Please, look at me," I whispered. The longer I waited, the harder my soul shook. It was like waking up in an operating theatre midway through surgery, unable to cry for help while doctors drilled and diced at your insides.

"He banished me," Esme breathed. "And as the months passed, I watched him, waiting for him to realise he'd made a mistake, waiting for him to take on the role he deserved, but what I saw instead made me sick," she paused, her pitch heightening with nasally revolt.

"He looked happy! After everything he claimed he wanted, I saw him laughing with his mother as if he had no recollection of all that he desired, and I knew I had to carry out what he lacked the strength to do. And so, I waited, and waited, and when the time was right, I possessed him."

My gut coiled as I stared at Nicholas, praying he'd lift his head.

Just look at me.

"When he first came through the trance, I expected him to thank me or at least marvel at the masterpiece I'd created. But the fool was desolate. Screaming and begging for forgiveness from lord knows who."

"Please wake up," I whispered, grabbing Nicholas's palm. It wouldn't work.

Why wouldn't anything work?

"Eventually they caught me, and do you know what they did?" Esme paused, then in a low, and almost sorrowful tone, she whispered, "They ripped out my eyes."

My lips parted. Peering up, I hunted her flayed face for some evidence she was telling the truth, and when her jaw trembled, I knew that she was.

"They pulled them right from the sockets," she howled.

Dropping Nicholas's palm, I shrunk back, failing to make sense of what Esme was telling me. Despite everything Esme had done to Nicholas, I couldn't believe he would act so callously, but then I'd seen him murder the Siren in a ritual he claimed was mandatory.

What if he claimed this was just as necessary?

"When the torture was over, they lit a fire," Esme growled, grabbing her minced face. "I could feel my skin slipping from the bone, my hair sizzling, my vocal cords bleeding as I begged for help, and he wasn't even there to stop it."

An anchor settled in my gut.

"What do you mean he wasn't there?" I whispered.

"He wasn't there!" Esme cackled, throwing her palms across her face.

"You mean, Nicholas had no part in what happened to you?" My chest heaved as I watched her; waiting for her to tell me it was Nicholas who had initiated the attack, or that it was him who lit the match, anything to make this hurt a little less, but instead, Esme shrugged.

The gesture was a punch to the gut with spiked fists.

"Where was he when it happened?"

Esme smirked, flashing me her pointy teeth.

"Where?" I screamed.

"Somewhere in the kingdom," she sang. "Probably mourning the loss of his parents."

Fighting to catch my breath, I bent lower. All I smelt was blood. I felt it embedding itself into my lungs, pressing itself against my throat, scarring my insides with a promise that after today, the scent would never wash.

"I could've killed him the night it happened," Esme was saying. Why? Why would she have killed Nicholas when all he'd done was refuse to carry out demands that were sick. "… After the death of his parents, Nicholas went in search of death himself, and I'd be damned if I handed him what he wanted on a plate. No, I had to be smart. I had a delightful strategy to have him butchered by the very thing he grew up detesting."

Unsure of what she was getting at, I lifted my head.

"You still don't remember do you?"

"Remember what?" staring into the abyss of her eyes, I felt I'd swallowed a bomb. "Remember what?"

Esme grinned.

Crouching lower, she pressed a dry lip to my ear and when she spoke those words, off went the bomb.

"You killed him, Raine. I possessed you."

Sweat pierced my brows as I shook my head.

"I wouldn't."

"Oh, but you did," she snarled. I threw my arms around my sides, fighting to keep myself intact. I was limbless. Arms and legs, ripped from their sockets. Esme was lying. She had to be lying. There was no way I would've harmed Nicholas, I would've remembered.

Bending lower, I glared at my hands. Glimpsing the dark gunk under my fingernails, my spleen coiled.

Blood.

The murky substance I'd seen earlier, was blood. Esme cackled as I pushed myself to find some logical explanation for why there was blood under my fingernails, but there was none. Eyes simmering, I glared at Nicholas's frozen face as my sight wavered. I blinked forcefully. The hall was slipping from my sight.

Was I venturing back?

Turning to Esme, I saw her wave, and before I had a chance to work out what was going on, I found myself in the corridor leading to the room I'd been in seconds ago. I spun around, disorientated, but the action wouldn't pass. I was being hauled towards the door at the end. My feet dragged forward in a trance. There was something heavy in my hand, cold.

A knife.

No.

I blinked, but I wasn't in control of my body. I wasn't in control of anything. I knew what Esme was showing me. I didn't want to see it, couldn't. I tried screaming, but the sound wouldn't arrive. I was trapped. In the shadows of my mind, I heard her laughing. Her hoarse voice scarped my cranium as my hand pushed the open door.

My feet continued moving, my heart continued screaming, and when I lifted my head and saw Nicholas smiling at me from the throne, it broken into a million irretrievable pieces.

"Nicholas get out," I shouted soundlessly.

It wouldn't work. Nothing would work. I was trapped in my own private horror movie and I couldn't even close my eyes.

"You took your time," he said.

Dizzy, I watched as my body carried me up the stairs to the stage. Nicholas cocked his head, his face gentle, his eyes unarmed.

Please, get out.

He rose from his throne as I approached him. I tried hurling myself backwards, shouting, flailing my legs, but nothing worked. My lips trembled as Nicholas held out his arms.

"Raine?"

I didn't want to see what happened next. In an effort to distract myself, I counted the seconds till it was over.

Three seconds.

I was in his arms.

He smelt of spring, and a future.

"Are you ready to go to the Blood River?"

His husky voice collected the tattered pieces of my heart.

Five seconds.

Nicholas pulled away, studying me thoughtfully.

He knew something was wrong. He knew.

His brow puckered as he drew back his shoulders.

Eight seconds.

His eyes sparkled with thought.

Earl grey tea eyes.

Earl grey tea.

Eleven seconds.

Nicholas's lips parted as his gaze flicked to the knife in my hands.

Twelve seconds.

It took twelve seconds to destroy a lifetime of happiness, Mia.

I flinched as the knife rained down on his spine. Nicholas flew back, his palms outstretched. I was sobbing, but I couldn't feel the tears, just the crunch the blade made when it ruptured his ribcage.

"I'm sorry," I tried to scream as I hit again, harder.

"Raine," Nicholas muttered, clinging to his chest.

Like mine, his palms were soaked in blood.

"I'm sorry, Nicholas. I'm sorry."

He couldn't hear my voice or see my tears. My heart wailed as he fell to his knees, staring up at me with this haunting look of betrayal.

Earl grey tea eyes.

His face paled as he lifted a hand. The veins in his neck bulged as he spluttered up blood. A trickle of it slipped down his chin and rested on the creases of his neck.

"Please," he whispered.

I shivered as my arm went up once more and the blade connected with his heart.

"No!" I screamed. This time the word soared out from my lungs, and when my focus came through, I saw I was back in the hall.

"Brilliant, isn't—"

Lurching forward, I grabbed Esme by her wrinkled neck. Her skull smacked the ground and her hair sprawled out in a silver puddle as she peered up gleefully. I had killed Nicholas. Me. It had all been my fault, and I hadn't even known. How weak must I have been to have allowed it to happen? When had it happened?

I screwed up my face, glaring at her, sprawled out and laughing.

"You played a part," Esme wheezed, her hot breath whipping my cheeks.

"I didn't know."

"Oh yes, Raine. Play the fool because it works so splendidly for you. Didn't he tell you to stay away? Didn't he tell you, you had no place here?"

My throat constricted as every conversation I ever had with Nicholas grazed my mind.

'Don't you know what you're doing to me, Raine.'

'There is a darkness here that shouldn't concern you.'

Harassed by a whirlpool of questions, I shook my head, forcing them away, but they wouldn't leave. Had the creatures outside known I was to blame? Had Nicholas known I was under a trance? What if he believed it was my intent to hurt him all along? What if he thought I'd been working with Esme?

"He tried to warn you," Esme hissed.

"Shut up," I screamed. "Shut up. Shut up shut up."

Esme stared up woefully. My teeth protested as I ground them harder, clinging to her neck with fingers that were ready to snap. I had killed Nicholas. Me.

Murderer. Murderer. Murderer.

The words went around in my mind like a barbed wheel, hacking away at my brain before Esme released a dry laugh and flung me backwards. A bright splatter of white flashed in my temples. A hammer to my skull. I winced but I didn't have time to acknowledge the pain, I had to fix this.

"Nicholas, get up," I demanded, crawling over to him.

"You did this," Esme sang.

Inches from Nicholas's bloody palm, Esme whacked her staff against the ground. From it, came a dazzling sea of carroty flames.

"Take some culpability and embrace the gift I have bestowed upon you, Raine," she cried as the flames encircled me. "I promised you would achieve greatness, now look, Creatures will talk about this for centuries to come. The tale of the human who executed the king, and gave birth to the queen who will set free the Sirens'."

"What do—"

"Did the Wolpel not tell you?" Esme snarled. "Can you not feel his seed festering inside of you?"

The fire gorged on my skin as I failed to make sense of what she was telling me, and when the words refused to come, Esme raced forwards then dropped to her knees.

"You're carrying his child."

"You're lyi—"

"Oh!" Esme gasped, clapping a hand to her mouth. "Did you not spread your legs and allow the buffoon to penetrate you?"

I shivered as the flames danced around us in a tangerine hurricane, nipping at my bloody summer dress and lifting strands of my hair. It was an accusation that brought down the sky, the clouds, the stars, and the moon, and for a second, I forgot where I was.

"I understand this may inconvenience you," Esme whispered. "Such damage the creature will inflict upon your life, and already such a pitiful life!"

I hung my head, straining to see some way out of this mess, but all I saw was the end.

"I have the power to save you, Raine."

Save me how? Esme had destroyed me, and now she was telling me I was carrying Nicholas's child. It was too much. Everything was spinning, and my teeth were melting.

"I can return you to your world with your mind rinsed of all the sins you have committed, all I ask is that you give me your child."

425

My heart tremored. My child? The infant I didn't even know if I was actually carrying? Is this what Esme had wanted all along? How long had she been planning this? And how had she known Nicholas and I would've become romantically involved?

"I didn't," Esme answered, sensing my thoughts. "Not at the beginning anyway, I planned on having you kill the buffoon the night you set eyes on him in the palace."

My eyes glazed over as I thought back to the night Esme had freed me. Her face in the flames. Her voice in my ears.

'Do not fear him' she'd whispered, and I hadn't.

"But then I saw the way he watched you when he let you go," Esme continued. "He was entranced by you, the fool, and I knew something marvellous would transpire."

My skin sweltered, and my lungs were charcoal.

"You were unwanted, and Nicholas always had a thing about saving the unloved."

"You want my child?" my voice came out a broken whisper.

"I can offer her a life you can't," Esme promised.

"Her?"

"A little girl who is destined be a queen amongst the Sirens."

Esme cocked her head so that her skin flapped to one side. Her lips parted, revealing a swollen black tongue.

"Do you truly believe you can raise a child after all those who have perished at your hands, Raine? Your mother drank herself to death because of you. Your father hanged himself because of you, Nicholas is dead because of you. Do you want the seed inside of you to meet an untimely death because of your frivolousness?"

A rough breath escaped my lips as I hunched lower. I was more than aware that Esme was preying on my weaknesses, Mia. Dragging up every gangrenous tragedy I'd ever blamed myself for, and trying to get me to doubt myself as I had in the past. But the person she was looking for no longer existed because Nicholas had changed me.

My face crumbled as I watched him, still waiting for him to lift his head. I knew it was a long shot, but what other choice did I have? I wiped my nose with the back of my arm, staring at his unmoving face. For so long I'd believed that humans are strongest on their own, Mia, but that's bullshit coming from the mouth of someone who is too afraid to love.

The truth is nothing makes us feel more invincible than having a friend we can count on. Someone who reminds us of how glorious it is to laugh, who watches us with understanding, and love, and compassion, who doesn't judge.

"Brave, Nicholas had said once, and if Esme thought I was going to forget that, she had another thing coming.

Lugging myself up from the heap on the floor, I staggered towards her.

"You're a liar!" I hissed.

Shock crossed Esme's face as the flames encircled us in a tangerine blaze.

"You killed Nicholas. You killed his parents, and for what? What did you gain from this? Nothing," I howled before she could answer.

Esme watched me with the spaces in her skull tightening. The papery scraps of flesh dangled from her jaw as she grinned menacingly, but I wasn't afraid of her, I pitied her.

"You did this!" I howled, fighting to keep my voice steady. "And all because you had some stupid school girl notion that Nicholas owed you something, but no one in this damn world owes us a thing!"

Esme shrunk back, rummaging around in my steely

face for the terrified woman she'd led into the woods months ago, but that woman was dead.

"Nicholas was your friend, and you betrayed him."

"You think I cared for that weak creature?" Esme growled, but she must have once because no one ever sought revenge from someone they didn't care for.

"As long as your child is bound to you, I will find her," Esme promised. "I will torment your dreams and plague your sanity until you have no choice but to throw her to the wolves."

"So do it," I challenged.

Fear grazed her face, and though she straightened up, it was a slip she couldn't come back from.

"Don't start wars with conquerors little girl," Esme spat. "Take a look at what I have done to Nicholas, do you honestly think I won't have the stomach to do the same to a child?"

I hung my head, glaring at my bloody summer dress with a sensation rushing through me like someone was chewing up my heart. Teeth puncturing my muscle, blood surging through the dents.

"Let me take away everything that hurts," Esme whispered, mistaking my silence for contemplation. "Wouldn't you prefer to forget this madness?"

"Forget?"

Esme nodded then placed a cold hand on my cheek. Studying the fleshy insides of her skull, I realised if ever I'd come across a monster in my lifetime, Mia, Esme was it. Only the thing about monsters is that they're not born like everyone believes, but created. Sculpted from isolation, and loneliness, and anger. Those are the true beasts we have to look out for, and if we're not careful, we too can become those monsters.

Watching Esme, I promised myself I'd never become as hell-bent on revenge as her, nor would I give you up because it was easy. I would fight. I would fight because it's what Nicholas would've wanted, and even though the memories of him would tear me apart on the brightest days, nothing hurt more than living in a world where he never existed.

"I'll never forget Nicholas," I promised.

Esme opened her mouth as I shoved myself free from her grip.

"And I will never, ever, let you take what's mine again."

"Raine—"

"No!" I howled, backing into the chestnut combustion. "Whatever you threaten me with, however much you antagonise or terrorise me, I will keep fighting because Nicholas..." I gritted my teeth, glaring at her with a feeling splintering through me as though I was no longer there. "He reminded me I was brave."

"You're cursed Raine," Esme snarled as I collapsed on the floor next to Nicholas. "No one who spends their life with you is safe. Mark my words, anyone you love will perish at your making."

Her words fell upon deaf ears as I traced Nicholas's chapped lips. To look at him hurt, and so I closed my eyes, trying to distance myself from this place, from Esme, from the flames. I needed to be somewhere safe, somewhere before all of this. Resting my cheek upon his bloody shirt, I thought back to the last time I'd seen him.

Two days ago, I'd woken to the sound of him playing the piano. Lying in the darkness of his room I questioned if I should leave him to it. We'd spent thirteen days together, and I imagined Nicholas needed his solitude just as much as I craved the feel of a paintbrush in my hand. Toying with the idea, I decided to go anyway. I hadn't seen him play, and if he wanted me to leave, I'd be able to tell by the way he watched me.

Following the melody out into the hall, I halted outside of a large entry. Pushing it open, I peered around nervously. The place was huge, with hundreds, maybe even thousands of empty seats circling the place where Nicholas sat at a polished black bench in the middle, his fingers pelting the bare surface of the piano like rain.

I watched his spine. Each time he threw down his hands, the muscles above the white sheet draped around his torso contracted. Impressed by the tune, I inched over to him, transfixed by the way his arms rose then fell, like the battle of an unregimented army. And when he gathered I was standing behind him, he looked over his shoulder and smiled.

"Spying on me?"

"Something like that," I replied, perching next to him on the bench. "I've just never seen you play. I mean, I've heard you, but seeing you, it's different."

Nicholas didn't push for an explanation, but I gave him one anyway.

"Seeing you play like that, it's like you're playing for yourself and you don't give a damn about anything but the notes."

"Forget the world," Nicholas whispered.

I nodded, thinking back to the first day he'd spoken those words. It was a joke between us now, a small reminder of how much we'd both changed. But what Nicholas didn't know, was that the first time he'd uttered those words, was the first time I knew liked him.

Sitting comfortably in the silence, I leant my head against his shoulder, before I had an idea.

"Teach me how to play," I gasped.

"Right now?"

I nodded, watching his tired eyes tighten.

"Yes, right now, you're good, and I want to learn."

Nicholas drew back his shoulders, pretending to look

annoyed, but the smile he wore rebelled against it.

"You need to make your hands into a sort of claw," he said.

"You mean like a crab?"

"I mean like a claw."

I rolled my eyes then did as I was told.

"Index finger down," he breathed.

I pushed my finger above the bare surface then jumped when a low note echoed through the silence.

"Little finger up," he said, the corner of his lip lifting. A higher note resonated.

"Now both thumbs down."

Nicholas pushed both my thumbs down, and as the rumbling of notes fell away, I grinned.

"I'll be better than you soon."

"Probably," Nicholas agreed.

Resting my head on his shoulder, I gazed out at the army of ghosts filling the red velvet seats. I was certain I'd drift back soon, Mia, and even though I knew it wouldn't be long until I returned, it still felt as though someone was sawing away at my limbs and asking me to carry on as I was.

"Nicholas," I whispered.

"Yes, Raine?"

"When we get back from the blood river will you teach me how to play?"

Nicholas bobbed his head.

"Promise?"

"I promise," Nicholas said, kissing my forehead. "All you need is a little practice."

"Index finger down, little finger up, both thumbs down," I muttered. "Index finger down, little finger up, both thumbs down." I'm not sure if minutes passed, or hours, or even days. But I whispered those words until my throat was dry, and my lips were numb.

Unsealing my eyes, I saw Esme had left. The flames were gone too. The only addition to the room was Candimore, kneeling beside me. When I lifted my head he just stared. His cloudy eyes locked on mine, his jaw clenched. I shuddered, too pathetic to speak the words strumming around inside of my head.

Nicholas is dead because of me. I'm carrying his child. Nicholas is dead. I killed him. I'm sorry. I'm so sorry.

"You didn't know," Candimore whispered.

Struck by rage he wasn't madder, my eyes flew open. I ached for him to scream, or shout, or call back the Cyclops to behead me for real this time.

"I should've," I said through my teeth. "She stopped me from saying her name. Why else would she have done it? I should've tried harder. I shouldn't have let her get inside my head like that… I can't—"

Candimore shook his head at his knees.

"Come on," he said, extending a scaled palm. "There's something Nicholas wanted to me to show you."

CHAPTER TWENTY-TWO

Watson scatters past me in a lint smothered suit. Collapsing in her seat, under the command of the clerk, she states her name, her credentials, the joint diagnoses made by herself and Pierce. Schizophrenia; a psychotic disorder categorised by hallucinations and delusional beliefs. I gnaw my lip as she runs through the process of their evaluation; the times and dates they conducted their interviews.

Gradually, her words thicken. She pauses, and as the room waits for her to continue, I wait, tasting hope. My eyes water, and before I can delude myself further, she starts outlining my symptoms in the lead up to Dan's death. Attempting to soften the blow, I wrap my arms around my chest, but her deception doesn't come as much of a surprise, Mia.

Everyone else had betrayed me; Pierce, Dan, Lucile, and worst of all Nicholas.

OCTOBER 5th 2018: the evening of the murder.

My eyes were on fire, and everything was too bright. I blinked at the flowers. There were too many of them. Each one whispered melancholy little songs that stung my ears like a fistful of wasps. I could barely remember the journey up to the garden. I couldn't remember leaving the hall or venturing through the broken-down icy currents of the palace.

All I remembered was my disappointment when I set eyes on the rusted swing set Nicholas had clung to weeks ago. Parts of the roof had caved in, and bits of rubble dusted the cobbled floor in blankets of auburn brick.

"How can we bring him back?" I mumbled.

Candimore stared at me in that same sad way he had each time I'd asked, but I didn't want his sadness, I wanted, no, I needed answers.

"Raine we can't—"

I threw myself round to face him.

"What do you mean we can't? This can't just be it. We can't just let her win." With a palm to my chest, I tried steadying my heart. Never had I been less in control of my body and it terrified me.

"Raine, Nicholas, is gone."

My lip twisted.

Gone.

Gone like he'd just popped out to fetch something, gone like he'd be back soon, gone like an old t-shirt that could be replaced, but Nicholas couldn't be replaced, I wouldn't let him be replaced.

"I did it to him."

"She possessed you," Candimore offered kindly, but I didn't want his kindness either. I wanted him to hurl insults at me, to scream and regard me as the barbaric creature Nicholas had assumed I was, because in the end, wasn't he right?

"He warned me, humans—"

"Stop," Candimore ordered, but the crunching sound the blade made when it connected with his spine rung in my ears like an old fire alarm, sounding louder, and louder, and louder until my head promised it would explode.

It was only a few nights ago I'd traced his spine with the tip of my finger, and when he turned and kissed my forehead, I knew no man, or city, or achievement would ever take his place because nothing would ever mark my heart the way Nicholas could.

"I killed him."

"Raine, you need to stop this."

"Why?" I snapped. "Isn't this what you said would happen all along, aren't you glad you figured it out?"

"Of course not," Candimore muttered.

"Then, why? Why all of a sudden are you being nice to me now? Why not execute me like you planned on doing before? why not show a little fury Candimore?"

Candimore shook his head at the floor.

"Because, Nicholas loved you, Raine."

His words ripped away my skin.

Trying my hardest not to cry, I bit my lower lip, but when I turned to the stone steps where we'd shared secrets, the tears fell anyway. I wiped my eyes furiously. I didn't have time to be upset. I had to be logical. I had to at least attempt to make sense of what had happened.

Esme had told me I was pregnant, even in my head it sounded wrong. Despite forcing a smile every time I saw a mother with her child at the park, despite the 'one-day' remark I'd throw Dan when Katie came around with George, I knew I wasn't ready to be a mother.

"Am I really pregnant?"

Candimore's eyes darkened.

"Candimore?"

Stooping lower, he managed a shaky nod.

"How can you be sure?" I whispered.

"Morgana could sense it."

"How?"

"She just can, Raine. She's a Wolpel, most Wolpels know the minute a child is conceived just by looking at you."

"But maybe she's wrong. People… creatures they can be wrong, can't they? They can get things wrong." I tried facing him, but my head kept lolling to my chest. "When?"

Candimore raised a hairless brow.

"When did she find out?" I snapped.

"A few days ago."

For the first time that afternoon a flicker of hope spawned inside of me because I thought if Morgana had found out a few days ago, she might've told Nicholas. I held my breath, studying him with too much hope.

"Did Nicholas know?"

Candimore stared right back at me, and when his luminous eyes pooled with tears, I felt myself breaking all over again. Puffing out my cheeks, I urged my body to be still, but it became insolent; crumbling and wilting under the substantial weight of the truth. I was carrying Nicholas's child, and he hadn't even known.

I glared the garden with nothing but unfiltered hatred. I had to get out of there, all I was doing was wasting time with Candimore. I had to get Nicholas to wake up. Pushing my palms to the cobbled ground, I fought to launch myself up, but everything was whirling around under mammoth tides of cold water, and the gap in the ceiling was burning a hole in my skull.

"I… I need to go back."

"Raine you need to see this mem—"

"Dragons' blood!" I gasped. "Morgana said it brings immortality. If we give him dragons' blood, he might wake up, and he'll know what to do. We need to get him dragons' blood." Even then I knew it sounded insane, Mia. Heartbreak can do that to a person; it eats away at our rationality until all we have left is hopeless prayers to a God we don't believe in.

"Raine,"

I wasn't listening. I had a plan; I'd take a bubble to the black-market stall and beg for dragons' blood. I'd plead, and cry, and wail, and pay anything to obtain it, and when I came back, everything would be as it was. Nicholas would be alive, and he'd take me to the blood river, and everything would be okay because I had a plan.

I fought to lug myself up, only when I got my feet to work it seemed I'd depleted all of my energy trying to stand. Seconds later, I smacked back into the concrete.

My chest punched the damp cobbled floor, my jaw clicked out of place. Rolling over and focusing on the dusty pink sky from the hole in the ceiling, I didn't even bother trying to sit back up.

"Why didn't he say anything?" I mumbled. "He had so many opportunities, why didn't he mention the curse, or Esme or any of this? I hate him. I hate him for doing this to me. I don't understand how someone could be so—"

"He didn't believe it."

My face crumbled as I forced myself upright. Pressing my knees to my chest, I turned to him with a face full of mistrust.

"What do you mean he didn't believe it?"

"I mean," Candimore sighed. "That after getting to know you, he didn't believe you would harm him, Raine. And after a while, Nicholas began to believe the curse was spoken in vain to stop him from living."

"But it wasn't," I pointed out. "I killed him."

"You were under a trance."

"Does it matter?"

"Yes!"

For a second, I was relieved to hear some fire in his tone.

"It matters because what you shared was real. Sirens are the strongest creatures known to our kingdom. Breaking free from their possession is impossible. It's the reason they're executed. They commit murder without a second thought, treating it as a hobby."

"But I—"

Candimore held up a hand.

"At first I admit I had my doubts about you," he said. "I believed you might have been working with her."

"I wouldn't —"

"I know," Candimore said, his voice softening. "I knew it the moment I saw you at breakfast. You had this look in your eyes. I saw how much you understood Nicholas, how much you cared for him, and when Nicholas watched you in the same manner, I admit I gave up trying to save him."

"Why?"

"Why save someone who doesn't want to be saved?"

I opened my mouth to tell him because it was the right thing to do, when he threw back his head. The gesture made the creases around his neck deepen as he blew out his cheeks.

"I knew Nicholas from the moment he was born," he said. "As a child, he had such enthusiasm for the world, such eagerness to immerse himself in culture and music. He liked the Mercreatures, did he tell you that?"

I nodded, but Candimore wasn't watching me. His eyes were glued to the hole in the ceiling where red light painted everything in a muggy shade of death.

"After his parents' passing, no one expected him to go back to the way he was. Nor did we anticipate what he'd become. For years, there was a darkness that bled through his eyes and left you haunted if you looked too closely, but when you arrived, he became the old Nicholas again. He was happy, and I couldn't ruin his last moments by taking that away from him."

"So, instead, you let him die?"

"It's what he wanted," Candimore replied, but all I heard in his voice was stale disbelief. I clenched my jaw, understanding Candimore hadn't wanted this either, he had tried to warn Nicholas, but Nicholas hadn't listened.

Why hadn't he listened?

If he told me the truth, I wouldn't have come back. If there was a chance I could've stopped it, I wouldn't have stepped foot in Wanderlust, even if it meant not seeing him again.

"He should've told me," I whispered. "If I'd known this was going to happen—"

"Then you would've acted differently."

"Then I wouldn't have come back!"

Candimore's face paled, and I had to look away because I couldn't bear seeing the hurt in his eyes, especially when he was the only creature bold enough to make Nicholas question what he was doing.

"I'm sorry," I said, and I was, Mia. I was so damn sorry for everything, but that remorse kept skyrocketing to rage because rage was easier to digest than sorrow.

"I just… I just thought we had more time. And now all of the things I thought I could tell him are useless. What am I supposed to do with these words?"

"Tell him," Candimore replied, nodding at the back of the garden. "That there, is his last memory. I planted it for him today. It's what I needed to show you."

My heart spasmed at the thought of seeing Nicholas alive, of being able to say goodbye. But I couldn't, not yet.

"Tell him what? That I'm livid he let me love him, knowing he wouldn't be around forever, or that I'm sorry I'm the reason he's dead?"

439

"Raine you're—"

"I am! You know I am! And what would good will speaking to a memory do anyway? He can't hear me. He can't see me, I can't even feel him. What good will any of this do?"

"It may help you to heal," Candimore said.

But I didn't want to heal. I wanted him back.

"What happens now?" I asked, skirting away from the topic of goodbyes.

"I'm sorr—"

"With the kingdom. What happens now that Nicholas is gone."

"There will be a new king," Candimore sighed. "Master Nicholas's once removed cousin from the fourth region, who will undoubtedly destroy Wanderlust with his madness."

The muscles in my chest tensed up as I tried to imagine someone else sitting in Nicholas's throne, or playing his piano, but I couldn't imagine a thing without him.

"I need you to see this memory," Candimore said. "I promised Nicholas I would show you." His voice bordered on a plea.

Refusing to answer, I scowled at my bloody summer dress.

"Raine," Candimore whispered, getting to his feet.

I lifted my head.

Candimore's eyes rippled with desperation, his face a portrait of anguish. Too weak to argue, I held out my hand then stumbled back as he hauled me up.

"Pick me," the flowers cried as we stormed by.

"I planted these in the passing months," Candimore told me while I forced my legs to march on. "The night Nicholas freed you, I thought something like this might happen."

"You did?"

Candimore nodded.

"So, what happened?"

"Without proof, Nicholas maintained we couldn't harm you. We argued about it after you disappeared. I told him it was senseless to ignore Morgana's prophecy, especially after he had disparaged it the first time, but he insisted…" He stopped when we halted at a fresh patch of soil bordered by green vines that reminded me of veins.

"Insisted what?"

Candimore released a patchy breath.

"Nicholas insisted that whatever was going to happen, would happen anyway, and he promised he wouldn't spend the rest of his life being afraid."

I looked away. Not wasting his life being afraid was something I'd encouraged Nicholas to do, and as Candimore perched down on the floor, I understood just how responsible I was for all of this.

"These are his last moments," Candimore said.

Collapsing next to him, I studied the petal he stroked with a claw. It was barely even a flower, and unlike the rest of the blossoms, it didn't have a face.

"This is what he wanted you to see," Candimore said.

My chest tightened as I glared at the flower. Part of me wanted to pick it, but the other part was terrified the moment I did, this would all be over.

"I'm scared," I admitted.

"I know you are," Candimore said. "It's only natural to be afraid, Raine. But that fear will persist on tearing you apart unless you face it. Saying goodbye doesn't mean forgetting. It doesn't mean you cared for Nicholas any less, or that the time you spent together was purposeless. But Nicholas isn't coming back, and not accepting that won't change anything. All you can do is acknowledge the pain that comes after that farewell, because the only way to escape grief, is to grieve."

I was about to argue when Candimore added,

"I had to do it with Nicholas's parents, and Marianne."

"Marianne?"

"Marianne was… is, my closest friend," Candimore said, his eyes fixed on the bud. "After the creatures attacked Esme that night, she struck all those who had been close to Nicholas. Marianne tried stopping the torture, Santos too."

Clearing his throat, he glared at the sunny garden with his forehead puckered.

"A blood bath filled the palace. Santos perished. Others we were close to too, but Marianne…" He shook his head at the floor.

"To behead a creature is monstrous. But to de-wing a Flemgril is beyond grotesque. She was a dancer once, a fine one, but after the attack she refused to dance, to leave the palace, to laugh."

"But you still have Marianne," I pointed out.

"And you will always have what you shared with Nicholas," Candimore replied. "It's the future you believed you had, that you have to let go of. The past will always belong to you."

The past.

That's exactly what I was afraid of, having nothing but the past.

"Go on," Candimore whispered.

I eyed the flower heatedly, thinking back to what Nicholas had asked me the day we ventured to the markets.

'Are you really going to waste your life scared of possibilities?'

I shook my head as if he was right there next to me. He was gone, but I still felt him everywhere.

My face blazed as my palm jittered over the petal.

My spine clicked out of place as the tip of my finger grazed the pollen, and before cowardliness could intervene, I plucked it hard.

Tumbling through a stormy combustion of the past, I shivered as I left the garden, Candimore, and the whispering flowers. Shifting through the darkness, I stumbled sideways when I saw Nicholas in the same place I'd left him hours ago, only this time, he was alive.

He was speaking to Candimore who knelt down beside him. I wondered how long it had been since Candimore exited the hall. If I had gotten there a little quicker would I have seen this exchange? Would I have been able to say goodbye properly?

Wiping my nose with a fist, I forced my legs to advance towards them. Sinking down next to Nicholas, I squeezed my eyes shut tight. I didn't want to see his face, or the wound cast across his chest, or the fear in his eyes. I didn't want any of this. I just wanted him back.

"You were right," Nicholas said.

His voice tangled itself around my heart, fooling it into believing he was still here.

He's gone, Raine. Accept it and move on. I couldn't—wouldn't.

"And just like the first time, I didn't listen."

"When have you ever listened?" Candimore sniffed.

A heavy silence followed.

"Master?"

"Can you... can you do something for me?" Nicholas asked.

"Of course," Candimore replied. "Anything."

"I need you to plant this memory for Raine…"

Something broke inside of me when he said my name. It was the same as he always said it. As if he were asking a question and answering it at the same time. My lip jerked when I realised this was probably going to be the last time I ever heard him say it again.

"I need her to know that I'm sorry. I'm sorry I dragged her into this mess. I'm sorry I wasn't better. I'm sorry I couldn't protect her. I'm sorry." His voice shook on the last word as I struggled to keep my eyes closed. Punching my thigh, my heart screamed for me to kiss him one last time.

Just one last time.

But I was terrified if did, my heart might forget it was broken, and I couldn't deal with the pain of reminding it.

"If she knew, she would've acted differently," Nicholas said. "And I didn't want our last days to be wasted with her trying to stop something she had no way of preventing, something I wasn't even sure would happen."

But it did happen. It happened, and now everything we shared was wasted, and I was sitting next to him, too scared to open my eyes. I clawed my palms, struggling to keep the tears from falling.

"She would've been prepared," Candimore said.

Candimore was right. If Nicholas had told me, I would've at least tried to prepare myself for a future without him, but instead I'd been hoodwinked into thinking this was the beginning.

"I couldn't do that to her," Nicholas argued. "I wanted her to see the world for what it was, not beside someone who might leave."

But you did leave. You left, and I didn't even get a real chance to say goodbye. Fighting to catch my breath, I gripped hold of my chest, but my heart wouldn't stop racing. It thudded against my ribs like a paddleball. Each thump resounding with the words:

Please come back. Please come back.

"She lived her entire life believing she wasn't enough, and I'll never understand how someone who could see the world so clearly would fail to see themselves."

I released a dry laugh, refusing to open my eyes, refusing to say goodbye. This wouldn't be the end if I didn't say goodbye.

"I loved her, Candimore, and you can think what I did was selfish. Perhaps, it was, but what other choice did I have?"

"You could have told me," I whispered, tears slipping from my clenched eyes. "You should have told me, Nicholas."

"The truth is it could've been anyone," Nicholas continued. "It wasn't Raine's fault, and I'm finally starting to understand my parents' death wasn't mine."

I forced a nod, glad Nicholas had finally found some solace in his end, but that didn't mean I had. Regardless of what he believed, I did feel responsible for his death, mainly because he wasn't here to convince me of anything else.

I sat there in silence, waiting to come out of the memory, waiting to go back to the garden so I could open my eyes. I clung tighter to my sides rocking back and forth, back and forth, when Nicholas spoke so gently I thought I'd misheard him.

"Forget the world."

Repressing a laugh, I opened my eyes, little by little. His eyes were sealed, his lips quivered each time the breath left his lungs. Looking at him was like going back to a childhood home that was about to be demolished. I recalled the laughter, the tears, the arguments, and suddenly I was taken by this feeling of homelessness.

"Nicholas," I whispered.

Nothing.

My friend was gone. The creature who'd taught me it was okay to be myself was just gone.

How could someone leave in the middle?

"Nicholas?"

His face remained motionless.

My heart heaved with the loss. Too heavy, too thick and the only words aching to spill from my lips were ones I still couldn't digest.

"I'm pregnant." I studied his vacant expression, waiting for a smile to graze his bloodless lips, waiting for a miracle, but nothing came.

"You know I loved you," I told him, fighting to keep my voice steady. "I loved you, and I don't understand why you didn't tell me any of this. I'm angry at you," I whispered. "I'm angry you let me love you. I'm angry at you for leaving without saying goodbye because this isn't a goodbye is it?" My voice shattered, and when his thick brows shivered, hot tears flooded my cheeks.

"I'm angry you didn't teach me to play the piano, or take me to the blood river, or back to the Unicorn farms like you promised, because you did promise didn't you Nicholas? You promised so much, and now I'm angry at the world because I feel like—" The words caught in my throat.

"I feel like you brought me back to the person I should've been, and now that you're gone, I don't know who I am anymore." My eyes throbbed as I waited for him to open his eyes.

Please just open your eyes, Nicholas. Please, just one last time, look at me with that baffled expression. Please.

"I'm pregnant." The words came out a question. "I'll teach her all of the things you taught me. Be brave, be strong, forget the world. And I'll protect her. I promise I'll protect her." Bending lower, I pushed my face to the ground, studying his vacant expression, trying to work out how I'd gotten to this point with him after a few short months. I'd spent seven years with Dan. Seven long and exasperating years, and he didn't know me a fraction as much as Nicholas did.

"If you can hear me, give me a sign."

Nothing.

"Nicholas, please, if you loved me just give me a sign!"

His face was the colour of day-old snow.

"Nicholas—"

A shuffling sounded up ahead of me. Prying my focus from Nicholas, I saw Candimore heading towards the door. My insides turned to dust. The memory was about to end, but I wasn't ready.

"I'll… I'll tell her about you," I stammered. "Whatever happens, I'll tell her that you were kind and gentle, and you believed in others."

I heard the clip of Candimore's shoes as he continued towards the door.

Please not yet. Don't take him from me, not now.

"I'm going to tell her this story. Even the bad bits. Everything that led me to this point, so if Esme does come for her, at least she'll be prepared." I wrapped a hand around my stomach, drifting from one shade of loss to another. "I'm going to name her Mia."

Then, for the briefest moment, Nicholas's jaw twitched.

I held my breath, waiting, praying, before he opened his eyes and smiled shakily. The gesture seemed to pain him, but he fought to keep it there.

"Thank you," Nicholas whispered. "You made me happy, Raine."

A painful laugh escaped my lips as the stage dimmed, the glacial walls, and those huge gold eyes I had fallen into so many times before. Only unlike the first time I'd met him, no longer were they filled with fear, but love.

I reached out to him as the hall blurred, my bones juddered, and when my focus came through, I saw Dan.

I flinched. Not only had I left the memory, but I'd left Wanderlust. Sweat blistered my brow as I raked over the fuzzy image of my studio.

"What the fuck, Raine?" Dan shouted, pulling me up to face him.

I saw myself in the reflection of his eyes; bloated face

and raggedy hair. This wasn't my life. I didn't belong here, not with him, not with any of this. Pushing past him, I prodded the mirror.

"What the fuck was that at my book launch?"

"Drop it, Dan. It's been weeks."

"Weeks? Raine, it's been two days."

I turned, bewildered.

Dan must've been mistaken. There was no way it could've been two days. I'd spent weeks with Nicholas. Weeks.

"You're lying."

"Raine—"

"Leave me alone!"

I jerked back when he grabbed hold of my shoulders.

"Why? What have I done that's so awful?"

I rubbed my eyes with a palm. I didn't have time to list Dan's indiscretions. I had to get back to Nicholas.

"Raine, we need to talk."

I ran my fingers over the glass, my nails, my palms, but nothing would work.

"Obviously with my book selling so well, and with you being a little… depressed. It's been a lot for you to take, especially when your paintings aren't doing too well, so whatever you think—"

"What I think, is that you've been fucking my best friend."

That shut him up.

For a second, all I heard were my fingers leaving smudges on the glass.

"Raine, I think—"

"No, you don't think. That's the problem." Swerving round I saw him eying me like a scientist trying to make sense of the moon.

"You don't know what you're talking about," Dan laughed. "You can go through my phone, Lucile and I, we're just—"

"Friends?" I didn't wait for him to argue. "Fine."

"What are you doing?" Dan asked. "And what are you wearing? It's barely two degrees outside. Is that blood?"

"I need to go back," I mumbled.

"Back where?"

"To him, to Wanderlust. I need to go."

"What the fuck is Wanderlust?"

I blinked at my pruned reflection, bloated and warped and barely human.

"Raine?" Hearing my name said by Dan did something to me. It sounded dirty. Wrong. Obsolete.

I snapped my eyes shut tight.

"I need to go. I need to get away from you, and this bullshit. I need to see Nicholas, I need to get through the mirror. I have to tell him I'm sorry."

For so long I'd wondered how Dan would regard me after I told him about Wanderlust, Mia. I thought he'd be shocked, maddened, bereaved even, but never had I imagined his reaction would be one of humour.

I saw his lip curl in the mirror, and I knew I hated him, then. I hated him so much I wanted to rip that smug grin right off of his face.

"Look," Dan said, scratching his beard. "Whatever you think you know about me and Lucile, it's not true."

"I don't care."

"Obviously you do Raine, look at you, look at what's happening. You're saying you need to get through a mirror. You keep hurting yourself. I've seen the marks. You need help, professional help." Dan straightened up, ogling the room as though this was all some big joke. Like I was a joke. "Where's the girl I met seven years ago?"

My face dropped.

"That girl?" I questioned, striding towards him. "That girl was never there to begin with, and if she was, you destroyed her when you fucked my best friend."

449

I waited for him to deny it again, to tell me I was crazy or obsessed. Too exhausted to keep up the charade, Dan sighed then lowered his shoulders.

"She didn't mean anything. She was just—"

"I don't care!"

Dan lifted his palms, but I didn't care if he surrendered, or he battled me till the world stopped spinning, all I needed was to go back.

"You need serious help," Dan repeated.

I ground my teeth to stop myself from screaming. There was a mallet in my chest and it wouldn't stop pounding.

"I love you."

That was all it took for my desperation to fire up into rage.

"Love?"

He nodded defensively.

"You don't know the first thing about love."

Dan pulled back his head, trying to decide if he needed a weapon to defend himself from the crazy stranger stomping towards him.

"Love is selfless, Dan. Did you think of me when you fucked my friend?"

His lips parted, but I wouldn't let him speak.

"Did you think of me when you heard me crying all those nights when you said you didn't want to hear it because you didn't want to see me like that? You've never loved me. You love what people can give you, what I gave you. Comfort, safety, someone to fuck, a body to keep the bed warm. Have you ever actually seen me?"

"You're not well," Dan said. "You're sick."

"I'm heartbroken!" Before he could argue I swerved back to the mirror. There had to be some way I could get back. "Esme," I whispered. "Esme," I called louder. "Let me see him!" Pushing my palms against the sweaty glass, I waited for the burst of uninhibitedness. I waited to be back in the garden with Candimore. I waited to be around someone who understood all this, but all I saw in the reflection of the mirror was Dan.

He was marching towards me. At first, I thought he was trying to grab, and when I registered what he was actually trying to do, I compressed my lips with my teeth.

"What are you doing?" I breathed.

"It's for your own good."

"Dan," I hissed. "Dan!"

I flung out my arms, but it was too late, Dan had already managed to shove me aside.

He was trying to pull the mirror off the wall. I heard the nail creaking from the plaster board as he gripped the corner with both hands.

"No!" I took hold of his shoulders, but the mirror had already come away, leaving a fresh mark on the wall. The surface covered his body; his arms were wrapped around the centre; his fingers touched. I stared at them, biding my time till I could lunge.

"How long have you known about us?"

I didn't answer. I glared at the cardboard on the back. If I charged then, it might work.

"How long have you known about Lucile and me, Raine?"

I watched his stubby fingers tighten, his fingernails twitched. Fear stained his eyes.

I pounced.

It happened so quickly, too quickly, a body bag filled with stones and tossed into the carnivorous depths of the ocean.

The mirror flew up in the air. I watched, praying I could retrieve it in time, praying this wasn't the end. A loud thud sounded as the frame hit the floor. A violent smash thundered as shards of glass twinkled to the ground, and all that followed were my butchered sobs as I dropped to my knees, understanding everything was over.

***

"Doctor Watson," the clerk continues. "In your professional opinion do you believe Ms Black should remain at Raven House for a minimum stay of up to one year, to ensure she is not at risk to herself and others?"

Watson's eyes slip to Pierce.

"No," she replies. "After eighteen sessions with Ms Black, I believe she is coherent, and after being arrested because of our incompetence as a justice system, I think anyone in her position would be riled up. Raine is not violent. She's heartbroken."

A whisper resounds in the courtroom as the judge pounds her gavel.

"Doctor Watson, you do understand a joint decision from yourself and Doctor Pierce should've been reached."

"Yes," Watson replies. "And I also understand the way in which Doctor Pierce conducted his interviews were unethical, and any hostility from Ms Black because of this, was understandable. I have informed the psychiatric board of Doctor Pierce's malpractice, and there will be an investigation into the matter."

"Doctor Watson—"

"He is at fault for any anger displayed by Ms Black and—"

"Doctor Watson—"

"He is a menace, and his license should be revoked immediately!"

CHAPTER TWENTY-THREE

After laying into Pierce, Watson wasn't given a chance to finish.

"Doctor Watson," the judge had barked. "This is a hearing to discuss Ms Black, not Doctor Pierce's incompetency as a mental health professional, any claims against him will be examined at a later date, not now."

Watson had nodded before she was escorted through the door by a stringy bailiff, whose bald head I watch from the window whilst attempting to make sense of what she'd just done.

She could've just waited. She could've bided her time and filed complaints appropriately, but instead, she'd chosen this moment, which would inevitably destroy her credibility as a psychiatrist, and all for something as trivial as me.

I push my hands against the desk as my neighbour shuffles to the podium. The final person to take the stand. Mr Thompson. Wrinkles peek out from the neck of his suit. His face is greyer than usual, with a hint of terror sewn into his battered blue eyes.

Mr Thompson had lived in the same decrepit house for nearly forty years. It was the same house in which his wife, Victoria Thompson had first announced she was pregnant inside of; the same house covered in scrawls, and paints, and Lego, and stuffed toys, right up until their three boys, Conner, Mark, and Aiden moved out.

It was the same house his granddaughter, Molly, had taken her first steps in, and the same house Dan and I had dinner at once before leaving abruptly when Dan complained it smelt of boiled lettuce.

The house had witnessed his wife, Victoria Thompson, married forty-three happy, and albeit some rocky years, after a brief fling in Mexico with the waiter some years before, come home after a routine check-up only to reveal she had cancer.

Eight months later, it was the same house Mr Thompson came home to, widowed, and crying so loud Dan and I heard him through the walls. But most importantly to the investigation, Mr Thompson lived in the house next door to a murder, and on the night in question he'd been spotted in his living room window.

"Mr Thompson, it took nearly three weeks for you to come forward, is that correct?"

Mr Thompson nods while the clerk waits for his response.

"Oh," he gasps. "Yes, but that was on account of the police not coming back to follow up on what I told them."

Staring into his aged blue eyes, I am taken back to the first time he'd greeted Dan and me at the front door with his stout wife who always smelt of homemade banana cake. Without her, he looks as if he's been pricked by a pin. The skin on his face droops and his eyes are so sunken they resemble grey craters.

"We will now read the statement you gave to the police on the 1st November 2018," the clerk begins. "At first I heard banging coming from the loft," he reads.

Mr Thompson shrinks in his seat.

"They were screaming at each other, and I thought it was odd because Raine never raised her voice, it was usually the fella."

I grind my teeth as the clerk's voice bounces across the room like a moth trapped in a burning bulb.

"I put on the telly, but I could still hear em' shouting. When asked if you were certain, you replied one hundred per cent because the walls were thin enough to hear them coming downstairs, which was later confirmed by the forensic team."

I huff as the truth showers the courtroom. The truth I'd tried hiding these past few weeks, and plain and dowdy Mr Thompson had heard it all.

"A car pulled up at around eight o' clock. About half an hour or so later, I heard running water. I thought everything was settled. When I heard the door go, I looked outside, properly like, and I saw her taking a pile of clothes out to the car. Is that correct?"

"Correct," Mr Thompson replies.

"Can you identify the woman you saw leaving the house?"

Like a child confessing to stealing a fistful of sweets, Mr Thompson peers up ruefully.

"It was her," he replies.

OCTOBER 5th 2018: Minutes before the murder

Shards of glass twinkled across the floorboards. Jagged pieces cut my palms as I scrabbled around pathetically. Dark pools of blood flooded the creases of my palms and left bloody handprints on my face as I gripped my cheeks.

"What did you do?" I kept sobbing. "What did you do?"

Dan backed away, his jaw stapled to his chest.

"Raine, it's just a mirror," he said. But it wasn't just a mirror, it was everything, and Dan had destroyed it all.

Crumbs of my reflection punched me as I crouched lower. My eyes were bulging. My lips, trembling. In one piece of glass I glimpsed half a powdery red smudge dragged down the skin on my cheek. In another, my swollen eyes.

I tried catching my breath, but everything was slipping through my teeth and the only thing I could think of to stop the feeling, was to pound at my face with my wet knuckles. The first blow thwacked my teeth. I felt the terrific pain of my fist ripping through my jaw. I hit again, harder. Blood erupted from my gums. About to hit again, Dan seized me by my shoulders.

"Look, I'm sorry!" he shouted, pulling me up to face him. "I didn't know this would happen. It's my fault. I neglected you. I should've been here. I get that now."

Even though my eyes were set on his, I wasn't looking at him. My mind was fixed on Nicholas, and on how everything that happened after this moment would fail to register. The pain of losing him was prolific, but the pain of losing him and having the world claim he wasn't real, that was a travesty.

"I love you," Dan was saying. "We're going to get you better. We're going to fix this." He spoke as if I were some sort of household appliance that needed rewiring. I wondered what tools were required to mend a broken heart.

Time? Acceptance? Reasoning?

What if I didn't want to be fixed? What if I wanted to stay broken, and detached, and unhinged forever because being complete would only bring back a nostalgic little feeling that would break me all over again.

Keep it together I reminded myself, not for myself but the child growing inside of me.

"I'm going to protect her," I whispered. "I'm going to fix this Nicholas, I'll tell her about you. I won't let Esme take her. I promise, I won't let Esme take her."

"I'm going to tell her it's over," Dan said.

My heart twisted when I saw him holding his phone.

"Don't," I breathed, wiping my bloody mouth with the back of my hand. "Please, Dan, don't."

"Raine, I have to." Dan's eyes expanded. For a second, I thought he was going to cry. I couldn't think of anything worse than him crying. Not then. "This isn't right. Look at you."

Using all the strength I had left, I crawled over to where he stood under the thin slit window. I didn't care if he was seeing Lucile. I wanted him to be happy. I wanted him to leave. I wanted to go back to the middle before all of this had happened, and then I could be with Nicholas.

Reaching his shiny black boat shoes, I held my breath as he pressed the phone to his ear.

"Dan, I'm begging you."

He wasn't listening.

"Dan, it's pointless, I don't want this. I don't—"

Lucile answered on the second ring.

"Hey," she purred.

"Listen, Luce," Dan said.

"Stop," I mouthed. He wouldn't, and his need to be a hero was choking me.

"Is everything okay?"

"Yeah, well, no."

Dan pawed his face, and when he glanced at me, it was clear he realised ending things with me glaring up at him with a dislocated jaw couldn't have come at a worse time, but the stage was set, all he had to do was say the words.

Don't. Please, don't.

"Luce, I can't do this."

I closed my eyes.

"Us."

Lucile was saying something. Her tone, shrill. Fear stained Dan's face as he scanned the broken glass glittering across the floor.

"I just can't Luce, listen Raine needs me, my wife." Dan didn't wait for an answer; he didn't argue or check she was okay. He simply clicked off the phone, shoved it back in his pocket, then crouched down next to me, smiling as though he expected some sort of light to flick back on in my eyes.

"See," he whispered, taking hold of my hand. "It's you, Raine. It's always been you. We're going to do this together. We're going to be okay."

Staring at my lacerated hand in his, I pulled away, wondering how it was possible for someone to jump from person to person like a greedy fruit fly, sampling more than its insipid body can digest.

Dan didn't care about Lucile. He didn't even care about me; all he cared for was the way he was perceived. After fucking my best friend, he'd finally decided to whack on a suit of armour, only now it was too late.

"I'll visit you in the hospital," he was saying. "We're going to get through this."

I wanted to laugh, but I couldn't remember how. I wanted to scream, but my vocal chords had been demolished. All I could do was speak quietly, but very clearly.

"You have no idea of how conceited you are, do you?"

Dan's lips puckered.

"I don't—"

"None of this is about you, Dan. None of it!"

Lurching forwards, I sent Dan flying back with his

hands cushioned by pieces of glass.

"My God, not everything revolves around you. I've known about you both for months, and the truth is a part of me was glad, because, because..." my voice trembled as the words I'd held back for years burnt cavities in my mouth. "I don't love you, Dan."

Swallowing the fuel in my throat, I searched his face, waiting for the jolt of realisation to knock him sideways, but not once did it flicker with grief. Instead, it melted into a muggy sort of disbelief.

"You do," Dan said in a tone so self-assured I wanted to scream. "Of course, you do, look at how you're behaving. You think you would act this way if you didn't love me?"

I compressed my fists, working hard to soften the blow, but the entire universe was imploding inside of me. I knew Nicholas was gone, I knew it was all over, but even with the facts, and evidence, bouncing around in my skull, my heart still couldn't understand it.

"How I'm behaving is because I have lost people," I said. "People I will never get back because sometimes life is cruel. But you, Dan, you left of your own accord, you chose to go. You chose to fuck my best friend and lie to me every day. How can you think I still love you?"

"Look, Raine—"

"Don't." I raised a palm, and for a horrifying moment, I thought Dan was going to laugh. "You don't even know me."

"I've been with you for seven years," Dan said.

"You could've been with me for seven hundred years and still not have a clue who I am, because you never tried."

Dan hung his head, then spoke three simple words:

"I love you."

I shook my head at my bloody dress. Love. That word, tossed around like a rampant dodge ball, flung anywhere, eager for it to connect, hungry for it to whack someone, anyone, to take them out and knock them sideways.

"Why?"

Dan's eyes brightened.

"Because you're sensible and kind, and you've always supported me no matter what."

"Have you supported me?"

"Of course! I support your art. When you said you wanted to focus on painting, I told you I'd pay the bills and—"

"That's not what I wanted."

"You may not have said it, but you needed it."

"You needed it!"

Dan stroked his jaw as I glanced behind him at an audience of canvases depicting a place in which I was certain I belonged, but not here. I didn't belong here. The palace, the Forkels, the centaur, tucked behind them, a portrait of two almond-shaped eyes that made my heart bunch up.

"Have you ever really looked at me, Dan?"

"Raine—"

"Have you?"

Dan's eyes slipped back to mine, but even then, I knew he couldn't see me, not in the way that Nicholas had. Dan saw me the same way he'd see a mouse. A compliant little woman whose best quality was knowing when to keep her mouth shut.

"You don't know me," I hissed. "You don't know how I feel when I paint, or the disconnect I feel when I'm surrounded by your friends, and you beg me to be normal. You don't know I cry myself to sleep most nights, thinking of all the bad decisions I made when I was a kid." I wiped my nose with my arm.

"In all the time I've known you, I always felt as if I wasn't smart, or polished enough to be your wife, and maybe it's my fault for not saying it sooner. Maybe I should've told you how lost I've felt all these years."

I trembled as my chest lightened from all of the unspoken words I'd held back for too long, coming up for air.

"Maybe I should've mentioned Lucile sooner. No, I should have mentioned her. But I was scared. I was so fucking scared no one else would love me. You made me believe that. You made me believe I was difficult, and that tiptoeing around your moods was normal."

"Raine—"

"I shouldn't have waited for it to get better. I've wasted so much time waiting for a feeling that was never going to come."

Dan tried reaching out to me when I leapt up.

I had to get out of there. I had to escape. Everything was fuzzy, and it hurt to keep my head up. Lumbering through the mess of smashed glass, I stumbled towards the hole in the floor. Dan called my name as I spilt through the hallway. His footsteps clattered behind me as I clung to the bannister, forcing myself down the steps, through the kitchen and into the living room.

Keys.

I needed my keys. Throwing myself onto the cold leather sofa, I pushed my hands into the creases, searching.

"You're not leaving," Dan said from the doorway. "Raine, did you hear me? I said you're not leaving. We need to talk about this."

Finding my keys, I leapt up, heading for the door. Pressing my hand against the handle, I was about to pull it open when banging from the other side made me fly back.

"Open the door," Lucile called.

I glared at Dan. His phone call had prompted her to make a final grandiose gesture.

"Go," I mouthed.

Dan wouldn't budge. He just stood in the middle of the room with this stricken look on his face.

"Go!" I shouted.

"Open the door, Dan. I know you're there, your car's here."

Stumbling backwards, I stared at the door with eyes bigger than my face. All I wanted was to leave, and I couldn't even do that. Reversing until my spine whacked the wall, I slid down to the floor, listening to her knuckles pound the laminated panels. My heart rattled as I ran my tongue alongside my front tooth, and the rough edge of where it had broken.

I had to be stronger for the child I was carrying. I had to keep her safe. I promised Nicholas I would keep her safe. Nicholas. Burying my head in my knees, I fought to block out the banging as it grew louder. The windows rattled, the letterbox jingled, and just when I thought Dan was about to run off and hide, a harsh breeze fluttered in from outside.

"What the fuck," Lucile shouted.

"Luce now is not the time."

From the gaps in my fingers, I saw her push past Dan.

"What's going on?" she asked, staring at me rocking on the floor.

"She knows."

"Knows what?"

"Everything."

Peering up, I admit a small part of me expected Lucile to deny it, or to lay on the waterworks, because for so long Lucile had been my friend, but when she answered, I felt my stomach roil with confusion.

"Good."

I glared at her, dressed in her flimsy beige blouse and tight black trousers, waiting for her to look my way, but she was staring at Dan.

"You said all you needed was to tell her, and now she knows, we can be together."

"We can't."

"What do you mean we can't?" Lucile tried touching Dan's arm before he ducked out of the way. "Seriously, Dan?"

"I think it's time you left."

Lucile's lip curled downwards as she pressed a hand to her scalp.

"Eight months," she breathed. "Eight fucking months and now you say you think it's best I leave?" The hope drained from her face. In its place, was a manic sea of fury. "You can't just throw this away. We had a plan. You can't just take that back, you can't." When Dan refused to meet her eyes, she took a deep breath then stared back brazenly. "No," she said.

Dan's eyes pricked with alarm.

"No?" he repeated. "What do you mean no?"

"I said, no. I'm not leaving."

"It's my bloody house."

"And I said no, Dan!"

"Luce, you need to—"

"No, you need to listen!"

I lowered my head as their raised voices took me back to when my parents fought. Squeezing my eyes shut tight, I promised myself I'd never do that to my daughter. I would never make her feel unloved or terrified or unworthy. I would protect her and shelter her from all things evil in this world and the next.

"I said get out!"

They were in the kitchen.

Someone was opening and slamming cupboard doors. I heard the slosh of liquid splattering into a glass.

"How the fuck can you want to be with her after everything. She needs help, Dan. Professional help."

"It's my fault."

"None of this is your fault, I've known her for years, she's always been weird."

Perspiration flooded my upper lip.

Was this how they spoke about me when I wasn't around? Is that what Lucile always thought?

"Luce, I can't."

"Why the hell not?"

"Because."

"Because? After everything you're going to brush me off with a fucking because?"

"Luce."

I heard her sobbing, venom tucked into each breath.

"Don't fucking touch me. Don't you ever fucking try and touch me, you weak, flaccid excuse for a man."

"Fine."

I bit my lip, willing the darkness to take me.

"Nicholas," I whispered.

"Nicholas, Nicholas, Nicholas."

Nothing.

"She's my wife."

"She's a mess."

"And what are you? Some spoilt little bitch who thinks she can fuck her way to the top? Face it, Luce. It was just a bit of fun."

"A bit of fun?"

"My wife—"

"Your wife? The same woman you said you couldn't stand to be around, the woman who drained the life from you, the cold bitch you couldn't bear to touch, that wife?"

My face sweltered. I had to leave, but I didn't even have the strength to stand. How would I drive through the night if I didn't even have the energy to lift my head?

"That was different."

"Of course, it was, because back then you wanted to

fuck me, you wanted to have a taste of me then throw me away like every other dick I've ever been with."

"It wasn't like that," Dan said, but everything in his voice told me it was.

"You make me sick," she spat.

I heard someone heading out of the kitchen; footsteps hit the brown hardwood floor before they were muffled by the fluffy beige carpet.

"Come on," Dan said.

I stiffened, inhaling the musky scent of his aftershave.

"Let's go."

I peered up groggily as Dan held out his hand. A boyish smile grazed his face. I wanted to refuse; to muster up the strength to tell them both to get out of the house that was under my name.

I shook my head, the words bulldozed my tongue.

"Raine," Dan pressed, and when I saw Lucile standing behind him with a knife, the sound of the world tuned down, and the colours thinned to black and white sketches.

The knife glittered in her palms.

Her eyes shone.

Two dents splotched black.

She bared her teeth.

Dan didn't know she was behind him.

He smiled as she raised her arm.

He wanted to help; even if he couldn't, he wanted to, and then, she lunged.

Trapped, I watched her lift the blade, the tip dripping an oily wine-red. Dan held up his palms as she hit again, ramming the knife into his front, over and over and over again.

He went down on the sixth blow.

On the seventh, his eyes rolled back.

His head smacked the coffee table.

Falling forward, I groped Dan's chest for a pulse.

"Call an ambulance."

"Raine—"

"Call an ambulance!"

Turning, I saw Lucile pushed against the wall, with everything she'd done in the last ten seconds, playing on a loop inside of her eyes. Her face was the colour of rain, and when she registered the knife in her palms, she dropped it, then winced.

She stood silently; a splatter of blood resting on her chin and her beige blouse sprayed in maroon confetti.

Swerving back to Dan, I pushed my ear to his chest. His heartbeat was slow.

"No," I whispered, making my hands into a fist and pounding his chest like I'd seen them do on TV. "No. No. No." This couldn't be happening. Not now. "Please." Sweat dripped from my brows as his eyelids fluttered closed. "Call an ambulance!" But I knew it would make no difference, Mia. Dan was fading fast, and when I pushed my palm below his nose, I heard his breathing cease.

"It was an accident," Lucile said.

I shuddered. Everything was going a million miles a second, and I couldn't catch my breath. Pressing my head to Dan's chest, I gagged as the muggy scent of his insides tangled with the air. Lucile had killed Dan. We had to call the police. This was a crime scene. Lucile had killed my husband. I couldn't move.

Why couldn't I move?

Clinging to my stomach, I forced my focus on Dan's unmoving face. His jaw was cracked; from the break, I saw his crooked tooth set below two straight incisors. His eyes were stretched in panic. I trembled, staring until his face became of a blurry pool of nothingness.

Esme was right. I was cursed. How else could I explain everyone I ever cared about dying? My father, my mother, Nicholas, and now Dan? I balled my hands into

466

fists, desperate to untangle myself from the pit of self-loathing I was falling into, but I couldn't help wonder if this was Esme's doing.

Was I to blame for challenging her? Had she found some way of possessing Lucile? She'd done it to me, what made me think she wasn't strong enough to do it to Lucile?

"Raine," Lucile whispered.

It seemed like seconds had passed, but when Lucile crouched next to me, I felt heat lifting from her skin as if she'd showered, and when I smelt the lavender shampoo we kept in the bathroom cupboard, I knew she had. Wrinkling my brow, I searched the Tardis of my mind for some clue when Lucile had left, but all that came was the sound of Esme's raspy voice:

'All you love will perish at your hands.'

She was right.

"I can't go to prison," Lucile was saying. She pushed a hand to my arm as I sunk into the blood-soaked carpet, that would later be trampled and bagged up as evidence. I thought of you coming into the world then, Mia. Copper eyes, and whiskey coloured hair, that new-born smell slipping from your skin.

'All you love will perish at your hands.'

Chest heaving, I glared at Dan's frozen face, going over the promise I made to keep you safe, Mia, and realising the only way to do so indefinitely, would be to give you up.

"We can say it was self-defence. Dan grabbed you and..."

Me? Lucile wanted to blame this on me?

"I'm sorry," I kept whispering. "I'm so sorry."

"They already have your records. They know you were depressed. We can say that's why you did it, Dan was abusive, you were scared. You called me from his phone. You told me you needed help. I came as quickly as I could, but it was too late. You did what you had to do. We don't even need to mention the affair. No one at work knows… just Katie."

Katie? Katie knew too?

"… And I'm sure she won't say anything. If they find out Dan and I were together, they might think you killed him because you were jealous. I'll go to prison if you don't. They'll lock me up. I'm your friend, Rainey."

I braced down hard on my lips, tasting blood. Lucile was right. Of course, she would go to prison. She'd acted irrationally to being scorned on more than one occasion. She'd smashed up houses; spray painted the word *cunt* on ex boyfriend's car windows, her criminal record backed it up, but she was wrong about being my friend.

There was a time, once. Nights I'd confessed the pain of losing my mother, afternoons I'd slipped out, exhausted by Dan's hunger for me to be the perfect wife. Then something had changed, all of the ghastly truths I had shared with Lucile, she had used against me. Like Esme, Lucile was a monster.

Hugging my stomach, I thought of what would commence in the following hours. The media were sure to be involved. I would be branded the victim, this placid little wife whose best friend had slaughtered her husband. They would glamorise the whole warped affair, but I couldn't be the victim, not after what I'd done to Nicholas. Nor could I give up the only thing I had left of him unless I was forced to.

Bringing my hand up to my face, I studied the blood under my fingernails. Nicholas's blood. I shuddered, recalling the look of betrayal in his eyes when the blade ruptured his spine. My heart broke, Mia, and with its disintegration, went all of the strength I'd built myself up of in the months before.

"I can't be the victim," I whispered. For that reason, I

decided to confess to a murder I didn't commit. It wasn't smart, or bold, or courageous, if anything, it was weak. I was weak, but the more I thought about it, the more I realised it was the only way to keep you safe. No judge, or jury, would ever allow a murderer to raise a child, and nothing I said after would even matter.

"…If you say it was self-defence nothing will even happen to you. We could say I came in to help and I found you this way and—"

"Fine."

I sensed her eyes glitter with uncertainty.

"Raine…"

I shook my head; I didn't want to listen. Closing my eyes, I went over the story I'd give the police when they arrived. A cover-up wouldn't be too difficult. The marks on my body would indicate Dan had been harming me for quite some time. The doctors' reports would back it up; the scars on my neck, the puncture wounds to my chest.

Could I claim Dan was violent after his death? The allegation seemed immoral, but what other choice did I have? Pressing my lips together, I recoiled from the sharp ache of my jaw as Lucile went over what she'd tell the police. She promised it wouldn't be so bad if I told them he grabbed me first. I was terrified, lost, battling with months of physical and psychological abuse. I did the only thing I could do.

I defended myself.

Silence stampeded around us.

Looking across, I saw her set the kitchen knife beside my face.

"I've wiped the handle," she told me. "It just needs your prints."

I forced a nod, waiting for her to throw me some wet apology, or break down crying, but all I heard was the dry shuffle of her trouser legs rubbing against each other as she shuffled to the door.

Cold air sprayed through the gap. The door slammed shut, and just as I began to question the repercussions of what I was about to do, I heard her scream,

"Police, I've just seen… my friends just stabbed her husband."

I stared at Dan's lifeless face, reminding myself I had to be brave. I didn't feel brave. I didn't feel anything, and I didn't expect to, ever again.

"I don't think he's breathing. You need to come quickly, she's still inside!"

Burying myself into the crook of Dan's neck, I exhaled as my mind fluttered back to the journey I'd taken. All of the creatures, and places I'd seen, flickering in my pensive eye like a glorious firework cast across a starless sky, then vanishing.

The last thing I promised Nicholas was that I'd tell you this story Mia, even the bad bits. Keeping true to that promise, I picked up the kitchen knife and I started at the end.

"I'm sorry, Mia," I whispered.

***

"Mr Thompson, you understand it was your statement that first launched the investigation into Lucile Fleetwood."

"I understand," he replies awkwardly.

"And by reading your statement, we are merely highlighting the reasons why Ms Black is no longer a prime suspect. You will be required by law to appear before a court at a later date for trial."

I blink at Mr Thompson, the smudge of a man who would most likely go home and stare at his TV screen for hours. Watching but not seeing. Hearing but not listening. I felt bad he had to go through all of the court appearances, and interviews, that would highlight his incompetency.

I felt bad he'd seen what happened. Not enough to implicate Lucile, but enough to turn the investigation on its head. He hadn't seen Lucile stab Dan or heard her hatch a plan with me. All he'd witnessed was her entering the house an hour before she claimed she had, before throwing her blouse and trousers into the boot of her car.

After his statement, the police had discovered blood in the boot of Lucile's dusty blue Toyota, Dan's blood, then in the bathroom sink that couldn't have possibly come from me, because there were no footprints to indicate I'd left the crime scene. And finally, after scouring her cluttered one bedroom flat, tucked in a bedside drawer full of contraception pills and old receipts, they'd found Dan's phone. Evidence Lucile had snatched to destroy traces of their time together.

"What now?" I mutter.

"We have to wait for them to make their decision," Peters whispers.

My heart stops as I stare at the judge raking through documents on the bench, understanding that in a few minutes my fate would be sealed. A fate I didn't even know I'd care for, until now.

CHAPTER TWENTY-FOUR

There are certain moments in life, that have the scope to shape an eternity, Mia. Some, are as gentle and as unexpected as a glance from a stranger. The instant their eyes miss ours, then settle slap bang on our souls. Then, there are occurrences we know will happen; the funeral of our parents, the morning of our wedding, the night we pack a bag and decide to leave a life that was devouring us.

We can spend weeks, months, even years, going over every minuscule detail of what we hope will transpire, only what we fail to anticipate is the inconsistent nature of our hearts, and of how, when that moment arrives, they can thunder inside us, protesting against everything we believed we wanted.

On the night I was arrested, I'd expected to feel numb when they read out the decision regarding my release. Back then, I believed I wouldn't care because I thought being incarcerated was the only way to keep you safe, Mia, but then something changed. An unexpected combination of events that causes my soul to quiver as the clerk stands behind me.

"Have the magistrates reached a decision?" the judge calls.

"We have."

The first domino to go down was Pierce. After being deceived by him, I hadn't expected the urge to fight to clinch down on my gut. A feeling I believed I'd buried after losing Nicholas. The second was Watson. In the aftermath of Dan's death, I'd forgotten all about human decency. I hadn't expected Watson to sacrifice everything she'd worked hard for for something as trivial as me, but then she had, and I was grateful she'd taken the time to see me, not as a mentally debilitated patient, but as a real person.

"Proceed."

The walls tremble, and the universe is crumbling.

Squeezing my eyes shut tight, I think back to the night I was arrested. Back then, all I saw was a silent stretch of black without a freckle of light. I admit when I started telling you this story, Mia, I hadn't expected to see that light again, but what I failed to acknowledge was the light was always there, all I had to do was open my eyes.

"We believe due to our own incompetence as a justice system..."

Cold sweat pricks the back of my neck, and the word please is lodged in my throat like century-old glue.

. "...We have failed Ms Black tremendously..."

I glance down at my stomach, promising I wouldn't get ahead of myself. Even if they did release me, I had no idea of what I would do, or where I would go.

"Evidence was not retrieved quickly enough, and as a result, Ms Black was falsely imprisoned..."

Lucile was facing a sentence of up to sixty years in prison without the possibility of parole for numerous charges, murder, tampering with evidence, perverting the court of justice, but where did that leave me?

"After her admittance to Raven House, reports from both Ms Black's psychiatrists' state that after medication her symptoms have diminished significantly."

The desk between my fingers is melting, and I am nothing but water.

"It is for that reason a unanimous decision has been reached that detaining Ms Black would no longer be in the publics' best interest."

Everything is white, a mighty paintbrush dipped across the creases of my battered black heart.

"Ms Black is due for immediate release under the premise she will continue taking her medication and agree to outcall visits from a licensed psychiatrist weekly."

I emit a muffled sound, the sonata of relief as hot tears pour down my cheeks.

"Ms Black?"

Gazing up, I glimpse an apology softening the judge's brown eyes.

"Legal proceedings are in place, and you are scheduled for immediate release pending the appropriate signed documentation." She pounds her gavel, and before I can thank her, a dry shuffle echoes around me as the jurors and magistrates head towards the door.

"You did it, Raine," Peters whispers.

But I didn't do anything, all of this could've been avoided if I told the police what really happened that night. Bobbing my head as Peters tugs me through the cautious glances, my mind flutters back to the evening I was arrested.

OCTOBER 5th 2018: Two hours after the murder

"Friend said she was a nutter," a female officer said

from the front of the police van. "Dispatch is already going over her medical files. It's all backed up."

"And the friend?" a male officer questioned.

"She's being interviewed, bless her, had a bit of a shock walking in on that."

"Imagine."

"Trust us to get called in."

"I hear a promotion."

Biting my tongue, I forced myself to keep quiet, because who in their right mind would believe a woman was travelling to an alternate universe through a mirror? The mirror. My chest throbbed as I glanced at the sky from the window, searching it for a sign I was doing the right thing, but all I received were the sounds of the officers cutting laughter.

"Come on, love," the male officer said.

Yanking me up by my cuffed wrist, he led me up the walkway to the station. I didn't spend much time being processed, or perhaps I did. Those first few hours are still a blur.

What I remember clearly, was the truth was there all night. A violent red mist, as I was made to undress in front of a female officer with bright plum hair. It was there when I pulled off my bloody summer dress that was tossed inside of a bag, marked 'evidence.'

I thought about telling the officers Lucile hadn't actually walked in on the crime scene, and that she had been the perpetrator, but when I saw myself in the mirror above me, I knew I couldn't, Mia. I blinked, and when the stranger with a lopsided jaw and puffy eyes blinked back, my insides turned to paste.

I thought of you then, Mia. Of how you deserved so much more than the brute who'd killed your father, and of how, if I kept you, as Esme had promised, I would only be endangering you. It was for that reason, after a brief medical examination, and before the grim-faced officers even had a chance to introduce themselves, I told them plainly: "It was my fault."

"Come on," Peters instructs.

Stalking her through the empty courtroom, I wonder what Lucile's heart sounded like when they turned up at her home. Had it rattled when the detectives asked why she hadn't mentioned the affair? Or was it just as placid as her conscience?

I wanted to believe that somewhere, deep down, she still bore traces of the brave little girl she'd been so many years before, but one of the saddest truths in life is that people change, Mia. And once they're gone, they're gone for good. Not because they can't change back, but because they don't want to.

Heading down the sunlit corridor, I squint at Peters's shoulders bathed under the hushed chatter of magistrates, and solicitors, rushing off to lunch when a familiar voice leaps out at me.

"Raine!"

Swerving around I see Watson rushing towards us with her brittle hair fluttering around her pink cheeks. Lost somewhere between my past and future, I come to a sharp halt as Peters glances between us undecidedly.

"I'll give you two a minute," she mumbles, slinking off and leaving us to broil in a crystal sort of silence.

"You did it," Watson says.

"I didn't do anything," I mutter, wishing everyone would just stop saying that.

"Of course, you did. You stayed strong."

Strong.

The word cuts through my spleen like a rusty penknife, because I hadn't been strong. If anything, by keeping quiet, I'd been weak. I shake my head, free to live my life with options I never dreamt I'd crave as much as I do now, and part of the reason is because of Watson.

"Why did you do it?" I ask.

Watson's face blanches, before she drops her head.

"Because it was the right thing to do, Elliot," she pauses, chewing the inside of her cheek. "He needed to be put in his place. What he did was more than unethical, it was sick, and if I didn't say anything, I knew he'd do the same to someone else." But there's something else, and before I can ask what it is, the confession bursts from her lips like air from a ruptured bagpipe. "And I kept thinking of Liam."

"Liam?"

"My son, he has autism."

My forehead pinches as Watson continues addressing the floor.

"He was diagnosed when he was four. Craig and I, we noticed something was wrong when he was a toddler. He would repeat things, simple words, phrases, nothing more." Tucking a strand of hair behind her ears, she lowers her voice.

"It was okay, at first. Craig and I promised we'd work at it together, I thought we'd be okay."

She shakes her head at her shiny black pumps.

"We weren't. I mean, I didn't think Craig was the kind of guy who'd just up and disappear. I thought he was someone I could count on, someone who'd stand by us. Then one day I came home from buying groceries, and I noticed all of his stupid baseball figurines were gone. I thought we'd been robbed," she emits a noise that sounds like a laugh.

"I was about to call the police when I noticed his CDs were missing, his clothes too, and then it hit me." Biting her lip, she looks up at me through the eyes of a lost child. "Craig couldn't handle it. He always wanted this perfect shiny family, and Liam and I– we weren't it. I guess Liam got too difficult, and I… well, I don't think he appreciated my parenting skills."

"Why are you telling me this?" I ask, hoping she doesn't mistake my curiosity for ungratefulness.

Dragging back her shoulders, Watson studies me with a sad smile.

"Because you were right, Raine. We were taking pieces of you without giving anything back. I understand it's a breach of ethics to discuss my personal life with you, but it made me think about humanity, and how in the grand scheme of things we're all the same. I'm sorry," she breathes.

"I'm sorry we had to poke holes in your beliefs because everyone's reality is their own. I mean, take religion for example. I could say a flock of people who believed in a man in the sky were all suffering from some sort of delusional disorder. But that's not the way the world works is it?" her voice catches in her throat, and her eyes swell with reluctance.

"We adhere to what we know. The norms in which we are taught by the mass of believers."

Taking a deep breath, she looks up at me, and for a second, I'm taken aback by the vulnerability in her face. In that naked expression, I see what she would've looked like as a girl. Blonde pigtails fastened neatly, lips that would tremble if they ever spoke lies.

"Seeing you today, all I could think of was Liam," she continues. "I kept wondering what would happen if he were accused of a crime, and a stranger saw him as an autistic kid, rather than the well-mannered man I know he will grow up to be, and I knew I'd never forgive myself for not forcing the world to see him for who he is, rather than the label tacked to him by people like me."

She skims the corridor undecidedly, before lowering her voice.

"I knew you didn't kill Dan the moment I met you," she tells me.

Thrown by her admission, I shake my head.

"How?"

"You looked… lost."

Before I can offer a lie, Watson holds up a hand.

"I've been there before, trust me. I know what it feels like to want to give up. To stare at the same ceiling for hours, days even, just waiting to come across a shred of salvation in that grey stretch of nothing you think is your life, but you have to believe in yourself again, Raine. Because that thing you're searching for is inside of you."

My heart heaves as I study the ground, torn between telling her she doesn't have a clue what she's talking about, and thanking her for seeing me for exactly who I am. Meeting her pensive stare, for the first time since losing Nicholas, I feel something I hadn't in a long time, understanding.

"Esme promised if I kept my baby, I would harm her," I blurt out. "And I couldn't—" my voice cracks as I take an unsteady breath. "After losing everything, I knew I couldn't give up the one good thing I had left unless social services forced me to."

"Then don't."

I wrinkle my brow.

"Pardon?"

"If you don't want to give up your child, don't," Watson repeats, firmer this time. "Have you heard Esme since taking your medication?"

Her eyes zero in on me when I shake my head.

"Do what you believe is right then, Raine," Watson says. "But keep in mind you're much stronger than you give yourself credit for. Most people would've fallen apart after everything you've been through, but you stand here sacrificing your happiness for the sake of hers. Whether you acknowledge it or not, you're already a mother."

Taking a step back, she watches me carefully.

"What?" I mutter.

"Do you remember what you told Nicholas?"

A hole in my heart twinges as I watch her, stunned. At a loss for words, I shake my head, and even though I'm certain Watson doesn't believe me about Nicholas, or Esme, or any of the creatures I'd told her about in our sessions, hearing his name said like that, like he existed, for a second, it's enough.

"You told him to stop punishing himself because—"

"I can't—"

"You can," Watson interrupts, her eyes softening. "Listen, Raine, I can spin you some rubbish about battling through thunderstorms, and hurricanes, and that after you defeat your demons the world will be stuffed with magic and pretty rainbows, but that's not the way the world works. The truth is, there's always going to be shitty days. You might come out of here and fall flat on your arse. You might be a terrible mother. You might relapse. The point is none of us have the answers, but to give up without trying leaves you with nothing but regret, and that in itself is losing."

Overwhelmed by her honesty, I'm about to tell her I wouldn't even know where to begin when she adds:

"Some of the magic exists in getting it wrong, of making mistakes and learning."

"You really think that?"

Watson nods with just enough conviction to stir something in my soul, and before I have a chance to ask where I would go, or what I would do, a silver haired man calls her name from down the corridor.

"I have to go," she tells me. "But remember what I told you Raine, and take care of yourself."

With that she saunters off, leaving me to stare after her outline fading in the pale winter sunlight. The first person since all of this to look at me like I was a person, the reason hope was moulding to iron in my chest, and I know I can't let her go, not yet.

"Wait!" I gasp.

Halfway across the corridor, Watson turns, bewildered. Racing up to her I throw my arms around her shoulders, waiting for her to flinch, or call security, but instead, she wraps a hesitant arm around my back.

"Thank you," I mumble into her suit.

"You know it's never too late to start again," Watson whispers. "Forget the world."

My heart stops as I pull away.

"What did you just say?"

"I said forget the world," Watson repeats, arching a brow. "It doesn't matter what anyone else thinks, all that matters is how you feel."

My eyes gloss over as I force a hefty nod, and as her words pour through the sunny corridor, I promise myself I will Mia, for both of us.

ONE YEAR LATER

We can never be sure of how a story is going to end, Mia. I guess that's because stories never do end. They stay with us and carry us forward, reminding us of who we are, and where we come from. Last year, when I was released, I believed it would be the end of this story. I thought that somehow, I'd leave the mental health facility and miraculously venture back to the woman I'd been with Nicholas; bright, sparky, and full of adventure, but as Watson had predicted, the journey I was about to embark on wasn't as straight forward as I first thought.

It wasn't a well-lit road swathed by glorious mountains and clear blue skies with birds singing overhead, and by no means was it the end. Caught somewhere in the middle, I'd ended up in a shabby B&B north of the M42, anticipating sleep that was always late in its arrival, searching for Wanderlust in any shiny surface that could pass as a mirror.

I didn't go back.

I never saw a glimmer of it again. Not Candimore or

Marianne, or any of the creatures who had once filled my life with colour. The only consolation I had, was that when sleep eventually arrived, it always brought dreams of Nicholas. I saw him playing the piano, and sitting across from me at the lake. I heard him calling my name from outside of the palace. Even in my sleep, I smiled when he called my name.

To say I missed him was an understatement, and I guess a part of me was still waiting for him to come back, because if ever you've loved someone, that hope never does go away. It took some time, but eventually, I began to accept that missing someone was okay. Hurting was okay. It didn't make me weak, if anything it made me brave, reminding me it hurt because I'd taken a chance, and despite losing Nicholas, loving him was one of the greatest gifts I could've given myself.

Life was a gift. A virtue I wouldn't squander with grief. And so, after too many sleepless nights, and mornings filled with fluctuating beliefs about life, and love, and death, I'd set up a canvas in that grimy B&B room and I turned my grief into art. Forcing myself to keep going, I'd plastered every memory that ripped through my skull on a blank sheet, losing myself in rich shades of nostalgia, and violent bursts of euphoria for hours, sometimes even days.

Eventually, I managed to sell most of my pieces to avid crime fanatics I believed were following Lucile's court case in a collection entitled 'Wanderlust'. Lucile wasn't that lucky. Despite her defence team fighting to pin Dan's death on me, insisting that someone who claimed she was travelling to an alternate universe through a mirror, had to have been disturbed and violent, justice prevailed, and after a lengthy court case, Lucile was convicted of murder and sentenced to sixty years in prison without the possibility of parole.

It was a small triumph that was short-lived, because

less than a week later, I went into labour seven weeks before my due date. 'Stress-induced,' the doctors muttered as I lay on the bloody hospital bed, groggy from an epidural with a beeping sound pulsing somewhere in the background. Beyond exhausted, I admit I wanted to give up then, Mia.

I wanted to let go when the doctors swarmed around me in green surgical masks, urging me to push with brows that were too furrowed. I wanted to drift off and disappear when your godmother Watson insisted everything was going to be alright with too much sadness wedged into her swollen eyes.

Yes, despite the many months' of working hard to put the past behind me, I wanted to let go, Mia, and had a memory not come to me that day, I might have.

It was somewhere in the middle of those thirteen days. The seventh, maybe the eighth. It came after we raced through the Valley Of Chosen Souls, and before that final goodbye. The day was lazy, and the smell of summer bruised the air mercilessly. Glancing at Nicholas, I felt him do the same to my soul.

"You know, that one sort of looks like you," I said, pointing at the sky.

Nicholas wrinkled his brow.

"Is this your way of telling me you see me like a shapeless blob?"

"Sort of, but you see, I sort of have a thing for shapeless blobs."

"Well, aren't I lucky?"

"Very."

Nicholas's face loosened as his eyes slipped back to the sky.

"Raine," Nicholas began unevenly.

"Yes, Nicholas?" I said, in the exact same tone.

"Do you think it will always be like this?"

"Like what? You mean me comparing you to shapeless blobs in the sky?"

"No," Nicholas said. "I mean, do you think we will always be happy?"

My lips parted as I watched him.

The question came as somewhat of a surprise, Mia, because in the last few days we'd spoken of our pasts, and the journeys we'd take. We'd bickered over lesser things, twice, and I'd cried after telling him about my parents' deaths, but we'd never really spoken of forever, and with the weight of it sitting heavy between us, there came a sudden fear that most things eventually end.

"I didn't expect I would ever feel this way," Nicholas continued. "After my parents' passing, I didn't believe I deserved to be happy. I didn't think I ever would be again, but now that I am, I'm terrified of losing you. Of losing this."

Certain if Nicholas didn't change his mind about me, it would always stay the same, I smiled, but when his eyes met mine, I witnessed a shadow of dread.

"What is it?" I asked, sitting up. "Nicholas?"

"If something happens to me," he muttered. "I need you to remember how strong you are."

I raised a brow. I thought he was being dramatic, overcautious. I didn't know. Nicholas's face hadn't changed, it was still a mess of fear and sadness.

"I mean it, Raine," he said. "Whatever happens, promise me you'll never stop fighting for the happiness you deserve."

I watched him like he was mad. But he wasn't, was he? He was simply preparing me for a future without him.

Taking his face in my hands, I bent lower and kissed his cheek.

"I promise you, Nicholas Werner, whatever happens, I will never stop fighting for the happiness I deserve. Now stop wasting all of this time being scared of possibilities." I teased in his voice. "Let's live for now, and let's get some food, I'm starving."

Nicholas lips parted.

"Raine," he started. Before he could finish, I stood then raced on up the hill.

Sometimes I wonder if I waited a longer, if he would've told me the truth that day, Mia. He looked like he wanted to, but then he'd clambered up from the lake and followed me to the palace, and we'd eaten in the dining hall, and we'd laughed about nonsense, and we were happy, we were so damn happy.

Looking back, I'm glad he didn't tell me. Despite my initial anger, in the months that passed I realised Nicholas was right. If he'd told me the truth about Esme, our last days would've been wasted, and those days were more than magical.

As I said, I thought of that afternoon when I went into labour with you seven weeks early, Mia. Drifting in and out of consciousness in the maternity ward, all I could hear was Nicholas's words strumming about in my head. *'Never stop fighting for the happiness you deserve.'*

I didn't, I fought so hard the blood vessels in my cheeks popped and my teeth powdered to dust, and when your tiny wail punctured the silence that day, I swear I saw him smiling beside me.

My heart flutters as I peer down at you sleeping in your cot. Gold light streams in from the bay windows to the left of me, dusting a bookcase in the corner, and the chalky mantlepiece ahead of me, littered with baby photographs and an assortment of bric-a-brac.

Three months old today, Mia, and it still terrifies me when I think of what I might've lost. Not only if the nurse hadn't unravelled the umbilical cord from around your neck in time, but before that, when I'd doubted myself all of those months ago in Raven House.

You, of course, are unaware of any of this, or any of the words I whispered to you back then. Though, at times, a part of me believes you understand when I tell you the story of the woman who got lost in the woods; and the king who traded his life for a portion of happiness.

Your face twitches as you wake slowly, peering up at me through eyes that are the exact same shade of earl grey tea in the light. 'A miracle child,' the doctors had called you, they had no idea how much truth lay in that statement.

Shattered from lack of sleep, and midnight feeds, I reach out to you, about to whisper your name when you lift a pudgy fist and grab the only thing I'd kept from the police in a bag marked 'evidence'– the ring Nicholas had given me another lifetime ago.

My heart stirs as your lip trembles.

You blink, once, twice before expelling a soft burst of laughter.

I laugh back, stunned.

Your first laugh, and in something as simple as that sound, I understand magic will always exist Mia, all we need is a little belief, not in the world, but in ourselves.

"Forget the world," I whisper.

A FINAL NOTE TO THE READER:

If ever you want to leave, go.

Don't force love, and don't run from it.

And if ever a venture, or another person should touch
your soul, embrace it and let love to destroy you

ACKNOWLEDGEMENTS:

Thank you to all of my Beta readers on Twitter who have given me the courage to publish, and to those who weren't afraid to critique. Thank you to my friends and family who have read Wanderlust at its earliest stage, and went over countless revisions with me; Samina Din, Fiona Faben, Hannah Tyler, Raheela Din. Thank you to Carl for being the plot twist in my own story and for your never-ending support. Thank you to my sister Molly, this book is dedicated to you. You've been there for me from the beginning and our saying 'it's not a shit life, it's just a shit day," carried me through this book. Thank you to my youngest sister Rose 8, for all of your advice about life. I hope that one day when you're old enough, you will enjoy this story. And finally, thank you to anyone who has read or purchased this book. Your support means the world to me.

ABOUT THE AUTHOR

L. Costevelos is the oldest of three children and grew up in Birmingham, UK. In her spare time, L. Costevelos enjoys travelling, reading, and of course writing. She is currently working on her second novel which is set to be published in 2020.

If you enjoyed this book please leave a review. Alternatively, if you would like to contact the author, or receive information on upcoming events visit: Lailacostevelos.com

Printed in Great Britain
by Amazon